THE SURGEON'S CURSE

THE SURGEON'S CURSE

BY

DOUGLAS VOLK

Please direct all correspondence and book
orders to: DanJon Publishing, LLC
PO Box 1011
Biddeford, ME 04005

ISBN: 978-1-086-62029-0

DEDICATION

This book is dedicated to my wonderful family, without whose endless love and encouragement I could not have written these novels.

To my wife, Gail, thank you for the never-ending love and support.

To my daughter, Danielle, and my son, Jonathan, special thanks to you for the many times you lifted my spirits and sent me back to the computer with a cheerful: "Don't give up, Dad. You can do this!"

I've written thousands of pages during the 37 years it took to publish *The Morpheus Series*. But no words can fully express the love I have for all of you.

Douglas Volk, 2019

ACKNOWLEDGMENTS

First, I would like to offer my deepest thanks to our nation's military veterans, in honor of whom I wrote *The Surgeon's Curse* and the other two novels in *The Morpheus Series*. I greatly respect the endless sacrifices that have been made by so many of the men and women who have served and continue to serve in our armed forces.

I'm also very grateful to my wife, Gail, and our two adult children, Jonathan and Danielle. All three gave me endless support and encouragement as I worked on these books for nearly four decades.

In addition, I'm quite thankful to many friends and colleagues, without whose help the books might never have been published: Dr. Jerome Slate, who spent many hours editing the hundreds of thousands of words in these volumes. Book producer Amy Nugent, who pulled together all the elements required to create three attractive and easy-to-read novels. David Swardlick, whose talented team of graphic artists helped greatly with the design, production and layout of the book covers and marketing materials. Retired Biddeford, Maine, police detective Richard Gagne, whose expertise on law enforcement techniques and crime scene analysis was immensely helpful. Dr. Stephen Soreff, who provided expert advice on the psychological dynamics involved in sleep and dreaming. Jessica Charak, DNA Technical Leader with the Las Vegas Metropolitan Police Department, whose advice on topics related to forensic science was invaluable. Journalist and TV Producer David Simon, whose book *Homicide* was full of helpful detail about the daily lives and work habits of a team of

Baltimore homicide detectives. Ken Rosen, retired University of Southern Maine English Professor, who was the very first person I went to for advice back in 1982. He encouraged me to take his Fiction Writing class and to attend the summer Stonecast Writers Conference where I began learning about the craft of writing. Thank you as well to Carol Fonde and Denis Ledoux for their expert advice and support.

And lastly, a special thank you to my current editor, dear friend and writing coach Tom Nugent, whose creative input, insights, editing skill and endless patience have been of huge assistance to me over the past twenty-five years that we have worked together.

Whenever I look back on the challenges that have been a part of creating *The Morpheus Series*, I'm reminded of one of my favorite children's books that has inspired me throughout my writing career, *The Little Engine That Could*! This classic children's story gave me some of the best advice I've ever received. "I think I can! I think I can! I think I can!"

I hope you enjoy *The Surgeon's Curse* and the other books in *The Morpheus Series*.

Douglas Volk

CHAPTER 1
A Nightmare at the Funhouse

A summer evening at the Dunwiddie County Fair.

High above the crowded fairgrounds, the August moon hangs like a fat gold coin against a sky that glitters with a billion stars.

And she's smiling. She's happy. She's watching Santuzzi the Fire Eater wow his audience with fiery tricks. Watching his huge mouth open wide . . . *hissssssttt!* as he spits a ball of blue flame directly at her!

She shrieks with terrified laughter . . . shrieks at the handsome young man holding her arm. "Eric, look out!"

He laughs . . . and she laughs with him. They duck away just in time to avoid the blazing fireball spinning and tumbling past them and then vanishing into the distance.

He gazes deep into her eyes. "That was close, honey! *Too* close, if you ask me. Let's get out of here! Are you in the mood for some ice cream?"

She nods. She pulls him close and gives him a ferocious hug. He laughs, then turns and leads her along the roaring midway toward the refreshment stands. There are a dozen of them—neon-lit Plexiglas sheds full of sizzling corn dogs and sugary fried dough and succulent Italian sausages. Beyond their brightness, looming 80 yards distant, is the mile-long harness track that rings the Dunwiddie Fairgrounds like a glowing noose.

Could anything be more perfect?

The summer breeze ripples through her soft blonde hair. She's enjoying herself thoroughly, as she listens to a circus calliope wheeze and grind through one of the old-timey popular tunes they so often play at these picturesque summertime fairs.

> *Daisy, Daisy, give me your answer, do.*
> *I'm half crazy, all for the love of you.*
> *It won't be a stylish marriage,*
> *I can't afford a carriage.*
> *But you'd look sweet upon the seat*
> *Of a bicycle built for two!*

He turns to her. "Chocolate, strawberry or vanilla—and they've also got mint chocolate chip. What'll it be, honey?"

She smiles, full of joy, full of love for him. Then she looks toward the illuminated ice cream stand—*The Big Lick*—and the elderly, white-haired woman leaning from the window, awaiting her order.

"Eric, I think I'll have . . ."

But now she hesitates.

How odd. For some reason she doesn't understand, the little old lady in the window is glaring at her. *Sneering* at her, with eyes full of icy hatred.

"What is it, ma'am?" she asks in a quavering voice. "Is something wrong? Is something the matter?"

The old lady doesn't speak for a moment. Then her mouth falls open. Her voice is cold, full of menace.

"What's wrong here is *you*, bitch."

"Me?" Stung to the quick, she recoils physically, as if she's just been slapped.

"Me?" she asks again. "*Me?*" Her stunned eyes are suddenly full of tears.

"Nasty bitch like you doesn't deserve to live!"

Amazed and horrified, she turns for comfort to her Eric—

He's gone.

Nowhere in sight.

Dazed and blinking, she watches a man in a filthy apron step up behind the elderly woman in the window.

"That's her, Elmer," says the ice cream lady. "That's the dirty cunt I told you about."

She can't believe she's hearing this. She's weeping now, weeping openly.

But Elmer doesn't seem surprised. He's nodding his head, nodding rapidly, and she's horrified to see that he has some sort of brownish-purple growth hanging from his neck. Is it a goiter? A hideous tumor? Is it full of tiny red bugs, vicious stinging insects crawling through the man's grotesque deformity?

"Bitch," says Elmer. He holds up his right hand—and now she sees the brutal-looking meat cleaver. The blade winks and glitters in the light from the electric sign, *The Big Lick.*

Elmer slides open the side door of the shed.

He shouts at his partner. "Let's *git* her, Edna!"

Now they're both lunging through the side door, their scowling eyes locked on hers. They're going to kill her!

She turns. "No, please!"

She runs. She staggers forward, nearly falls, twists an ankle. Hobbling now, and desperate, she looks back over one shoulder . . . and sees how they're gaining ground on her. The cleaver whistles through the air, blade glinting, and she hears the old lady shouting again and again: "Chop her to pieces! Chop her to pieces!"

She runs! Runs! But after a few steps she stumbles sideways, loses her balance, falls through an open doorway marked:

SUMMERTIME FUNHOUSE!
HALL OF MIRRORS!

Dark in here—pitch-dark—and snarling, guttural laughter.

A voice shouts, "Squirt her! Squirt the bitch!"

Something wet, slimy . . . it's all over her face! And then a light winks from a wall—and she catches a sudden flash of silver—and a blade sizzles through the air, a gleaming blade, blue steel, a hissing blade—*just missed her*!

"Help me!"

SUMMERTIME FUNHOUSE!

She screams it again, "Help me!"

But now the wood-plank floor starts to bend. It buckles in the middle, she's sinking into the floor, and she reaches out wildly for something to hold onto. She clutches at something rubbery, spongy, full of liquid, and now it's squirting yellow-wet onto her clean white blouse.

It's a giant pig bladder, expanding, leaking, stinking, and fouling her neatly combed hair with its spreading filth.

HALL OF MIRRORS!

"*Grab* her, Elmer!"

A hand darts from a wall, a rubber hand, blood-soaked. It jams straight into her shuddering gut—"I GOT HER, ELMER! BRING ME THE CLEAVER!"

And then something cold, wet, slimy . . . wrapping itself around one side of her neck, an eel, a poison eel, needle-sharp teeth going for her jugular—

POW!—she crashes through a wall of canvas . . . and all at once she's back out in the air, with the stars wheeling and glittering high above her sweating head.

Once again, it's a summer evening at the Dunwiddie County Fair.

Frantic, she lurches toward the distant harness track. It's her only hope now. If she can just reach the grandstand, if she can just reach that big crowd sitting in the bleachers, if she can just scream for help . . . surely help will arrive and she will be saved. Saved!

For a few terrible seconds, her life hangs in the balance.

Sobbing with relief, she realizes she's going to make it. She's going to win this race around the harness track. Already she can see the crowd in the grandstand watching her run along the damp turf . . . already she can see how amazed they are to watch a woman racing down the homestretch. A frantic woman who staggers on every other step, screaming desperately:

"Help me!"

"HELP ME!"

Ten more steps, only ten steps and she will be safe— She skids to a stop.

Stunned by a wave of paralyzing horror, she realizes the worst—

All of the people in the grandstand . . .

They *all* have white hair. They *all* wear pale blue smocks with the same logo stitched over the left pocket: a huge red tongue licking a vanilla ice cream cone. All of the men have masses of diseased flesh hanging from their brutally disfigured necks.

Her mouth falls open.

Her eyes are huge, huge, as she sends up the most terrible, the most agonizing scream of her life: "Noooooooooooo!"

But her scream will go *unheard, unheard*, as the entire world collapses inward on itself, goes utterly and forever black.

***

The sleeper opened one bloodshot eye. She focused it on the team of researchers—and then she began shrieking like a maniac trapped in the depths of Hell.

"You must . . . make them . . . STOP!"

A moment later she came howling off the laboratory bed, her fists whirling and saliva flying from her distended mouth.

"I'll *kill* you, *all* of you, you dirty motherfuckers!"

Her first blow landed on the right shoulder of a red-haired woman in a white lab coat. She wore a plastic I.D. tag above the front pocket.

Alix Cassidy, Ph.D., Assistant Director
Sleep Disorder Center of Atlanta

"Sandra, Sandra, hang on, it's me!" Dr. Cassidy shouted as the sleep subject's fist slammed into her shoulder, momentarily knocking her off balance.

"It's *Alix*, Sandra—everything is okay, do you hear me? You're at the Sleep Disorder Center. You're gonna be *okay!*"

But the terrified young woman heard none of this. Crazed with fear, she was struggling to crawl down off the bed, while thrashing wildly about and cursing a blue streak.

Responding instantly, two other research laboratory workers were now struggling to hold the flailing Sandra Nadeau in place, along with Alix.

"It's me, Sandra. It's Alix! You're in the sleep lab, honey. You're gonna be *okay!*"

For a few moments, these calming words appeared to soothe the nightmare sufferer. Now her features sagged and her eyes flooded with tears. "I went to buy ice cream," she moaned, "and then the bitch came after me!" She sobbed once and rubbed her inflamed eyes. But then, all at once, she flared again: "Hey, fuck you! Okay? Fuck all of you! They were going to kill me! Don't you get it? Filthy bastards, dozens of them— they were going to cut me to pieces!"

With a ferocious kick, she managed to thrash one leg free. A moment later she was sliding halfway off the bed and dangerously close to breaking their grip entirely.

Dr. Cassidy had seen enough. "Dr. Kidder!" she shouted at the psychiatry resident, "we need help over here, now!"

Nodding calmly, Dr. Russell Kidder was already holding up a hypodermic needle full of enough diazepam to bring down a runaway horse.

A few seconds after the injection went in, the patient stopped struggling.

Mumbling softly, she fell back against the bed and was soon fast asleep.

***

The Sleep Disorder Center team took a deep breath.

"Wow," said Cindy Taylor, RN, Dr. Cassidy's long-time assistant at the SDC. "That was a nasty one!"

Nodding reassuringly, Alix patted her rattled aide on the arm. "She'll be fine, Cindy, nothing to worry about."

7

Alix turned to the psychiatrist, who was in the middle of inserting his spent hypodermic needle into a biohazard sharps container: "Thanks for the assistance, Russ. She should sleep for several hours now."

"No problem. Glad to help," said the somber M.D. He was a tall, slender man with a neatly trimmed beard and thick glasses set in heavy black frames. "I think we just got a glimpse at how violent nightmares are often linked to clinical depression.

"As you may recall from our discussion on Wednesday, this subject's post-sleep behavior seems to have a totally unconscious element—almost as if the nightmare were invading her cognitive functioning.

"A very interesting phenomenon, I must say . . . and rather important for your research on nightmares, I would imagine."

Alix smiled. "It sure is, Russ. Although I must say, I don't think we've even begun to scratch the surface, when it comes to understanding the links between nightmares and mental illness."

She sighed and turned to her assistant. "Cindy, if you'll take over here, I'd like to start pulling some files together for Dr. Kidder to review in treating this patient."

Cindy looked up from a nearby computer screen. She'd already begun her survey of the chattering data monitors that surrounded the subject's bed. Now she sent the two of them a bright, cheerful smile.

"No problem," she said. "Listen, there's a fresh pot of coffee and some hot water for tea waiting for you in the conference room."

CHAPTER 2
Leaving . . . on a Jet Plane

It was nearly midnight, as Alix hurried back to her office and quickly assembled the nine Sleep Disorder Center folders on Sandra Nadeau. A 29-year-old Atlanta resident, Nadeau worked as a receptionist for Xerox on Peachtree Street downtown. Sitting at her desk, Alix scribbled a few introductory notes on the folder marked *SDC—Nadeau Sleep Disturbance Episodes: Lab Monitoring*.

"Terror upon awakening, accompanied by difficulty separating dream content from conscious awareness."

For at least the hundredth time in her 12-year career as a sleep researcher, Alix was absorbed in the notes she'd taken while studying a dreaming sleep subject. She was most interested in the physiology of the brain activity she'd just witnessed. After many years of study, she understood that deep inside the neuronal tissue which regulates basic cognitive and intellectual functions is where the electrochemical mechanism known as "dreaming" takes place. As always, Alix was intrigued and fascinated by what she'd observed.

"Cognitive impairment, physical symptoms of panic still evident at sixty seconds post-awakening."

Frowning thoughtfully, she stopped writing and lifted the steaming cup of tea to her lips.

This patient was struggling with psychological deficits, of course. She suffered from a borderline personality disorder with occasional psychotic features—which meant that her reaction to nightmares was bound to be atypical. For most people, a nightmare was no more harmful than a summer thunderstorm . . . a brief eruption of thunder and lightning followed by a few minutes of driving rain and roaring wind.

For most people, after that, the skies cleared, the sun came out, and the birds resumed their peaceful songs in the still-dripping branches.

But every now and then, at the height of the thunderstorm, disaster would suddenly strike. Like a bolt of sudden lightning that sends death and destruction into a Fourth of July picnic, some nightmares had the power to blast right through the human psyche. Those with mental illness seemed especially vulnerable to the fearsome power of their own terrifying dreams.

"All set, Alix?"

She looked up. Dr. Kidder was standing in the doorway of her office and holding a cup of freshly brewed coffee.

"I'm ready," said the eager sleep researcher. "Let's get busy."

***

They spent the next 45 minutes reviewing Nadeau's psychiatric history and the results of half a dozen overnight sleep studies like the one that had just taken place in the fifth-floor lab at the SDC.

"I hope what we just saw wasn't a step backwards," said the psychiatrist, who'd been treating Sandra for the past six months.

"How so?" asked Alix.

"Well, she had been making some impressive gains," said the doctor. "Much better ego-control of her affective deficits, for example. She also managed to significantly reduce her dependence on alcohol."

Dr. Kidder paused for a moment and tapped his pencil on the tabletop. "All that is very encouraging, of course . . . but her post-REM sleep behavior tonight suggests that her affective issues may actually run deeper into the cognitive nexus than I thought."

He sent his colleague a somber look. "I hope we aren't seeing the kind of image disruption that can lead to a complete psychotic break."

Alix nodded. "I hear you, Russ. But I don't think I'm as troubled by her panic reaction as you seem to be."

He was studying her carefully. "Why not?"

"Well, I've watched people wake up from nightmares dozens of times in recent years. There's *always* some panic involved—even if it's only transitory. She got carried away for a minute, that's true, right before you gave her the sedative. But I'm not convinced that her panic was anything more profound than the usual inflection-point cascade most people experience right after a bad nightmare."

Dr. Kidder was smiling at her now. "That's what I like about you, Alix. You're the eternal optimist." He took a sip of coffee. "Okay, ask Cindy to send me the workup later in the week, will you? I'll do my best to weave it into her therapy."

"Sure thing," said Alix. The two of them were on their feet now.

"So today's the big day?" said the psychiatrist.

Alix grinned back at him. "That's right, Russ. I'm leaving . . . leaving on a jet plane; don't know when I'll be back again! Remember that old song? I'll be flying out of Hartsfield around two o'clock this afternoon, nonstop to Portland, Maine. Big Pine, here I come!"

The psychiatrist laughed and shook his head. "Alix, you never cease to amaze me. You're going to be spending eight weeks at a center on paranormal psych-research—in the wilds of rural Maine! Hey, I wish I could go *with* you. Talk about exploring the far frontiers of neurobiology!"

Alix sent him a good-natured grin. "I like pushing the envelope, okay? I also like hanging out on the cutting edge of science. It's why I got into sleep research in the first place. As for the 'paranormal' aspects . . . well, what's wrong with venturing out into the unknown a little bit now and then?"

He was smiling again, smiling and teasing. "I understand you're actually going to be giving a series of lectures on Somnambulistic Telepathy up there. Have I got it right?"

"Yes, you do."

They were walking down a long hallway, beneath a series of overhead fluorescent lights. "I've spent the last several years collecting data to prove my often-maligned theory," said Alix, "so why would I want to stop at this point—especially when they invited me to lecture at Big Pine?"

He was shaking his head, exaggeratedly wide-eyed and still pretending to be astonished. "So I take it you're going to be unveiling your outlandish findings at Big Pine? Can I expect to read about you on the *Science* page of the *New York Times* this summer? I can see the headline now: *Paranormal Researcher Claims Some Sleepers Can Control Other People's Nightmares*!"

Alix laughed out loud. "Yeah, read all about it!" she chortled at her companion. "Stop the presses—ST is real!"

They had reached her office; she opened the door and flicked on the light.

"Straight out of *The Twilight Zone*, no less," said Dr. Kidder.

Alix chuckled again, but then her expression grew more serious. "Actually, I suspect there may be a provable scientific basis for Somnambulistic Telepathy, although it hasn't made any of the major science journals yet."

He was peering at her now, thoroughly intrigued. "Really?"

"That's right," said Alix. "There isn't a lot of lab data—it's too early for that—but what we do have strongly suggests that some dreamers may undergo a kind of 'biochemical cascade' during REM sleep, when most nightmares take place. At the neuronal level, there's a huge eruption of energy . . . what we call a 'REM explosion,' if you will."

Dr. Kidder was nodding earnestly at her now; the jokes had stopped. "Very interesting, Alix, to say the least. I really hope you'll do great things up there in Maine, you know that. Like Dr. Jacobson, I don't always agree with all that paranormal stuff—but I *am* a big fan of your courage and your willingness to go out there on the edge and take some real risks now and then."

She offered him a smile of deep gratitude.

"Just remember, I'll be around," he said, "if you run into any problems or just need to talk to somebody up there in the Maine woods."

"Absolutely," she replied.

"Russ, I can't thank you enough."

***

By ten o'clock the next morning, after catching a few hours of sleep and attending to some packing chores at her apartment, Alix was standing in front of Dr. Stanley Jacobson's huge folder-cluttered desk. The director of the SDC had been hard at work since 7 a.m. As always, he'd shed his white lab coat in favor of the baggy gray sweater and drab-looking tie he preferred on the job.

"How'd that sleep subject do last night, Alix?"

"Well, she struggled a bit at first," said the researcher, "but then she settled down and did okay. Dr. Kidder and I went through our usual debriefing and Cindy did the follow-up and discharged the subject. She left about an hour ago."

"Good work," said the doc. He was tapping on a folder with the knuckles of the first two fingers on his big right hand. "I understand things got a little bit dicey in the lab at one point?"

"That's correct," said Alix. "You should have heard her description of the dream narrative—and especially the way it ended. But she pulled out of it after the sedative knocked her out. She slept another few hours—and Cindy says she was fine after that."

Dr. Jacobson was tapping the folder a little harder now, a sure sign that he was about to express some emotion. Jacobson was an extremely competent scientist and an administrator of the first rank . . . and yet, like many dedicated researchers, he often seemed uncomfortable when it came to sharing his feelings.

"Alix, I'm really going to miss you."

Alix laughed. "I'm sure you'll be just fine," she said. "Things aren't that busy around here in the summertime. Hey, I'm only going up to Maine; it's not like I'm headed off to spend two years at the North Pole or something!"

The two of them beamed at each other. During more than 12 years of working together on sleep research at the renowned Atlanta institute, they'd become as close as father and daughter. But now Alix was leaving; she'd be flying off to Portland in only a few hours for her summer-long sabbatical.

Isolated in the remote hardwood forests of Maine, the Big Pine complex was the site of some of the world's most cutting-edge research on the mysteries of clairvoyance and imaging-at-a-distance . . . along with half a dozen other disciplines located at the far frontiers of psychological science. Dr. Jacobson was proud of his loyal assistant, but he wasn't crazy about the topic she'd be lecturing on during this summer. Grim-faced and obviously concerned, he was tapping the table even harder.

Alix watched his huge knuckles at work and felt a sudden flash of affection for this tireless, soft-spoken researcher, the rock-solid mentor who'd been at her side for so many years. "Don't worry, Stan," she said gently. "The weeks will fly past, and I'll stay in touch by telephone."

He sent her a melancholy smile. "Yeah, yeah, that's what they *all* say. But what happens if you get so caught up in that weird stuff at Big Pine—it's borderline science, no offense!—that you can't break away from it by September?"

He ruminated for a few moments, and then his long face grew truly somber. "Quite honestly, I'm a little worried, Alix. We both know what happened back . . . back twelve years ago, when you got caught up in all that paranormal stuff with the unethical psychiatrist and the troubled Vietnam vet."

Alix didn't say anything. She didn't have to.

For a moment, her eyes were full of fear.

"I mean . . . hey, you know I have the greatest respect for your interest in paranormal research," Jacobson was hurrying on now. "But I don't trust this stuff, I really don't. As far as I'm concerned, the science involved isn't rigorous enough and the controls are lacking. The metrics are often weak as hell. You know it and I know it. And the risks of potential abuse are sky high. I'm still troubled by what happened to you back in '74—a kidnapping, an attempted murder and a suicide.

"That ugly situation ended in a man shooting himself to death, for God's sake!"

He paused for breath, and his gaze seemed deeply troubled. The knuckles had stopped rapping the desktop. Alix wondered if she'd ever seen him looking this downcast, this worried before. "I'm serious, my dear. Go ahead and do your lecturing and research—but I want you to be extremely *careful* up there at Big Pine, do you understand?"

But Alix was chuckling out loud by now . . . chuckling and waving him away.

"Good Lord, you make it sound like I'm going off to become the Bride of Frankenstein or something. Let's get back to reality, can we? Big Pine is probably the most respected paranormal research center of its kind."

He frowned. "I know, I know. But I took a quick look at some of their course offerings the other day, and they didn't help my confidence level one bit." He sighed heavily. "I mean, how the hell am I supposed to get comfortable with seminar titles like 'Can We Really Remember the Future?' and 'Encounters with the Dead'?" He gave her a long, mournful look. "Just promise me you'll be careful, okay?

"And whatever else you do, stay in touch!"

She promised to do both, and they exchanged a quick hug.

***

Ten minutes later, she was zooming along I-85 in the Chevy Sprint, headed back toward her tiny apartment in suburban North Druid Hills, her home for the past six years.

Stevie Wonder's smash hit was playing softly on the car radio. *I just called to say I love you; I just called to say I care. . . .*

She glanced at her wristwatch and groaned out loud. Nearly noon . . . and she still had a list a mile long of things to do before she could head to the airport. *It'll be all right*, she told herself. *That stuff with David and Laura and the terrible nightmares, and then David's suicide . . . that's all ancient history now.*

The green exit signs were flashing past, one by one. Only three miles to go . . .

But then, just as she was passing the exit closest to her own, she got a sudden shock.

All at once a battered pickup truck came barreling up the entrance ramp. Tires howling, the rusted-out vehicle yawed dangerously, rocked wildly back and forth . . . and then shot from the ramp directly into her path!

Alix hit the brake pedal, and the Sprint went into a terrifying sideways skid. For a second or two, she waited for the sound of exploding metal and glass, while her pulse raced and she didn't dare breathe.

But the freeway traffic was light that morning—lucky for her—and she was spared the disaster that for a moment had seemed inevitable.

With her heart pounding in her chest, she looked toward the jerk who'd cut her off . . . and was amazed to see him hanging out of the driver's-side window and glaring back at her.

He wore a dirty royal blue *Braves* baseball cap, and beneath the bill his scowling eyes were full of hatred. Astonished, she watched him waggle his tongue at her in an obscenely lustful gesture—a vicious redneck display of naked sexual aggression.

What the hell is the matter with him? What an asshole!

Still shaking, she made her way home without further incident. After piloting the Sprint into her parking space and flicking off the radio, she pushed the car door open and immediately felt a cool summer breeze gently touching her face and soothing her tired eyes. All at once her spirits began to lift.

Why should she let that idiot darken her mood? Hey, the summer was about to begin and the good times were about to roll! All at once she felt energized. After more than two years of planning and dreaming, her summertime adventure was finally about to begin!

A moment later, she was hurrying through her front door. She had only a few minutes to make sure everything was put away, then check all the appliances and move Puddy—her emerald-eyed Maine Coon feline—into his comfortable travel cage.

She was going to miss little Puddy a lot . . . but she felt relieved knowing how much her friend Jan adored the cat.

Her travel plans had been carefully arranged. After parking the Sprint in Jan's garage and giving her beloved pet a final hug—"See you in eight weeks, Puddy!"— Alix would be hopping into her pal's car to be dropped off at the Atlanta airport.

Five minutes after turning off the lights and locking her apartment door, Alix was back in the Sprint and headed toward her friend's suburban rancher.

If all went according to plan, she'd be walking the wild forestlands of Central Maine before the sun went down.

Chapter 3
Hello Darkness, My Old Friend

It was four-thirty p.m. at Mulligan's Pub in downtown Boston, and the shamrock-decorated banner above the nearly deserted bar said it all.

Welcome to Mulligan's—Home of the Second Chance!

Directly beneath that vivid banner—which also featured a grinning leprechaun in a Boston Celtics basketball jersey—sat a balding fat man named Arthur Forbes. He was in the middle of his third straight bourbon-and-Coke.

"Hey, Tracy!" blared the florid-faced booze hound from his perch directly below the word *Chance*, "I asked you not to forget me, didn't I, sweetheart?"

Tracy sighed. What a pest! But her job was to serve her customers, whether she liked them or not. The endlessly chattering Arthur had become a late afternoon regular at Mulligan's during the past couple of weeks. His arrival at the popular sports bar had coincided almost exactly with his having been fired from his job as a corrugated box salesman.

A total pain in the ass! The feisty bartender shook her head at the idiot on the second stool. "I *haven't* forgotten you, Arthur, not at all. Hey, I poured your last double five minutes ago. Give the bar lady a break, will ya?"

She laughed good-naturedly and then pushed a refilled bowl of salted peanuts back toward the middle of the bar, as she waggled a scolding finger directly at the barfly's bloodshot eyes. "If you don't slow down, I'll end up peeling you off the linoleum!"

"No chance, Little Miss Tracy," Arthur wailed, pretending to be hurt by the warning. "No way can six little shots of bottom-end bourbon slow this guy down. You just keep on pourin', and I'll just keep on *soarin'*, whaddya say?

"Now that I've been canned, Mulligan's is my home away from home—so you gotta treat me right!"

Tracy was waving him away now. "I don't get it, Arthur. If you've been fired, why are you sitting in here lapping up the hooch? Don't you think you oughta be out there job hunting?"

He glared. "Miss Tracy, who's gonna hire a 56-year-old with a dismal sales record—to say nothing of the major league paunch I've developed since I stopped giving a shit about meeting my monthly quota? You think they're gonna give me the corner office at Gillette?"

Moaning with self-pity, he gestured toward the long row of bottles stacked below the big mirror behind the bar. "Instead of lecturing, how about pouring?"

Tracy shook her head—and reached again for the Kessler rotgut on the bottom shelf.

"That's more like it," leered Arthur, who by now had settled back on his stool and was eyeing her with naked lust. And why not? Tracy Donovan was a flame-haired Irish beauty, and she knew it. Blessed with a pair of jade green eyes that could cut through steel and a terrific set of boobs, the fetching bartender had long ago learned how to parlay her good looks into the big tips that were paying her way through Suffolk University.

"There you go, sport," she wisecracked as she slid Arthur's next double toward him. "If you sip that instead of gulping it, you might have an easier time staying upright on that stool."

"Ten-four, boss lady," said Arthur, whose x-ray vision was now locked onto Tracy's tits and the cute little "Lucky Shamrock" bow tie that dipped and bobbed above them. "Whatever little Tracy wants, little Tracy *gets*."

Now his bleary eyes were sliding down her plaid skirt toward the black patent leather boots that gave her the sassy dominatrix look he so craved.

What a piece of ass, Arthur told himself. *If only I could get her to sit on my face!*

Deep down, of course, he knew his quest was hopeless . . . but he couldn't help himself. "Miss Tracy, I've got a question," he blurted with one hand raised in the air like an eager schoolboy's.

"Ask it, dipstick."

But the smart-ass remark wasn't malicious; Tracy's bottom lip was sticking out in mock belligerence.

Arthur took a deep breath and then took the plunge. "What time you gettin' off tonight, hon?"

In a flash, her green eyes went cold and her Irish smile evaporated.

"Sorry, but I have to finish a paper for school," she said. "I'm in the middle of pulling together—"

But at that moment she was interrupted—by a strange, singsong voice coming from the other end of the bar.

Hello, darkness, my old friend,
I've come to talk with you again.

The two of them turned to stare at the stocky, broad-shouldered man who until now had been sitting hunched over his solitary drink.

Apparently oblivious, the silent boozer way down at the far end of the bar had been minding his own business. But now he was singing to himself—rumbling through the Simon & Garfunkel classic in a harsh baritone that showed he had no musical talent at all.

> *Because a vision softly creeping*
> *Left its seeds while I was sleeping.*
> *And the vision that was planted in my brain*
> *Still remains*
> *Within the sound of silence.*

The two of them stared at the chunky stranger in the faded navy-blue blazer as if he'd just arrived from Mars.

Arthur, who wanted Tracy all to himself, finally broke the silence.

"What the fuck was *that*, mister, and who the fuck are *you*?"

The stranger didn't reply. He merely smiled. It was a thin smile, and cold, and Tracy felt a sudden flash of intuition: *This guy is one mean sonofabitch.*

For a moment, responding to the hint of violence in his eyes, she felt a flash of real fear.

"Simon and Garfunkel," said the stranger at last. "That was 1965. That was another world. Our beautiful bartender is too young to remember it, but I do.

"I remember it very well."

Arthur was scowling now. His face was an open book, and the message on it was easy to read: *How dare this rude fucker step between me and my luscious bartender?*

"What's your story, pal?" the fat man finally barked. "What's with the history lesson?" The questions

23

sounded like threats, but the singer only chuckled somewhere deep in his throat.

"Tracy knows my story," he said.

Tracy froze. *How does he know my name?* But then she remembered the plastic name badge she wore beneath the leprechaun bow tie.

"It's a story as old as the hills," said the crooner in a low, ominous voice. "It's a 'She Done Him Wrong' story, isn't it, Trace?"

The bartender stiffened. "I'm sorry," she said in a voice shakier than she'd intended, "but I really don't know what you're talking about."

Arthur was eager to help. "Leave her alone, mister. Let her be. You got that, pal?"

But the man at the other end of the bar pretended not to hear this.

"Bright red hair and vivid green eyes," he said with a barely audible chuckle. "I knew a girl like you once, Trace. A real *hottie*, believe me.

"An Irish lass with sweet dimples just like yours."

Tracy remained silent. She was trying to look away, but her gaze remained locked on the singer.

He's mean all the way down to the bone, she told herself. *Better stay clear.*

"We were an item, me and her," the newcomer rumbled on. "We were going to spend the rest of our lives together.

"But then our dreams all turned into nightmares."

He paused for a moment, sighed, and reached for his drink.

"Oh, I can tell you a thing or two about nightmares, my friends. I truly can."

Now he was leaning toward them and holding up his heavily bandaged right hand so they could see it clearly.

"Just last night, for example, I had a very strange nightmare. Are you with me, dear hearts? I dreamed that I was being burned, here on the back of my hand—burned with the image of a venomous snake, its fangs bared and ready to strike. . . ."

He smiled and drank. Amazed, nearly hypnotized, they watched him unwrap the bandage and turn the hand toward them.

"Yes, it was a deadly snake. I know you won't believe me, of course, but when I awoke this morning, the snake had been burned into the living flesh of my hand!"

They stared. He smiled. "Sounds crazy, doesn't it? The idea that a nightmare could actually become real?

"The idea that a dream tattoo could become a *real* tattoo?"

He was holding the tattooed hand above his head now, teasing them with it. "Do you see . . . do you see how it's still bleeding? Freshly cut, dear hearts. Freshly cut!"

Tracy didn't want to look. But her gaze was already darting toward the hand, toward the bleeding tattoo of the snake.

He laughed once, a growling sound—was it pride that made him laugh? "Say, do you happen to know The Spear, my friends? Do you know the works of Shakespeare—the greatest dramatist who ever picked up a pen?"

Astonished, they waited. "Do you know one of his greatest works, *The Tempest*, and that amazing moment when he has Prospero—the aging and gifted magician, Prospero—utter what may be the most powerful lines he ever wrote:

*"'We are such stuff as dreams are made on,
And our little life is rounded with a sleep!'"*

They gaped. The barroom had fallen utterly silent now. Mesmerized by the stranger's eloquence, they could only wait for the rest.

"Nightmares! Do either of you have any idea how terrible a nightmare can become?

"Can you imagine how much it hurts, in a nightmare, when the knife goes deep into your belly, when the knife blade slices again and again through your shuddering intestines?

"That's what *she* did to me, Tracy. A woman who looked exactly like you. She ruined me . . . this flame-haired woman who had made such passionate love to me. Naked, crawling across the carpet, her mouth blood red with wine, her tits gleaming in the candlelight, her nipples so taut and so hungry for my mouth, and she's pleading again and again: 'Fuck me and *keep* fucking me until I beg you to stop!'"

He fell back on his stool, eyes blazing.

Nothing moved. Listening, they were statues of frozen metal. They were paralyzed, until at last Tracy recovered. "Excuse me, but that language doesn't cut it in here. Either clean it up or take it somewhere else!"

But the newcomer ignored her warning. "And then," he went on with his tirade, "less than a year later, she put the knife in me. The cold steel, Tracy! She destroyed my career, destroyed my life forever . . . left me sitting in this third-rate barroom in downtown Boston.

"Left me sitting here with you and your pathetic loser friend—that guy over there with his belly hanging over his belt buckle."

But Arthur had finally heard enough. Gasping with the effort, he climbed down off the barstool and lumbered toward the man who slouched at the far end of the bar.

"Hold it right there!"

The new voice—icy and authoritative—belonged to Jerry Benevento, former Pro Bowl football star for the Boston Patriots and now the six-foot-five, 250-pound owner of Mulligan's, the Home of the Second Chance. He wore an old AFL jersey with his number emblazoned on the back.

Nobody moved.

"Okay, gentlemen," said the former defensive end, who'd been an all-star fixture in the AFL from 1961 through 1969, "here's what we're going to do next.

"We're going to finish our drinks and pay our tabs. Then we're going to say goodnight to each other and make our way out to our cars."

He smiled his cheerful smile—which featured the three gleaming new teeth he'd acquired after taking a savage hit in a playoff game with the New York Jets—at the two unhappy-looking men. "Tell me: does everybody here *like* my plan?"

The Simon & Garfunkel fan didn't respond. Moving slowly, unhurriedly, he tossed a ten-dollar bill on the bar.

Then, just before turning on his heel and heading for the front door:

"You'll be seeing me around, Tracy. You can count on that. You'll be seeing me in your nightmares."

And he was gone.

Benevento looked anxiously at his frowning and obviously rattled bartender. "Has that asshole been harassing you, Tracy?"

She shook her head. "Nah, he's just a jerk, that's all."

The giant in the Patriots jersey nodded thoughtfully. "That whacko fucker must be totally out of his mind. What was all that weird stuff he kept babbling about nightmares, anyway?"

Tracy was still shivering a little. "I have no idea, Jerry. What a creep!"

Jerry glowered. "If he ever comes back here, let me know and I'll throw his ass out on the street. Okay?"

She smiled. But it was a wobbly, uncertain smile.

"Will do, boss."

The two of them watched poor Arthur make his slow, shuffling journey across the barroom and out the front door.

CHAPTER 4
A Scream of Horror

Five hours later, as Tracy did her best to relax over a glass of chilled white wine in her tiny East Boston apartment, she couldn't stop thinking about the customer with the snake tattoo on the back of his hand.

That weirdo had freaked her out. But with her boyfriend out of town for two days—Brian Kearney's landscaping company was finishing up a new golf course down in Hartford—she was on her own and would have to soothe herself as best she could.

After pouring another generous helping of *vino*, she flipped on the TV . . . just in time to catch a rerun of *Laverne & Shirley*, her all-time favorite sitcom. Tonight's episode was a real screamer—with the two scatterbrained girls somehow getting themselves locked up after hours inside the massive Milwaukee brewery where they worked.

Alone and *very* tipsy—the two of them had been enjoying a lengthy "Shotz Brewery Happy Hour Testing" session before wandering off and getting lost somewhere in a labyrinth of storage tunnels and test tanks located beneath the Main Plant Boiler Works—they wandered from one security-bolted door to the next, while giggling and hooting about their ridiculous predicament.

Laverne: Geez, it's almost eight p.m., Shirl! Are we gonna have to spend the rest of the night down here or what?

Shirley: Well, if we do, at least we'll have lots of draft on tap!

Hah-hah-hah!

The audience "laugh track" buzzed with canned hilarity—but the still spooked Tracy didn't join in.

She reached again for the wine bottle. . . .

The popular sitcom rerun was followed by a documentary on the "Endangered Mountain Gorillas of Rwanda," but Tracy had seen enough. Soon she was stretched out on her narrow bed and drifting toward sleep. The wine did its job quickly enough; within ten minutes or so she was breathing quietly and even snoring a little.

Then the early REM phase set in.

***

About half an hour later she woke abruptly, startled by a loud clanging sound—as if someone were striking a metal pipe with a hammer.

For a moment she wondered if the janitor might be at work somewhere nearby. But the alarm clock on the night table said it was 2:13.

No way would Mr. Kovach be pounding on the water pipes in the middle of the night.

Lying motionless in the dark, she blinked slowly and waited for her eyes to adjust to the dim streetlight filtering through the window. *Uh-oh.* Was this the beginning of another nasty insomnia attack? They occurred about once a week. Stress related, probably. They often left her twisting and turning on her mattress for two or three hours at a time.

Just stay cool, stay relaxed.

Hoping to float back into dreamland, she closed her eyes and tried to project a pleasant, soothing scene on the backs of her eyelids. *Ah, yes, the beach at Hyannis!* As a child, Tracy had spent several summers running happily across the grass-covered dunes that made the Cape Cod seashore such a popular vacation spot.

What a joy it was, watching the creamy surf rise and tumble across the sand. Summertime at the shore . . . *and soon she'd be hurrying up the beach for another ice-cold strawberry lemonade!*

But then her eyes jerked open.

Something had made . . . a sound.

A groaning sound—like an old wooden door creaking slowly across a battered cement floor.

She felt a stab of alarm. Then a quick jolt of adrenaline—as she spotted a shadow above the TV set. That shadow didn't look right; it didn't *fit*.

The shadow was round, and flat . . . and moving slowly along the wall.

She looked closer and saw that it was the shadow of a hat, framed now in the pale streetlight falling through the window.

The shadow was moving. A man's hat, moving toward her.

She shot up into a sitting position, stunned, with her heart hammering painfully in her chest.

Her apartment door was open, wide open. A man was standing in the open doorway. A man in a slanted hat.

Amazed, she saw how he was tilting his head back a little, as if he intended to sing her a song.

Her gaze crawled slowly upward. She didn't want to look at his face, didn't want to see who he was—because she knew already (she had *always* known) that it was him.

It was *him*! But she couldn't stop herself from looking, and now she watched him step toward her with the light gleaming behind him in the open doorway and she couldn't stop herself from looking and seeing that it was *him!*

It was the face of the man in the bar, *the psycho at Mulligan's*. He was singing again. That same old song . . . the one he'd crooned at her earlier that day:

Hello darkness, my old friend,
I've come to talk with you again.

"Hello, Tracy."

His voice was low, flat, without inflection.

"So we meet again, my dear."

Numb with shock, she watched him lower himself slowly onto the room's only chair.

She heard it groan beneath his settling weight.

She looked around wildly, intent on escape . . . and was stunned to discover that the room seemed much larger now, and the ceiling appeared to be much farther away.

The distant walls had taken on a metallic shine—as if she'd been sleeping inside an enormous metal tank of some kind, a huge tank designed to hold thousands and thousands of gallons of . . . what?

A light-bodied draft on tap?

He uttered one word.

"Tracy." Just that one word. The two syllables went flashing and darting into the blank, terrified space behind her eyes.

"Tracy," he said again. He smiled a dead smile, and his laugh was cold and flat and without real mirth.

"Tracy, don't you think it's time we changed your name?"

She had begun to tremble, to shiver. Had the temperature fallen somehow? With a shock, she felt something even colder than the air brush her knee, her right knee, just below the place where her pajama shorts ended.

His hand!

"Hello, Alix," he growled. "Nice to see you again."

Tracy had stopped breathing.

Paralyzed with dread, she turned to speak to him, desperate to get him to make sense.

But her rushed words were full of holes, full of breathless gaps.

"Who are you and why are you calling me 'Alix'?"

He only smiled. His cold eyes, icy blue eyes, stared at her face.

Slowly, slowly, he lifted his right hand . . . and then gently placed it where her thighs met.

She shuddered. "What . . . what are you doing?"

He smiled. "Don't trouble your pretty little head with questions, Alix. All you have to do is remember one simple thing."

"Wha . . . what?"

He smiled again.

"Remember that I'll be back," he said.

The voice that had been struggling deep in her throat at last broke free and exploded in a scream of horror.

"No, please . . . don't hurt me . . . NO!"

***

She woke up a moment later . . . and vomited on the sweat-soaked mattress.

Heaving and retching, with the acid puke dribbling down her chin, she dragged herself into the bathroom and knelt helplessly for a good half-hour beside the toilet.

After that, she felt sick all afternoon . . . too sick to report for the start of her regular Friday shift at four o'clock. But as the hours dragged on, she saw that she had to find a way to make it in. For one thing, she needed the bigger tips she would earn on the weekend. And deep down, she feared that if she once started missing work over these kinds of psychological issues—over what was nothing more than a painful nightmare, after all —she might *really* start to fall apart, might *really* start to lose it.

You gotta get in there, Tracy, regardless of how you feel!

It was a struggle—but she finally managed to step into the shower, shampoo her tangled, sweat-damp hair and apply her usual makeup.

By four o'clock sharp, she was striding through the back door at Mulligan's. Her strong mouth was set now, and her eyes were blazing with determination.

Things went well . . . until about eight-thirty, when the front door of the Irish tavern swung open and in walked a stocky, shuffling, grinning man whose image sent a bolt of dread into the middle of her gut.

She studied him. Studied the same unshaven face, the same stained and faded navy-blue blazer.

"Hello, Tracy," he said. He was looking right at her. Boldly, even arrogantly. "Nice to see you again, babe."

She stared at him. "What do you want?"

He laughed out loud. "What do most people want, Tracy, when they walk into a bar? I want a drink!"

He chuckled, and the sound was cold, cold in her ear.

"Oh," he said then, as if it were a sudden after-thought, "I also wanted to ask you how you slept last night."

She gasped.

"How I . . . *slept*?"

He chuckled. "I hope you had pleasant dreams?"

She gasped again, and one terrified hand shot upwards to her mouth.

"My . . . *dreams*?"

He smiled. "I hope you weren't bothered by all that banging on the pipes . . . by the clanging of the pipes in that beat-up old brewery where you live?

"Really . . . don't you think you should tell Mr. Kovach not to make so much noise at night?"

Her eyes widened.

She screamed: "Jerry! Jerry! Help me! Please, Jerry!"

The swinging doors behind her slammed wide open as the former pro football player came blasting his way out of the kitchen.

"Jerry . . . it's him. It's *him*!"

The big man in the green apron stepped toward the bar. "Listen, you asshole. . . ."

But her sneering visitor was already hurrying toward the front door of Mulligan's.

He pushed it open . . . and then turned back for an instant.

"I'll be seeing you!" he shouted at her.

The bartender felt herself beginning to faint, as the giant in the apron waved his huge fist.

"I'll be visiting you again real soon, Tracy. I'll drop by late at night, okay? Pleasant dreams, sweetheart!"

Then Dr. Michael Rogers closed the door and vanished into the darkness.

CHAPTER 5
Big Pine, Here We Come!

Alix was enjoying a pleasant daydream—big yellow butterflies hovering above a cobalt blue New England lake—when a polite hand tapped her gently on the shoulder.

"Excuse me, miss. I need you to bring your seatback to the upright position for landing."

Alix opened one eye. "Oh, sure, no problem!"

The attendant smiled, nodded, and continued her journey down the narrow aisle.

Awakening slowly from her bright reverie, Alix yawned once, stretched, and then hit the button on the armrest and felt the seatback instantly respond.

A few minutes later she was gazing through her window as the harborside city of Portland, Maine, rushed up toward the wheels of the descending jet.

It was Wednesday afternoon, about 4:30. Alix Cassidy's summer-long adventure at the Big Pine Research Center for the Study of the Paranormal was about to begin.

As she felt the thump of the landing gear vibrate through her feet, Alix was asking herself what the next couple of months would be like. After studying half a dozen scientific papers that had recently been authored by conference participants, along with a detailed lecture schedule, she had a pretty clear fix on the arcane topics such as "The Dynamics of Precognition" and

"Understanding Reincarnation" that she'd be hearing about in the days ahead.

In between attending those lectures, of course, she'd also be lecturing on her own highly speculative topic, the controversial phenomenon known as "Somnambulistic Telepathy."

Alix knew a great deal about that often hotly debated area of psychic research, and for good reason. As the author of a recent breakthrough paper on the topic in the authoritative *Journal of the Paranormal*, she was now regarded as a budding authority on the theory that says some human beings are capable of "invading" the nightmares of others.

According to Alix's article, this amazing phenomenon had been accomplished more than once, via a telepathic process known as "dream travel"—a so-far-unexplained psychic activity in which certain gifted individuals are reportedly able to cross the physical boundaries that separate them from other people and then temporarily inhabit their sleeping brains.

A fascinating quest? You bet. Fortunately, and in spite of Dr. Jacobson's good-natured but very real skepticism, Alix had been allowed to pursue her interest in "ST" without hindrance at the Sleep Disorder Center of Atlanta . . . even though the roots of that interest lay in the notorious 12-year-old "Laura and David" case.

That sensational 1974 incident, violent and macabre in the extreme, had dragged the famous Atlanta research institute into a lurid medical scandal that read like the script from a Hollywood sci-fi melodrama. . . .

But all of that was in the past now.

As the jet's straining engines went into full-thrust reverse, Alix Cassidy was located very much in the present. For the next two months, she'd be living among a group of cutting-edge scientists who wouldn't automatically assume that her ideas about ST were "far out" or "unscientific".

This was to be Alix's "summer of paranormal vindication"—or so she hoped. At this moment she felt fully prepared for whatever might lie ahead.

Bring it on, she told herself as she climbed to her feet and reached toward the overhead storage bin for her carry-on luggage.

Whatever's coming next . . . bring it on!

***

The crowded Portland International Jetport terminal was a swirl of bright summer colors, but there was no mistaking the big cardboard sign—*CASSIDY*—or the smiling but frumpy-looking woman who held it.

"Dr. Violette?"

"Dr. Cassidy?"

A moment later, the sign lay in a nearby trash receptacle, and the two women were both laughing and talking a mile a minute.

They were also looking each other over carefully.

Dr. Roslyn ("Call me Rozzie!") Violette turned out to be a chunky, broad-shouldered woman whose drab-colored skirt and wire "granny glasses" gave her the look of an old-fashioned schoolmarm.

But that first impression was subtly countered by the low-cut, purple-hued Birkenstocks on her very large feet, and by the fire engine red polish that gleamed from her jutting toenails.

Eyeballing the jovial paranormal researcher, who was also a highly regarded academician with a doctorate in her field, Alix felt a wave of instant affection wash over her.

This lady looked *interesting*. She also looked like *fun* . . . and when she spoke, Alix's initial take on her was promptly reinforced.

"Alix, I can't tell you how pleased I am to shake the hand of an accomplished sleep scientist, and especially a scientist who's famous for having an open mind. I read your paper on ST for the third time last week, and then I spent half the afternoon pacing around my office while my poor brain positively *whirled* with questions!"

A moment later, the longtime Big Pine Executive Director was once again grasping Alix's hand. "I'm really looking forward to your lectures on ST!"

Understandably enough, Alix was thrilled to the core by her colleague's upbeat assessment of her work.

"How very kind of you, Rozzie!" she breathed as the two of them made their way toward Baggage Claim. "I hope you'll let me return the compliment—by pointing out that I just finished your article on precognitive experiences among adolescents last week!"

Chatting happily, the two women soon collared Alix's two suitcases and made their way out to the parking lot.

When Rozzie pointed to her ride—a battered old Ford pickup truck with more than 300,000 miles on the odometer—Alix found herself laughing out loud.

"Wow! You're driving an American classic. Nice set of wheels!"

"Give it a good yank!" Rozzie barked as Alix approached the passenger side door. "That damn latch likes to stick, so you gotta start by teaching it a little *respect!*"

Nodding, Alix pulled on the balky handle with all her strength.

The door flew obediently open, triggering a wild laugh from the woman in the purple Birkenstocks.

"That's it, Alix. Welcome to the great State of Maine. Did you know, we've got more pickup trucks per capita than any other state in the union? It's true . . . and it's *also* true that we don't take shit from any of them!" Rozzie roared again and turned the ignition key.

Two minutes later they were exiting the parking lot and swinging north onto the I-95 Maine Turnpike for the first leg of their four-hour run to Moosehead Lake—the isolated woodland home of the Big Pine Research Center for the Study of the Paranormal.

CHAPTER 6
A Sudden Warning

After enjoying a quick snack at a Burger King on the outskirts of Augusta, the two women jumped back into the truck and rolled north again. Soon they were clattering past the exit signs for Fairfield, Waterville, and a series of other Central Maine towns, with both of them prattling away.

They exited I-95 at Palmyra and continued onto a rural blacktop that ran off toward the foothills of the Longfellow Mountains. From time to time, Alix would catch a flashing glimpse of pale blue water glinting beneath the warm June sunshine.

"Absolutely beautiful," she told the woman perched behind the wheel. "I bet that's Moosehead Lake off in the distance."

"Sure is," said Rozzie. "Biggest lake in Maine—and also the biggest *mountain* lake east of the Mississippi. You aren't gonna believe Big Pine, honey. The center is located on a giant pine bluff above the southeast shore of the lake. The setting is majestic."

"So I gather," said Alix. "I read a lot of stuff about nearby Mount Kineo and Sugar Island. They both sound wonderful."

"Looks like you've been doing your homework," said Rozzie with a chuckle. "Well, I can promise you one thing: you won't be disappointed by the landscape. The only problem with putting a research center in the middle of a lakefront paradise is that you're constantly tempted to go swimming or canoeing—or maybe even bass fishing—instead of attending your next lecture!"

Alix nodded. "It sounds fabulous, Rozzie — especially if you've never been to Maine before. I visited Boston a few years back, but other than that, I've spent zero time in New England. So this is all new to me."

Now the woman at the wheel was laughing out loud. "You better not tell anybody at Big Pine that you think the northern half of Maine is part of New England," she said with a hoot of delight. "Once you get up around Moosehead Lake and environs, you've got Canada lurking on three sides of you . . . and the terrain feels so wild and remote it's hard to believe you're still in the good old USA."

She roared at her own joke, and then tapped the brake pedal with a purple sandal.

The old pickup shuddered in response, and their speed quickly diminished. Soon they were approaching an old-fashioned wooden sign that featured a hand-carved arrow indicating an approaching right turn.

Beneath the arrow were two words in capital letters and a number that told them all they needed to know. BIG PINE 11.

"Hang onto your hat," Rozzie shouted as the old Ford rattled through a series of deep ruts.

"From here on, the ride's gonna get a little *bumpy!*"

***

They drove slowly through the lakeside campus—a modest assemblage of five wooden buildings, each one story in height—that loomed high on a bluff above the pearl blue waters of Moosehead Lake. It was late afternoon by now, and the declining sun hovered like a ball of molten gold above the dark green spruces and firs fringing the study center.

"This is really quite lovely," enthused Alix. "Look at all those canoes. Is Big Pine an academic study center or a summer resort for nature lovers?"

"Both," said Rozzie. "Just kick back and enjoy!"

She turned the wheel sharply, and the truck's worn tires skidded across a patch of white gravel. "Hey, before I take you down to your cabin—also known as 'Yurt Streamside'—I want to show you our pride and joy."

She had pulled the Ford into a space marked "Rozzie's Spot!" Now they were parked alongside a low-slung building fronted by a green-painted triangular sign that featured a majestic-looking loon and a hand-painted legend, *Welcome to Big Pine*.

The two women climbed down from the pickup and Rozzie led the way across the gravel toward the swinging wooden doors at the center of the building.

But then she stopped walking and held up one hand.

Startled, Alix lurched to a stop beside her.

At the same moment, a powerful gust of wind rolled over both of them. The sharp breeze was cold . . . at least ten degrees colder than the surrounding air . . . and when it hit the branches of a nearby pine, they responded instantly.

Bending and scraping against the tree trunk, they sent up an uncanny, moaning sound. For a moment, Alix could have sworn it was the voice of someone (some desolate, tormented woman?) weeping in hopeless sorrow.

Then the sound deepened, became a low mutter, almost a growl, before gradually fading off in the direction of the surrounding lake.

"What in the world was *that*?" said Alix.

Rozzie was smiling back at her. "Who knows, honey? But you better get used to it, because it happens all the time at Big Pine! We don't know if it's an Indian spirit who wants his tribal lands back, or maybe some long-dead pioneer settler who got stuck on this side of the afterlife."

She laughed. "Whatever it is, it seems quite harmless. And also very *interesting*, don't you think?"

She turned then, while Alix stared at her in amazement, and resumed her march toward the front doors of the center. Moving with surprising grace for a woman with such big feet, Dr. Violette took her guest on a quick tour of the facility, which consisted of half a dozen gleaming laboratories and a small auditorium containing about 150 seats and a state-of-the-art movie and TV projection system.

Together they strolled down to the pocket-sized stage, where a large yellow placard still advertised a lecture session that had taken place earlier that day.

Can the Dead Really Live Again?

How Effective Are Randomized Controlled Trials at Determining the Accuracy of Reincarnation Narratives?

(Or . . . Did Stephen King Actually Get It *Right* in *Pet Sematary*?)

Panel Discussion Follows

Moderator: Dr. Gunther Sverdlow, Geneva Paranormal Institute

"That was Dr. Sverdlow's presentation at ten this morning," said Rozzie. "Are you familiar with his studies in precognition?"

"I am," said Alix. "I take it he's a very influential figure in his discipline."

Rozzie nodded. "And a dynamic lecturer as well. Wait 'til you see him in action. It's like watching Houdini at work—quite mesmerizing."

Alix was intrigued. "He came here all the way from Geneva, am I right? For the entire summer?"

"Sure did," said Rozzie. "He's this summer's superstar, no question. The Boston *Globe*'s top science writer was up here last week interviewing him—and me, too—for hours on end. We were both properly impressed.

"We're told there's going to be a story about us in next week's *Sunday Globe Magazine*—who'd a-thunk it?"

They both laughed . . . and then stopped short when the doors at the front of the auditorium swung open.

All at once a tall man in a neatly pressed lab coat was leading a tiny white-haired woman toward them.

"Oh, hello, Dr. Andrews!" Without hesitating, Rozzie was reaching out to shake his hand. "This is Dr. Alix Cassidy, you know, from the Sleep Disorder Center in Atlanta? I just ferried her up to BP from the airport in Portland. Alix, this is my colleague and fellow researcher Dr. James Andrews."

Dr. Andrews smiled broadly, and a ray of sunlight from the nearby windows flashed in his horn-rimmed glasses. He shook their visitor's hand, pumping it up and down with great enthusiasm.

"Alix, I read that last article you wrote on ST. Wonderfully interesting stuff. Welcome to Big Pine!"

He turned to the tiny woman at his side. She stood well under five feet tall, but with a strong chin and penetrating brown eyes that gave her weathered features a look of fierce intensity.

"Alix, I'd like you to meet Melinda Birdsong. She's the Chief Medicine Woman of the Abenaki Tribe, right here in Central Maine. She also has an outstanding reputation as a psychic and healer with remarkable powers of clairvoyance."

Alix's eyes widened. "Melinda, it's an honor to meet you. I've been looking forward to learning more about your remarkable work with the Abenaki, ever since I heard you'd be in residence here this summer."

Beneath her shock of snow-white hair, the tiny woman didn't respond at first.

For at least ten seconds, she remained utterly expressionless.

Then she opened her mouth . . . and the sound that emerged was like nothing Alix Cassidy had heard before.

It was a thin, fretful singsong . . . a moaning sound like the wind going through a forest of snow-laden pine boughs.

Amazed, Alix stared in wonder at the psychic . . . while her eerie voice rose and fell like a siren.

Naaaaaii-eeeeeeh-wah!
Naaaaaii-eeeeeeh-wah!

A moment later the windows at the rear of the auditorium began to go dark . . . as a pair of enormous black wings appeared to suddenly block out the sunlight.

Alix gasped. Somehow, this brightly lit space was now sinking into deep shadow, sinking beneath a wave of sinister darkness. At nearly the same instant, the temperature in the BP auditorium plummeted almost to the shivering point.

Alix gasped with the shock of it. Was she the only one feeling the sudden cold?

Naaaaaii-eeeeeeh-wah!

The world stood still for a moment.

And then the Abenaki Medicine Woman sent up another terrible shriek.

It was an earsplitting scream, a nightmare scream that cut into Alix's ears like a flashing dagger and froze her on the spot:

"CURSED!"

Blinking with amazement, both Dr. Andrews and Dr. Violette were leaning in closer to Alix now, as if trying to protect her from the medicine woman's gathering wrath.

Then the spell finally broke. Like a handful of icicles flung against a brick wall, the Abenaki psychic's voice rang out on the air one last time and fell silent.

A few seconds later—it seemed like a month to Alix—Dr. Andrews had wrapped one arm around the Native American's shoulders and was leading her back up the center aisle of the auditorium.

But he couldn't prevent her from pausing in the doorway and turning back . . . turning back to wail out one final and unholy imprecation:

"CURSED!"

Staggered to the teeth, Alix felt her heart hammering against her ribs.

For a terrible second or two, she wondered if she might actually faint.

Cursed . . . cursed . . . it was the same terrifying word she'd heard 12 years before, back during those terrible struggles with Laura and David—and that viciously twisted psychiatrist, Dr. Michael Rogers!

Struggling with the memory of it, she took a step and nearly fell.

I will not be terrorized again, she told herself as she fought to control her shaking hands. *I do NOT believe in the power of the curse!*

"My God, Rozzie," she gasped at the heavy-shouldered woman who was now doing her best to help her up the center aisle of the auditorium.

"What was *that* all about?"

CHAPTER 7
Remembering a Brutal Suicide

The next day—Alix's first full day at Big Pine—began with a short hike on nearby Rattlesnake Mountain, where the early morning mist swirled through the dripping branches and the cries of distant loons echoed faintly through the chilly air.

After a quick shower and a cup of coffee, she hurried from her cabin to the lecture hall. She was just in time for the start of the globetrotting Dr. Sverdlow's lecture, "Precognition and *Dasein*: Did Martin Heidegger Establish a Philosophical Basis for ESP?"

Amazed, Alix listened intently from her seat at the front of the auditorium as one of the 20th Century's most highly regarded researchers on paranormal topics discussed the links between psychic phenomena and mainstream existentialist philosophy.

Again and again, as she reflected on how several of her era's most powerful thinkers—Heidegger, Sartre, Buber, Jung—had speculated that the human mind actually operates in dimensions far beyond the reach of most human beings, Alix was challenged to keep up.

During lunchtime, while she and Rozzie sat munching turkey-and-Swiss sandwiches in the locally famous Big Pine *Kaffee Klatch,* Alix talked excitedly about her own highly experimental research in Somnambulistic Telepathy—the widely debated psychological phenomenon in which a few uniquely gifted humans are reportedly able to enter into (and participate in) the nightmares of others.

Rozzie was deeply interested and very supportive, of course, but when she expressed some old-fashioned skepticism about whether or not two sleepers could share the same dream, the animated Alix jumped into high gear.

"Believe me, I was just as skeptical as you are at first," she told her new friend. "But something happened to me about twelve years ago—something very strange. As a matter of fact, it was the strangest thing I've ever witnessed in my life."

Rozzie's left eyebrow rose slightly. But it was obvious that she loved a good story, especially if it contained a dash or two of weirdness.

"I was doing some research on this young woman at the sleep lab in Atlanta," said Alix. "She was suffering from brutal nightmares that were apparently subjecting her to insomnia, weight loss and half a dozen other health problems."

Nodding intently, Rozzie soaked up every word.

Alix paused for a second to collect her thoughts. "I know you'll find this difficult to swallow, Roz, but I uncovered a ton of objectively verifiable evidence to show that the young woman involved—Laura —was being attacked in her sleep by a man named David.

"He was a deeply disturbed Vietnam War combat veteran who was suffering from what we later learned was PTSD."

Rozzie picked up her coffee cup but didn't drink from it. "All right, I'll take your word about the scientific evidence," she said after a bit. "But what was the upshot,

Alix? What were the actual implications in psychological terms?"

"Great question," Alix shot back. "To answer it, I need to tell you what happened. After I'd worked with Laura for a few months, it became clear to me that David was torturing her in her sleep. He had somehow gained access to her nightmares.

"It also became clear that David himself was being manipulated by this unscrupulous psychiatrist in Boston—a really sleazy Svengali-type named Michael Rogers, who'd discovered the reality of ST and was determined to hype it for his own purposes.

"Rogers was a pathetic liar and deeply pathological himself. He was hoping to garner all the rewards that would flow from having achieved this huge breakthrough in understanding the true dynamics of human dreaming. He continued to manipulate both Laura and David—without trying to get them any real medical help at all—until the poor Vietnam veteran finally crashed and burned."

Alix had been stirring a packet of sugar substitute into her coffee, but now she stopped.

"Here's the part you *really* aren't going to believe," she told Rozzie. "After a while, it became quite evident that this Rogers guy knew all about David's strange nightmares, and that he was using that knowledge in an effort to control David *and* his girlfriend Laura."

Rozzie's hazel eyes had widened noticeably by now. "You're right, honey; I *don't* believe it." She sent up a ringing laugh. "Still, we should never let facts get in the way of a good story, right?"

Alix sighed, but good-naturedly. She'd long ago grown accustomed to this kind of skepticism.

She'd also learned how to let the facts speak for themselves . . . and instead of arguing with her new pal, she was now digging into her dark brown zippered purse.

"I finally called the police in an effort to save Laura from David. By then he'd already abducted her and was holding her in a filthy basement in Boston. He had a knife to her genitals, and he also had a gun."

She handed a yellowed newspaper clipping to her skeptical friend. "Somehow, Michael *also* found out that Laura was being held in the basement, and he showed up there as well. Don't ask me how he knew this, but he did. When the police finally arrived, they had to break the door down.

"As they did so, David shot himself in the head and died instantly. It's all right there in that Boston *Globe* clipping from 12 years ago."

Rozzie didn't speak for a minute. Wide-eyed with amazement, she was eyeballing the wrinkled piece of newsprint on the table before her.

Boston Vietnam Vet Takes Former Fiancée Hostage, Before Shooting Himself in Grisly Basement Suicide

A deeply troubled Vietnam War veteran who was reportedly suffering from "Post-Vietnam War Syndrome" shot himself to death in a basement in the Mattapan section of Boston yesterday afternoon, according to state and local police.

The alleged hostage-taker, 25-year-old David Collier (address unknown) reportedly kidnapped his former fiancée and was holding her at gunpoint in a basement at 1012 Revere Street, according to a police spokesman.

Police said the suicide victim was being treated for depression and recurring violent nightmares by a Boston VA psychiatrist, Dr. Michael Rogers, who was also on the scene when the tragic incident occurred. . . .

After nearly a minute of deep concentration, Rozzie looked up from the *Globe* clipping.

"Holy moly," she blurted at the woman on the other side of the table. "Are you telling me this David fellow was . . . like . . . traveling in and out of Laura's nightmares at *will?*"

Alix nodded. "That's exactly what I'm telling you, Rozzie."

"But how? How? I mean, I'm a psychic . . . but even for me, it just doesn't seem possible, not given the ordinary rules of logic—to say nothing about the ordinary rules of physics."

Alix took a sip of coffee. "I don't *know* how, Rozzie. I've spent the past dozen years trying to answer that very question. And to tell you the honest truth, I'm not sure that I've made a whole lot of headway in figuring the puzzle out!"

She frowned thoughtfully, and then her vivid green eyes took on a faraway look. "The whole thing was very strange, very uncanny. And there were elements of the supernatural as well.

"It was truly weird, let me tell you. Mike—Dr. Rogers, I mean—was convinced that David had been attacked by some sort of *curse* while he was fighting in Vietnam."

But now Rozzie was staring at her, openmouthed.

"Mike? *Mike*? Alix . . . if you don't mind me asking: how close were you and this . . . this corrupt psychiatrist?"

Alix didn't answer for a bit. Her eyes had gone to the big picture window, to the distant, looming vista of Moosehead Lake and Rattlesnake Mountain.

"Oh, my God," said Rozzie. Her coffee cup made a ringing sound as she banged it on the table. "Are you telling me that this . . . this Dr. Rogers and you were . . . *tight*?"

No response.

And none needed.

After a few seconds, Rozzie sighed heavily. "Alix, I don't want to intrude, but the suspense is killing me, and I gotta ask: where is this Mike Rogers today? What happened to him? Is he still working as a shrink at the Boston VA?"

Once again, Alix didn't reply. The faraway look in her eyes had been replaced by a look of icy disdain.

"I don't know what happened to him, Rozzie, and I don't *care* what happened. As far as I'm concerned, that chapter of my life is over now.

"He's part of the past, and the past is gone forever."

Is it? Rozzie's eyes were riveted on Alix now. *Is the past ever really "gone?"* she was asking herself.

Or does it linger on and on—ready to pounce again at any moment?

Perhaps Alix was thinking the same thing.

All at once, the sleep researcher's eyes were full of tears.

CHAPTER 8
The Chase

Lunchtime.

Two City of Boston detectives—Jake Becker and Tony Rizzo—were standing in line at Murray's Jewish Delicatessen on Commonwealth Avenue.

Detective Rizzo, decidedly un-Jewish, was studying the hand-lettered sign above the pickle barrel: "*Ess Gezunterheyt.*"

Tony was also scratching his prematurely balding head.

"*Ess Gez*-what*?* What the fuck does that mean?"

Jake gazed calmly back at him. "It's Yiddish for 'Eat in good health.' And you know I don't appreciate that street language. Do me a favor and clean it up."

Tony glared. An Italian bulldog whose Sicilian grandparents had been enormously talented glarers themselves, Jake's new partner had the icy stare down pat.

"Hey, I'm a wop, pal—as in 'Without Papers'! My parents were Italian immigrants and I grew up on the streets. Plus, I just spent the last ten years taking down drug dealers for the Boston PD. Sorry, but this is how I *talk.*"

Jake sighed and shook his head. "What? A second-generation Italian-American police detective has to sound like a moron? Is that the idea?"

Tony snorted, but without real rancor. "Okay, Jake, I'll agree to knock off the street lingo—if *you'll* promise to stop talking like a Harvard English professor, okay?"

They both laughed. At the 13th Precinct— headquarters for the Boston Homicide Division—they had a nickname for Jake Becker.

They called him "The Professor." Becker was a Jewish egghead. Everyone knew that. Also a raging liberal on most social issues. But he was one hell of a detective, so they tolerated his wackiness, if grudgingly.

Now he said: "Let's stop debating and start eating. My treat. You can pick up the check next time we hit Regina's in the North End."

Rizzo opened his mouth to reply, but was interrupted.

A heavyset man in a silver-flecked handlebar mustache was pointing at them. "Will you look at what the wind blew in?" growled Murray Fisher, the longtime deli owner.

"How you been getting by, Jake?"

"Doing okay, Murray. This is my new partner, Tony Rizzo. He was a heckuva narcotics detective for a lot of years, but now he's decided he wants to work in Homicide. We're just getting to know each other, and Tony decided he wanted to experience the gustatory wonders of the classic Jewish delicatessen."

"Welcome, Tony."

"Thank you," said Rizzo. "Goose-a-tory wonders? Murray, there's something *wrong* with this guy."

"I know," said Murray.

"He talks funny," said Rizzo. "Uses words nobody can understand."

"Tell me about it," said Murray. Then, addressing the slender man in the pale gray suit: "How's that wonderful daughter of yours doing, Professor? She still giving you fits?"

"Absolutely," Jake replied. Then he groaned. "Charly's fourteen, after all . . . what else should I expect?"

"Teenagers," said Tony. "I got two, as we speak. For a while there, I thought I might have to cut my wrists."

The other two laughed and nodded.

"She's at the stage where she knows everything," Jake went on. "Einstein was a dimwit, compared to Charly." He sighed. Smiled. "But she's a good kid, Murray—I love her madly."

"I wish I could say the same about my two," said Tony. "This morning at breakfast, they were talking about sticking up a Brink's truck. I'm pretty sure they were serious."

More laughter all around. Then: "It can't be easy for you, being a single parent," Murray said to Jake. He was looking away from the two of them now, looking at the big menu board on the far wall. "A teenage girl needs a mother."

"We get by," said Jake, "but thank you for asking, Murray. I do miss Ruth a lot. As a matter of fact, as soon as I feed my pal Tony here, I'm going to head over to the cemetery for my yearly visit to her grave."
"Good, that's very good."

Nodding and smiling, the deli maestro had begun rubbing his chubby hands together. "All right. Let's get you two fed. How about a couple of cheese blintzes? The wife just made 'em. Her grandparents brought the recipe all the way from Russia!"

"Cheese blimps?" Tony was frowning. Uncomprehending.

"*Blintzes*," said Jake. "It's a thin pancake filled with cheese. Jeez, I can't take you anywhere."

"They're sweet as the life-giving manna from heaven," rhapsodized Murray, "and that's a quote directly from the great Yiddish writer, Sholem Aleichem."

"Well, pardon me for not being one of the tribe," said Rizzo.

"How about I order up some *real* lunch—maybe a cheeseburger and fries?"

Jake laughed good-naturedly. "Don't chicken out on me, Tony. I promised you an amazing sandwich, and we're not leaving here until you eat it." He turned back to Murray.

"How about a Reuben on dark rye for my fellow detective? He'll never stop thanking us."

"I'm on it," said Murray. "You?"

"The same. And give us a double order of the potato *latkes*, with some apple sauce and sour cream on the side."

"Potato *latch*-keys?" said Rizzo. His Sicilian face had morphed into a swirling mask of incomprehension.

"I never heard of any potatoes like that. Hey, how do I even know this stuff is safe to eat?"

"You'll have to trust me," said Jake. "You have no other choice."

"Gimme five minutes," laughed Murray. The chunky man in the apron turned away, and the two cops headed for a table against the back wall. They settled in beneath yet another Yiddish motto (*A Bi Gezunt . . . Don't worry so much, whatever it is, you've still got your health!*). Once seated, they unhooked their cumbersome belt radios and slid them off to one side.

A moment later Tony reached into his shirt pocket and retrieved his pack of Camels. But Jake shook his head.

"Don't even think about it."

"What? I can't smoke? Jews don't smoke cigarettes?"

"Some do. Then they get lung cancer and die. I'm not breathing that poison—so please put 'em right back in your shirt."

Rizzo was glaring again. "I can't believe this shit. Man, you are so uptight . . . Freud would have had a field day with you."

"You think so? Well, Freud was *also* Jewish—so go figure."

Rizzo made a chuckling sound somewhere deep in his throat. "Okay, I'll lay off the weed, at least until the end of the workday. But that don't mean I won't light up as soon as I pour that first cold brew at night!"

Jake smiled back at him. "Your call, Tony. And I certainly agree. You have a perfect right to undergo the agonies of emphysema and heart disease and stroke . . . all for the sake of a few puffs of—"

But his next words were cut off. Suddenly, both belt radios were chattering at once. Jake had turned the volume down on his—he didn't like advertising the fact that he was a cop. But during his two decades on the force, he'd learned how to listen to the lower-voiced device with one keenly attuned ear.

ALL UNITS, TEN-FORTY-SEVEN.

Both men froze. The numerical code meant: *Robbery in Progress*.

TEN-FORTY-SEVEN INVOLVING A TEN-THIRTY-TWO. LOCATION IS MARTIGNETTI LIQUOR STORE, WORTHINGTON AT AMORY. ALL UNITS IN THE VICINITY OF

WORTHINGTON AND AMORY RESPOND
IMMEDIATELY. SUSPECT CONSIDERED
EXTREMELY DANGEROUS.

"Ten-thirty-two" meant: *Armed Suspect.*

The two cops stared at each other, and it was Becker who spoke first. "Worthington and Amory. That's only a few blocks from here."

Tony was blinking fast. "You're right."

"Grab your portable and gimme the cruiser keys."

Tony's eyes widened. "You want the keys? Why?"

Jake was already on his feet. "I'm driving, that's why. Gimme the keys." Tony looked unhappy, but he didn't speak. As a veteran sergeant in CID—the Criminal Investigation Division of the Boston PD—and a homicide detective with more than 15 years of experience, Jake didn't have to ask twice. He had rank.

Tony handed over the keys.

Now they were running for the door. And feeling the adrenaline. During the past six months or so, Boston had been awash in convenience store holdups . . . sometimes perpetrated by drug-zonked crazies outfitted with blazing handguns.

Only three days before, Vincent and Jane Cantrello — they'd been running a mom-and-pop liquor store on Blue Hill Avenue for the past 40 years—had been taken down by a .38 revolver in the hands of a street thug sky-high on crack. They'd been shot point blank. Both of them. Now they lay side by side in a Catholic cemetery in South Boston.

Adrenaline! They pounded across the parking lot behind Murray's, running for their unmarked car.

"Get on the horn," Becker thundered. "Tell Dispatch we're responding."

Tony fumbled for his radio. Behind them, they could hear a distraught voice wailing in their direction: "Hey . . . what the hell, guys . . . your *sandwiches* are ready!"

Murray got no reply.

As they dove into the car, Tony was already barking into the radio: "Unit Twenty-Four—copy. We are responding to armed robbery at Martignetti Liquor Store, from Commonwealth and Essex."

Tony glanced at Jake, who was holding up three fingers. "ETA . . . three minutes."

The radio screeched once, then crackled with static: COPY UNIT TWENTY-FOUR, I HAVE YOU RESPONDING TO TEN-FORTY-SEVEN FROM COMMONWEALTH AND ESSEX, ETA THREE MINUTES.

Jake shifted into reverse, and the big tires on the unmarked spat gravel as they skidded backwards across the lot. "Hit the blue, Tony!"

His partner nodded, then yanked the bubble flasher from the dashboard and clamped it onto the roof, where a powerful magnet would keep it stable. The black plastic cord's loose end snapped into the cigarette lighter.

With his free hand, the younger cop hit the toggle switch that triggered the wailing siren.

"Shut if off!" roared Jake.

"Huh? *Off?*" Tony was gaping at him.

"Why don't you just send the perp a telegram telling him we're on the way?"

Tony hit the switch again. "Okay, whatever you say, Professor."

The unmarked was a silent phantom now, flashing blue. Intent behind the wheel, Jake had narrowed his eyes to slits as he scanned the busy traffic ahead. At Worthington and Amory, he caught a flash of movement to his left.

Look out!

With a lightning-quick response, he crunched the brake and the unmarked car fishtailed through a long, shuddering slide, then walloped into the curb.

"Jesus, Jake! What the hell?"

They'd barely missed a tiny Asian woman carrying a big paper bag of Stop & Shop groceries. With her vision partially obscured by the bag, she'd stepped into traffic against the stoplight—and she'd nearly paid for it with her life. Now the groceries were flying. Jake watched a huge yellow squash go tumbling end over end through space.

A moment later the old lady was screaming bloody murder at them both: "Fucky you, you beeg Ah-mer-ee-can *po*-lice, you stupid plicks!"

Tony didn't sound much happier: "Jeez, Jake, you nearly killed her."

"That's correct. Your adverb is on target, Tony: *nearly*. She'll be okay." Jake gritted his teeth.

ATTENTION RESPONDING UNITS—SUSPECT HAS LEFT THE LIQUOR STORE. WITNESS PUTS HIM IN THE ALLEYWAY RUNNING SOUTH FROM AMORY.

Jake eased the unmarked past a giant cement truck with a revolving mixer.

SUSPECT DESCRIBED AS WHITE MALE, SIX FEET, ONE HUNDRED EIGHTY POUNDS, EIGHTEEN TO TWENTY-FOUR YEARS OLD. WEARING BLACK-BILLED BASEBALL CAP WITH

RED SOX LOGO, DARK SUNGLASSES, WHITE
SNEAKERS.

APPROACHING UNITS ADVISED TO USE
EXTREME CAUTION—SUSPECT ARMED AND
DANGEROUS.

They were less than two hundred feet from the liquor
store.

Leaning forward, Tony peered through the
windshield. He saw a gleam of light wink against plastic
sunglasses. "There he is! In the alley . . . hope you
brought your running shoes, Professor!"

The car rocked to a stop as the tires bit at the asphalt,
and the doors flew open on both sides. Now they were
running, flying across the tiny parking lot that bordered
the store, headed for the alley.

Forty yards ahead, the suspect was hightailing it, with
the outline of his handgun clearly visible below his right
hand.

Tony was on the radio again: "Dispatch, we've got the
suspect in sight. He's in the alley behind the liquor store.
We're now in pursuit. Need backup."

COPY, UNIT TWENTY-FOUR. BACKUP ON THE
WAY.

Jake's hand had gone to his shoulder holster by now.
His standard-issue Smith & Wesson semi-automatic was
already clear of the leather holster. "Police officers!" he
shouted at the retreating figure. "Drop your weapon and
put your hands high in the air so we can see them."

But the thug kept going. And he was fast. Tony's 12-
shot S&W was also out by now, muzzle at the ready.

Lunging forward, already breathing hard, the two
cops were accompanied by two giant black shadows,

also armed. The shadows flickered weirdly against the rundown buildings on the right side of the alley.

Then the suspect turned around. Like a defensive cornerback covering a wide receiver, he was suddenly running backwards. They soon saw why. Amazed, they watched his big right arm swing through space. . . .

The gun flashed once, twice . . . and the rounds went slashing into a row of empty beer kegs.

"Fuck," shouted Tony. "*Fuck!*" Yet he was also smiling. His life was on the line . . . but he looked like a man who was actually enjoying himself. Crazy!

They were deep into the alley now, and the suspect had turned his back on them again—but not before kicking a trashcan into their path. Tony had played some flanker back at Boston College, however; now he buttonhooked neatly and slipped past the spinning trash receptacle.

But Jake's reflexes weren't as good. With a resounding crash, he went head-on into the can—which instantly spewed a dozen beer bottles and one startled rat onto the filthy pavement.

The suspect had turned to glare back at them . . . and he never saw the frightened cigarette smoker in the green apron coming. The collision knocked the startled break-taker's butt right out of his hand and sent him toppling to the pavement, where he lay inert for a moment while screaming: "Watch where you're *going*, asshole!"

The two cops zoomed past him without a word. But because their eyes were on the downed kitchen worker, they didn't see the wino staggering into their path, intent on obtaining a handout.

Ka-*BOOM*! Jake ran right over him.

The wino went to one knee, yet somehow managed to remain upright.

Stunned and disoriented, he nonetheless was able to croak out his usual request: "Got any spare change?"

On the word "change," *Tony* ran over him and knocked him cold.

But now they were approaching a major obstacle—an eight-foot-high chain-link fence. Jake read the single word printed on the sign: *Cyclone*, and he groaned out loud. At his age, fence hopping was definitely not a fun sport . . . but he seemed to have no choice. The Bad Guy was already starting to make the climb.

Gritting his teeth as he struggled for a toehold, the older cop watched several loose bills escape from the suspect's right pocket . . . then flutter away like bright green butterflies on a summer breeze.

Tony got his feet hooked into the fence and began climbing, while roaring at the Bad Guy: "Get down or we'll shoot!"

With an Olympic-sized leap, the younger cop vaulted skyward . . . and actually managed to grab the culprit's left sneaker!

It came off a second later . . . even as Tony was absorbing a vicious blow in the face from the *other* sneaker.

"Goddamnit . . . shit! My shoulder!"

Now Tony was lying flat on the pavement, gasping, with the wind knocked out of him.

The suspect already had one leg over the top of the fence. "Hey, fuck you, pig!" he shouted at the downed man. "How you like me now, you cop mothafucker?"

And he jumped.

He soared for a moment against the royal blue sky, but he'd made a mistake: he'd accidentally lost the gun, which discharged as soon as it hit the pavement. The round went sizzling away into the branches of a stunted tree near the end of the alley.

Jake was halfway up the fence by now. He wasn't enjoying the climb.

Sure enough, he'd caught his belt on a metal snag in the fence . . . and when he reached down to free it, he lost his grip.

Down he came, in an explosion that sent more trash cans flying and triggered a wholesale panic among a dozen pigeons who'd been feeding on some scattered popcorn.

But then he spotted an open doorway in the fence. In a flash he was back on his feet and through the doorway and back in the alley and running again . . . with Tony trailing him by ten yards and holding onto his injured shoulder.

Looking down at the pavement, Tony spotted the thug's gun. In a flash, he grabbed it and stashed it behind his waistband.

Seconds later, the two cops got a big surprise.

Suddenly, there was no thug in sight. He'd vanished without a trace. The alley appeared to be empty now . . . except for the giant, green-painted dumpster that stood on an apron of scarred asphalt off to the right.

In big black letters, four words had been painted on the jumbo-sized trashcan: *Property of Speranzo Bros.*

The two detectives looked at each other. *What the fuck . . . where'd he go?*

Gun at the ready, Jake had begun to inch his way around the dumpster. His heart was hammering in his chest, and he could feel the cold sweat seeping from his forehead.

"Watch it," said Tony in a low voice. "Careful, Jake."

"Got it," said Jake. He inched forward. The Bad Guy had dropped his pistol, which would not be a factor now. But Jake had learned a long time ago—as every veteran cop sooner or later did—that you can get hurt or killed in a hurry if you made assumptions during a collar. So Jake was *not* assuming that he now faced an "unarmed" suspect.

What if the Bad Guy happened to be carrying a *second* gun, just like Jake's own backup weapon?

Slowly, slowly. Step by step, the older cop inched forward. Nothing. Ten seconds passed. Then, with a ruffle of feathers, a pigeon took off—*squaaaawwwkk!*— and he flinched badly. *Shit!*

Jake took another step . . . and caught his breath.

The suspect was kneeling on the pavement, directly behind the dumpster, with both hands high in the air.

"What the fuck?" the Bad Guy growled. "Where'd *you* come from?"

"See that open door?" Jake pointed. "And you're under arrest."

The suspect stared woodenly at him for a moment. "You found an open door? What the shit . . . you mean, I climbed that fucking fence for *nothing*? I'm going to jail?" The assailant was kneeling on the asphalt, his hands in the air. "Hey, I didn't do nothing!"

"Really?" said Jake. "Then why'd you rabbit on us, friend? And why'd you fire that popgun in our direction, if you didn't have a reason to run?"

But Tony had arrived by now, and he was screaming. "You're under arrest! It's over, you asshole! Get on your stomach—hands behind your head so we can see 'em."

The assailant looked up at Tony's bristling gun. Then he rolled onto his stomach and twisted his arms so his hands were braced against the back of his skull. "I'm clean, pig—you ain't got shit on me and you know it."

The younger cop had his knee on the suspect's back now, as he snapped on the cuffs. Then he stepped back. "Really? Tell that to the witnesses back in the liquor store."

Rizzo moved the muzzle in closer.

"Do you have any idea how much I'd like to pull this trigger, after what you just put us through?"

"I got rights," snapped the thug.

The younger cop's right index finger tightened noticeably.

"Tony, back off," said Jake. "You heard me. *Do* it."

Tony obeyed and stepped back. Reluctantly.

"You have the right to remain silent," said Jake, as he launched the familiar ritual. "Anything you say can and will be used against you in a court of law. You have the right to an attorney. If you cannot afford an attorney, one will be provided for you.

"If you decide to answer questions, you have the right to stop at any time. . . ."

It was over.

Finally.

***

Four hours later, after the suspect had been loaded into the wagon and rolled off toward the 13th Precinct lockup—and the two cops had been fully debriefed by the Police Deputy Commissioner—Becker and Rizzo sat at a back table in the Irish-run Bunratty's Tavern and talked about their very interesting day at work.

Tony's hands were still shaking a little as he joked with his partner about the collar. "Shit, I think I separated my shoulder again—just like in the Notre Dame game."

Jake sipped his brew. "Want me to run you by the ER?"

Tony shook his head. "Naaah . . . I'll give it a day or two, see what happens."

Rizzo looked at his new partner. Grinned slyly.

"Has it occurred to you yet that you may be getting too old for this stuff, Professor?"

Jake bristled. "No, it has *not*."

Tony smiled. "Hey, the thought never crossed my mind."

He paused for a moment, then: "Say, we never did get to eat lunch. Maybe we can go back to Murray's tomorrow for those cheese blimps and potato latch-keys!"

They laughed then—together—and lifted their beer mugs in a mutual salute. It was late afternoon and raining by the time he arrived at the Temple Etz Chaim Memorial Cemetery in West Roxbury.

***

He sat in the unmarked car for a few minutes, preparing himself for the ordeal ahead.

For Jake Becker, this was the saddest place on earth. Yet it was also a place of spiritual nourishment . . . a place to renew his unshakable commitment to Charly and his own frequently repeated vow to work night and day to become the best homicide detective he could be.

Still, the emotional pain was difficult to face.

As always, he just sat in the car at first, watching the rain trickle down the windshield . . . until all at once he was remembering Rachel, his murdered sister.

Raped and killed at the age of six by a sadistic monster, and then buried in a tiny grave here at the Temple Etz Chaim Cemetery.

Only ten years old at the time, in 1954, Jake had been stunned by the tragedy, nearly paralyzed by it. For a while, they'd even taken him out of school, and he'd spent several weeks at home, except for regular visits to a child psychologist.

How many hours had he spent sitting in his room and staring at the pages of his picture books without seeing them? Or watching the toy train with the little yellow flag above the caboose, *B&O RR*, as it clattered around and around the toy track, making the same endless circuit again and again?

By his late teens, he'd fallen into the habit of visiting Rachel's grave every year on the anniversary of her *Yahrzeit*. When Ruth died of leukemia only a dozen years later, it had seemed fitting and proper that she also be buried here, along with both of Jake's parents and only a short walk from the site of Rachel's final resting place.

The ritual was always the same. For a few minutes, after paying his respects to Ruth and his parents, he'd stand in front of the child's memorial, quietly meditating.

Jake wasn't a religious man, not really . . . so he'd simply ask himself again and again: how could God have let it happen?

He had no answer, and he didn't expect to find one. But his visits to Rachel's grave had left him with a burning vocation, a passionate commitment. Taking these evil monsters off the street—the same kinds of monsters who'd killed his beloved sister—would be his lifelong mission!

No child would suffer as his sister had suffered, if he could prevent it. He'd spend his entire career hunting down the "bad guys" and putting them away.

After only a few years, repeating that solemn vow had become an important part of his annual remembrance at the cemetery.

He always brought a big bouquet of pink French tulips with him. Those flowers had been Ruth's favorite . . . and he gently placed a few on each grave, while being careful to provide an extra one for Rachel. Once the flowers had been settled reverently into place, he would gather a few small stones to place atop the gravestones.

It was the Jewish way of letting the deceased know they hadn't been forgotten.

Memories . . .

Sighing heavily, he climbed out of the police cruiser and started toward Ruth's gravesite.

The next hour or so would be hard for him.

But he knew he'd never stop coming back here, year after year, to remember the four people he'd loved so much.

CHAPTER 9
Home Again, Home Again

He was desperate.

He hated that word—Dr. Michael Rogers, *desperate*!—and he hated the situation in which he now found himself.

But most of all, he hated the man whom he was about to beg for help . . . the famed Chicago thoracic surgeon and inventor of an award-winning technique (the pioneering "Rogers Procedure") for cracking the chest before heart surgery: Hoyt Woodrow Rogers, M.D.

(Also known—at least to Dr. Mike—as "The Prick.")

His father.

It was three o'clock on Wednesday afternoon, and Michael Rogers was sitting in yet another shithole bar, this one located on a back street in grimy South Chicago. *The Circus Show Bar*. He'd come here on The El in search of some cheap booze, so he could work up his courage for the brutal humiliation that surely lay ahead.

Down to his last few bucks and totally *desperate*.

He'd flown economy class from Boston to Baltimore to Chicago and then taken a transit bus into the city, a six-hour exercise in degradation.

Unshaven and badly in need of a shower, with all his hopes shattered, all his youthful dreams shipwrecked . . . and now he'd have to beg The Prick for help!

"Please, Dad . . . I'm in real trouble . . . can't you help me out?"

Dr. Mike looked around. The "Show Bar" was nothing more than a shabby neighborhood tavern . . . a home away from home for sad sacks who looked almost as pathetic as he did. Bleary-eyed, he studied the washed-out clown painting above the bar, along with the two faded White Sox pennants that flanked it at either end. He groaned out loud.

He was nearly flat broke now, having spent the biggest part of his ready cash on this quick trip to Chicago. . . .

He hadn't dared to call the old man on the phone. That would have made it too easy for him to say no.

His only hope now, his only remaining strategy was to let himself be fully humiliated by the cold-blooded bastard. Because once The Prick's anger was spent, he might feel a moment or two of compassion for the black hole his younger son had become. That moment was all "Little Mikey" had going for him. If only he could take advantage of it!

If he begged a little bit—if he whined and blubbered—while pointing out how well his super-successful older brother (the beloved Hoyt Woodrow Rogers, *Jr.*, already a managing partner at one of the Windy City's top law firms) had been doing in recent years. . . .

If he sobbed once or twice ("Hoyt's a millionaire, Dad, but what about *me*?"), the old man might feel a molecule or two of pity for his loser of a son.

Pity.

It was the only card left in his hand now, and he had to play it. Another month or two without new funds and he was sure to be evicted from the rundown, roach-infested apartment where he spent his tortured nights. And then what? A homeless shelter?

Or would it be Life on the Street . . . a vicious decline into the world of the winos, and sleeping in the parks, and begging for change on tony Newbury Street, and his silver-streaked beard gone ragged and filthy?

He looked at the bartender, a fat man in a ketchup-stained sweatshirt, *Da Bears*—and his heart sank toward his shoe tops.

"Gimme a double shot of Kessler, rocks."

The obese booze jockey lowered his copy of the *Herald* sports page. Eyed him suspiciously.

"You got two bucks?"

***

The now-retired Dr. Hoyt Rogers lived in the upscale Lincoln Park section of the city, in a restored Victorian mansion that had recently been featured in *House Beautiful* as a "classic example of graceful American-style Princess Anne renovation." The mansard-style roof featured two cupolas and several gables with impressive gingerbread molding. The layout included a gazebo surrounded by Japanese lanterns.

The sumptuous backyard was highlighted by a luxurious fern garden that had long been the envy of the Chicago Horticultural Society.

Little Mikey arrived at 7:15. It was a muggy evening in early summer, and the lightning bugs were already out. Above the immaculately trimmed lawns along Imperial Drive, the amorous insects swarmed like glowing coach lamps in a Charles Dickens novel about high society.

He trudged slowly down the sidewalk, watching the lawn sprinklers fling their silver ribbons of water through the fading twilight. Goddamn, but he hated this world . . . hated these steep, proud houses with their ranks of silent windows . . . hated the purring Cadillacs and the BMWs that cruised along wide avenues named *Imperial* and *Westminster* and *Cavendish* and *Bellefleur*.

This was the world of success, the world of men and women who'd made the grade in life. These were the winners!

And who was he?

Driven out of his profession by a tawdry scandal, and then forced to make a shitty living by teaching Psychology 101 to classrooms full of bored community college students . . . and how had it all happened? Honest to God, there were days when he couldn't even *understand* what had been done to him, days when he struggled to make sense of it.

Exhausted and half-paralyzed, he could find refuge only in a single thought: the disaster had been orchestrated by *her*—that bitch in Atlanta, the one who'd fucked him over royally!

But he had arrived at last. Teeth clenched, he stood at the foot of the elegant veranda that fronted 470 Imperial Drive. The tall house loomed through the dusk like a mighty fortress, and for a few moments his heart trembled with fear.

Did he really have the guts to mount those wide, polished steps and punch the illuminated button on The Prick's mahogany-trimmed front door?

Yes. He did. There was nothing left to lose now, and he actually smiled—*What the fuck. Go ahead and do it!*

As if imbued with a will of its own, his right index finger stabbed the doorbell.

He waited. No response. A white Ford Mustang convertible drove slowly past the mansion, its stereo system throbbing with a Carole King classic from the 1970s: S*o far away. Doesn't anybody stay in one place anymore?*

He punched the bell again. He felt a surge of panic. What if the old man was off in Asia somewhere, off on one of his extended trips as a celebrated art collector with millions to spend?

But no. There were two lights burning somewhere on the upper floors–

Bingo! The front door finally swung open and all at once he was looking into the somber, hooded gaze . . . not of Wilma Jefferson, the housekeeper (was this her night off?) . . . but of The Prick himself!

"Dad!" he stammered absurdly. "It's me, Michael."

"I know who it is, Michael."

The old man's face was expressionless. "I was upstairs, working on my book—I didn't hear the bell at first."

Michael nodded. Of course. His "book" . . . his pompous, self-congratulatory memoir: *A Heart Surgeon's Journey: My Life on the Frontiers of Cardiology.* The old man had been writing his autobiography for at least a decade but seemed unable to finish the project—probably because he couldn't stop talking about himself and his glorious career as an award-winning surgeon whose name already adorned an entire wing at one of America's most highly regarded hospitals.

The older Rogers stared unhappily at his prodigal son. Clad in a raw silk smoking jacket—probably one of his recent Hong Kong purchases—the illustrious medico was a tall, leonine figure blessed with a shock of elegantly cut snow white hair. Like one of those elder statesmen from the American Deep South—*Step right up and meet the Senior Senator from the great state of Alabama!*—the old man actually seemed to have gained physical stature with the passage of the years.

Tall and silver-maned, he loomed several inches above the stumbling younger man in the stained makeshift outfit and the frayed running shoes who had somehow landed on his front porch.

"Come in, son."

A moment later he was leading Mikey into the ornately furnished living room.

Yes, it was all exactly as he remembered it. There was the great central fireplace with the old man's sour-faced oil portrait hanging above the fire screen. There were the two pricey ottomans and the $12,000 Persian carpet and the Chinese porcelains full of freshly cut lilies and lilacs and gladioli, and all of them arranged to perfection. . . .

"Sit down, Michael."

As always, it was a command rather than an invitation. And he obeyed, as always. Soon he was perched on one of the backless sofas, directly across from the old man, who'd now crossed his silk-clad legs and was staring disapprovingly at his wayward son.

"What brings you to Chicago, Mikey?"

Mikey looked around helplessly. *Is this my father*, he wondered, *or is it a cold-blooded stranger who's afraid I might ask him for a loan?*

"Dad . . ." his voice was trembling and hesitant. "Dad . . . I'm sorry to bother you, but I'm in trouble. I lost my teaching job at the community college."

"I didn't know that, Michael—but frankly, I'm not surprised."

The cold blue eyes were locked on Mikey's face, judging him, always judging him.

"I know I've made some mistakes. . . . ."

"Mistakes? *Mistakes*? You utterly disgraced yourself, that's what you did. Not to mention disgracing our esteemed family. You lied about your research and betrayed your VA patients. Those aren't mistakes. They're crimes, and you know it."

He could hear a clock ticking somewhere in the background. Was it the sound of his own approaching doom?

"Dad . . . I need your help."

"So what else is new?"

"I'm . . . I'm going to be evicted from my apartment."

The legendary surgeon frowned intently. Then he growled. "I knew it would come to this, sooner or later, with you sitting in my living room and begging for a goddamn handout."

"Dad . . ." he swallowed hard. "Won't you please help me?"

The surgeon's pale white lips were firmly compressed. *Disgust.*

"How much are we talking about?"

Mikey hesitated. His heart was laboring painfully in his chest. The ticking had grown louder and more insistent, as if the invisible clock had somehow taken up residence in his brain.

"Well . . . I was thinking about . . . maybe twenty-five thousand dollars?"

The eyebrows shot upwards again, but this time with incredulity.

"Twenty-five thousand *dollars*? Are you out of your mind? You have the temerity, after what you've done to my family name . . . after what you've done to my reputation . . . you have the insolence to come into my home and ask me for that much money?"

Mikey didn't move. He crouched stiffly on the ottoman, his back radiating pain, and a stray thought flashed through his struggling brain: *The Matisse above the sofa is worth much more than that.*

But it was now or never. *Go for it.* "Dad . . ." he moaned in a cringing voice that broke into a stifled sob, "won't you please help me, Dad? I'm desperate!"

The man on the other side of the room reflected for a moment.

Then his face hardened and the bit of light that had been gleaming in his flat eyes suddenly evaporated.

"No, I'll give you nothing." He was scowling at his son. "You need a lesson in self-reliance, and you're going to get it, whether you like it or not!"

Mikey was blinking at him now. Blinking fast. "Dad . . . please? I'm down to almost nothing, don't you understand? I'm going to be out on the street in a couple of months."

He sobbed again, much louder, and a wave of despair rose like bitter acid in his mouth. "What about Hoyt, Dad?" He was whining now, whining unashamedly. "He's got millions! My brother is a millionaire many times over, you know that.

"He won't listen to me, but he'll do whatever you ask him to! Couldn't you speak to him for me? Please!"

The older man's mouth was clamped shut by now. He shook his head.

"You expect me to do your begging for you? You want me to beg your older brother for *money*? I just told you I don't intend to help you—and I'm certainly not going to ask him to!"

Hoyt Rogers Senior snorted with utter disdain. "Hoyt Rogers Junior is a damn good lawyer, a *great* lawyer. He earned every nickel he's got! And you expect me to go to him—where is your pride, son? Where is your goddamn *pride*? How did you turn into this . . . this spineless loser, this pathetic derelict begging me to have his successful brother put him on the dole?"

Little Mikey was on his feet now. The clock in his head was ticking so loud he thought his brain might explode.

"Dad . . ." He was struggling desperately against the urge to vomit all over the Persian carpet. He could feel it building inside his strangled gut—wave after wave of bitter black vomit, greasy vomit that would burst from his gaping mouth and wash everything away on a tide of stinking putrescence.

"Dad . . . I think I'm going to be sick . . . can I at least use the bathroom before I leave?"

"Of course, of course," the old man frowned. "But don't go making a mess in there—Wilma is off tonight, and I don't want to be cleaning up after you!"

Nodding . . . Dr. Mike dragged himself across the living room and down an adjoining hallway. A moment later he was in the bathroom and hanging onto the sink.

He was throwing cold water into his feverish eyes and struggling not to puke.

He waited . . . and then waited some more. The attack was easing now. At last he took a huge breath and squared his shoulders. And then suddenly his eyes lit up. *That trophy case in the Family Room*—this was his chance!

For more than a year now, he'd been planning to steal the old man's most prized possession—the gleaming scalpel he kept on a mahogany display board located only a few feet down the hall from the bathroom.

Crafted from sterling silver and engraved with the doctor's initials, "HR," the scalpel was surrounded by gold-framed photos of the famous clinician shaking hands with celebrities and high-profile politicians. In one of those smarmy photographs, Hoyt Senior and Hoyt Junior could be seen with a beaming U.S. President who'd scrawled out a personal message for them: "To Hoyt Rogers, Sr. and Jr.—best of luck, Richard M. Nixon."

There were no photos of Little Mikey, however.

Whenever he thought of the scalpel on the display board, Dr. Mike ground his teeth in impotent rage. That glittering surgical instrument had been a shining, symbolic gift from the Academy of American Surgeons, which had presented the old man with it eight years before, as part of his Lifetime Achievement Award. . . .

Did he really have the balls to steal the goddamn thing? Yes! And it was now or never!

Instead of hurrying back to the living room, he took four bounding steps in the opposite direction . . . and found himself standing in the middle of the sumptuous Family Room. At center stage, of course, loomed the gleaming Lifetime Achievement plaque, buffed to a high gloss.

The scalpel had been fastened to the mahogany with three evenly spaced metal clips. All Dr. Mike had to do was give the instrument a hard pull and a twist and . . . presto!

Now he looked down at the steel-covered blade in his hand, the symbol of his father's proudest accomplishments, and he smiled as he read the six letters that had been embossed on its side: *RIBBEL*.

At last his dream had come true.

The Ribbel was his!

Slipping the device into his pants pocket, he hurried out to the living room.

The old man had been waiting impatiently for his return; now he rose hurriedly from his chair and stalked toward the staircase that led to his upstairs office.

"Goodbye, Michael," he said, looking back over one shoulder. "I hope you can find a way to put your life back together, I really do. I wish you luck . . . but that's your struggle, not mine, and I can't do it for you. I have to get back to work.

"Please contact me when you have something positive to report!"

He turned away and began to climb the carpeted stairs.

Dr. Mike didn't speak. What was there to say?

Somehow, he managed to make it to the front door.

Somehow, he was back on the wide, polished front steps . . . was staggering forward, nearly collapsing, then landing on the sidewalk, then walking, staggering, lurching forward into the twilight, with the lightning bugs glimmering all around him.

But then he stopped for a moment, and an ugly smile creased his thick features.

"You sonofabitch," he told himself. "You dirty bastard. Hope you don't have a heart attack, the next time you go looking for your Ribbel!"

Muttering with rage, the renowned surgeon's son lurched down the sidewalk and vanished into the oncoming summer night.

CHAPTER 10
"I Am The Surgeon!"

He bought another pint of rotgut and then stumbled back to the airport. The clock had stopped beating in his head.

Had a vein burst or what?

He was so exhausted that he could barely hold his head up. He had finally come to the end.

It was over. Everything was over. All his hopes and all his dreams: blasted. And he was headed for the street. The gutter.

His worst nightmare—eating out of trash cans and sleeping on steam grates—was about to become monstrously real.

He groaned. And then he remembered. *Nightmare*.

Yes, he had just remembered that one word—that one single word: *Nightmare!*

He smiled, because all at once he was remembering. He had the power. He did! He had one last weapon remaining in his arsenal: *The Nightmare*.

Ever since that dream of the tattoo . . . ever since that night about a week earlier, when he'd awakened from a terrible dream of being burned with the image of a writhing, blood-dripping snake . . . yes, he'd awakened to find *a real tattoo cut into his right hand, and blood still leaking from the raw flesh below it, from the wound the tattooing had left behind. . . .*

He had the power now!

Just like that pathetic David Collier, his former patient, that deranged Vietnam vet with the bloody snake knife –

Little Mikey had the power now!

And he could use it against *anybody he wanted.*

Now he leaned back in his airliner seat and sneaked a long pull from the pint bottle of cut-rate rum.

He smiled again. He grinned . . . huge!

Because it was after 11 o'clock in Chicago . . . and he knew the old man's habits, all the way down to the smallest detail.

His father would be sound asleep at this very moment.

At this very moment.

Little Mikey lay back against the seat. He drifted slowly, slowly toward unconsciousness . . . and as he drifted, a single word kept returning to him, returning again and again in a sweet and soothing refrain.

Ribbel.

Ribbel.

The world's foremost manufacturer of razor-sharp surgical scalpels!

***

He slept.

He dreamed.

He brought the triangular blade of the Ribbel #11 gently up against the soft, wattled flesh that encased his father's ribcage.

"Hello, Dad."

The old man's cold blue eyes flashed open. They were a dazed lizard's eyes—icy, emotionless, dead.

"You!" hissed the famous medical doctor. "So it's you again, is it? Little Mikey has come back to badger me again! Why? I told you, no money. No money! So why are you here? What is it you want?"

Mikey moved the Ribbel closer to his father's straining eyes. Showed him the blade.

"This, Dad. *This* is what I want!"

His arm flashed . . . and the cold steel went flashing between the famous surgeon's ribs . . . went slashing deep into a shuddering artery. There was time for only a single terrible scream . . . as the surgical blade whipped back and forth again and again, and the blood of the dying man went roaring out through his torn ribcage and flooded the expensive Oriental carpet beneath his bed.

The old man was bleeding to death. Rapidly. And Little Mikey stood above him, gloating and shouting: "Tell me: Are you proud of me *now*, Dad? Are you proud of my powerful new surgical technique?

"I am The Surgeon. Do you hear me? I am THE SURGEON!

"How does it feel to have *your* chest cracked open, you heartless prick!"

CHAPTER 11
For in That Sleep of Death, What Dreams May Come?

Try as she might, Tracy Donovan couldn't fall asleep.

Her insomnia was easy to understand.

Having been terrified within an inch of her life by the maniac who had somehow managed to creep into the worst nightmare she'd ever experienced, the youthful Mulligan's bartender was in the middle of a full-scale anxiety attack.

After twisting and turning on her bed for nearly two hours, Tracy couldn't stand it any longer. She had to tell someone about the agonizing nightmare in which she'd been threatened by a psychopath.

The nightmare had been bad enough. But her terror over the dream confrontation in the abandoned brewery seemed positively *trivial* when compared to the horror of knowing that her dream-assailant *also* remembered many of its details.

How could she even begin to explain the fact that the torturer in her nightmare was *also* a customer at Mulligan's . . . or the fact that he had then returned to the bar to describe her awful dream—before finally threatening to invade her sleep and torture her again?

Sleep is impossible, face it!

After downing two glasses of wine and watching an hour's worth of insipid television, Tracy did her best to fall asleep. But as the minutes ticked away one by one, her heart sank. Face it: Tracy Donovan was too damned *terrified* to sleep!

It was eight minutes past two in the morning when she finally gave up and decided to call a close friend, regardless of the late hour.

With a trembling index finger, she punched the seven numbers into her phone.

"Hello?"

"Judy, don't hang up! It's me, Tracy!"

"Tracy? What time is it?"

"It's two o'clock."

"Are you okay, honey?"

"No, Judy, I'm not. I'm . . . I'm in some kind of terrible trouble. I'm in a situation . . . it's so weird. I think I'm in danger—and I don't even understand what's going *on*."

"Danger, Tracy? What kind of danger? What are you talking about?"

"Well . . . see, this guy came into the bar the other night . . . and he was some kind of sick . . . well, a psycho. A real psycho, Judy! He was singing real weird at first . . . and then he told me about some woman he hated. Some woman who'd hurt him terribly many years ago. He said I looked just like her. And he vowed revenge."

There was a long pause on the other end, before Judy asked: "Revenge against that other woman from back in the past . . . or revenge against *you*?"

"That's part of the problem, Judy. I couldn't really tell which."

Tracy was shivering hard now. Her voice shook badly. "Anyway, he told me he would see me in my dreams. And then later I had this nightmare and he was *in* it!

"He called me by this other woman's name . . . and I could tell he wanted to hurt me in some awful way, some horrifying way. . . .

"I started screaming. I screamed so loud I woke myself up. It was dreadful. But that wasn't the worst part."

"There's more?" Now Judy's own voice was shaking, as she absorbed the details one by one.

"What happened next was . . . Judy, I know you're gonna tell me I'm crazy."

"No, I won't."

"I swear to you—the very next night, I was working the front bar, and he showed up again. And he mocked me. He made fun of me.

"He asked me if I remembered my nightmare . . . and then he hit me with several exact details that proved he had actually *been* there. In the nightmare, I mean."

Judy made a low, moaning sound: disbelief. "You're kidding."

"I'm not. He was *there*, Judy."

Now Judy let out a long, unhappy sigh. "Come on, Tracy. That's impossible and you know it."

"I knew you wouldn't believe me."

"Tracy, I'm your best friend. I love you and I know you never lie. But . . . are you trying to say that this—this creep was actually *present* in one of your nightmares and then returned to tell you about it in *real life*?"

"That's exactly what I'm telling you."

Another long silence.

"Honey . . . you haven't been taking anything, have you?"

"What, drugs? Of course not."

Her friend sighed again. "Well, it's just that . . . you

. . . I'm sure you can under . . . look, people can't share each other's dreams like that, Tracy. It's physically impossible."

Tracy was fighting back tears. "You're right. Of *course* you're right. But how can I explain it? I swear to you, it happened just like I'm saying it did. How can I explain it to *myself*?"

Another long silence. Then Judy brightened. "Look, I've got an idea, babe. Okay? How about if you don't even *try* to explain it?"

"Don't even try?" Tracy was gasping, trembling.

"That's right, sweetheart. What if you just leave it alone for now? How about just trying to get a good night's sleep—and leave all the complicated explanations for later? How would that be?"

All at once, Tracy felt a little better. "Okay, maybe you've got a point. I'll take a sleeping pill, and I simply won't allow myself to think about all of this. I just won't think about 'the nightmare man'."

"Good plan, Tracy. You get yourself some rest and we'll go out for coffee tomorrow and see if we can figure it all out."

They both hung up, and Tracy headed for the bathroom and the medicine cabinet. *I won't think about him. I won't!*

A few moments later, she was gulping down a 200-milligram capsule of Nembutal.

***

Ninety minutes after Tracy finally drifted off, part of her left eyelid began to twitch.

It was a tiny movement, barely perceptible . . . but soon the entire lid was twitching.

Five minutes after that, both eyelids were flickering through the Rapid Eye Movement (REM) phase of dream-filled sleep.

At first, her dreams were calm and soothing. She was standing on a beach at sunrise, watching the creamy surf ripple across the sand. Revere Beach! She was a child once again, running on tiny feet through the lapping seawater and watching the seagulls feed along the shoreline.

Wonderful. She could feel the cooling breeze against her youthful skin. But then . . . a shadow. She looked up. A gull was hovering only a few feet from her left shoulder, and the squawking bird held a tiny yellow fish in his beak.

She watched, fascinated, while the gull's merciless hold closed tighter and tighter . . . until all at once the fish's terrified eyes burst open, showering Tracy's arms and hands with bright red blood!

She turned away and hurried back down the beach. *I don't want to see any more of that; I don't want to know about it.*

But now she was watching a crab stagger across the sand, not ten yards distant. She skidded to a stop, fascinated, unable to tear her eyes away. *What's wrong with him? Why is he crawling like that?*

She moved in closer; to her horror, she saw that one leg had been torn away—and the ripped-open stump was trailing a dark liquid across the sand. And his mouth . . . something had happened there—somehow his gaping mouth had been slashed apart . . . and now she saw it, a huge fisherman's hook dangling from the twisted orifice.

How would he be able to eat that way? *How will the poor thing ever manage to eat?*

Her heart was pounding against her ribs now, and her breathing had become labored and painful. Then all at once the light began to fade. The beach grew dark and the details blurred away to invisibility, and at last the world was entirely dark.

Pitch black. All she could hear was the sound of a faucet dripping somewhere, dripping slowly, on and on, somewhere in the far distance. . . .

Plink.

She strained to hear it better, that dripping.

Plink.

Where? What? Was it a *sink* of some kind? Was she sleepwalking? Had she somehow wandered into her own bathroom? Was her bathroom sink dripping on her? Oh, dear, that was wasteful, she really needed to see if she could fix that–

No.

It wasn't the bathroom sink.

Astonished, she realized that she was now staring at a huge wooden barrel, and the barrel had a slow leak in it, and the barrel was dripping, dripping. . . .

Beer!

The brewery!

With a stab of horror, she realized that she was back *there* again. That TV sitcom, she remembered it now— once again, she was locked up inside the Shotz Brewery plant! Now the darkness was beginning to fade a little. With growing unease, she watched the light rise slowly, almost imperceptibly . . . until at last the stark reality of her surroundings was plainly visible.

She was trapped in a gigantic cement-floored warehouse . . . an enormous underground room crowded with giant kegs and barrels and metal vats full of gurgling liquid.

She blinked. Her eyes grew huge. She was looking down at her own body now, and she saw that she was stark naked and tied to a big metal rack with leather straps that bound her arms and legs so tightly she could barely breathe!

Plink.

Her mouth fell open, and she tried to scream. But all that emerged was a dreadful gasping sound: "Please . . . h-h-h-h-elp me!"

Gasping! With bulging eyes, she watched a huge hairy spider creeping toward the metal rack on which she lay bound and helpless.

Plink.

Gasping! Straining against her bonds! *Plink.* Then she saw it.

There. Against the wall . . . right above that jagged crack.

A shadow.

"Hello, Alix."

The words hung on the air. She looked down at his right hand . . . saw the gleam of metal there.

"Whhhh . . . what? Why?" Her voice emerged a low moan, desperate. "Why . . . are you calling me *Alix*? My name is *Tracy*!" She gasped . . . strained against her bonds. Wailed at him: "I don't know what you want! Please let me go. You're hurting me . . . please!"

He took a step toward her, and she saw that he was smiling.

"You let me down, Alix. You hung me out to dry, babe.

"I was the one who discovered the secret power of nightmares . . . not you."

Her mouth hung open now; all at once her thighs were wet with her flowing, uncontrollable urine.

"It was my discovery, Alix, not yours. Somnambulistic Telepathy—it was going to win me the Nobel. I was going to show them all: The Prick, and that bastard Hoyt, my golden-boy brother.

"I was going to fly off to Stockholm to receive the Nobel."

Fighting for air, she watched him raise his hand. Saw the blade there. Watched him run a thumb along the gleaming steel.

"I've brought you a present, sweetie! It's a wonderful device that surgeons use—a Ribbel!" He laughed happily. "This was once my father's proudest possession. But I took it from him. It's mine now, mine to keep forever.

"But before I show you how I use it, may I ask you a question?"

Tracy's mouth was hanging open. "Wha . . . what? What question?"

He grinned. He seemed quite pleased with himself. "Why did you fuck me over, Alix?"

She shook her head. Once . . . twice. She moaned. "No, no, I don't . . . I never . . . I don't know what you *mean*!"

She fell silent for a moment, eyes full of horror, breathing in ragged gasps like a winded horse. Then she started begging, "Please, please, I don't know any Alix. Please stop—I don't *know* her!"

He was grinning again. Enjoying himself fully. "Why did you tell the world that ST was your discovery, Alix . . . when you knew it was *mine*?"

"Please, please . . .", and now she was vomiting, vomiting and struggling to escape, with the pale yellow vomit oozing from her gaping mouth.

"Wrong answer, Alix!" His arm whipped the blade, and this time it was the middle of her ribcage that parted like butter and then the scarlet blood surged out of her slashed aorta and sprayed the wall and then ran dribbling down to the floor.

She had stopped breathing. She had stopped thinking. She was a block of stone, cold dead stone, watching the blade rise above her. Watching it rush toward her at the speed of light. Her mouth flew open. "Nooooooo!"

Her life ran down the side of the gleaming metal tank until there was nothing left.

Just the occasional scarlet drop, falling slowly and randomly from the nearest tank.

Plink.

He smiled. How he smiled. Little Mikey, happy at last!

With the last of her dissolving strength, she heard his rumbling, guttural laughter.

CHAPTER 12
Interrupted at the Dunkin' Donuts

They were cruising along Hanover Street in the North End, with Tony at the wheel and Jake yakking a blue streak about the latest techniques for identifying hair and fibers taken from a crime scene.

"Honest to God, Tony, the things they can do in the lab now are astounding. I mean, really—they can go right down to the molecular level, you know? They can look at a single hair taken from a crime scene and use it to determine if a suspect comes from European, Asian or African ancestry."

Nodding, Tony turned and stared at his partner. "Okay, fine. But how's that stuff going to tell you if the sonofabitch pulled the trigger or not?"

Jake stared back. They were sitting at a red light. "Tony," replied Jake, "I refuse to believe you're devoid of imagination."

Now the Italian's jaw was sticking out. "Whaddya mean?" he joked. "Devoid of *who*? How about talking English for a while, Dr. Becker?"

Jake smiled. "Are you telling me you can't imagine a situation—a situation in front of a grand jury maybe—where knowing whether or not the defendant was an Asian, let's say, might help to place him at a murder scene?"

Tony groaned with disgust, then stepped on the gas. The unmarked Crown Victoria jumped away from the light. "Hey, I got plenty of imagination, Jake. Just ask the fucking drug dealers around Blue Hill Avenue how imaginative I was, when it came to finding ways to park their asses in the slammer."

The older detective looked at him, deadpan. "Tony, I've asked you many times before and now I'll ask you again: please dispense with the vulgar street lingo already, okay?"

"Yeah, yeah, sure. Whatever you say, Professor!" Tony hit the turn signal, and the car swerved to the left. "You know, Jake, I finally figured out where you picked up all that fancy talk of yours."

"Really?"

"Yup. I asked some of the guys in Homicide, and they told me all about your Ivy League background."

"Did they now?"

"That's right. They said that's where you first got started in your career as a big-time Boston egghead." Tony looked over at his partner and grinned. "Well, I grew up in Southie, as a street kid—and you can bet none of *us* was gonna make it to the Ivy League! Know what I'm sayin'?"

Jake shook his head. "Northeastern University is hardly the Ivy League, good buddy. They told you wrong. And nobody gave me a nickel, either. I worked nights in a tannery to pay tuition, and I had to borrow food money—hold it! Stop the car!"

He was pointing to the right side of the approaching intersection. Reacting instantly, Tony jammed on the brake so hard that they nearly went into a skid. "What the hell's the matter?"

"Dunkin' Donuts," barked Jake. "Over there! It's five o'clock, Tony.

"I could really use a cup of coffee, and so could you."

On the other side of the intersection, the doughnut chain's familiar sign—a cup of steaming coffee and the famous logo, "DD"—beckoned to the two hungry cops.

Tony nodded. He grinned again. "At last, we agree on something!"

***

The front door banged open, and the two of them stepped up to the Dunkin' counter.

Sure enough, both of their belt radios immediately began to chatter.

Thirteenth, this is Dispatch. Code Yellow at 1414 Davis Street, Apartment 512. Repeat: the homicide scene is 1414 Davis Street. The Holton Arms Apartments, Number 512. Do you copy?

They looked at each other. "Too bad," sighed Jake. "Looks like we gotta go back to work. No caffeine fix for us today."

"Aw, *fuh* . . ." said Tony, barely managing to catch himself.

Jake lit up. "Congratulations, Tony," he laughed as they hurried back toward the unmarked. "You stopped yourself just in time!"

CHAPTER 13
Questions, Questions

After months of preparation, Alix Cassidy was finally about to take the stage at Big Pine for her first lecture on a highly controversial subject: Somnambulistic Telepathy.

Striding into the Big Pine Main Auditorium at nine a.m. sharp, she was fighting a swarm of jetliner-sized butterflies. After gulping a cup of black coffee—*bad idea!*—she had quickly succumbed to what felt like a case of the terminal jitters.

Her momentary panic only deepened when she spotted the large display board at the entrance to the auditorium.

Oneirology, Quantum Entanglement and
Somnambulistic Telepathy:
Some Intriguing Questions

Dr. Alix Cassidy
Big Pine Conference
June 14, 1986
9—11:00 A.M.

Blinking rapidly, she peered at the billboard for a few moments . . . while her heart pounded in her chest. But the attack of nerves didn't last long. Alix was eager to tell this audience of world-class paranormal researchers about her astonishing theory—worked out over many years of research—that some human beings are capable of invading the nightmares of other people and then *participating* in them.

She felt confident about her science, but she also knew that there would be many skeptics listening this morning. Hence the butterflies.

Still, they were only a minor distraction, and for good reason: Alix had spent a good portion of her professional life working to understand the phenomenon known as "Somnambulistic Telepathy" . . . and she'd gradually become convinced that the term described something real.

ST was as real as Laura Resnick, the desperate young woman who'd apparently been one of its first victims . . . and as real as David Collier, the tragic Vietnam vet who seemed to have been its first practitioner.

And what about Dr. Mike Rogers, the twisted psychiatrist who had exploited them both? Sick bastard that he was, Rogers claimed to have *also* experienced ST and had concluded that it was very real indeed.

She wouldn't think about Mike Rogers now, however. Not at this supremely important moment, with more than a dozen of the world's foremost paranormal investigators sitting out there in the cushioned seats of the Big Pine auditorium and analyzing her every word.

Starting right now, she needed to focus on the research findings she'd come up with during so many years of hard work. It wouldn't be easy. Although today's audience would be full of amateurs who loved all things paranormal, it would also include a significant number of no-nonsense scientists. Alix knew she would be tested to the max.

As always, her best hope for success would be to present a simple, lucid description of the physiological dynamics of ST. Because this lecture would be an "overview" of the topic—rather than an in-depth assessment of the results that had been generated by recent scientific studies of the phenomenon—she knew she wouldn't have to fight "the Battle of the Data" today.

(The complicated number crunching of the statistical evidence in favor of ST would come during her *next* lecture a few days hence.)

Yes, she was ready. But all too soon, her mental review of the upcoming lecture was noisily interrupted.

"Alix? *Alix!* How you feeling, honey? Are you all set to take center stage?"

It was Rozzie, of course, with her big hazel eyes gleaming excitedly as she sipped from a Styrofoam cup of steaming coffee. "Hey, good luck, sweetheart—now you go on out there and knock 'em dead!"

Alix sent her new BP friend a huge smile. "Can't thank you enough, Roz!"

The auditorium was filling up fast now. Soon Alix was listening to the silver-haired Big Pine Executive Director tell the scientists about ". . . a nationally recognized researcher whose provocative theories about what takes place during a typical nightmare are these days opening new vistas in sleep science.

"Ladies and gentlemen, may I introduce Dr. Alix Cassidy, the Assistant Executive Director at the renowned Sleep Disorder Center of Atlanta. Let's give Dr. Cassidy a warm welcome!"

Alix rose from her chair. Somewhere in the distance, the sound of their welcoming applause rose and fell like the surf at an oceanfront beach. She took a deep breath. Then she walked out to the center of the stage to greet her rapt audience.

She began with a simple definition.

"We call it *oh-nye-ah-RAW-loh-gee*," she told them with her best smile, "which is one of those fancy scientific words that often leave people scratching their heads and complaining: 'That sounds like Greek to me!'

"Well, it *is* Greek, or at least, it's *transliterated* Greek. What it literally means is 'the study of dreaming.' Oneirology! It didn't *start* with the Greeks, however. As a matter of fact, the Ancient Egyptians were busy studying dreams (and also writing some very interesting papyrus manuscripts about them) more than 3,000 years ago.

"Since those early investigations, which were followed by numerous other groundbreaking studies during the Renaissance and the Enlightenment—and then by the paradigm-shifting contributions of modern thinkers such as Sigmund Freud and Carl Jung—the 'science of dreams' has grown more challenging with each passing decade."

She paused for a moment, and her eyes scanned the packed auditorium . . . until they suddenly met the calm, intensely focused gaze of Dr. Gunther Sverdlow, undoubtedly the biggest scientific name at the entire conference.

Slender and athletic looking, the renowned Swiss researcher was watching her carefully. Was he smiling at her skeptically—or did she only imagine it?

That question would have to wait—she had a case to prove, and she needed to begin proving it *now*.

"Ladies and gentlemen," she told them, "I think the best way to describe Somnambulistic Telepathy and how it works is to tell you a quick story.

"Everybody likes a good story, right?"

A murmur of assent rolled over the audience, and she smiled. "All right then, fair enough. And this story begins the way Snoopy would want it to! You remember good old Snoopy, the novelist-wannabe from *Peanuts,* and his immortal opening line: It was a dark and stormy night?

"Well, it *was*, my friends. Especially in London, England, back in 1977, where an American Army sergeant named Walter Sandoff lay sleeping peacefully in his apartment, at about five o'clock in the morning. And of course, that meant it was *midnight* back in Hartford, Connecticut, where Walter's dear mother, Clara Sandoff, *also* happened to be asleep.

Anyway, the point is that on this October night in '77, dear Clara suddenly began to dream. It was an ominous dream—because it focused on a fire that appeared to have broken out at an apartment complex on a city street."

Now Alix clicked a remote device in her left hand and the audience gasped . . . as a large screen on the back wall of the auditorium momentarily appeared to erupt in leaping scarlet-hued flames.

"Watching the fire build in her nightmare, poor Clara was understandably frightened. Imagine her anxiety a moment later, when her son's face suddenly appeared to her. Horrified, poor Clara watched the flames moving closer to him. What could she do? How could she save her boy?

"Finally, desperate to help, she summoned all her strength and produced a scream so powerful that it tore through her paralyzing nightmare and woke her up: 'Walter, your apartment is on fire!'"

Alix paused again, while her audience sat rapt, waiting for the punch line.

"As I'm sure many of you know, the description of what happened next has been the subject of widespread scientific debate in recent years.

"What happened was that poor Walter, who'd been sound asleep on this dark and stormy night, suddenly woke up and jumped to his feet.

"Terrified, Sergeant Sandoff had just experienced his own nightmare vision of roaring flames devouring his apartment . . . and right in the middle of that very frightening dream, he'd heard the unmistakable voice of his mother shouting those same six words at him—six words that would forever imprint themselves on his shocked memory:

"Walter, your apartment is on fire!

"That warning came just in time, and the badly frightened sergeant was able to wake up his wife and two kids and get them to safety."

Alix paused. Once again she hit the clicker. Now the intrigued audience was eyeballing a jet-black title projected in jumbo-sized letters onto the screen behind her:

QUANTUM ENTANGLEMENT, OR WHAT EINSTEIN LIKED TO CALL: "SPOOKY ACTION AT A DISTANCE!"

Moments later the letters were replaced by a photograph. The photo was of a man with a gray-streaked mustache. He held a smoldering pipe.

They were now looking at one of the most famous faces in human history: the face of Albert Einstein.

Alix waited two beats and then sent her listeners a huge grin. She was having fun now, and her passion for her topic was evident in every word she spoke.

"My friends, the story of what happened to Clara Sandoff and her son Walter on that stormy night has never been explained. Or at least, it has never been explained *scientifically*.

"But there's no doubt that when Clara and her son talked later about what had taken place, they both remembered their identical dreams. And they both remembered those six words. They'd never heard of 'somnambulistic telepathy,' of course . . . but that's what they had apparently experienced."

She clicked again; now the screen showed two fiery electrons dancing around each other in gigantic figure-eight orbits.

"Ladies and gentlemen, I think it's safe to say that science still doesn't fully understand what occurred that evening.

"Did Clara Sandoff actually discover a previously unknown pathway that allowed her to leave her own body and enter her son's nightmare, which was taking place more than 3,000 miles away, on the other side of the Atlantic?"

She smiled. She was in full command and she knew it.

"Well, in order to grasp how Clara could be in two places at once, we need to spend a few minutes thinking about a very curious phenomenon known as 'quantum entanglement'—a phenomenon in which two nuclear particles millions of light years apart can actually interact with each other.

"And how do they accomplish this uncanny feat? According to the physicists, they accomplish it via 'quantum entanglement'—or what the great Albert Einstein called 'spooky action at a distance'."

Her listeners were leaning forward on their chairs now. They didn't want to miss a word.

"Thanks to the revolutionary insights developed by Max Planck, Werner Heisenberg, Erwin Schrodinger and their colleagues in the first half of the 20th Century, we now have a completely new understanding of quantum physics. And that understanding depends primarily on our recognition of a key scientific fact—a concept which the quantum physicists refer to as 'The Uncertainty Principle.'"

She paused and clicked.

UNCERTAINTY PRINCIPLE

Once again, her green eyes scanned the silent audience; once again, she found herself meeting the inscrutable gaze of Dr. Gunther Sverdlow. He was smiling again, and she couldn't help wondering: *Does he think I'm over the top? A crackpot?*

But her words were still flowing and she rushed ahead. "According to Werner Heisenberg's Uncertainty Principle, it's impossible to accurately determine the position of an atomic particle—down at the quantum level, that is—while at the same moment measuring the *speed* of that same particle. It simply can't be done, my friends! Nor can we simultaneously calculate both the spatial relationships and the speeds of *other* particles

. . . including the bosons, the muons, the quarks and all the rest of the incredibly tiny entities that make up the Standard Model in physics.

"As all of you know I'm sure, the physicists have been struggling for years to come up with a unified theory that would connect these particles—along with their controlling forces, such as gravity and electro-magnetism—in a single, coherent design . . . or what my colleagues in the world of quantum mechanics refer to as 'A Theory of Everything.'"

She clicked.

THEORY OF EVERYTHING

"Alas, that quest for the ultimate theory remains elusive, up to and including the present moment. Of course, more than a few of our top physicists are now predicting that they will one day manage to discover a 'God particle'—such as the recently promulgated concept of the 'Higgs Boson'—to link all these entities in one grand design.

"But that mind-bending discovery is still decades away, since we don't at present possess the tools (such as a giant particle accelerator 15 to 20 miles long) that will probably be required to make it.

"All we know for sure right now is that many of these swarming atomic particles are somehow *connected*—and they're somehow able to affect each other across both time and space."

Another click, and the audience was startled by an odd phrase that had suddenly jumped onto Alix's screen:

THE HAIR ON THE BACK OF YOUR NECK

She was closing in on her target now, and about to hit them with the most important concept of all. Leaning forward, she studied their deeply attentive faces and smiled.

"So where are we then? What does quantum mechanics—and specifically, quantum entanglement— tell us about the very strange phenomenon known as dreaming? Why is it that the period of unconsciousness known as 'REM sleep' so often produces nightmares which leave us feeling shaken and disturbed, even terrified at times?

"How is it that some dreamers—people like Clara Sandoff and her son Walter—seem able to communicate with each other through their dreams, by keying into what I call 'Somnambulistic Telepathy'?

"Questions, questions! Aren't they *fun*?"

She smiled as a wave of delighted laughter rolled over her audience.

"There's no doubt that these are fascinating puzzles for all of us who work in sleep research," she said. "But where are the *answers*, my friends? How can we explain a phenomenon that seems so uncanny and mysterious, when we lack the tools to even understand the basic dynamics of dreaming?"

She had stepped away from the microphone by now; she didn't need it anymore. Fully energized by her topic, her excited voice boomed through the crowded auditorium.

"Perhaps the best way to attack these questions is to take a lesson from the quantum physicists. And what is their bottom-line message, here in 1986? As best I can determine, it's simply that the particles which make up ordinary matter are connected in ways we don't understand.

"Apparently, they're able to affect each other by linking up outside the boundaries of space and time, via Einstein's 'spooky action at a distance.'"

She was pacing across the stage now, pacing and talking a mile a minute.

"All right then: I think it's time to ask ourselves a crucially important question. Aren't human beings *also* connected to each other in ways that appear to lie outside time and space? For example: while riding on a bus or sitting in a subway car, how often have you experienced the weird tingling that occurs when you feel the hair rising on the back of your neck?

"We've all had that experience at one time or another, right? And what usually happens next? Sooner or later, you turn in your seat and crane your neck . . . and discover that another passenger has been staring fixedly at you from behind. And then you tell yourself, 'Why, I absolutely could *feel* his eyes on me!'"

She had stopped pacing now. Clear-eyed and focused, she hit them with the punch line: "Spooky action at a distance, my friends! Just like the quarks and the bosons of quantum physics, it would seem that human beings are connected in ways we can't fully explain.

"And it is here—*deep inside the mystery of this uncanny human connection*—that we should look for the clues that will explain Somnambulistic Telepathy.

"Ask yourself: when a dreamer's neuronal synapses flash with energy during a nightmare, are there physiological processes taking place at the quantum level which somehow transcend the limits of space and time?

"I believe there are. What I'm suggesting to you today—and I have now come to the heart of the sleep research I've been conducting over the past twelve years—is the idea that the electrochemical process of neuronal signaling during sleep may very well contain quantum aspects.

"And those same quantum aspects may turn out to be what actually make it possible for people to *share the same dream* . . . via some as-yet-unexplained mechanism involving spooky action at a distance!"

She had them now, and she knew it.

Eyes blazing with passion, she had come to a full stop at center stage. "So much for the quantum physics involved in ST. But what exactly *causes* the chain of physiological events that seems to bring on this rare brain activity?"

She paused and sighed. "Unfortunately, we don't know much about that part of the process. Up to now, there have been very few studies and the data are sketchy. Apparently, some humans are affected by an abnormality during sleep . . . a sudden 'biochemical cascade' that occurs only in REM sleep. This cascade somehow provides a gateway to the world of ST. In my own research, I've come to think of it as a kind of 'REM explosion' that is the necessary precursor of dream travel.

"As I noted just now, we still know very little about the so-called REM explosion. But it's clearly a crucial part of the process. In my next lecture on Thursday, we will go much deeper into the complex biochemistry of human dreaming. Together we'll explore the amazing world of neuronal and synaptic signaling that looms behind every nightmare.

"But for right now, I think we really do need to stop and catch our breath. Let's take a 15-minute break and meet back here at 10:15 for a very interesting video presentation called 'Dreams and Mysteries: What Really Happens When We Sleep?' by some cutting-edge researchers at the University of Chicago."

Nodding and smiling, Alix began moving toward the stage-right exit . . . and was pleased to hear the waves of enthusiastic applause that were now rolling through the auditorium.

Approaching the steps that led down to the lower level, she suddenly found herself on the receiving end of an exuberant hug.

"Way to go, Alix!" clamored Rozzie.

"I told you to knock 'em dead—and you did!"

CHAPTER 14
Enter the Devil's Advocate

The video on "Dreams and Mysteries" was delayed, however.

Moments after the Big Pine audience settled back into its seats, the proceedings were interrupted.

All at once, the internationally renowned Dr. Gunther Sverdlow had his hand up.

"Dr. Cassidy," he said in the easygoing, drawling voice of an established scientific icon, "I hope you won't mind if I ask you a question before you start your video. Is it okay if I take a few moments to play the devil's advocate regarding your earlier comments about ST?"

Alix braced herself. "Of course, Dr. Sverdlow. Please proceed."

"Thank you," he crooned. "First of all, I want to thank you for your outstanding presentation a few minutes ago. Your description of the psychological dynamics involved in Somnambulistic Telepathy was both interesting and provocative."

He paused for a moment, while the audience waited for the other shoe to drop.

"I also found your example—the telepathy that allegedly took place between dreaming subjects in Connecticut and London—to be quite intriguing. It was not particularly convincing, however. As a matter of fact, I'm quite sure there's a simple and easy-to-understand explanation for what actually went on."

Alix waited calmly. *Keep your cool*, she told herself. *Don't overreact, regardless of what he says.*

"That explanation is, of course, mere *coincidence*."

The audience responded with a murmur of consternation, and several listeners craned their necks to get a better look at the questioner.

"Rather than assuming that the sergeant and his mother were communicating via their dreams, I suspect they merely happened to experience similar dreams by *chance*."

Alix frowned back at him. "Chance?" she asked in a briskly assured voice.

"Are you suggesting that what happened in London was nothing more than a series of random, coincidental events? If so, I must say that such a scenario seems unlikely."

The famed Swiss scientist was smiling broadly now. Was he patronizing her? Now she felt a flash of anger: *Who the hell does this guy think he is?*

But the devil's advocate was rushing ahead with his critique. "If you think about it for a minute," he said calmly, "I believe it will become obvious that events of this kind occur quite frequently each day. A woman in Arizona dreams that she is communicating some vitally important warning to a friend or family member who's thousands of miles away.

"But later, when she calls to check on that friend or loved one, she discovers that the warning never got through—and that the danger she was warning against didn't exist!

"Really, Dr. Cassidy." He smiled again, infuriatingly. "Don't you think hundreds of such false alarms occur daily, all around the world?

"This is undoubtedly the case. But every once in a while, purely through coincidence, there is a random event in which *both* parties report having experienced a telepathic communication of this kind. And if that communication is *also* related to a dangerous threat (such as the house fire that your Army sergeant claims to have experienced), then the so-called 'telepathy' aspect draws everyone's attention."

Now the celebrity scientist slowed his delivery in order to emphasize the bottom line. "Such apparently telepathic events make great newspaper stories, Dr. Cassidy, but the fact remains that they probably involve nothing more paranormal—and nothing more *spooky*—than ordinary, everyday coincidence!"

The auditorium fell silent, as the audience waited to see how Alix would handle the challenge from Dr. Sverdlow.

She didn't hesitate. Still smiling, and with her gaze locked on his, she rose to the occasion.

"Dr. Sverdlow, thank you for your candor and for your appropriately skeptical attitude. If you don't mind, I'd like to respond to your question by asking *you* one."

His thick eyebrows flared suddenly: surprise. "Why . . . of course, Dr. Cassidy. Please go right ahead."

Leaning forward at the podium, Alix took a deep breath.

"My question is this: what does the relevant research tell us about the numerical ratio between incidents in which both subjects believe they have communicated telepathically while asleep . . . and incidents in which we later learn that there is no confirming evidence to show that their accounts of such 'shared dreaming' were based on anything more than mere coincidence?"

A loud buzz went through the audience, as her listeners struggled to make sense of her complicated question.

Dr. Sverdlow also appeared to be struggling a bit.

Frowning deeply, he scratched his wrinkled forehead. "All right, I think I see where you're going. And my answer, of course, is that there *is* no relevant research of this kind. To my knowledge, no one has ever collected this kind of data. Why would they? These are not the kinds of questions that normally *occur* to science."

Now Alix was the one smiling. "But surely you can supply us with some approximate metrics? After all, *you're* the one who's suggesting that some fraction of the reports of Somnambulistic Telepathy will occasionally appear to be accurate, merely through coincidence, am I right?"

"Well, yes . . . but—"

"Then don't you think it's fair," she cut him off smoothly, "to provide us with a sense of scale here, Dr. Sverdlow? How often do these 'mere coincidences' occur, anyway? Do they occur in 95 percent of all reported cases of ST? Or only in 50 percent? Thirty percent?

"How can we hope to measure the likelihood that such coincidences actually *do* occur often enough to explain the large number of reported examples of successful telepathy, if we don't have any definitive data?"

"Well, I'm afraid I can't tell you. . . ." and he trailed off.

"No?" said Alix. "Well, I do think that's unfortunate. Because there *are* indeed three large cohort studies from the 1970s—two in Denmark and one in Germany—that measured the incidence rates for such 'mere coincidences' in great detail. These studies were not published in English-language journals, so many of you may not have read their findings.

"But the studies *did* identify dozens of subjects who had reported ST experiences—while providing firm evidence (such as the fire in Walter Sandoff's London apartment) to suggest that their ST communications had actually taken place in reality, while the subjects were sound asleep."

Now she sent him her best, brightest smile. "I'm not going to get into the actual data on those compelling studies, Dr. Sverdlow—not until my next lecture, anyway—but I can assure you that they *do* exist, and that they are highly persuasive.

"And although you don't seem to be aware of them, I *do* want to thank you for what I'm sure we'll all agree was an extremely interesting question!"

***

He was so impressed with Alix that he wound up asking her out to dinner the following night at the famed Blair Hill Inn, located about an hour's drive south of sprawling Moosehead Lake in Greenville.

They settled down in the elegant hostelry's highly regarded Parlor Room—the chef was a graduate of the renowned Le Cordon Bleu in Paris—and they talked for nearly three hours about sleep science and Somnambulistic Telepathy. They also discussed their heady plans for thrilling projects that would break new ground in paranormal research.

By ten o'clock, as they sipped at goblets of Courvoisier and basked in the glowing candlelight, Alix could feel the old fires beginning to rise deep within.

Gunther Sverdlow was world-famous as a scientist, and rakishly handsome. His eyes had never once left hers. "How I wish I could bring you to Geneva," he murmured against a background of dreamy violins. "You and I would make such a team, Alix. The world of the paranormal would never be the same again!"

She nodded and smiled. Amazed that this powerful man was paying such close attention to her—a woman who'd been more than five years without a lover's touch—she struggled to remain above the waves of giddy euphoria that threatened to swamp her.

It was a delicious evening, to be sure, and his lightly accented European elegance was difficult to resist. But she kept her wits about her somehow. She hung onto the table and listened carefully to every word. . . .

And it didn't take her long to discover that—except for a few overheated compliments about her "mysterious eyes" and her "charming smile"—Gunther Sverdlow talked almost entirely about himself.

A narcissist then?

Be careful, she warned herself. A man like that . . . a man who sees you only as a reflection of himself . . .

Been there. Done that . . . with one Dr. Michael Rogers, thank you very much!

At the end of the long evening, as he dropped her off at her Big Pine cabin, she agreed to think about joining him on another date in a few days.

But she had no intention of rushing into anything . . . and when Sverdlow bent his head to put his lips against hers, she quickly turned away.

With a hurried "Thank you, I had a lovely time!", Alix darted across the gravel driveway and disappeared behind her cabin door.

Chapter 15
The Enigma of the Locked Bedroom

The Crown Victoria pulled into an empty parking space beneath a green canvas awning marked HOLTON ARMS.

A Boston PD black-and-white patrol car was stationed near the big glass doors that led into the front of the nine-story complex . . . and the entrance was cordoned off inside a noose of bright yellow crime-scene tape.

Jake put his hand on the car door but didn't move. His belt radio had begun to chirp.

EMT says victim appears to have died of stab wounds.

Jake didn't hesitate. He had the radio in his hand now. "If EMT's still there, tell them not to touch the body."

"Ten-four that, Homicide."

"Off at the scene."

"Copy that, Homicide."

Jake and Tony stepped out of the car. As they approached the glass doors, both men reached for their gold shields. The uniformed cop positioned just outside the doors waved them through. A moment later, they were eyeballing the lobby. It was the typical layout for a mid-priced apartment complex in Boston: scuffed parquet floorboards, a couple of dusty potted plants, two vinyl-covered easy chairs and a battered black sofa.

They nodded to another police uniform at the entrance to the elevator and then stepped inside. The old elevator car's fixtures were made of tarnished brass and the mirror had a chunk missing.

Tony hit the "5."

The two detectives rode up in silence, except for the occasional metallic rattling of the lift device.

"Wouldn't want to get stuck in here," said Tony as they neared the end of the ride.

Jake looked at him. "What's the matter, you claustrophobic?"

"You bet. Getting locked inside a small space flips me out. Always has. Got shut up in a linen closet by accident one time as a kid. Six, seven hours it was before they found me.

"No fun at all . . . especially wondering if the oxygen would run out."

"Ever tell a shrink?"

"Naaah . . . those guys don't know shit. Couldn't find their dicks in a rainstorm."

They were walking down a long narrow hallway. The light came from a series of overhead fixtures, but one flickered erratically—was it about to give up the ghost? They passed several doors. When they reached 512, they greeted the uniform on duty outside the victim's apartment.

He held up his metal clipboard. "Hello, Detective Becker. I gotta log you both into the crime scene."

He scribbled on the clipboard for a moment, then looked uncertainly at Tony's gold shield. "Detective Tony Rizzo," said Tony. "I'm the new guy in Homicide." The uniform nodded and scribbled again. "Okay, no problem. Thanks, guys."

They stepped past him and got a small surprise: a brightly painted poster had been taped to the inside of the door. Now they were gazing at Paul McCartney's round dopey-looking mug. The famed Beatle was sucking on a red lollipop above a legend printed in giant boldface: *All You Need Is Love!*

They moved through the doorway and encountered a heavyset, balding man in a white coat with three words stitched in red above the front pocket: *Herb Pulaski EMT*.

"Hey, Jake," said the chunky technician. He nodded at Tony. He was sweating profusely.

"Hello, Herb," said Jake. "Glad to see they haven't canned you yet."

"Give 'em time," said Herb. "Listen, guys, I was just leaving. There's a uniform back there with the body. Better snap on your jock straps—this is a nasty one."

Rizzo glared at him. "Nasty how?"

"He cut her a bunch of times. Lot of trauma to her ribcage."

"We'll be fine," said Tony. He and Jake were already slipping on their plastic gloves, along with the plastic booties that would be needed on the blood-smeared floor.

Nodding, Herb turned away and began collecting his gear. The other two proceeded into what was obviously the victim's living room. The furniture was mismatched and scarred here and there with cigarette burns—typical college-apartment stuff. A knee-high coffee table held several unlit candles and a small incense burner.

The walls were hung with more music posters: Fleetwood Mac, The Police, Madonna. At the far end of the enclosure a door frame curtain made of long strings of colorful beads marked the entrance to the only bedroom.

Jake was the first one in. He said hello to the uniformed patrolman standing on the other side of the room. The uniform nodded back at him but didn't speak. At first glance the entire layout seemed to have been painted in bright scarlet. But as his eyes adjusted to the gloom, Jake saw that a lot of the surface area—walls, floorboards, big floor-to-ceiling mirror—was splattered with dried blood.

Jake stepped toward the bed. The victim lay spread-eagled. Some of the blood on her midriff and groin was still wet. She'd been slashed dozens of times, mostly in the chest.

"Goddamn," said Tony. "What kind of sick sonofabitch . . ."

"Officer," said Jake, "please don't lean against that window."

"Okay, no problem," said the uniform. He stepped toward them—a young cop with a lick of blond hair grazing his forehead.

Jake didn't touch the body. He just stood above the dead woman for a couple of minutes, looking and thinking. "Narrow incisions," he said at last, as if talking to himself. "A fine-edged blade, and he swung it in a downward arc with his closed fist, like he was punching her again and again.

"Angry."

He looked at the youthful cop. "We got an I.D. yet?"

"Yup. Name is Tracy Donovan. Been living here about a year."

The uniform had removed a spiral notebook from his shirt pocket. He flipped the pages. "The apartment manager—that's Mrs. Teagarden, down in 101—says the victim worked at a sports bar not too far from here. Mulligan's."

Jake blinked slowly at him. "A bartender?"

"That's it," said the cop. "Worked nights mostly, so she could attend day classes over at Suffolk."

"Who found the body?"

"Her boyfriend. A kid named Philip Hatch. He let himself in with a key apparently, about two hours ago. After he saw *this*, he passed out. Got real sick. When we arrived on the nine-one-one call, he was puking his guts out.

"Then he started having chest pains. He's in the ER at Boston City right now."

Jake stared calmly at the patrolman. "Okay, thanks. We've got somebody with him, I assume?"

"Correct. We rode with the ambo. He'll have a BPD escort until you two can get to him."

Jake nodded. "We'll speak to him shortly."

Soon they were joined by Dr. Stuart Pino, the medical examiner, who arrived with two stretcher-guys from the BPD meat wagon.

"Gentlemen," said Jake.

"Hello, Detective Becker," said Dr. Pino. He was a tiny man with highly skilled hands. Soon those hands were at work on the victim's eyes, temples and fingernails. It didn't take Dr. Pino long to complete his task. He started by activating a mini-tape recorder no larger than a pack of cigarettes.

"Report by Dr. Stuart Pino, unexplained death, Holton Arms, Apartment 512, June 10, 1986. Numerous cutting wounds. No obvious signs of struggle. No apparent tissue residue under fingernails. Time of death approximately eight hours ago. Probable cause of death, blood loss from more than twenty wounds by a fine-edged blade, maybe a scalpel. Wounds especially extensive in the thoracic area. Major blood loss probably from aorta, which could have been slashed by deep penetration of weapon."

Dr. Pino stopped dictating. Jake had stepped over to the window by now. He studied the clear glass panes and the balcony beyond.

"Locked," he said to Tony. "No paint flakes, no scrapes on the latch—the perp didn't break in or out through here."

The younger cop nodded. "Same story on her apartment door. No sign of forced entry. And Mrs. Teagarden—the manager—says she came home alone last night. A quiet evening . . . no problems at all, according to Teagarden."

Jake thought for a minute. "Probably somebody she knew. Maybe someone from the bar?" He looked at Tony. "Did you notice the white stuff on the bathroom mirror?"

"What stuff?" growled Tony.

"That cloudy white substance, milky-white. Looks like semen to me."

"Didn't catch it," said Tony. "He jerked off on the mirror? How the hell could he have pulled that off?"

Jake shrugged. "It's a floor-to-ceiling mirror. He stands in front of it and watches himself masturbate."

"Truly weird," said Tony.

"Anyway, we'll have to wait for the lab guys to tell us what it is," said Jake. "Meanwhile, let's talk to the apartment manager, then head for Mulligan's.

"Gonna be a late one, Tony."

"Copy," said Tony. "That's fine with me, Jake. Looking at this"—and he gave the corpse a melancholy wave with one gloved hand—"makes me want to work all night long."

Jake smiled quietly at his glowering partner.

"Me, too," he said. "But first I gotta call Mrs. Whitney and tell her I'll be working late tonight."

"Mrs. Whitney?" said Tony.

"Charly's nanny," said Jake. "She covers for me when I work at night."

***

Mrs. Teagarden turned out to be a large round-faced woman in a flowing green bathrobe and bristling hair curlers.

Her brown eyes were huge as she greeted them at her door. It was obvious that she'd been waiting anxiously for the arrival of the police.

"Come right in, gentlemen."

She led them into a brightly furnished living room dominated by a half-dozen toy poodles on the mantel above a small non-working fireplace. A living French poodle lay supine on the armrest of a nearby sofa. Suspicious, the dog raised his curly head to inspect the newcomers.

"Can I serve you some coffee, officers?"

"Thank you," said Jake, "but that's not necessary."

They sat down. Mrs. Teagarden lifted the tiny, white-haired dog from his perch and gave him a quick hug. "This is Buster Boo. He's my best buddy."

Then, pointing to the toy dogs above the fireplace: "Those are all his cousins up there on the mantel!"

"Hello, Buster Boo," said Jake. He and Tony glanced at each other for a moment.

The dog made a low, growly sound somewhere deep in his throat. The two men were now perched on the sofa and the apartment manager had taken a seat in a facing easy chair.

"We won't keep you long, ma'am," said Jake. "I'm sure this has been a terrible shock."

"Dear heavens, yes," she said. "Oh, that poor girl. How could such a thing happen to a wonderful person like Tracy?"

She stared at them, wide-eyed. "And what if he comes *back*?"

Jake smiled reassuringly at her. "Don't worry. We'll have a couple of patrolmen stationed here around the clock for at least a week, Mrs. Teagarden. They'll provide enhanced security. No problem."

He thought for a moment. "Do you have someone you can share all of this with? Somebody to talk to?"

Mrs. Teagarden sighed. "Yes, I've already called my friend Mildred, thank God. She's coming over here in an hour." She brightened a little. "Mildred has been my savior, ever since I lost Alfred. My husband? He's been gone six years now. Can you believe it?"

She gave the little dog a mournful hug.

"I'm sorry. We won't hold you long," said Jake. "We just need to know if you saw or heard anything last night."

Mrs. Teagarden's eyes had filled with tears. "No, I never heard a peep, gentlemen. Not a *peep*. And I've already talked with all the other residents up on the fifth floor. Tracy was in 512 as you know. Some of the tenants I spoke with live right down the hall from her. But nobody heard a thing last night."

Jake waited. He'd learned over the years that it was sometimes best *not* to ask questions. Just let the witness talk freely, in a totally disconnected fashion, and then focus on whatever came up.

"Really, it's horrible," she said. "And that poor young man? He found her body, and I think he had some kind of breakdown. Her boyfriend? I think his name was Philip?

"He fainted, the poor thing, and they took him away in an ambulance."

"So we heard," said Jake.

"Really, Tracy was such a nice girl. Always polite, always respectful. Not a bit of trouble from her. And very quiet. A college student, you know? Most of the time she worked at night and went to classes during the day."

Tony had one hand up. "How about last evening, ma'am?"

The apartment manager leaned forward on her chair and gazed at them intently. "Same story, I think. I saw her in the hallway around one a.m., walking toward the elevator. I was taking Buster Boo out for his nightly constitutional, right before bed. We spoke together briefly."

Her eyes lit up for a moment. "Sometimes she gives . . . *used* to give . . . Buster a treat. You know, a little doggie-snack?"

"Was she alone when you saw her?" asked Jake.

"She was," said Mrs. Teagarden. "She was still wearing her uniform from work, this place called Mulligan's."

The two detectives looked at each other: *we're headed there next.*

"How'd she seem?" asked Tony. "Cheerful? Friendly?"

"Absolutely," said Mrs. Teagarden. "She even asked about Buster Boo. She's a huge fan of this particular poodle, lemme tell ya!"

She gave the dog another terrific squeeze. "Anyway, I watched her get on the elevator and I never saw her again."

Now the woman in the rumpled housecoat was frowning thoughtfully. "That's really all I know, officers.

"The rest of the evening was completely routine. Very quiet. Not a peep! Nobody on five heard a sound from 512. How could such a terrible thing happen?

"Trust me, these walls are just thin plywood, really—not much insulation left at all after so many years. You can hear *everything*. My next-door neighbor can't flush her toilet without me hearing it!"

The two detectives nodded as they rose to their feet. "Mrs. Teagarden, thank you for helping us," said Jake. "Detective Rizzo and I will be interviewing all the tenants on the fifth floor and another team of investigators will be talking with the people who live on the other floors.

"Is there anything else you've seen or heard in recent days that might help explain what happened to Tracy last night?"

The manager was also standing up by now. Blinking slowly, she walked them toward the door. "Well . . . not really. No, wait. There is one thing. She had a friend. Very close."

"A friend?" Jake was watching her carefully.

"This other girl, about her same age," said Mrs. Teagarden. "I think she's also a student over at Suffolk. Her name is Judy. I don't know her last name. Just Judy. But she was in Tracy's apartment a lot.

"They were best pals, those two," added Mrs. Teagarden. "Just like me and little Buster Boo."

She rubbed her nose against the dog's nose, as the two men said goodbye.

CHAPTER 16
Judy Remembers "The Creep"

"Goddamn," said Jerry Benevento. He looked like he might burst into tears at any moment. "Fuck! You gotta be fucking kidding me! I can't believe it!"

"I'm sorry," said Jake.

The big man in the Patriots jersey kept rubbing his forehead.

"Jesus, this is just terrible. Aw, goddamnit, this is *horrible!*"

He made two fists and looked wildly around the bar, as if preparing to punch something, anything. Then his hands relaxed, and he went back to rubbing his forehead and muttering curses.

"She was a great kid," said Jerry. "Man, what's happening to this country? Can you answer me that? This country is going straight down the toilet, man."

"I'm sorry," said Jake. "Did you know her boyfriend?" He studied his notes for a moment. "Philip Hatch?"

The former gridiron hero stared unhappily at them. "Philip? He was cool, man. Treated her like a queen. There was never a harsh word between them, believe me. You don't think—"

"We're just getting started," said Jake. "Did she have any enemies, Jerry? Was anybody mad at her?"

Jerry made a sour face. "Tracy? Hell, no. Everybody loved Tracy. Count on it. She was the most popular bartender ever worked for me."

"I hear you," said Jake. "But I'm also thinking . . . you know, like maybe an old boyfriend, a jealous type, something like that?"

"Naaah, I never heard anything like that."

Jerry shook his head back and forth. Then he froze.

"Wait a minute—there *was* this guy, I don't know if it means anything, but there *was* this guy."

"What guy?" said Tony.

"This guy came in the bar, you know, a customer? He gave her a bunch of lip. Seemed real angry. Like . . . you know, he hated women or something? He was mad at an old girlfriend . . . and, like, you know, he was trying to take it out on the bartender.

"She was a little afraid of him—especially after he told her that he'd be coming back to see her. She told me about it. She called him 'The Creep.'

"Said he'd threatened her in some way."

Jake was scribbling in a spiral notebook.

"The Creep, huh? Any more details?"

"Nope. Sorry. I mean, in a place like this . . . shit, half the people who come in here could qualify as creeps, know what I mean?"

He sighed wearily. "The bar business—trust me, it's a breeding ground for whackos."

"I hear you," said Tony. "So, okay. What'd you say to her when she told you she was afraid of this guy?"

Jerry's two fists were back in the air again. "I told her not to worry about him. Told her I'd break his fucking neck in a heartbeat if he touched a hair on her head."

"Entirely understandable," said Jake. "But you never heard any more about him?"

"Nothing, man."

"Tracy also had a close friend. Judy something?"

"Judy Bell," said the bar owner. "Yeah, they were very close."

His eyelids flickered. Then his broad face lit up. "Hey, Judy applied for a job here about a month ago, but we haven't had an opening yet.

"Anyway, I got all her contact info back in the office—won't take me but a minute to get it for you."

***

Judy Bell screamed once and nearly fainted.

They got her onto a kitchen chair, white-faced and trembling. Tony fetched a glass of water.

"Oh, my God, oh Tracy, Tracy. Oh, sweetheart, how could anyone do this to you?"

"I'm sorry," said Jake.

He'd been saying those two words to people all day long. Par for the course when you worked homicide.

After a while, Judy poured herself a drink and began to calm down.

She was a slender young woman in her early twenties. She had China blue eyes and close-cropped bangs that gave her a pageboy look. As the alcohol took hold, her pupils expanded until they were almost nickel sized. They were also inky black with shock.

Jake waited until she'd relaxed a little and then asked her if Tracy had maybe been fighting with Philip Hatch in recent days. "Never," she said. "They were total lovebirds, those two."

"He wasn't the jealous type?"

"Not at all. No way. She was completely devoted to him."

Jake meditated for a few moments. "Anybody else who might have wanted to hurt Tracy?"

The woman at the kitchen table fell back against her chair.

"Oh, my God," she said.

The two detectives stared at her.

"What's the matter?" said Jake.

"You okay?" said Tony.

"Oh, my God."

"What?" said Jake.

"You aren't gonna believe this."

"Try us," said Tony.

"Oh, my God. There was this guy . . . this guy came into the bar. A real weirdo. She was afraid of him."

Jake and Tony looked at each other. "So we heard," said Jake. "And?"

"You won't believe me. You'll say I'm crazy."

Judy's upper lip had begun to tremble. Her knuckles turned bone white as she clung to the table.

They waited.

"The weirdo came into the bar a few days ago. He told Tracy he knew how to sneak into her nightmares."

The two cops traded glances.

"Try that again, why don't you?" said Tony.

"He told her he could . . ."

Judy groaned. Then she sobbed once—a sob full of desperation, full of horror.

"He said he knew how to invade her nightmares . . . and that he would hurt her when he did."

Jake and Tony stood there, expressionless.

"What?" said Jake. "He threatened to attack her while she was asleep?"

"No!" cried Judy. Her voice was loud, almost a shout.

"Not while she was asleep and *having* a nightmare. He threatened to attack her from *inside the nightmare itself.*"

Jake squinted at her, dumbfounded.

"Wait a minute, Judy. Let me get this straight. This guy said he would hurt her in a *dream* . . . and that the attack would somehow be *real*?"

"That's right," said Judy. Her voice was rising like a siren, rising toward what would soon be a terrified shriek.

"Tracy told me he'd actually appeared in a nightmare of hers . . . and then he came back to the bar the next day and described many of *the exact details from that same nightmare!*

"She was terrified. Absolutely terrified. She kept telling me over and over again: 'He says he's going to come after me again in my next nightmare, Judy.

"'He's going to hurt me—maybe even kill me—while I sleep!'"

Chapter 17
A Shocking Lab Report

It was time for Jake Becker to put his foot down.

Time for the veteran homicide detective to stand tall. Time to go *mano a mano* with the bully who'd been pushing him around for several days now.

Crouched over a plate of Mrs. Whitney's dinner-time baked salmon croquettes, the hard-nosed cop took a deep breath. Then he looked his relentless adversary straight in the eye.

"I hate to disappoint you, young lady," the frowning detective told his 14-year-old daughter, Charly, "but the answer is still *no*."

From beneath her helmet of wavy, pink-streaked hair, the peeved teenager glared back at him.

"Did you hear me, Charly? That's n and o—as in NO. You may *not* sleep over at your friend Margie's house tomorrow night."

The bully scowled at him. Her eyes had widened, and her face was turning bright red. Her mouth was expanding like a Disney helium balloon at the start of the Macy's Thanksgiving Day Parade.

Here it comes, Becker told himself. *Get ready*.

He braced.

"Dad . . . *Daaaaad*! How can you do this to me? All my friends will be there, while I sit at home like the biggest loser on Planet Earth!"

She began to wail. "It's not fair. You *know* it's not fair!"

Jake closed his eyes for a moment. Raising a teenager was a Herculean endeavor under the best of circumstances . . . but doing it alone—as a single parent—was absolutely impossible. His responsibility on this one was clear, however; having overheard Charly talking to a friend on the phone about "smoking some pot at the sleepover," he knew that he couldn't allow her to attend the all-night get-together.

"Not fair!" his darling daughter yowled again, while one hand tugged at the pink fringes of her bizarrely styled hair, which had been engineered by her "best friend in the world"—the same Margie who was hosting the sleepover.

"All the cool kids will be rocking to Jon Bon Jovi— but *I'll* be rocking in grandma's old chair, right here in our stupid living room!"

Now she shot him a dagger frown of scornful disdain. "How come all the other parents will let their kids go? Margie's mom even offered to bake us brownies!"

Jake sighed. "Charly, I've told you before: I don't *care* what all the other parents do or say. And that includes Margie's mom. Got it?"

"But why? What's wrong with the idea?"

Jake sighed. "Let's just say I heard about some of the activities that will be taking place at the sleepover and leave it at that."

She was on her feet now; her plate of spaghetti (specially prepared for her by Mrs. Whitney, since she "hated" salmon) had somehow overturned . . . sending a wet mass of tomato-red pasta skidding halfway down the dinner table.

"I hate you, do you hear me?"

"You don't mean that, sweetheart."

"The hell I don't!"

Having demonstrated her grownup ability to curse, the bully glared at him triumphantly.

"Charly, I've asked you before not to use that kind of language."

She rolled her eyes dramatically. "Oh . . . what a terrible curse! What a horrible word: *hell*. You better hope I never decide to *really* start cursing—"

"Watch it now, young lady."

"Because if I do, you'll hear some stuff a whole lot worse than *hell*!"

Charly turned. A moment later she was running toward the living room stairs. At the top, she whirled for a final salvo: "You're the . . . the worst dad who ever lived!"

Two seconds later, her bedroom door slammed louder than a pistol shot.

Jake shook his head. *Teenagers.* He sighed. Meanwhile, the kitchen phone was ringing and ringing.

Moaning with frustration, the worst dad in the world climbed slowly to his feet.

Still shaking his head, he lumbered across the linoleum squares to where the infernal device hung from a hook above the countertop.

"Hello?"

"Jake?" It was Tony. He sounded completely out of breath.

"What's up, Tony?"

"A whole lot."

"What? Something new on the Donovan case?"

"That's right. Something real nasty. According to the lab guys, that *was* semen on the bathroom mirror. Which means he must've hung around for a while, jerking off . . . while she lay there bleeding to death."

Jake tightened his grip on the phone. "I knew it. Are they sure about the semen?"

"Absolutely. I talked with Harrelson myself. He's already reviewed the two lab techs' findings. They ran a test on the specimens we sent 'em. It was human semen. No question about it."

"I don't understand that, Tony. We've got no forced entry into the room, no signs of struggle and no noise from the victim's apartment."

"I can't figure it, either—especially after talking to Donovan's boyfriend. He was discharged from the hospital after a few hours. Seems to be doing okay now. Anyway, he told me he'd talked to her on the phone for half an hour that night, right as she was falling asleep.

"She was scared, he said—terrified of her own nightmares. So he sweet-talked her to sleep, right there on the phone."

Jake reflected for a minute. "Okay, so after they sweet-talked, another guy shows up at her apartment. She had a *second* visitor, right?"

"He says no. He swears the two of them were totally tight. Says they were even planning to get married."

Jake was blinking slowly, helplessly. "Wait a minute, Tony. Are you telling me she was alone all night, no signs of forced entry, nobody heard anything . . . and yet she winds up stabbed to death?

"Sorry, but you're violating the laws of physics, my friend. She had a second boyfriend and he dropped by for a visit. Get over it."

They were both silent for a while. Then Jake said: "I know you looked at the autopsy findings again on

Monday. See any indications of rape? Skin under her fingernails?"

"Nope. Nothing significant. But vaginal trauma from rape is usually hard to pinpoint."

Jake mulled it over. "So what's your guess?"

"Don't have one," said Tony. "Right now, all I can say—"

His next few words were lost in a howling cacophony of guitar riffs and screamed lyrics from upstairs:

Shot through the heart,
And you're to blame;
Darlin',
YOU GIVE LOVE A BAD NAME!

It was Jon Bon Jovi, of course, roaring through his recent hit single, and Charly had the volume up so loud that the entire house was trembling as if struck by an earthquake.

Jake cupped the mouthpiece and shouted toward the ceiling: "Charly, turn that damn thing down this minute!"

He waited.

The Bon Jovi band went right on screeching. They were a bunch of dope-dealing anarchists outfitted with 10,000-watt amplifiers and enough voltage to light up Fenway Park for a night game!

Jake closed his eyes and gritted his teeth. "Tony, I gotta run. Let's meet up at the station, eight o'clock sharp?"

"You bet," said Tony.

CHAPTER 18
Looking for a Redhead with Emerald Green Eyes

Dr. Mike was drifting again.

Drifting.

Tonight he'd decided to spend a few hours in the city's notorious Combat Zone. Nothing too exciting. All he wanted was to sit in a strip joint like the Teddy Bare Lounge for a while, nursing a beer and looking for the kind of flame-haired, emerald-eyed beauty who would remind him of . . . *her.*

Little Miss Alix.

Or maybe he'd drift on down to the Two O'Clock Club? Yeah. He'd keep an eye out for her as he loafed along Washington Street, then swung left onto Kneeland and headed for LaGrange. The heart of the Zone! No problems for Dr. Mike. He was just keeping an eye out for the *woman of his dreams.*

Slouched on a barstool at the Naked I, he gazed happily at the big neon sign on the other side of the dirty plate glass. First the image on the sign flashed blue—and became a staring human eye—and then it flashed red and became a woman's fully bared breasts.

Yeah! The Naked I.

He lifted the glass of sour brew to his lips. Dr. Mike hadn't shaved in more than a week. He didn't smell so hot either. But so what? He hadn't come to the Combat Zone to socialize, had he? He didn't need any new friends . . . not with his best friend hugging his right hip.

Not with his pal "HR" tucked away so carefully in the back pocket of his ragged jeans.

His loyal sidekick, good ole HR!

Folded up neatly inside its leather sheath and ready to go.

You bet! With his asshole daddy's scalpel at the ready, how could Little Mikey ever go wrong?

An hour later he was sitting in the Hollywood Haven, nipping at a Tequila Sunrise and listening to Survivor pound through *Burning Heart.*

In the burning heart, just about to burst,
There's a quest for answers, an unquenchable thirst.
In the darkest night, rising like a spire—
In the burning heart, the unmistakable fire.

He watched a topless dancer shuffle mechanically to the driving beat. She was a tall blonde, well-built, but her eyes were deader than yesterday's newspaper and the green lizard tattoo on her belly made his stomach roll over with disgust.

He didn't want a blonde, goddamnit. He wanted a redhead! *The girl of his dreams . . .*

After a while he climbed off the stool and headed into the can for a leak. Standing at a filthy urinal, he read the usual third-rate inscriptions from the usual platoon of strip-club morons: *Go fuck yourself! Don't need to—yo momma just sucked my dick!*

Dr. Mike stumbled out of the club without looking back. It was raining a little now . . . a thin, cold rain that slicked the electric signs, made them look like glistening popsicles in the glaring drizzle. Near the corner of Kneeland and Tremont, he saw a flash of movement in a doorway, as a hulking wino in a battered baseball cap lurched to his feet and approached him, obviously in search of a handout.

"Hey, mister, can you help me out with some change?"

"Get lost," said Dr. Mike.

The wino refused to give up, however. Moving in closer, he flashed a smile at his quarry . . . a smile that revealed a ragged lineup of yellow-stained teeth. "How 'bout a cig, mister? Can you help me out with a smoke?"

Dr. Mike had heard enough. "I told you: get the fuck away from me."

But the vagrant persisted. What the hell was the *matter* with this guy? Weaving unsteadily on his feet, the derelict made a weird croaking sound . . . a grotesque attempt at a laugh? Then he lurched toward his target, bleary-eyed, both hands in the air.

"All I'm askin' for is a bowl of soup, mister! I ain't had nothin' to eat in two days. Gimme a break!"

Dr. Mike's right hand had gone to the sheath in his back pocket. "I don't give a fuck if you ever eat again, you hear me?"

Soon the doctor's hand held a gleaming length of steel. "Back off, loser—I'm not gonna tell you again."

But the wino was too intoxicated to understand. "Mister, I been walking these mean streets too long. You hear me? I need me a boost, don't you get it?"

With that, the beggar reached out to poke Dr. Mike in the chest.

His hand never got there.

Because the length of steel had sprung open, and the infuriated ex-psychiatrist was gripping a cold blue blade.

Swooosh!

The polished Swiss scalpel went hissing through the air.

Stunned, the derelict stared at his hand, now missing two fingers and spouting bright red blood.

Dr. Mike turned away. He was already wiping the scalpel clean and returning it to the sheath. "Don't say I didn't warn you, numb nuts."

The wino sent up a thin, pathetic cry: "Awwww . . . fuck! I been *cut*. Goddamnit . . . somebody help me . . . I been *cut*!"

He was on his knees and holding his stricken finger-stumps high in the air, with the blood running down his forearm onto the muddy sidewalk.

Nobody gave him a second look.

Dr. Mike, halfway down the block, had already forgotten him.

I want me a redhead. An icy smile flickered across his whiskey-swollen mouth.

I want me a redhead with emerald green eyes!

***

They sat over cups of steaming coffee in Jake's cubicle.

"Okay, Tony," said the senior detective. "Thanks for rescuing me from Charly."

His partner sipped—and winced as he burned the tip of his tongue. "A big tough cop like you, twenty years on the force," Tony said with a chuckle, "and somebody's got to save you from a fourteen-year-old?"

Jake groaned. "This isn't any fourteen-year-old, pal. This is Grendel, my man. One false move and she'll rip your sternum out."

Tony was staring at him. "Grendel?"

"He was the monster in *Beowulf*," said Jake. "You don't know about *Beowulf*? He's only the most famous ogre in all of Old English Literature."

Tony sipped and winced again. "Ogre? Hey, you'll pardon me, Professor, if I ain't that well-read. Okay? I majored in Phys Ed at Boston College, remember? The big mental challenge at BC was badminton . . . and the toughest class at the Police Academy was called 'How to Work a Crime Scene.'"

Jake was grinning at him. "Grendel hung out on the bottom of a lake. All the Anglo-Saxon tough guys would swim down there to take a crack at him.

"But only one tough guy actually got it done: Beowulf!"

Tony's long Italian face was a mask of boredom. "Thanks for the lit class, Professor. Like, you know, I really give a shit?"

"Quiz on Monday," said Jake.

"Right. I'll study hard." Tony waved him away . . . then brightened. "Hey, I brought doughnuts. You want one or not?"

"Sure."

They were silent for a while, eating. Then Tony said, "Let's get serious here. As I told you on the phone, Harrelson and his guys at the lab came up with semen. They say there was plenty of it on that floor-to-ceiling mirror."

Jake considered it. "Very possible, I guess. But I'm more interested in another question right now."

"Go for it."

"How the hell did the killer get into her room? We've got no physical marks on the doors or windows—and nobody heard a peep out of 512 all night long."

Tony pushed the doughnut box away. He propped his elbows on the table. "Good question. Wish I could answer it."

"Yeah, well, here's one more for you. Who's the blade man? According to you, we've got Tracy Donovan's totally credible boyfriend on the record now, and he says he was about to marry her. Says he was talking with her on the phone as she drifted off to sleep that night."

Tony nodded. "Right. She conked out while he was in the middle of a sentence. So what's your point?"

"I don't have a point. I'm just not understanding how the intruder got in. Something doesn't work here, that's all."

Tony blinked slowly at him. "Get real."

"I *am* real."

"Really? Doesn't sound like it—because what you're telling me is, nobody actually broke into the apartment. And if nobody broke in, the killer materialized out of thin air. So you're saying our suspect is Casper the Friendly Ghost?"

Jake reflected for a few seconds. "Maybe she hangs up with the boyfriend and then gets a *second* phone call?"

Tony shook his head. "Nope. I already talked with my source at Ma Bell. No calls after the fiancé's call at 11:37."

Jake looked at him. "You eyeballed the phone company logs?"

"I did."

"Without a warrant?"

Tony's left eyebrow inched upward. "You're kidding, right?"

"You violated the Constitutional right to privacy, Tony."

"Oh dear. Did I really?"

"Don't do it again, you hear me? Not without a proper warrant."

Tony frowned. "Okay, will do. You're the boss. I was just trying to speed things up a little, that's all."

"We don't break the law, Tony. You heard me. Get a warrant. That's an order."

Jake lowered his coffee cup and continued. "Okay . . . so apparently there was no second call. What next? Maybe after she hangs up with the fiancé, an old friend shows up unexpectedly at her door?

Or maybe somebody had been hiding in her apartment the entire time?"

Tony shook his head. "Somebody shows up at midnight? Unannounced? Or maybe somebody was playing hide-and-seek in her bedroom all night long? Not very likely, Jake."

Jake kept going, however. "Maybe the new arrival brought her some news she didn't like. They started arguing . . . one thing led to another. They fought, and he killed her during the fight?"

"It's too big a stretch," Tony said. "An unannounced visitor, middle of the night. Somebody she knew. They talk . . . and then he decides to knife her and jerk off on the mirror? Still doesn't work, Jake."

Jake frowned. "You're probably right. It doesn't fit. There's something about this whole thing we're not understanding."

Tony sighed. "There's gotta be a way. And we gotta *find* it, pronto. We need to burn some shoe leather, starting bright and early in the a.m. Talk to her past friends, her family and her co-workers at the bar. The whole ball of wax."

They sat quietly for a bit. Then Jake's features brightened.

"I keep thinking about that old girlfriend of hers, that Judy Bell. Maybe she knows something that could help us."

Tony blinked. "We already interviewed her."

"Once is never enough," said Jake. "She was very close to Donovan, remember. They were close friends. Maybe she forgot a detail or two about the creep who visited the bar that night. That crazy fucking nightmare guy who was making threats at the bar? Who knows? Let's try her again, whaddya say?"

"Ten-four," said Tony. "I'll set it up, pronto."

Chapter 19
Caught on the Horns of a Dilemma

Dr. Violette lifted her cup of Earl Grey decaf and peered into it, as if searching for an intruding insect. Or was she trying to read her friend's future in the tea leaves?

"Alix, you need to be careful."

Dr. Cassidy, enjoying a cup of fragrant English Teatime, gazed calmly back at her friend.

"Careful of what, Roz?"

"You know what . . . or should I say *who*? That Swiss hotshot Sverdlow. Trust me, Alix: I've been around the track a few times. That Sverdlow . . . he oughta be wearing horns! He's got the look, know what I mean?"

"The look?"

Alix was at a loss.

"The 'horns look,' dear girl. As in: 'I'm horny all the way down to my socks.'"

Rozzie took a long satisfying pull at her Earl Grey. "Did you know the medieval world usually pictured the devil wearing horns?"

Alix laughed. "Nope. I'm afraid I haven't spent a whole lot of time studying the medieval world, Rozzie."

"It's true, hon. And what about the satyr? *That* particular image goes all the way back to Ancient Greece. The satyr often wore horns, too—and you know what *he* was after."

Alix was still laughing. "What?"

"Well . . . they have a word for it down where I come from, down in Charleston. They call it *poon*-tang."

Alix frowned. "Wait a minute, Roz. I grew up mostly in Wisconsin, so please pardon me, but I have no idea what you're referring to. What did you call it?"

"*Poon*-tang!" thundered Rozzie. "A man like that Gunther Sverdlow . . . you can see it right there in his eyes. Take it from someone who knows. That sonofabitch is hornier than a four-balled tomcat!"

Alix was nearly doubled over with laughter. For a few moments she feared that she might swallow her teacup.

"Rozzie, you're in the wrong business. Have you ever thought about doing stand-up comedy?"

Rozzie was snickering and waving her friend away. "Thanks, honey, but flattery won't work with me. I'm *way* too old for a career in showbiz, and we both know it.

"Seriously, Alix, I want you to be careful. That damn Sverdlow is a top-ranked philanderer with a triple-A reputation for wooing his female colleagues and then leaving them stranded on the beach. He's been married before, you know."

Alix stiffened. "Really? He didn't mention that to me."

Rozzie snorted. "Why would he? Picture it. He's got a beautiful redhead drinking wine with him at an elegant restaurant, against a glowing backdrop of flickering candles and Mantovani strings. The candles are glowing and the orchestra is doing *Some Enchanted Evening*. He knows damn right well that talking about how he ditched his dumpy wife 17 years back in Geneva for a 24-year old Givenchy model—that's what I heard, anyway—isn't going to take him where he wants to go."

Alix blinked. "Which is where?"

"Straight into your pants, honey-chile. Pardon my French, but I'm telling it like it is!"

Alix picked up her cup. "I'm afraid you've grown cynical with the years, Rozzie. That dinner we shared was terrific, and Gunther was the soul of politeness throughout."

Rozzie's upper lip curled back on itself. Skepticism. "Was he really now? No physical moves at all?"

"Well . . . he *did* try for a goodnight kiss as he dropped me off at my cabin."

"Uh-huh." Rozzie scowled, then guffawed. "So what happened?"

"I turned away, that's all. I thought it was way too early in our relationship for that kind of move."

"Good girl. I can guarantee you, Alix: if you'd let him put his mouth on yours, he'd have followed you straight into your cabin. No question about it. He'd have jumped your bones in a New York minute."

Alix sipped. "Well, it didn't happen."

"Right. And if I were you, I'd make sure it *never* happens."

Rozzie thought for a minute, then brightened. "Anyway, he's onstage in the main auditorium tomorrow at ten-thirty a.m."

"Dr. Sverdlow, you mean?"

"The very one," said Rozzie. "According to the program, he'll be giving a one-hour lecture: *Human Precognition—the Facts versus the Myths*."

Alix smiled. "Very interesting," she said. "Can I expect to see you there?"

"You can," said Rozzie. "I'll be there, and I'll be watching *you*."

"Me? Why?"

"Why do you think? Somebody's gotta protect you from the four-balled tomcat!"

***

It was almost certain to be the most interesting—and entertaining—lecture at the 1986 Big Pine Conference. The excitement in the auditorium was palpable.

Showtime!

Obviously, Dr. Gunther Sverdlow was up to the challenge.

Attired in an elegant gunmetal-hued suit by Armani, he sported a silk tie with a pattern of black and white diamonds . . . along with a pair of cufflinks cut from glittering topaz.

Supremely confident in his neatly trimmed Van Dyke beard and his possum-sleek razor haircut, the research superstar strolled out to center stage at precisely ten-thirty.

Microphone at the ready, he took a few moments to scrutinize his audience. When he finally spoke, his voice was smooth as chilled yogurt.

"Good morning, fellow researchers. Thank you all for attending what I hope will be a most entertaining and informative lecture. Before I get started, I want to say that it's both a pleasure and a privilege to talk with you today about a subject that's very dear to my heart.

"Tachyons!"

A low murmur of surprise rippled over the audience. *Tachyons?*

"That's right, my friends. Tachyons! What are they? Well, the simple answer is, they're subatomic particles—but particles that have been blessed with a certain remarkable talent."

He looked around the silent auditorium for a few seconds. His smile would have been the envy of the Cheshire Cat.

"And what *is* this extraordinary talent that only tachyons seem to possess? It's very simple, my good friends.

"They know how to move faster than the speed of light! Which is very important—please trust me on this—because it means that they also know how to perform another amazing trick: *They can travel backwards through time.*"

Wow! With the flick of a jeweled wrist, the Swiss showboater triggered an electrical switch concealed in his left shirt cuff—and the back of the stage suddenly blossomed into greenish pulsating light.

"Ladies and gentlemen, *voila!*" boomed the celebrity researcher, as a series of transparent light bubbles shot from the screen toward his amazed listeners.

"What you are watching is a cinematic representation of how tachyons move through extra-dimensional space in a mode that allows them to completely ignore the ordinary laws of physics!"

He smiled again—the Cheshire smile—and then stepped toward a small table that contained several ordinary-looking objects.

One of those objects was a magazine. Like a magician at the start of a clever trick, Dr. Sverdlow was waving it high above his head.

"Ladies and gentlemen," he crooned at his nearly hypnotized audience, "I am delighted to present you with a copy of *People* magazine, dated May 18, 1980. In that issue, *People* reported that only one person in the world—a Swiss scientist named Gunther Sverdlow—

accurately predicted that the Iranian fundamentalists in November of 1979 would kidnap dozens of Americans and hold them hostage in Tehran for more than a year."

He stood silent for a moment, letting the drama build. Then he hit them with the crusher. "My dear friends, as you will see in this cover story, *I made that exact prediction three weeks before the event took place in 1979!*"

Once again, a murmur of amazement rolled over the scientist's listeners.

With a look of triumph, he leaned back and asked them: "So how did I accomplish this remarkable feat? It was quite simple actually.

"I found an algorithm that got me some help from my gifted friends, the time-traveling tachyons!"

Seated in the middle of the tenth row, Alix leaned toward Rozzie and hissed in her ear: "He's good, Roz. He's damn good."

"You got that right," Rozzie hissed back. "But how good is his *science*?"

The lecturer had returned to his table of props by now. Beaming happily, he reached over and picked up what appeared to be an ordinary push-button telephone. With a conspiratorial wink at his audience, he lifted the handset from the base and put it to his ear.

With his free hand, he began to push the buttons.

"Ladies and gentlemen," he said with a mysterious smile, "I'm sure you know exactly what I'm doing. I'm calling someone on this telephone, right?"

Nods all around. What could be more obvious?

Next the Swiss experimenter spoke loudly into the mouthpiece. "Hello, I'm calling Gunther, please. Gunther, is that you?"

A moment later, he cupped the mouthpiece with one hand and told the audience: "The person who answered this call just said to me, 'Yes, it's me, Gunther Sverdlow. Thank you very much for calling.' So now I will respond to him."

Into the phone he said: "Hello, Gunther. My name is also Gunther!

"How are you doing today, my friend?"

He listened for a few seconds, then said to the audience: "He just told me: 'I'm feeling fine. Today's date is June seventeenth.'"

(Alix whispered to Rozzie, "What the hell is he *doing*?" Rozzie whispered back, "Beats me!")

A moment later, Dr. Sverdlow was replacing the handset on its cradle and returning both to the table.

"Ladies and gentlemen," he said with the same assured smile, "the telephone call you just witnessed seems perfectly routine. But it's not. Not at all. Why? Because the device which I just used to make the call is not an ordinary telephone. It's actually what Albert Einstein—in one of his papers on special relativity— referred to as a 'tachyonic anti-telephone.'

"In other words: the signals in this particular telephone are transmitted by faster-than-light tachyons . . . which means they're capable of traveling backwards in time.

"By using the anti-telephone, in short, I can perform the rather remarkable feat of calling myself up and having the call go through prior to having *made* it.

"To illustrate my point, let me show you a brief videotape of the telephone call, please. As you will see in a moment, the tape captures me in the act of answering the call I just made to the phone in my cabin. Perhaps you will ask: 'So he called his cabin phone. Big deal! What's so unusual about that?'

"Well, what's unusual is the fact that in this upcoming video, you will see that I answered the telephone call you just saw me make . . . *and I answered it yesterday morning.*"

Dr. Sverdlow smiled confidently. "Now, please allow me to show you the video of the conversation you just heard."

Stunned, the Big Pine audience responded with a series of gasps and exclamations: "What? Are you serious? But that's impossible! He called himself just now, and then took the call *yesterday*? And he's gonna show us him doing that on the video—so we can see it for *ourselves*?"

For her part, Alix was laughing out loud and tugging at Rozzie's sleeve.

"I can't believe it, Roz. He isn't doing science—he's doing theater. This guy is from outer space!"

But there was no time for Rozzie to respond. The videotape was already running.

Totally astonished, the onlookers watched a casually clad Dr. Sverdlow pick up a telephone and answer it. After listening for a moment, he told the caller: "Yes, it's me—Gunther. Thank you very much for calling, Gunther! Today's date is June seventeenth."

Next came the video image of an immaculately clad Dr. Sverdlow, who stood onstage and listened to the man he'd just called for a few moments. Then he said to his audience: "He just told me: 'I'm feeling fine. Today's date is June seventeenth.'

The man in the silk tie beamed happily. "But as we all know, today's date is June *eighteenth.*"

A moment later the "earlier" videotaped version of Dr. Sverdlow—but this time casually clad and in his cabin—held up a copy of the New York Times front page.

All the News That's Fit to Print
June 17, 1986

From center stage, Dr. Sverdlow now sent his audience a magician's triumphant smile.

"As you could plainly see on the video, my dear friends, after I made that phone call to myself on this stage just now—a phone call via the tachyonic anti-telephone—I was able to answer it myself . . . and I answered it in my cabin *yesterday morning*!"

***

It took the mind-boggled audience several minutes to figure out that the entire "scientific demonstration" had been nothing more than an elaborate ruse . . . a fact that Dr. Sverdlow happily admitted, right after the 15-minute coffee break.

"Please forgive me," he said with a gleam of mischief in his eye, "but I could think of no better way to show you how the tachyons are capable—by outrunning the speed of light—of transporting information from the present to the past.

"Yes, I *staged* that video—but wasn't it *fun*?"

He paused for a moment, then raised a cautionary hand. "Of course, I readily concede that the actual physical existence of tachyons is still being debated by physicists all across the globe. Until quite recently, in fact, most particle physicists have regarded these tiny fragments of the atom as mere *theoretical* particles—and there continues to be considerable doubt as to whether or not they actually materialize and then almost instantly vanish somewhere in the depths of the quantum field.

"But that question, I would suggest to you, remains secondary to our concern here today. Because what we are attempting to do here at Big Pine this morning is to simply describe a theoretical model that could serve as a viable explanation for the psychic phenomenon known as *precognition*."

With that explanation, the Swiss genius was off and running. During the next 45 minutes he regaled his audience with one dramatic disclosure after another, as he did his best to show them how faster-than-light particles might help a so-called gifted "psychic" to "read the future."

Totally captivated, his three hundred listeners were treated to an astonishing laundry list of "precognition breakthroughs" that Dr. Sverdlow claimed to have achieved since being featured on the cover of *People*. Among the highlights, along with his prediction regarding the Ayatollah's kidnapping of the 52 U.S. Embassy employees in 1979 in Tehran, were several shockers that left his audience buzzing with surprise.

Item: As early as 1983, the hawk-eyed prognosticator had been warning that the U.S. Space Shuttle program would be struck by a "major disaster" involving "a tragic loss of life." That disaster, he had predicted, would dominate the news for months to come.

Outcome: The tragic explosion aboard the U.S. Challenger, the worst disaster in the history of the U.S. space program, had taken place three years later, on the 26th of January, 1986, and only a few months before this Big Pine gathering . . . with seven crew members killed instantly over the Atlantic Ocean just off the coast of Florida.

Item: During the summer of 1982, Sverdlow had raised eyebrows among dozens of political scientists around the world by predicting that the iron-fisted dictator Ferdinand Marcos would soon be ousted from power and forced to leave the Philippines.

Outcome: Toppled from power after a series of stunning political missteps, the once-invulnerable Marcos had fled Manila in disgrace on the following February 26th—only four months prior to the Big Pine Conference.

Item: During much of the late 1970s, Dr. Sverdlow had been warning that "a Soviet power plant was in jeopardy of exploding, with horrific consequences for tens of thousands of people in Eastern Europe."

Outcome: The April 26, 1986, disaster at Chernobyl Reactor Four in the Ukraine was still making front-page headlines everywhere—two months after triggering worldwide panic over the nuclear energy industry's potential for causing horrific destruction.

After astonishing his eager audience with these dazzling examples of his ability to "read the future," the world-famous paranormal researcher wrapped up his lecture by pointing out that "at this stage, to be quite honest, we don't really know for sure if faster-than-light particles—such as our friend the tachyon—hold the secret that can explain the thousands of precognitive experiences which have been reported in recent years.

"But one thing does seem certain, as we continue our scientific inquiry. Precognition is *real*, my friends. It's happening daily all around us. And as thinking people with a boundless curiosity about the physical processes that shape our world, we owe it to ourselves to find out *how* it happens . . . and *why*.

"Thank you, my very good friends!"

Then, bowing deeply from the waist, he rose back up to his full height and sent his vigorously applauding audience a grinning thumbs-up.

The Cheshire Cat had triumphed once again!

Alix was more than impressed.

"I'm totally blown away, Roz!"

"Me, too," said her astonished colleague. "And I'm also just a tiny bit suspicious."

Alix stared at her. "Suspicious of what?"

"His cheap tricks," said Rozzie.

Eyes narrowed, she was watching Gunther Sverdlow take a series of additional bows.

"I can't tell if we were watching a scientific researcher give a lecture just now . . . or a nightclub performance by The Great Santini!

"Apparently, he thinks that because this conference is devoted to the paranormal, he can rely on a bunch of showbiz stunts to make his points—rather than basing them on solid science. It's outrageous!"

Now Rozzie turned to her smiling friend.

"You gotta keep an eye out, Alix. Be careful, will you?"

Chapter 20
A Fatal Misstep

"Wait until you taste this *Barolo*!"

The two of them were seated on lawn chairs near the boat dock at Big Pine. It was nearly midnight. They'd already enjoyed a mouth-watering lobster dinner with plenty of chilled white wine. Now they were relaxing beneath a nearly full moon on the waterfront.

In the distance a loon cried out once . . . twice . . . and then went silent.

"I am very serious about this, Alix! In Switzerland, everyone knows the Italians are the *real* winemakers. The French are too refined. They are obsessed with bouquet and with grace notes. And the Germans? Don't even think of it. Except for a few sparklings and a few light whites, the Germans know nothing about wine.

"Most of them live for beer, and nothing else!"

Gunther Sverdlow held up a bottle of one of Italy's most famous red *vinos*. "These *Barolos* aren't just the best full-bodied wines made in Italy. They may very well be the best in the entire world. This wine is from the Piedmont region, of course—the hilly country in the north of Italy—and the grapes they use, the *Nebbiolos*, are absolutely exquisite."

Alix watched him apply the corkscrew for a few seconds, as he prepared to pour the expensive wine.

"This was very thoughtful of you, Gunther. You're really a piece of work, you know that?"

"Truly? How so?"

"A world-class expert on the paranormal . . . who *also* turns out to be an expert on Italian wines? Pretty impressive, I must say."

He shrugged—and she heard the gentle *thwack* that told her the cork was out of the bottle.

"We must live, no?" He smiled gently, thoughtfully at her. "What is the point of knowledge—what is the point of *science*—if not to increase the joy of living?"

He was pouring the wine now. Somehow, he'd just retrieved two glittering wine glasses from the front pockets of his smoking jacket. She looked on, amazed.

"These are Riedel Vinum glasses," he told her with a knowing smile. "As you can see, they're unusually curved—a special step that allows for better aeration of the vintage."

He handed her a half-full glass of Barolo and lifted his own with a savvy flourish. "I drink to you, Alix. I drink to your great skill as a scientist, and I drink to your great beauty as a woman."

She smiled and sipped . . . and the wine went flashing over her taste buds like a school of excited fireflies.

"This is terrific, Gunther. I taste cherries . . . and also a hint of flowers. Am I getting it right?"

He nodded. "Absolutely," he murmured. "Cherries . . . flowers . . . and just a touch of licorice. What did I tell you? These northern Italians are the true masters of the vineyard, my dear.

"When it comes to extracting joy from the grape, they simply cannot be matched."

They fell silent after that. Alix was watching a long shimmering streak of moonlight undulate on the breeze-riffled surface of Moosehead Lake. She'd been expecting many good things at Big Pine—thrilling lectures, stimulating conversation, new scientific insights—but romance had not been among them.

And yet here she sat, listening to the loons and sipping *Barolo* with a man whose reputation as a paranormal researcher had helped to change the world of brain science.

"So," he said after a bit, still smiling warmly in her direction. "You must tell me: who is Dr. Alix Cassidy and what does she think she wants most out of her life?"

Alix thought for a moment. "Well . . . I'm not very good at talking about myself, Gunther. But I suppose I would say, if pushed . . . that I'm a very hardworking scientist who wants very much to prove that her findings regarding Somnambulistic Telepathy are accurate."

She paused and stared off over the moon-streaked water.

"Most of all, though, I think I'd like to know that the research I do is helping people live healthier, more creative lives. And I also want to better understand dreams—both my own and the dreams of others."

Nodding thoughtfully, he was already pouring more wine into her glass—without having been asked to do so.

"That is precisely what I *expected* to hear you say, Alix." He sent up a cheerful laugh. "You know, it's really true what they say about you Americans, all of you."

She peered at him. "What do they say, Gunther?"

"They say you're all incredibly idealistic . . . and you work too damn hard—and you're too naïve about the world for your own good!"

Alix laughed. And drank. "Why, that's just plain ridiculous! I know plenty of American researchers . . . all they care about is seeing their name in the headlines and nailing down that next half-million-dollar research grant from the NIH!"

Then she hesitated.

Suddenly she was tempted to continue: *I'll give you an example. I knew a psychiatrist once, a guy named Rogers. He was a leader in his field. And you know what he did? He stole my private notes on a patient, and he betrayed a patient of his own . . . and because of it, a very sad and tragic young Vietnam War veteran from Boston lost his life.*

How's that for idealistic and naïve, Gunther?

Yes, she was tempted . . . but in the end Alix decided she wouldn't tell this man about Dr. Michael Rogers. Call it an instinct, call it an inner voice that warned: *Don't go there with this particular gentleman, Alix. You won't like the results.*

Instead, she laughed brightly—too brightly—and drank some more of the excellent *Barolo*. "Well, I think that's probably enough about me," she said after a bit. "Let's hear the latest update on the wide, wide wonderful world of Dr. Gunther Sverdlow, whaddya say?"

He gazed calmly back at her. "What would you like to know?"

"Your goals, I guess. Your scientific goals? That was an amazing lecture you gave this morning, Gunther. When you called yourself on the telephone—called yourself *yesterday*!—I felt like I was watching P.T. Barnum at work!"

He grinned. "The famous American circus man?"

"The very same!"

He laughed, and his eyes flashed with something she couldn't quite decipher. Did he really like being compared to the showboating circus entrepreneur?

"I think that a little bit of circus is good in science," he said, looking directly into her eyes. "Sometimes you need a little spectacle in order to make your point. In that moment, of course, I was simply trying to show the audience how it would be, if you really *could* use the tachyons to travel back in time."

He was pouring again. Pouring and frowning. "I am hardly the first scientist to make this point about the tachyons," he said in a low murmur. "Einstein himself often joked about building an 'anti-telephone.' And of course, we all know how playful, how fun-loving Einstein could be. He said something once that, as a scientist, I have never forgotten.

"He said: 'Never forget that imagination is more powerful than knowledge.'"

Alix shook her head again. She was still sipping. "Gunther Sverdlow, you are quite remarkably wonderful."

"Thank you. In what way am I wonderful exactly?"

Huh? She was a little surprised at that. She'd expected him to brush off the compliment, rather than asking her to *elaborate* on it. All at once, she found his self-centeredness quite comical. Was the wine getting to her?

"Well, I mean . . ." she was struggling now, fighting a sudden impulse to blare at him: "Remind me—what *are* the tachyons again?" and now she giggled out loud (that damn *Barolo!):* "I mean, you seem to know a lot about everything! You really do, Gunther! ESP, time travel, Italian wines, Einstein's most quotable quotes," and she actually hiccoughed with laughter, *Jesus, I sound totally drunk,* "and it's all just a little bit *overwhelming* when you first encounter it, know what I mean?"

Sverdlow smiled. He seemed cool, and even a little haughty . . . and once again she caught that brief flash of something she couldn't quite fathom, something cold and dark in his face, in spite of his gleaming smile.

And then for an instant she was remembering Rozzie's warning about him: *Something tells me this guy is bad news.*

It was only a brief moment of doubt, however. Mostly she felt wonderfully relaxed and powerfully intrigued with this hugely accomplished man of the world.

Soon he was purring softly at her, "Alix, you are a very beautiful woman. Do you know that?"

She stared back at him, a bit uneasy. "Well, thank you, but I . . ."

"I've been asking myself for days," he sighed: "Is it her fiery red hair that makes me feel such passion? Every time I look at your hair, I remember that old Swiss saying: 'Smoke on top, flame down below!'"

He sent her his most dazzling smile. "Shall we go back up to my cabin?"

She didn't answer him with words.

She simply took his hand. Together they rose from the lawn chairs.

She took a last look at the perfection of the moon-dazzled lake . . . and felt the midnight breeze go rippling through her soft red hair.

***

Things did not go well, however.

There was something unsettling in his kiss—something metallic and baffling that she couldn't figure out—and as soon as she felt it, her heart sank. But she did her best to brave it out. She told herself that if she could just get caught up in the rhythm of it, just swing along with *his* rhythm, she might be able to join him in his pleasure. She might be able to help him make their two separate voices sing together in a single unified harmony.

It didn't happen.

He was too rough with her, for one thing. He seemed to think that throwing her around on his narrow camp bed would excite her . . . that she'd respond to being dominated, but the idea of having "rough sex" with him didn't interest her.

What she wanted most was to simply melt *into* him . . . to use their carnal connection as a kind of communication channel over which she could tell him (in a language older than mere words) of all the hurt and fear and loneliness that had blighted her world ever since the long-ago days of the treacherous Dr. Mike.

But Gunther Sverdlow wasn't really *listening* to this woman he'd bedded at the cabin beside Moosehead Lake.

Instead he seemed intent on trying to gouge some excitement out of pushing her around in bed. Again and again, he tried to mount her from behind, "doggy style," in the parlance of the sex manuals. When she seemed reluctant and unresponsive, he simply tried all the harder to break down her will and establish her subjugation.

Finally, unbelievably, he took a swing from way out in leftfield and gave her a powerful, stinging slap on the ass!

She was infuriated, and she was lost.

Suddenly the wine she'd drunk tasted like acid in her throat and the distant keening of the loons sounded to her stricken ears like a hopeless summons to some bleak underworld.

What an asshole, she told herself with an angry sigh. *I need to leave. This just isn't working out!*

But it was too late by then.

They'd taken too many wrong turns in their lovemaking. Her behind was still smarting from the slap, and there was no way back to the spontaneous joy she'd felt while sitting beside the lake. Yet the relentlessly intent Sverdlow plunged doggedly ahead, refusing to give up.

After jamming a condom onto his half-erect penis (*that* flaccid organ hardly seemed large or imposing to her now, given his great stature in the world of "scientific affairs"!), he'd finally managed to insert himself into her and was now rocking energetically back and forth, grunting heavily and repeating again and again in a loud voice: "Yes, yes, yes, *mais oui*!"

Alix could hardly believe her ears. "*Mais oui*"?

Then for a terrible instant she was afraid that she might burst into sudden laughter, might erupt in waves of rollicking, uncontrollable merriment that would leave him hating her forever.

It was grim. It was dreadful.

She hung on as best she could, praying that he'd get off soon, so she could make her escape. But then came the worst moment of all . . . the moment that completely destroyed whatever remained of Alix's fast-vanishing interest in this shallow-minded lightweight from Geneva.

It happened right before he came, when the bellowing Swiss superstar—"*Mais oui*!"—thrust a long forefinger into her anus and shoved it deep inside her.

"Ow! Hey . . . what the hell do you think you're doing?" she yelped.

"That *hurts!*"

A moment later she was pulling away from his wine-sodden embrace. With a loud *pock!* (not very different, she thought, from the sound the cork had made leaving the *Barolo* bottle), his rapidly deflating member parted company with hers.

Then she was somehow on her feet and shimmying back into her sundress and heading for the door.

"Thank you, Dr. Sverdlow!" she shouted absurdly from the cabin's entrance, as if using the honorific would somehow make up for what she knew would be regarded as a mortal insult.

"I enjoyed the dinner and the wine –" But she couldn't finish the sentence. She couldn't pretend anymore! How many times, in situations like this, had she simply run away from a potential confrontation? How many times had she given in to panic and simply fled the scene . . . only to regret it terribly, forever after?

No, she told herself. *Not this time!*

In a flash, she whirled back to confront him.

"No, the truth is that I *didn't* enjoy the damn dinner—and you're an enormous bore," she snapped directly into his stunned face.

"You're so full of yourself that you can't see what's right in front of your eyes. All that crap about Einstein and relativity and the tachyons—you may be able to fool a few undergraduates with it, but you aren't fooling me, you pompous ass."

His mouth fell open, but nothing came out. He was too amazed to respond.

"As for your lovemaking—it sucks! I don't know where you got the idea that slapping a woman and sticking your grubby finger in her ass is a turn-on . . . but I can assure you the *opposite* is true. Good evening, Dr. Sverdlow!"

She ran.

Sverdlow tried to follow her. Somehow, he'd retrieved her pale blue panties from the bed, and now he held them out. "Wait, wait, Alix, you will need *these*, won't you?"

But then the swinging screen door caught him head-on, and he stumbled sideways and nearly fell.

Ignoring his reminder about the panties—he could use them to jerk himself off with for all she cared!—Alix staggered along an overgrown path. It took her more than a minute, but she eventually managed to find her own cabin and yank open the door.

Ten seconds later, she was spread-eagled on her cabin bed, face down, weeping hysterically into her pillow.

If only she'd listened to Rozzie's warning about that fatuous asshole!

Swamped beneath a wave of bitter anguish, she was remembering how the same kind of incident had destroyed a night of lovemaking with Michael Rogers twelve years before.

"Michael," she cried out in the silence of her lonely waterfront cabin. "How could you do that to me?

"How could you *do* that to me?"

CHAPTER 21
Into the Underworld

The two of them were sitting on the tiny pine-plank deck that fronted Rozzie's waterfront cabin.

It was twilight, the best time of day at Big Pine, with the late afternoon sun hanging like a ball of molten copper above the wind-rippled surface of Moosehead Lake.

"Rozzie, I'll be honest with you," said Alix. "I feel like absolute dog shit today. Please pardon my French."

Rozzie looked across the deck at the gloomy face of her newfound pal. "Dog shit? That isn't French," she said with a chuckle.

"It's pure American-ese . . . and if it helps you describe the way you're feeling right now, you go right *ahead* with it!"

Alix gave her a warm smile. "I'm a total idiot. I thought Gunther and I might be able to light a fire last night," she said quietly. "But now it's the day after and all I'm looking at is a great big pile of ashes."

"Uh-oh," said the loyal Rozzie. "That doesn't sound so good, dear. Didn't I warn you about that gentleman?"

"You did, but I didn't listen. Why can't I learn anything, Roz? I'm dumb as a slab of cement."

"No, you're not!" All at once, Alix's porch buddy was laughing out loud. "Come on, honey. It's not *that* bad. Don't forget, you know a hell of a lot about sleep science. As a researcher, you're wearing the pants at this conference!"

Alix sighed. "That's nice. Thank you, Roz. But we both know my personal life is a howling disaster. And we both know why. *You* saw through Gunther in about five seconds. That's how long it took you to peg him as a narcissistic asshole."

Alix groaned out loud. "You nailed him cold, while I took the bait like a half-starved trout! Tell me: why do I always go for the heartless shitheads?"

Rozzie didn't speak for a while. She was looking out over the lake and watching a million diamond-points of light wink along the wave tops. A bird cried out once— a cry of mourning, or a cry of delight? Who knew? "I can't answer that, Alix. What can I tell you?

"The world is a beautiful place at times—and the world is also a hellish nightmare at times."

She turned to face her unhappy friend. "Maybe your heart's too big for its own good, honey. Maybe you respond to things out of feeling . . . while your mind trails behind. You were hungry for something with that Sverdlow idiot.

"What was it? Do you know?"

Alix reflected.

"You want the truth?"

"Absolutely."

"I think I wanted to have a strong man—a man of many accomplishments—tell me he wanted me more than anything else. But instead of getting what I wanted, I discovered that the 'strong man' didn't even know I was stretched out beside him.

"He didn't know I was *there*, Rozzie, and that hurt like hell."

The two women sat together quietly after that. The night's first loon had begun sending up its melancholy cries, and a slice of pale vanilla-colored moon had risen above the bluff that flanked the lake.

"Rozzie, I hope you don't mind . . . but I think that in some ways, you've become like a mother to me."

"I don't mind," said Rozzie. She was smiling again. "But what *about* your mother, Alix? You've never once mentioned her, do you know that? What was her name, anyway?"

Alix was rocking slowly back and forth on her chair. "Maeve McNeil Cassidy," she said in a low, unsteady voice. "She was a tough old Irish broad, worked in a textile factory in small-town Indiana and then later in Milwaukee, where I mostly grew up. Ran a sewing machine 40 hours a week and prayed for all the overtime she could get.

"She'd managed to finish high school before that . . . but there was no money, and the idea of going to college simply lay outside her experience.

"She was tough . . . but she was kind."

Rozzie nodded. "Knowing you, I'm not surprised."

"We lost her early. My sister Mary and I were both teenagers when the first heart attack struck. She was gone before I turned twenty-one. By then I was already off at Wellesley, studying biology on a full scholarship.

"Mary and I both managed to escape from her world, Roz. We never worked a single factory shift growing up."

Roz was patting her friend's shoulder. "Bless the lady," she said. "I'm sure that's what she wanted for you two girls."

Alix had begun dabbing at her eyes. "I'm feeling a little blue, Roz."

"I know, honey. It's okay. You can forget that Swiss nerd, if you really want to. You can find a man who'll *see* you. A man who'll love you as you are."

"I can," said Alix. "I will."

Rozzie was hugging her now—hugging her unashamedly and rocking her back and forth on the pine-plank deck.

"You're home, girl. You're *home*, and everything is gonna be okay."

The loon cried out again—a long, slow note that echoed for a moment and then sank away into the encroaching darkness.

***

Sunday afternoon. Another scorcher.

Dr. Mike was listening to the weatherman on WBZ 1030, one of Boston's most popular radio stations.

"Brace yourself, folks. Today's high could break the record set back on July 13, 1954, when the thermometer hit 104 degrees. And with one hundred percent humidity also expected, you're gonna be real glad you're sitting near that air conditioner!"

Clicking off the broadcast, Dr. Mike scowled angrily. *I hate this fucking heat.*

He bent over and caught a whiff of his smelly armpits. *Whew! Only one way to fix that.*

For at least the third time that day, he reached for the English Leather cologne and doused his upper torso, so nobody would notice his stink.

Yeah, his cock needed some sucking. Needed it bad. But that action would have to wait until the Dreamtime, when his highway into other people's nightmares opened up for business.

Who'd be his lucky victim tonight?

All in good time. Right now all he wanted was to cool off.

Twenty-five minutes later, walking down Washington Street through the heart of the Combat Zone, the angry shrink was approached by a strung-out hooker with an ugly face and a huge ass.

"Hey, fella. Want some booty?"

"Go fuck yourself," Dr. Mike growled back at her.

"Oooh, Mr. Tuffy. We got ourselves a Mr. Tuffy here," Big Ass barked.

"Fuck this, you ugly piece of shit," he yelled as he shot her the finger-fuck sign.

He swung left onto Kneeland Street. Looking up, he spotted a giant knife painted in blazing neon on the billboard of the Orpheum Theatre. It was a knife the size of a tire iron, and it glittered fiercely in the clenched fist of *Crocodile Dundee.*

This was the hit movie of the year, and everybody was talking about it.

Why not, Dr. Mike asked himself.

For the price of a movie ticket, he could escape the oppressive heat—while cheering on the hotshot Australian shit-kicker with the jumbo-sized blade.

Soon he was pushing his way through the ornate double doors and striding up the right side of the carpeted aisle towards the ticket counter.

And there she was: the girl of his dreams!

The ticket seller's name badge identified her as "Elisa." She was a dead ringer for Alix Cassidy. Amazed, he stared at her swirly-red hair, at her penetrating green eyes, at the luscious lips that had been *his* to suck on once. Back before the disaster. Back before she'd destroyed his life and ruined his reputation. Back before she'd poisoned his world forever.

"One for the Crocodile, sweetheart." He gave her a great big naughty wink and then slid a twenty dollar bill across the counter.

She gazed calmly back at him. No expression.

"When's your shift end, good looking?"

The big green eyes widened slightly as she mulled her response.

Then her gaze went cold, unfriendly. "That'll be four dollars, sir."

Poker-faced, she handed him back his change.

Dr. Mike was staring right into her eyes, making her very uncomfortable.

"You know how they came to name this theatre, sweetheart?"

She was avoiding his stare. But Dr. Mike didn't wait for her to answer. "The Orpheum? Well, there was once a Greek god named Orpheus who fell in love with a luscious redhead just like you."

Dr. Mike was having fun.

"Excuse me, sir, but we have other customers waiting to purchase tickets."

The pest just kept on talking.

"That Orpheus, he was quite the guy—oops, meant to say, quite the god. I bet you don't even know anything about Orpheus, do you? His story is very sad. He loved this woman so much that he traveled deep into the Underworld, the land of the dead, to bring her back. He wanted her that much!"

"Excuse me, sir. . . ." Elisa tried again to interrupt him.

Dr. Mike ignored her and continued his rant.

"Orpheus was an ancient Greek musician. But what he's really famous for was his attempt to retrieve his wife, Eurydice, from the Underworld. That poor babe stepped into a nest of vipers and suffered a fatal bite on her heel. And it was on her wedding day!

"Talk about fucking bad luck."

She was looking away from him now, with fear in her eyes.

"See this?" Michael stuck his burned and tattooed hand in her face.

She responded for a moment; she couldn't help herself.

"Oh, what happened to your hand?"

"I'll tell you all about it. But first . . . why don't you and me go on a journey, sweetheart? A journey to the Underworld? The land of nightmares, the land of pain and agony!

"Just you and me, whaddya say, sweet lips?"

Before she could answer, they were interrupted.

"Hey, pal, you gotta *move*. Now! We got a lot of customers here."

At the far end of the counter stood Tommy Ellington, the movie theater shift manager . . . a lonely guy who lusted after Elisa himself. Growling.

"We've heard enough of your bullshit, mister. Either go inside or we'll have to ask you to leave."

Tommy was pissed. Why should he have to listen to this asshole talking all sweet to *his* Elisa? Why let him get away with this ridiculous Orpheus bullshit?

But the man harassing Elisa *still* refused to move. Instead he began chanting:

"Hear me, O Death, whose empire unconfined,
Extends to mortal tribes of ev'ry kind.
Thy sleep perpetual bursts the vivid folds. . . ."

Tommy blinked. And glared. "If you don't move along, I'll have to call security."

A moment later he turned and yelled. "Frank, I need your help over here."

The Pinkerton Robo-Cop started moving toward them. At six-three and built like an armored truck, Frank wouldn't have any problems handling Dr. Mike.

Now the truck swaggered up to the counter, ready to confront the intruder.

"Is this man causing you a problem, Tommy?"

"Yeah, he sure is. He's being a pain in the ass."

To the sneering Dr. Mike: "Well, in that case, we gonna have to ask you to leave the theatre, know what I mean?"

"Fuck you, Robo-Cop."

Frank grabbed the man's arm. Twisted it violently. Hauled him towards the exit.

"Hey, whaddya think you're doing? I got rights, man! I didn't do anything wrong. That bitch was coming on to me."

"Yeah, right. She was coming on to *you*? Do you really expect me to believe that?"

Struggling, Dr. Mike wailed at her: "Sweetheart, will you tell this Robo-Cop—"

Too late.

Dr. Mike was not destined to see *Crocodile Dundee* today.

With a final shout at Elisa, he roared his goodbye. "I'll see you in your *dreams*, baby. I'm coming after you tonight, you cunt. You'll pay for this, wait and see. . . ."

But then he was airborne and landing in the street.
Lying helpless on his ass.

Just another bum muttering curses on a Combat Zone sidewalk.

CHAPTER 22
Strangers in the Night

Midnight. Relaxing at the butcher-block table in her kitchenette, Elisa Mayhew poured herself a double shot of Bacardi over six cubes of ice, then added four inches of RC Cola. With a groan of satisfaction, she settled back in her plush cushioned chair.

For Elisa, midnight was the best time. While her stereo played Sinatra ballads in the next room, she could kick off her sneakers and drift into a romantic reverie full of handsome strangers who were madly in love with her. After a couple of rum-and-colas, these glamorous daydreams seemed much more real than her dull little life as the afternoon cashier at the Orpheum.

Barely thirty, she'd already been divorced from two worthless husbands, Max and Ike, both long-haul truckers. Those two fly-by-night operators had given the state of matrimony a terrible name. Yes, they'd put her through absolute hell . . . and Elisa meant it each time she told herself (usually after ingesting half the Bacardi bottle): "I really hope both of those bastards are stone-cold dead!"

Tonight was no different. The clock above the stove said *12:24*, and as usual, Elisa was already fully inebriated and feeling no pain.

Crooning along with Ol' Blue Eyes, she floated happily above the sweet melodies that filtered through one of his greatest hits:

Strangers in the night,
Exchanging glances;
Wondering in the night,
What were the chances
We'd be sharing love
Before the night was through?

Elisa sighed with longing. By now her eyes were brimming with tears. *Oh, my, my, Frankie, Frankie,* she told herself, *how I wish that door would swing open right now . . . and there you'd be, with that sexy fedora of yours pulled way down low over your eyes. . . .*

But then she caught herself.

She was being ridiculous! Frank Sinatra making love to *her*? Ol' Blue Eyes was a world-renowned entertainer, a giant of the music industry . . . and what was Elisa Mayhew?

The afternoon cashier at the Orpheum, that's what.

A nobody. Well, she still had her looks, at least. Yes, she still owned her piercing green eyes and the striking red hair that curved and rippled along her neck like a swatch of delicate, windblown silk. And her breasts . . . yeah, they were still firm, still supple, and her rosebud-nipples could still go taut and perky when she wanted them to. . . .

But all of that would begin to change soon, and she knew it. Elisa was in her thirties now. She could read the score. The truth was that she'd wasted her best chances at happiness and a comfortable life on those two lowlife truckers . . . and why, why, why?

She'd been so stupid! So thoughtless. And now it was probably too late. Sighing, she shook her head. She poured. The black hands of the clock above the stove read: *12:51*. She settled back in her chair and lifted the Bacardi to her lips.

Then she started writing out the latest entry in her pocket diary—while doing her best to describe the man who'd threatened her at the theater that afternoon, the insane wacko who claimed to be able to visit the "underworld of dreams."

After that, she put her pocket diary away and settled back. She drank deeply and then relaxed, her head sinking back into the soft cushions. . . .

> *Something in your eyes*
> *Was so inviting;*
> *Something in your smile*
> *Was so exciting. . . .*

***

Brrrrinnggg! The phone on the kitchen wall suddenly begins to jangle.

Groaning, Elisa stands up. Moving slowly, and thoroughly irritated by the incessant ringing, she eases her way across the beige linoleum squares of the tiny kitchen and reaches for the damn thing.

"Hello?"

Nothing at first. Just the sound of someone breathing heavily on the other end.

"Hello?" she says again.

Another few seconds of silence . . .

Then: "Guess who this is?"

Elisa takes a sharp, sudden breath, almost a gasp. "Pardon me?"

"You heard me. I'm wondering if you know who I am."

The voice is low, flat, without inflection. Elisa wants to hang up, but something keeps her on the line. Something keeps the green plastic phone against her ear.

"This is Orpheus," says the voice on the other end. "I've just returned from a brief visit to the Underworld . . . thought I'd give you a ring!"

Elisa blinks wildly. "You . . ." she says after a bit. "*You!* The one who harassed me at the theater this afternoon!"

Laughter on the other end. Slow and deliberate, a rippling baritone. Her heart is pounding furiously. She can't seem to catch her breath.

Yet she can't hang up. Moving with agonizing slowness, she limps back to her chair.

The elastic cord dangles behind her as she topples back into her seat beside the butcher-block table.

"Look at the clock, Alix."

Startled, bewildered . . . she jerks her eyes toward the black hands of the clock above the stove. Nothing at first . . . and then . . . *what's that shadow? What's that shadow on the face of the clock?*

Her mouth twists sideways. It's a huge centipede, silver and black, oozing from a hole in the glass face of the clock!

A hundred legs wiggle obscenely in the light from the ceiling fixture. Now it's crawling down the clock-face. Wriggling.

Everywhere it goes, it's leaving behind an oozy trail, bright scarlet.

She opens her mouth to scream, but no sound emerges. Nothing. *I'm dreaming,* she tells herself.

I must have fallen sound asleep in my chair . . . and I've begun to dream.

The giant centipede, easily the size of a small snake, has already reached the wall beneath the clock.

That wall is painted eggshell blue . . . and now the creature's wriggling legs are smearing the blue wall scarlet.

"Hello, Alix," says the voice on the other end.

She jerks upright. She shouts into the phone. "You! It's you! I remember everything you said. Tommy heard it, too. He's gonna call the cops!"

More laughter on the other end. "Is he? Is he now? Tommy's home in bed, Alix. He's sound asleep, dear. And he's dreaming, too. Do you know what he's dreaming about?"

"No!"

"I'll tell you. He's sucking on your tits, Alix. He's sucking and he's moaning, 'So good. So good.'"

"Stop it!"

But she's hardly listening anymore. The centipede has reached the beige linoleum squares at the bottom of the wall. Already, it's inching across those squares toward her cushioned chair.

She must get up, must get *off* this chair before it arrives. But her limbs are so heavy, so weary . . . her limbs are paralyzed! With growing panic she realizes that she can't move—*she is powerless to move.*

Faintly, playing so distantly and so faintly in the background that she can barely hear it:

> *Strangers in the night,*
> *Exchanging glances . . .*

"Please," she breathes into the phone. "Please . . . why are you doing this to me?"

Another nasty chuckle. "Me? I'm not doing anything to you, Alix. You're the one having the nightmare, aren't you? Why don't you just go ahead and wake yourself up, sweetheart?"

She sobs once. "I can't. I *can't* wake up . . . and you *know* that!"

With a shock of horror she realizes: the centipede is climbing one of the legs of the chair! *Wake up,* she screams at herself. *You must wake up!*

"I knew a girl like you once," says the voice on the other end. "A lovely girl with the sweetest green eyes.

"But she did me wrong, Alix. She let me down in the worst possible way."

On the word "way," Elisa's eyes widen until they're huge.

The centipede is crawling along her left thigh! Her inner thigh . . . and with a stab of blind terror she realizes what its final destination will be.

Desperate now, she's shrieking into the phone: "I don't know you! I *never* knew you! You must let me go . . . please! You must let me go!"

The wriggling legs are inching along her panty line.

The creature's obscene head is already burrowing into the soft wet flesh.

"PLEASE!"

But the cold dead voice on the other end never changes its tone. "You let me down, dear. You turned me in. You blew the whistle on me . . . destroyed my world forever."

She's writhing in the chair now . . . twisting . . . turning . . . but she cannot stand up . . . cannot move. *He's inside her! He's inside her!*

She feels the first bite of the flashing scalpel slicing into her ribcage!

She screams once: "Nooooooo!"

She looks up to find . . . *him* looming above her, *him* with the surgeon's tool clasped tightly in his right hand.

"Why, Alix? Why did you betray me, sweetheart?"

Her mouth flies open: "I don't . . . I'm not—"

"Wrong answer, bitch!" And his arm whips out at her like a darting snake, and the scalpel bites at her ribcage again. She gasps. Her vision blurs. Her gut heaves, and she wets herself everywhere.

"Why did you turn me in, Alix?"

Gasping. Suffocating. "I'm . . . please, please, don't you see? My name is Elisa, I am NOT—"

His arm whips out and the scalpel bites into the great artery that feeds her body: the aorta. "WRONG ANSWER!"

She screams one more time . . . and the scream goes on and on. *Has she been screaming for hours—or does it only feel that way?* The wet red ooze is running and running along her sopping panties and running down her convulsing thighs . . . running into a thick scarlet puddle on the linoleum . . . then into a second puddle

. . . oozing and oozing along the linoleum squares toward the doorway that leads out into the hallway of Apartment 477 at the Granada Apartments.

"Goodbye, my sweet."

It's the last thing she hears.

Sinatra has stopped singing now. The night is silent. The black hands of the clock jerk forward. Stop. Jerk forward. *2:46.*

"Goodbye, my sweet."

Darkness after that.

Smiling contentedly, he stands for a moment above her in the dim kitchenette. With one hand he gives the

silver heart-shaped locket around her neck a quick jerk.
The thin gold chain parts easily.

Mine, he tells himself. *All mine!*
HAPPY, DAD?

CHAPTER 23
Readings from a Dead Woman's Diary

Eight a.m.

The janitor was mopping the fourth floor hallway at the Granada Apartments, a rundown building less than half a mile from the Boston Combat Zone.

His name: Ernesto Gutierrez.

Just pushing the mop back and forth across faded yellow tiles. Just whistling a tune he'd heard the night before on his portable Zenith . . . a golden oldie from way back in 1971, the year he'd arrived in Boston from Old San Juan. A smash hit by the pop group known as Tony Orlando & Dawn.

> *Oh my darlin',*
> *knock three times*
> *on the ceiling if you want me. . . .*

Ernie Gutierrez' pint-sized but muscular figure was outlined in the early morning sunlight that fell through the dusty windowpanes to his left. Quick-footed and cheerful most of the time, he wore a chocolate brown yellow-feathered hat.

One gold tooth up front glinted from time to time in the dazzle of sunshine flooding through the panes.

> *Oh my sweetness . . .*
> *twice on the pipe*
> *means you ain't gonna show.*

Two-thirds of the way down the hall, he stopped. Sniffed.

What was that powerful odor? Something strong and metallic . . . like rusted iron. What? Another leak in the cranky old air conditioning system? The damn thing kept breaking down . . . sometimes it seemed like Ernie spent half his time working on it.

Was it malfunctioning again? Shit!

He'd forgotten about the mop and Tony Orlando & Dawn. He sniffed again. It was weird . . . but he could feel something tingling at the back of his neck. The hairs back there had gone stiff and electric.

He felt a flicker of anxiety go racing through his gut.

What the fuck? Truly weird! What was that smell? Rusted iron? A leak in the pipes?

Then he saw it.

Holy fuck!

Seeping from beneath the door to 477.

A spreading puddle, bright crimson . . . a puddle that oozed and shivered beneath the fluorescent lights in the ceiling.

Holy *fuck*!

Ernie threw the mop handle on the floor. His eyes were opened wide. He blinked once . . . twice . . . and then his eyes went to the rusty metal plaque beneath the imitation-brass knocker:

477
Elisa Mayhew

He turned.

He skidded across the wet tiles, moving so fast that the chocolate brown hat flew from his head and bounced along the sun-bright hallway.

Ernie didn't notice. He was running now, sprinting down the long hallway toward the EXIT door and the stairway that flanked it.

"Help!" he shouted again and again as his feet thudded down the rickety staircase.

"I need me some help, man . . . *pronto!*"

***

Jake and Tony arrived on the scene a few minutes before nine.

They'd heard the first 911 call from Dispatch, and they'd beaten everybody else to the scene. They stared through the open doorway of 477, amazed.

"Jesus," breathed Tony. "That floor's an inch deep in blood."

It was true. The two cops were eyeballing what looked like a small lake of hemoglobin.

At the center of the lake a woman appeared to be floating, drifting aimlessly. Her head was thrown back against her chair, and her half-clad body was stiff with rigor mortis.

Tony gaped. But Jake was already sliding a pair of plastic booties over the soles of his shoes.

"Get on the horn," he told his partner. "We're going to need everything the lab techs can give us. The works. Tell 'em to bring along the full cart—and you better tell 'em they're going to be here awhile."

"Got it," said Tony. He didn't move. He was frozen, and glassy-eyed. One look told you he'd gotten way out of his comfort zone.

"Take a breath," said Jake. "It's just blood, Tony. Nothing new about that, not for us. You've seen blood before, haven't you?"

"Not *this* much blood," said Tony. "Not a pond in the middle of somebody's kitchen." But then his face slowly relaxed. The spell had broken. Within a few seconds, he was on the radio to headquarters with his first report.

The daytime medical examiner, Dr. Pino, soon arrived. As always, his movements were brisk and businesslike. He carried a black medical bag and his face was expressionless.

"A bad one," he said. He'd covered her face with a sheet of green plastic. "She's all cut up inside—just like that last one we had. When was that one, about two weeks ago?"

"That's right," said Jake. "At the Holton Arms."

"You made any progress on that one yet?"

"Nothing definitive," said Jake.

"She's been cut to ribbons all over her body, it looks like," said Dr. Pino. "Same M.O., it would appear." He paused for a moment.

"The wounds look almost exactly like the ones I saw at the Holton."

"Interesting," said Jake.

"Same slash pattern. Looks like he sticks a sharp blade between the ribs, then yanks it around. I'd say she's been dead four or five hours."

"Over here," interrupted Tony. He was standing beside a full-length mirror that flanked a set of kitchen cabinets.

"You aren't gonna believe this, Jake."

Jake walked over. He eyeballed the cloudy white substance on the mirror. Then he looked at Tony.

"I got twenty bucks says that's semen," said Tony. "Just like last time."

"No, thanks," said Jake. "Why should I give you my hard-earned money?"

The medical examiner had his hand up. "I'll have to confirm this back in the morgue lab," he said, "but it looks to me like these cuts may have been made with a scalpel."

"Vicious bastard, whoever he is," said Tony.

He was on the radio again, this time calling for the morgue wagon.

Jake was frowning harder now. He walked slowly across the kitchenette floor, stepping gingerly around the crimson pools beneath his feet. "What's this?" he asked the other two.

He reached down to the chair that held the victim . . . and retrieved a small red spiral-bound notebook wedged behind the seat cushion. He held it up for the others to see.

Using his right hand, now in a plastic glove, he opened the notebook to the first page.

May 17, 1985

> *Dear Diary: Got another call from Ike this morning. Can you believe that asshole wants to get back together again? I told him, fool me once, shame on you. Fool me twice—shame on ME! That man was the sorriest excuse for a husband in the entire history of the human race!*

Jake smiled for a moment. Then he looked at the other two. They could hear footsteps outside in the hall by now—the morgue guys were approaching. "She must have been keeping a diary," said Jake.

He went back to the notebook. Still frowning, he flipped to the last page that had handwriting on it.

June 23, 1986

Dear Diary: Weird day at work. Guy tried to pick me up—some nut job with a snake tattooed on his hand. And get this: when I told him to buzz off, he started ranting about nightmares. Told me he'd sneak into MY nightmares, if I didn't do what he wanted! Well, this girl don't scare too easy, okay?

I finally had to call Tommy over. He read the asshole the riot act, then called the security guard. The two of them kicked the nut job out onto the street, which is where he belongs. And right away, he starts screaming at me, threatening me. Says he's going to meet up with me in my dreams! Guess you better be on the alert next time you fall asleep, right, girl? Or else, just stay awake all night?

What a creepy bastard. Looks to me like that guy's entire LIFE must be a nightmare!

"Tony?"

"Yeah?"

The junior detective was at the door now, letting the morgue guys in.

"You've got some reading to do."

Tony stared at him. "What, the diary?"

"That's right, pal. The diary. You may not believe this . . . but she was talking about nightmares in her final entry."

Tony's eyes widened. "You're shitting me."

"Not in the least, detective. She wrote that this guy tried to pick her up at work. The Orpheum Theater, you know, over by the Combat Zone? She shot him down. And he didn't like that."

"Pissed him off, did it?"

"That's right," said Jake. "He swore he'd come after her—in her nightmares."

Jake thought for a minute. "Orpheum Theater, huh?"

"Correct," said Tony. "Combat Zone."

Nodding slowly, the Professor went silent again.

Thinking.

Then: "Okay, I think it's time we put together a composite."

Tony nodded.

"We have four witnesses now. We've got the bar owner, that guy Jerry at Mulligan's. And also that customer who was drinking in there that day—Arthur Forbes. They both got a look at the man who threatened Tracy Donovan and talked about nightmares. And now we have Tommy at the Orpheum, and the security guard who helped give the 'nut job' the boot.

"According to this diary, they both saw the customer who was making threats about nightmares. Four eyewitnesses—so we're now talking about 'a person of interest'."

"I'm with you," said Tony.

"Next step: we bring all four of them down to Homicide and sit them down with the artist."

"Okay," said Tony. "I'm on it like a hornet."

CHAPTER 24

Tommy was "Smitten"!

They found Tommy Ellington two blocks south of the theater, at the Hungry Guy Hot Dog Stand on Washington Street. He was sitting on a metal stool, hunched over a chili-and-cheese-slathered dog about twice the size of an NFL football.

Jake held out his gold shield.

"Boston PD, Homicide. You Tommy Ellington?"

The diner's eyes narrowed. "Cops? I'm on my dinner break."

Jake smiled. "That's okay. You can eat while we talk. How's the dog?"

The little man on the stool swiveled his eyes from one detective to the next.

"Good. Real tasty. They make a good dog here. They're famous for it."

"So I hear," said Jake.

"Am I in any trouble?"

"Not yet," said Jake. "But we do have a few questions for you. You know Elisa Mayhew, the cashier at the Orpheum?"

"Sure. Sure. Of course, I know Elisa. I work with her." Beneath his flaring eyebrows, Tommy's eyes were agape. His mouth jerked a little to one side. "What's wrong, officers? Has something happened to Elisa? Jesus, I hope she hasn't . . . Goddamn, just don't tell me she's been hurt."

"I'm sorry," said Jake.

"What?" said Tommy. His mouth jerked again. "Is she okay? What the fuck happened? Is she hurt? *What*?"

"I'm sorry," said Jake. "She's dead. Stabbed to death."

Tommy didn't move for a while. Then his face began to crumple. Like a rubber mask under great pressure, his face slowly collapsed. His features ran together, and his grieving mouth swelled until it looked like a swollen gash that might bleed at any moment.

"Somebody stabbed her?" Tommy's cheeks had gone white as paste.

"But how? Why? Oh my God . . . *why*?"

"We'll get to that later," said Jake. "Right now, we're just wondering if you might remember an incident from yesterday afternoon."

Tommy was blinking fast. "What, an incident at the movie theater?"

"That's it," said Jake. "We've got some information that says Elisa had a visitor yesterday. A weird-acting customer—tried to pick her up. A guy with a snake-tattoo on one hand."

Tommy didn't respond for a bit. Then he lowered the Hungry Guy Dog back down to the paper plate. A car passed in the street, a big Oldsmobile 98. The passenger-side window was open, and for a few seconds Mick Jagger growled at them: *I can't get nooo . . . SATISFACTION!*

"I think I know the guy you mean," said Tommy. "He was there, all right. At the theater, I mean. A total weirdo—I had to call the Pinkerton guard on him."

Jake thought for a second. "Did you see the snake-tattoo?"

Tommy nodded. "Sure did. Ugly as sin. It was bleeding."

Tony leaned in. "The tattoo was bleeding?"

"Right," said Tommy. "Trust me, this guy was bizarre-o all the way down to his socks. I heard everything he said, and it was some of the creepiest stuff ever came out of anybody's mouth."

Jake smiled. "You heard everything he said?"

"Sure did."

"But why?" Now Jake wasn't smiling anymore. "Why were you listening in, Tommy?"

Tommy's mouth jerked again—this time to the opposite side.

"Okay . . . I'm sweet on her, okay? I'm sweet on Elisa. All right by you? Ain't no law against that, is there? I look after her, that's all. I keep an eye out."

He picked up the hot dog, but then forgot about it. "I know she don't care about me. Huh? I'm too old for her . . . shit, I know that. But a guy can hope a little, right? Maybe dream a little now and then, know what I mean?"

"I do," said Jake. "It's okay. You were smitten with her. Is that the story?"

"That's it." Tommy grinned back at him. "You're on it. I was smitten."

"No problem," said Tony. "Smitten, that's all."

"So what did he say?" asked Jake. "The weird guy? What'd he say to Elisa?"

Tommy deliberated. "Okay, he started in on this weird rap about some place he called the Underworld. It made no sense, but that's what he said. He claimed to be some kind of God. Orphey . . . Orphey-somebody.

"He said he knew how to travel through the Underworld, because he was the Orphey-guy. Said he knew how to sneak into a person's dreams. Then he threatened her. I heard it all. I heard it loud and clear. Every word. He said: 'I'll see you in your dreams, baby.

"'I'm coming after you tonight, you cunt!'"

Jake and Tony stared at him.

Jake said: "What happened next?"

Tommy leaned toward them. His face was flushed now, full of hatred.

"Pinkerton guard grabbed him, threw him out on the sidewalk. Lifted him right up and *threw* him outta the goddamn lobby."

Jake nodded. "You think you could describe him accurately? His features?"

"Goddamn right. I got a good memory, everybody says that. That's one thing about me. Everybody always says—"

"Okay, fine. Tommy, we need you to come downtown. It's important. You can help us create an artist's rendering."

The hot dog was back on the plate again. Tommy looked scared. "The police station? Geez, I don't know. What would I have to do down there?"

"It's not difficult," said Jake, "and it won't take long. We'll just ask you some questions, that's all. We'll want as much detail as you can give us about the guy's features. You know. Eyes, hair, nose, chin, any scars, that kind of thing."

Tommy blinked back at them. "No trouble for me?"

"No trouble," said Jake. "You'll be doing a public service, actually."

He looked closely at the theater manager for a moment. "You'll be doing it for *her*, too."

Tommy glanced up at them. His chin was trembling harder now. "For Elisa?"

His mouth sagged and his eyes filled with tears. "Okay," he said. "I'll come in. I'll do it for her." He gulped again. "Goddamn, I can't believe it. Is she really dead?"

He looked up at the two of them. He pushed the hot dog plate away, and they could tell he wasn't hungry anymore. "She's really gone?"

Jake patted him on one shoulder.

"I'm sorry, Tommy, I really am."

"Me, too," said Tony.

Tommy nodded. Reached for a paper napkin to wipe his eyes.

"She was beautiful," he said. "I think I was the only one who saw it.

"She was *beautiful*, goddamnit!"

CHAPTER 25
An Intriguing Phone Call

Thursday afternoon, four o'clock.

Seated at her big desk in the Big Pine Main Office, Roslyn Violette, Ph.D., was engaged in an urgent administrative task: massaging her swollen feet. Having led another strenuous nature hike up the side of Rattlesnake Mountain that morning, Rozzie was struggling through a very familiar and very painful process to which she often referred as "resurrecting the howling dogs."

I'm too damn old to be climbing that monster, she told herself with a groan, while her eyes scanned the list of BP lectures and labs for the upcoming week. *Maybe we oughta install a cable car so I could ride up in comfort.*

But then her ruminations were interrupted by the jangling of the office telephone.

Would her aggravation never end? Duty called, however. Sighing wearily, she waited for the fifth ring. Like most psychics, Rozzie was thoroughly superstitious, and never answered before the fifth jangle . . . having years ago become convinced that the number five, the precious link between Heaven and Earth in many systems of dream interpretation, was the supreme guarantor of happy tidings.

She grabbed it just as No. 5 began. "Hello, Big Pine. This is Rozzie Violette speaking."

"Ah . . . yes. Big Pine?"

"Yup, that's us," said Rozzie. "How can I help you, sir?"

By now she was struggling to get a mangled sock back onto her left foot.

"Thanks . . . this is Homicide Detective Jake Becker calling from the Boston Police Department."

The voice was deep and commanding.

Rozzie stopped fumbling with her sock.

"I'm trying to reach one of your people . . . a Dr. Alix Cassidy? She's an expert on human sleep and nightmares, apparently."

"That's correct," said Rozzie. "Dr. Cassidy."

She frowned.

A police detective? She felt a shiver of apprehension and a moment later she was blaring at him. "I hope Alix isn't in any trouble?"

"No, no trouble at all. I'm just hoping to speak with her for a minute, that's all. I looked at that profile of her in the *Globe Sunday Magazine* the other day, and I read how she'd helped the Philadelphia Police on a murder case a few years ago.

"She did a great job for them and we're wondering if she might be willing to advise us on some crimes that have been occurring down here in Boston."

Rozzie was nodding now. Her eyes were bright.

"Wasn't that a terrific story? The *Globe* reporter was up here for three days. I thought he did a great job."

"I agree," Jake replied. "That's why I'm trying to reach her now. These recent crimes in Boston that I mentioned . . . they've raised some questions about nightmares and I'm hoping to ask Dr. Cassidy a few questions."

Rozzie didn't hesitate. "You got it, Detective Decker, say no more. And please pardon me for giving you the third degree! We get a lot of crank calls up here at Big Pine, as you might imagine, given that our specialty is ESP."

"I understand. Can you put me through to Dr. Cassidy?"

"Absolutely."

Rozzie was out of her swivel chair by now and reaching for her other sock.

"I'll have her ring you right back!"

***

"Hello, this is Dr. Alix Cassidy. Am I speaking with a Detective Decker?"

There was a slight pause on the other end.

"That's me, but it's Becker—'B' as in Big Pine."

"Sorry, detective. Rozzie must've gotten it wrong."

"No problem."

"So what can I do for you?"

"Well . . . I wanted to ask you a couple of questions. I'm a homicide detective with the Boston Police Department, and we're dealing with something that we can't quite figure out."

Alix nodded on her end of the line. She was intrigued. She liked puzzles, and if they included some aspect of sleep science . . . why, so much the better!

"I saw in that *Globe* story the other day how you helped the homicide detectives on that case in Philadelphia a few years ago. You know, where the perp . . . where the killer claimed he wasn't responsible for strangling those two women to death because a voice in his nightmares made him do it?"

Alix was frowning and nodding. "Yes, of course. That was a very challenging investigation. I was glad I could help a little bit."

"Well, we've got a situation here in Boston where two women have been stabbed to death. It happened in the past two weeks, and some of the circumstances surrounding the killings appear to be identical. Both murders involved nightmares."

"Really? In what way?"

"Shortly before they died, both women claimed to have been threatened by the killer—who vowed to attack them while they slept, during nightmares in which he would actually show up in the flesh."

Alix took a sharp breath.

Attacked during nightmares?

It had been a dozen years since the ghastly tragedy involving David and Laura and Dr. Mike—and in all that time, Alix had never heard of another case of homicide via Somnambulistic Telepathy.

But she'd never stopped looking for one, either.

And if her theory about the reality of ST was accurate, Jake Becker might be able to help her prove it.

"I'm putting together what we call a 'personality profile' of the killer," the detective was hurrying on. His voice was low and urgent, and she could tell that he was under a lot of pressure. "After reading the *Globe* article, I thought maybe you could help us better understand our suspect's obsession with nightmares.

"Dr. Cassidy, have you been following the news about the two murders I just described?"

"Not really, detective. I just got here from Atlanta a couple of weeks ago. The conference is being held on Moosehead Lake—way out in the boonies—and I haven't looked at a newspaper or watched the evening news since I arrived. We're off the grid."

Jake pressed on. He needed this scientist on the case. "Uh-huh. Well, the *Globe* piece raised some interesting questions about this . . . this dream-travel stuff. So I wanted to ask . . . in your opinion, what kind of man would come to believe he could actually assault women while they sleep?

"I mean, he seems to think that by entering their nightmares, he can assault them in *reality*. And according to the article . . . well, didn't you work on a similar case back in 1974?"

Alix didn't respond for a moment.

"I believe you told the reporter that something like that had happened in seventy-four, am I correct? Something involving the idea of dream travel?"

Alix had begun holding her breath.

"Well," she said. Then she stammered, "I . . . okay, the thing is, there was this tragic situation in Boston. A young man, a deeply troubled Vietnam vet, came to believe that he could invade other people's dreams."

"Uh-huh," said Jake. "Yes, I think I do remember the case . . . but I didn't work on it personally. Unfortunately, we've had a whole lot of Vietnam War-related suicides and killings over the years, so it didn't really stand out."

He paused, waiting for more.

But Alix was having some difficulty speaking. Suddenly, she was back in the midst of that brutal summer. Once again she was listening to Laura's desperate screams. For a moment, in her mind's eye, she was watching Nixon board the helicopter, holding both hands out in the famous "V" sign and exiting the White House in disgrace. *Your President is not a crook!*

For an instant, she had difficulty believing that the shocking events of 1974 had actually occurred.

But at last she found her voice. "I'm not quite . . . I don't know exactly what you need from me, detective, but I'll do my best. The thing is, that Vietnam vet—he committed suicide. He couldn't endure the suffering he faced. I was there when it happened. He shot himself and died.

"A young Vietnam veteran who was struggling with what we later came to understand was actually PTSD.

"It was terrible. A young man who'd been drafted into the Army and sent to Vietnam to fight a faceless enemy . . . and yes, he did come to believe that he could invade other people's nightmares. Then he died at his own hand. What a tragedy.

"I do hope we've learned our lesson about invading other countries and trying to force democracy down their throats!"

Listening to Alix on his end, Jake was frowning hard. He needed to get *moving* on this thing, and fast. "Let's go back to nightmares for a minute. Do you think they can be symptoms of mental illness . . . maybe part of a distorted personality that might drive a serial killer to murder young women?"

Alix nodded. She could see what he was after now. "I do think so, Detective Becker. There's some very convincing research out there to show that recurring violent nightmares are often a symptom of the kind of psychopathic behavior you're talking about.

"If you could learn more about the nightmares the killer is supposedly experiencing, they might give you some valuable clues to his personality and his motivation for committing these crimes."

Jake deliberated for a few seconds. Then he made a snap decision.

"Dr. Cassidy, what you're telling me is very helpful. I think it might help to give us a window into the killer's personality, and I'd like to talk with you in more detail. Any chance I could interview you at Big Pine in a couple of days?"

Alix's eyebrows rose.

She hadn't counted on this. "Well, I'm not sure you know . . . do you have any idea how far we are from Boston? You might get a surprise. I can tell you—I flew all the way to Portland from Atlanta, and we *still* had to drive for three or four hours to reach Moosehead Lake."

Jake was nodding. Frowning. The clock was ticking and the city of Boston was becoming increasingly alarmed. Did he really have time for this?

"I hear you," he said at last. "I know it's a long drive."

Then it came to him. Out of the blue. What if he rang up Commander Wills at the Coast Guard? Ask him about borrowing the Guard's seaplane for an afternoon? What if he *flew* up to BP, instead of driving? Yes, it might work. And Wills owed him one . . . from two years before. The commander's screwed-up nephew had gotten his tit in the ringer in Boston, after getting caught with some stolen gym equipment from a health club in Brighton. A really dumb move—the kid was probably learning-disabled—but Jake had managed to intervene.

In the end, the young man had copped a plea and had gotten nothing more painful than a few months of community service.

Jake thanked her, promised to call back, and quickly hung up. Five minutes later, he had Commander Wills on the line.

CHAPTER 26
A Face in the Mirror

Big Pine prided itself on the quality of its cuisine. The Friday night menu included fresh-caught brook trout, fresh-picked corn on the cob and homemade Maine blueberry pie *a la mode*. It was a mind-bendingly delicious dinner, and nobody enjoyed it more than Alix Cassidy.

"My compliments to the chef," she told Rozzie after finishing her last succulent bite of dessert. "And my compliments to *you*, Roz. Are you sure you didn't major in hotel and restaurant management?"

The two of them laughed heartily. "Glad you liked it!" bubbled Roz. Then: "See you in about thirty minutes?"

Rozzie had invited Alix to her cabin after dinner so they could "chat" a bit. The sleep expert wanted to freshen up a tad before joining her pal.

After hurrying back to her cabin, she brushed her teeth, gargled, and even flossed. She added a bit of crimson lipstick and a couple of puffs of makeup to her cheeks. Energized and looking forward to the gab session, she strode over to the mirror and began to brush her hair.

As the brush swept back and forth, she was rehearsing a couple of urgent questions that she'd been preparing for the BP Director.

For one thing, she wanted to learn more about Melinda Birdsong, the Abenaki medicine woman who'd frightened her so badly with talk of a mysterious "curse." According to Roz, the woman was a gifted psychic whose insights into the hidden side of reality were full of provocative—and supremely *interesting*—clues to the workings of the paranormal.

With her hair carefully brushed, Alix felt like a new woman. Only one step remained now, not one she enjoyed. Eyes scrunched with distaste, she sprayed her neck and arms with the insect repellent Rozzie had given her.

"Uck!"

The greasy stuff smelled of chemicals—not exactly the kind of scent she wanted on her skin. But it was necessary: without it, walking outdoors near Moosehead Lake was a recipe for being eaten alive. If there was a single bloodthirsty mosquito in the neighborhood, it was certain to find Alix Cassidy, with her fair skin and red-haired complexion.

Done. How did she look? With a quick glance, she examined the woman in the mirror—and got a sudden shock.

What the hell?

Suddenly, fleetingly, she was looking at a man's leering face beside her own in the reflecting glass!

She whirled—cried out: "What?"

There was no one standing behind her.

She spun around full circle . . . and stared again at the mirror.

Nothing.

No face.

What the hell was going on?

Was her mind playing tricks on her?

For an instant, she had clearly seen a man's face, hideously distorted and grinning back at her!

Or had she?

Alix stood motionless before the mirror. My God, was she losing her wits? Had that been a hallucination?

All at once she was remembering what Dr. Jacobson had told her back in Atlanta: *Be careful up there, Alix. You'll be getting into some deep paranormal stuff. Watch your step.*

How weird could things get? First there had been the sudden drop in temperature and the dark, wing-like shadows during Rozzie's introductory tour of Big Pine.

Then that mysterious Indian medicine woman had shrieked at her. Unbelievable! And now here she was . . . struggling with the fact that some distorted image of a face had looked back at her from her own mirror!

Calm down. It was a trick of the light, that's all.

You're still a little shaky after what Gunther pulled on you.

Let it go. Let it go.

***

Ten minutes later, Rozzie was offering her a glass of wine.

"Just what the doctor ordered!" said Alix. "A bit of the grape will steady my nerves, and they *do* need steadying."

Rozzie laughed out loud. "Too much work-stress, lately? Don't worry, this stuff will blot out whatever ails ya!"

She held up a greenish bottle covered with wax seals and twists of elegant ribbon. "May I have the honor of pouring you a glass of 1973 *Pouilly-Fuisse Chardonnay*?"

"Wow, Rozzie! Sounds like a high-toned vintage, all right. Where'd you get it?"

Rozzie couldn't hide the huge grin on her face. "Gunther Sverdlow, who else?" she said proudly. "Don't worry, he won't miss it. After the way he treated you the other night, I think it's only fair that we give the douchebag some payback! You in?"

Rozzie was roaring now, totally cracked up by her own dirty deed. "That pompous piece of shit had three cases of his finest wine sent to Big Pine, two weeks before he even arrived."

Alix laughed—but by now she was staring a bit nervously at her friend.

"How many glasses have you had, Roz? No offense . . . but you sound like you're already half in the bag."

The older woman waved her away. "Nah, I'm fine. Perfectly fine! Hey, I had to taste it first to make sure it was worthy of our imbibement." She paused and frowned. "Say, is that a word? *Imbibement*? Come on. Let's go sit out on the porch so we can talk. It's all screened in, so you won't have to worry about being bitten."

Reassured—but not entirely—Alix followed her boisterous buddy across the living room to the sliding glass doors that led outside. "Roz, I don't mean to be ungrateful, but that insect repellant you gave me smells just awful."

Roz laughed again. Her round cheeks blazed with good humor . . . and with lots of high-powered *vino*. "It is what it is, sweetheart. Let it do its job. You'll be grateful, believe me. At Big Pine, we've got mosquitoes the size of Buicks!"

She raised her glass in a toast. "Here's to Gunther Sverdlow, may he rot in the nether regions!" She guzzled happily—and didn't notice the splotch of *Pouilly* that splattered against her wrist.

Alix returned the salute, then took a healthy swallow of the French libation. "Roz, you are truly a piece of work. Hear, hear!"

Rozzie howled, then sang in a booming *basso profundo*: "Gunther, may you never get laid again!"

They settled down gradually. From the vantage point of the porch, Alix had a clear view of the pristine waters of Moosehead Lake. Above them, the night sky blazed with millions of stars, each pouring out its rays from unimaginable light years away.

"So what did you want to chat about, Rozzie?"

Her friend didn't hesitate. "Well, I wanted to discuss that incident with Melinda, the Indian Medicine Woman. What do you think she saw that day? Why did she start yelling at you?"

"I don't really know. I have no idea what she might have seen," said Alix. "But that scream of hers, and all that stuff about the curse? I have to admit, it left me pretty rattled.

"Whaddya think? You know her a lot better than I do."

The BP director frowned thoughtfully. "Well, for starters, I can tell you that Melinda is one of the most gifted psychics I've ever met. She's also a totally free spirit. You haven't seen it yet—but that little lady rides around Big Pine on a thundering Harley Hog!"

Alix was staring at her. "A Harley *what*?"

"A Hog! It's a big old motorcycle, Alix . . . a 620-pound Softail with white-walled tires, a 1540-CC engine and enough glittering chrome to burn a hole in your retina. Melinda only weighs 95 pounds, dripping wet

. . . but trust me, she handles that chopper of hers like a pro!"

"Wow!" breathed Alix. "A motorcycle-riding Indian medicine woman? What will they think of next?"

"She's something else, all right," said Roz. "And she's also *feared* by a lot of people up here . . . because she's got what the Abenaki tribal people call 'Big Medicine.' Melinda is a highly regarded psychic . . . which is why her strange reaction to meeting you left me feeling a bit shaken.

"I think she must have felt something dark around you—some kind of dark spiritual energy, perhaps? I mean, that word she used: *Cursed*. What do you think she was getting at?"

Alix sipped her wine uneasily. "I honestly have no idea, Rozzie. And it's been bugging me all week. Maybe she was seeing into the future—reacting in advance to the idea that a homicide detective would be coming here soon? That Detective Becker? You spoke with him, right?"

"I did."

"I mean, he works on murders day in and day out. Talk about living in darkness all the time! Maybe Melinda was responding to that? Maybe she was connecting with the spirits of some of Detective Becker's murder victims?"

Rozzie mulled the idea for a bit. "Well, judging by her reaction, whatever the hell she saw was pretty powerful." Now she turned to face her friend. "I guess we'll have to stay tuned on that one, huh?" She took another drink of wine. "Got anything else on your mind, sweetheart?"

Alix deliberated. "Well . . . you know, just the usual stuff. I keep asking myself: should I change my life? If I don't, will I regret it? And if I *do* . . . will I regret *that*? What's the psychological term for this kind of uncertainty? Cognitive dissonance?"

She gave her friend a long pleading look. "Honestly, Roz, there are days when I'm just not sure what my next move should be."

Roz nodded. "Welcome to the club, dear."

"I mean, right now . . . well, I'm really not sure if I want to stay at the SDC. I keep asking myself: Is this really the work I want to do for the next few years? I'm just not sure. Quite frankly, the research you're doing up here seems a hell of a lot more interesting than my sleep studies in Atlanta. It's refreshing to be in a place where the sky's the limit . . . a place where you're encouraged to push the envelope, instead of constantly being told that you're 'going too far.'"

Alix paused for a moment to watch a loon settle onto the moonlit surface of the lake. "Of course, I really admire Dr. Jacobson . . . but the bottom line is that the brass at the SDC . . . they think this dream research I do is a bunch of malarkey. I didn't say anything to you about this before . . . but right before I left for Big Pine, Dr. Jacobson hinted that he might be retiring soon and suggested that I consider applying for his position."

She looked at her friend, who was nodding encouragingly.

"He told me I'd get a 'glowing recommendation' from him—and that it would be very helpful. He told me just to think about it, that's all, and that we'd talk about it when I got back.

"But then he added, 'You *are* coming back, aren't you?'"

Rozzie was watching her carefully. But she remained unusually silent, and Alix picked up on it instantly. "What's the matter? You don't think running the SDC would be a good fit for me? Is that it?"

The BP director sighed, then set her glass down carefully on the porch railing. "Alix, I'm sure you'd make a fabulous Executive Director. But I wonder . . . would that kind of detail-filled administrative work be adventurous enough for you?"

Neither of them spoke for a while. They listened to a bullfrog thrumming a mating song, somewhere down near the water's edge.

At last Alix broke the silence. "Well, that's enough about me! Let's get back to *you*. What I really want to know is: when are you going to retire, Roz?"

The older woman laughed. "Not until I meet my maker! Seriously, Alix, I'm not the retiring type. Besides, what would I do with myself if I didn't have a money-losing research facility to run day in and day out?"

The two women were quiet until Rozzie finally launched the question she'd been waiting to ask all night."

"Alix, do you want to tell me any more about what happened to you back in 1974?"

Startled, Alix suddenly remembered the terrifying image she'd spotted in her mirror. *Him.* The man who had broken her heart. All at once she was sure of it, totally certain: that menacing figure in the mirror had been Michael Rogers!

Rozzie was peering at her curiously. "You okay?"

Alix nodded. "Yeah, I'm fine. Just thinking, that's all."

But deep down, she knew she *wasn't* fine, not at all.

"Oh, Rozzie," she sighed after a bit, "I've had such terrible luck with men. I really have. Is something wrong with me? Why do I always make such bad decisions about these guys I wind up with?"

Rozzie gave her a friendly wave. "Aw, don't be so hard on yourself, Alix. If somebody puts on an act, how are you to know they aren't being honest?"

Alix blinked back at her. "You're right, Roz. Still, that guy back in 1974 really did mess me up. And you're going to think I'm off my nut . . . but the fact is, right before I left my cabin to join you tonight, I thought I saw his face staring back at me in the mirror!"

She took a deep breath. "If you want the truth, it scared the hell out of me." She gave Rozzie a searching look.

"Roz, you really do have some strange stuff going on here at Big Pine, you know that?"

Rozzie was nodding, but she wasn't laughing anymore.

"I most certainly *do* know, honey. It's what makes this place so special, huh? Anything goes! Spirits of death and faces in the mirror.

"I could go on and on, but I think you get the point."

"I do, I do. Loud and clear!"

Rozzie reached for her glass. "Well, it's getting late—and don't forget, we've got Detective Becker coming in the morning. I'm enjoying this thoroughly, but we better get some rest. Want me to walk you back to your cabin?"

"That's okay." Alix was on her feet now. I'll be fine, but thanks for offering."

"Here, take my flashlight. You'll need it."

Alix leaned over and gave her new friend a powerful hug. "Thanks for the gabfest, and thanks for treating me to some of Dr. Sverdlow's most expensive wine.

"I had a blast . . . catch you tomorrow!"

***

Four a.m. She awakened suddenly. Something wasn't right. She sat up on her bed, peering through the cloudy glass of the cabin's only bedroom window. *Where have all the stars gone?* It was very strange—a cloudless sky, and moonlight on the distant water, and yet . . . no stars!

Where have all the stars gone?

Then she began to hear it, rising slowly in the distance, like a wailing siren.

Naaaaaii-eeeeeeh-wah!

Growing louder and louder. Coming nearer and nearer.

Amazed, astounded, she felt her mouth falling open and she shouted into the darkness outside the cabin: "Who are you? Come closer so I can see you!"

Nothing at first.

Then a low, moaning voice, almost a growl: *He is coming now. You have brought him here. The Dark One is coming.*

She froze at the foot of the bed. Her eyes were straining, but they couldn't penetrate the surrounding blackness.

"Who are you?" she shrieked at the voice. "Why are you after me? What have I ever done to you?"

Evil spirits surround you, woman. You are in grave danger. You have brought him here. The Dark One. He is coming for you, and he will take you soon. Naaaaaii-eeeeeeh-wah!

Cursed!

Alix tried to scream again. And failed. For a moment, looming in the cloudy window, she thought she saw the face of Melinda Birdsong.

No . . . now there was something else crawling on the glass . . . a creature that wriggled obscenely, centipede-like. It lifted its head to show her a set of bleeding fangs. Teeth glinted in the dim light from the moon—teeth that looked scalpel-sharp!

Teeth like polished daggers . . . and two black-printed letters stood out among them: **HR**.

What could those two letters mean? Were they somehow connected to the Dark One?

As if answering her question, a low, sinister voice growled somewhere deep in her mind: *I'm going to let you look at HR, Alix. I'm going to cut you open with it, and I'm going to watch you die. Slowly. Painfully.*

You'll pay dearly for what you did to me.

She shrieked.

"Please, no . . . spare me!"

Ten seconds later, she woke from her nightmare.

She was trembling. Shuddering. Would she vomit? She could feel a trickle of icy sweat on her forehead, while her mind raced, raced.

Who is the Dark One?

Who is he and when will he appear?

CHAPTER 27
A Catfight at Filene's

Saturday, 5:24 a.m. After a drunken binge that had kept Dr. Mike on the prowl until long after midnight, he lay stark naked on his urine-stained, vile-smelling mattress.

He'd gone out to celebrate the nightmare-killing of that bitch from the Orpheum . . . but no matter how much he drank, he felt no joy and no real vindication.

If anything, he felt worse now.

He was doomed and he knew it. His fate was sealed. Alix Cassidy had put the dagger in him, and there was no way to escape the ugly truth she had revealed to the world.

Dr. Rogers is a fraud who steals other people's research!

The pain of her betrayal was even worse than the pain from the poisonous snake venom burning into the back of his hand.

He snarled with rage. He knew what had to be done!

He would have to kill again. He would have to find another woman like Alix and take her out during a nightmare!

Today!

***

7:50 a.m. Walking down Kneeland Street, Dr. Mike spotted the Orpheum and immediately crossed to the other side.

Seething with anger, he yanked down on the visor of the New York Yankees baseball cap he'd found sitting atop a trash can. After pausing for an instant to flip a fuck-bird at the dingy-looking movie house, he resumed his steps. There would be no movie today for Dr. Mike. No way. He had far bigger plans. . . .

A few blocks past the Orpheum, near the corner of Washington and Summer, loomed Boston's renowned downtown department store with its legendary discount department.

Filene's Basement.

Amazed by what he saw, the disgraced shrink stopped walking.

The scene before him was pure craziness, utter mayhem. Throngs of young women were pushing and fighting their way through the swinging doors and down a flight of stairs into the basement store. Dr. Mike had never witnessed anything like it. Why were these broads screaming their lungs out? Were they high on something or what? What the fuck was going on?

Hoping to figure it out, he gazed long and hard at the banner that hung above the entrance doors.

THIS SATURDAY ONLY!!!!!

Find Your Dream Wedding Dress at Filene's Basement RUNNING OF THE BRIDES!

Although Dr. Mike didn't realize it at first, he'd just wandered into one of the biggest events of Filene's entire year.

He was standing in the heart of the action . . . the place where bargain-hungry young women flocked in order to locate their "perfect wedding dress"—at rock-bottom prices. And it was total insanity. Once again this year, hundreds of future brides had camped out the night before in order to be among the first through the doors at 8:00 a.m.

By day's end, many of these frantic shoppers would be leaving with the wedding gowns of their dreams, at remarkably low prices. Although a sizable percentage of the gowns were worth thousands of dollars each, the luckiest of the shoppers would be required to pay only a few hundred bucks for them.

Wow! Dr. Mike's timing couldn't have been better. What could be more perfect than to stumble upon dozens and dozens of women out of their minds in a shopping frenzy? Bring them on! Responding to his excitement, his tattooed hand had begun to bleed again, as he eased his way into the swirling mob outside the department store.

Soon he was wandering among hordes of young women who were crowding the racks, grabbing their favorite gowns and trying them on. Incredibly, many of the maniac bargain hunters were clad in nothing more than bras and panties, or in bathing suits. . . .

Drifting among them, Dr. Mike couldn't help wondering: how many of these girls were virgins, chaste young things who'd decided to wait until their wedding night to be fucked for the first time ever? He broke into an ugly grin at the thought, and his mouth watered with pure lust as he tried to decide which ones might be still un-ravished.

Uh-oh, look out!

Only a few steps away, two girls were fighting over the same gown. Shrieking at each other, they pulled at the delicate fabric until it ripped. Wasn't this fun? Dr. Mike *loved* watching such catfights. He stood there observing the action . . . until a platoon of security guards finally arrived to separate the combatants.

Dr. Mike wandered on.

I wonder what's happening upstairs?

As if on cue, a flight of stairs appeared before him. They led up to the full-price section of the department store . . . where he was delighted to be met by a Lancôme sales lady wearing a mini-skirt and a low-cut blouse. She was handing out free samples.

"Excuse me, sir. Would you be interested in sampling our new fragrance, Tigress?"

He gave her his sweetest smile, looked her up and down, and then gazed deep into her eyes.

"Go fuck yourself, lady."

And he walked away.

"Wow, you're a pig," she shouted after him. "A pig!"

Dr. Mike ignored the insult. He kept walking, and it wasn't long before he reached the Elizabeth Arden counter . . . where he noticed an elderly woman sitting on a stool and staring into a gigantic magnifying mirror. The beautician was attempting to make her look presentable.

"Hi there, ladies," said the cheerful Dr. Mike.

He wagged a long finger at the beautician. "Say, you'll need a whole lot of makeup, if you're hoping to make *that* old bag look pretty!"

He roared with laughter. Resuming his odyssey through the makeup department, he flung one insult after another at these silly bitches. But then he stopped dead in his tracks as a familiar fragrance tantalized his nostrils. He turned around, searching for the source, which had to be nearby. Yes, it was growing stronger by the second.

Then it hit him smack in the center of his olfactory nerve. That was *her* fragrance! He was sure of it. The bitch had worn this same perfume almost every day! Her sheets and pillows had carried its scent long after their lovemaking had ended.

He scanned the crowded perfume department.

Then his eyes stopped moving.

There she was, working at the Chanel counter!

With her crimson hair, her penetrating green eyes and those endearing dimples on each cheek, she could have easily been mistaken for Alix.

So what if her name tag said "Tiffany"?

"Good afternoon, sir. How may I help you?"

She saw instantly that he wasn't wearing a wedding band. "Looking for a gift for your girlfriend?"

"Ah . . . yeah, I am." Dr. Mike would play along.

"So what did you have in mind? Some perfume, perhaps? Our most popular fragrance is Chanel No. 5. Would you like to sample it?"

"That would be very nice, thank you."

This girl is perfect.

An exact replica of the bitch who ruined me.

Dr. Mike had struck gold!

But he would behave—at least for now. Smiling, he launched an inquiry. "How long have you worked here, Tiffany?"

"Just six months," she replied.

"Then I'll bet you don't know much about the history of Chanel fragrances, do you?"

"A little." She frowned at him. "Why, do you?"

"Do you know why they decided to call it Chanel No. 5, and not Number 4 or Number 8?"

"That's a good question. I have no idea. Why?"

"Madame Chanel chose the fifth fragrance she was given by her chemists."

"That's interesting. Thanks for sharing it with me. Let me have your hand and I'll spray a bit of it on your pulse spot."

Dr. Mike extended his right hand, palm up.

"See if you like this. It's by far our most popular perfume."

She sprayed his wrist and then suggested that he give it a second to dry.

"Did you know that in 1952 Marilyn Monroe revealed to the world that she wore a few drops of Chanel No. 5 to bed every night . . . and nothing else?"

The salesclerk wasn't impressed by this bit of trivia, however.

"I don't mean to be rude, sir, but I'm very busy today. Would you like to make a purchase?"

Dr. Mike ignored this remark. "A woman should wear perfume where she would like to be kissed," he crooned now. "Where do *you* like to be kissed, Tiffany?"

"Really, sir. I don't have time to fool around. Would you please make up your mind?"

He grinned. "When I'm ready, Tiffany. And I'm not quite ready just yet. You didn't answer my question, dear. Where do you like to be kissed?"

"That's really none of your business. Either make up your mind or please leave."

This broad is a fighter. I like that.

"I bet I know the answer, sweetheart. I bet you like your pussy kissed, don't you?"

Her face darkened. "That's disgusting. You need to leave right now."

But once again, fate intervened.

At that moment, an older woman appeared at the Chanel counter. She was a society creature for sure, impeccably dressed. *What a pompous piece of shit.* Right away Dr. Mike noticed that she was showing off what had to be at least a five-carat Marquise cut diamond ring. From each delicate ear hung a glittering diamond solitaire earring that had to be three carats, if not more. Around her neck she wore an antique crystal necklace . . . a necklace he could use to strangle her if she became too much of a pain in the ass!

She was wearing a St. John knit jacket and slacks and carrying a Louis Vuitton handbag with Manolo Blahnik pumps gracing her feet.

"Hello, Mrs. Lodge," said Tiffany, eager to please the moneyed aristocrat. "Thank you for stopping by again today."

Mrs. Lodge sent her a patronizing smile. "You may call me Marilyn, dear."

Nauseated by the exchange, Dr. Mike rudely interrupted: "Tonight, Tiffany, when you go to sleep, put a few drops of Chanel No. 5 on your pussy. You won't be sorry, I promise."

Mrs. Lodge gasped with alarm. The word "pussy" probably wasn't in her daily working vocabulary—but she clearly knew its meaning. And it didn't have anything to do with felines, either. Dr. Mike was enjoying himself fully.

"That's okay, sweetie pie, no worries—I'll just come back another time, okay?"

He laughed happily . . . while watching the stricken Mrs. Lodge flee the area.

Tiffany was now alone with this crude man and she didn't like it one bit. Astonished, she watched several drops of bright red blood suddenly appear on the perfume counter. From where? They seemed to have materialized out of nowhere.

Then Dr. Mike stuck his hand directly under her nose, and she understood where the blood had come from. "My God, that's awful! What happened to your hand?"

Horrified, she stared at the deranged doctor's big right hand. Against her will, she was peering at the tattoo of a blood-oozing snake—and at the tiny drops of greenish-yellow pus that leaked from the tips of its menacing fangs.

The smirking intruder didn't bother to answer Tiffany's question. He just kept on ranting. "Madame Chanel wanted to create a woman's perfume with a woman's scent," he told her.

Then, mockingly: "Jasmine! It's a fragrance that resists the whims of passion and the passage of time. It's the most precious of essences. . . ."

"That's him, officer. That's the man who's harassing Tiffany. I heard him use profanity!"

The security officer glared. "Is that true?"

"Nah, I haven't been harassing her at all," whined Dr. Mike. "You got it all wrong. I just came in here to buy my girlfriend some fancy perfume. She came on to *me*. Asked me to slip into her dreams and kiss her . . ."

Tiffany began to shout. "I didn't say anything of the sort. He's lying!"

The rent-a-cop instantly bought her story.

"Sir, you need to come with me. I'm going to have to escort you out of the building."

The guard didn't wait for an answer. Grabbing Dr. Mike by the shoulder, and not so gently, he pushed him in the direction of the nearest exit.

When the fuming doctor tried to resist, the security officer twisted his arms behind his back and marched him away.

Dr. Mike looked back over one shoulder. "You won't get away with this, baby doll!

"I'm coming after you tonight, in your nightmares. Got it? *Got* it? You haven't seen the last of me, you bet. I'm going to kiss that pussy of yours. You bet.

"I'll lick it like an ice cream cone! And that's not all I'm going to do, you cunt."

At the door, the security officer warned Dr. Mike: "If I ever see you in here again, I'll use your face to mop the floor. You got that, asshole?" When the vagrant didn't respond, the hired cop asked again, "Did you hear me? I asked you a question."

Then he shoved his prisoner out the door and gave him an extra push onto the sidewalk.

Dr. Mike landed on his ass. Once again, he'd been manhandled.

Once again, he'd been treated like a piece of shit.

So what? Now he was laughing.

See you tonight in your dreams, baby doll!

CHAPTER 28
Charly's Nightmare

Midnight.

Stretched out on his rumpled bed, a restless Boston Police detective named Jake Becker was having a lot of trouble falling asleep.

For some reason, he couldn't stop thinking about his telephone call to Big Pine earlier that day. If this Alix Cassidy knew her stuff—and she certainly sounded knowledgeable about nightmares and psychology—she might turn out to be a valuable resource in putting together a personality profile of the killer. . . .

He needed help, and he knew it. How long before the maniac struck again? Anxious and impatient, he thrashed around on the mattress, trying to find a comfortable spot. But it was hopeless. Try as he might, he couldn't relax enough to drift off into the refreshing kingdom of blessed sleep. How had Shakespeare described it in *Macbeth*?

Sleep that knits up the raveled sleeve of care . . .

Forget it! He was sitting upright on the bed now, feet flat against the warm wooden planks of the floor. Maybe a glass of milk would help . . . followed by another chapter of *Lord Jim*? Yes . . . a few pages of Conrad's marvelously rich prose were always the perfect prescription for insomnia.

He yawned and slipped his toes into the deep cotton slippers that waited at bedside.

A minute later he was standing in a pool of fluorescent kitchen light, with the refrigerator door open in front of him. Still yawning and stretching, he surveyed the contents. Plenty of healthy fruits and vegetables for Charly, along with plenty of yogurt and cottage cheese and kosher dills for him.

Then he spotted the quart of milk located just to the right of the cold cuts.

He reached for it and got a surprise.

Something flashed. Or did it glimmer? A bit of light. Headlights from a passing car? He leaned in closer to the small window that flanked the refrigerator . . . was somebody out there, walking around with a flashlight?

What? *What's that?*

He jerked his head back as if he'd been stung.

For just a moment, he'd been watching a thin wriggling snake flow sinuously across the windowpanes!

At the same instant, he'd felt something cold—icy-cold, and unpleasantly wet—go shuddering through his lower gut.

Jake never cursed. It was a point of pride with him.

But now he forgot himself and bellowed out loud: "What the fuck?"

He blinked . . . stared . . . and blinked again.

Just like that, the snake was gone. Vanished. Had he really seen it? Had it really *been* there? Perplexed and more than a little frightened, he reached for the glass bottle of milk.

The moment his hand touched the dank skin of the jug, he heard a sound that made his blood run cold.

It was a sobbing sound—the racking cry of a young girl terrified of something.

He looked up from the milk, astonished.

Charly was standing in the kitchen doorway.

Her face was wet with tears.

"Dad . . . Dad. So horrible! So horrible!"

He lunged toward her, his heart pounding in his chest. "Charly . . . my God, what's the matter?"

She was swaying back and forth . . . a thin, wild-eyed figure in a white nightgown covered with tiny pink roses. Now he stood before her, a hand resting on one of her shoulders.

"What?" he said. It was nearly a shout.

"Dad . . . I just had this nightmare. I dreamed that you were *falling*. You'd fallen off . . . like, a tall escalator in a high-rise building. You were screaming, so terrible, and while you were falling, this tattoo thing was eating your face!"

He gaped at her. He was swaying a little himself now. For a shaky moment he wondered if he might fall down right there in front of her, and then never *stop* falling.

"A tattoo?" he blurted. "I fell off an escalator? Hey, honey, it's okay. It was just a nightmare, sweetheart; everything is going to be okay."

He gave her a comforting hug, but she just kept on talking. "The tattoo thing was eating your eyes, Dad. It was eating the light in your eyes.

"I watched your eyes filling up with darkness! The tattoo thing had all these legs, wiggling legs, like a giant caterpillar or something, a huge bug with this . . . this bleeding tattoo on its back, and it ate the light out of your eyes.

"Then I heard this creepy voice, like, it was singing and laughing, a deep ugly voice singing these words over and over again: *Hello, darkness, my old friend.*"

She was weeping openly.

"I heard it, Dad, and I knew that voice was talking about your *eyes*, about the light that was bleeding out of your *eyes*. And I couldn't do anything to stop it. I couldn't stop the voice.

"I wanted to turn it off, I really did. But there was nothing I could do and your eyes kept bleeding light, and the voice kept talking on and on, so horrible, laughing and growling: *Hello, darkness, my old friend*!"

He held her close. "It was only a nightmare, Charly. Only a nightmare, that's all. It wasn't real, do you hear me? There was nothing real about it. Just a bad dream. Just a terrible dream. Do you understand?"

She didn't answer him. She was shivering violently now. "Dad . . . is something bad going to happen?"

"Of course not, Charly."

"Is something dark coming, Dad?"

He shook his head furiously, again and again. "Of course not. Everything's fine. You're at home. You're standing in your own kitchen. You've had a nightmare, but it means nothing, nothing. . . ."

With one hand gently cupping the back of her head, he was leading her back to the warmth and safety of her bedroom.

Yes . . . there it was . . . the poster of the Beach Boys wearing the bright yellow straw hats . . . along with Eeyore the donkey doll and the little brown teddy bear he'd won for her only a few weeks before at the Boston Latin School Springtime Fair.

It seemed to take forever, but she gradually calmed.

She lay silent on the bed, and her breathing slowly returned to normal.

He sat on the chair beside her desk for nearly an hour, until he was sure she'd fallen asleep again.

Then he returned to his own room and did his best to knit up the raveled sleeve of his fretful wakefulness. But it was difficult. It was a test, and he wasn't sure he could pass it.

He'd been deeply shaken and more than a little frightened by Charly's terror.

He struggled ... and the pale gray dawn was breaking in the corner of his bedroom window before he finally drifted away into broken, troubled sleep.

CHAPTER 29

A Thrilling Ride in Rozzie's Canoe

The DHC-3 Otter turned in the bright sunshine and began its descent.

With an eardrum-assaulting roar from its piston engine-powered single prop, the seaplane with the United States Coast Guard insignia on its side dropped like a diving hawk toward the bottle green surface of Moosehead Lake 5,000 feet below.

Perched on her cushioned seat directly behind the pilot, Charly sent up a cry of pure delight.

"Wow!"

Then she gave her father a double thumbs-up.

Having recovered her cheerful spirits entirely—a good night's sleep had done wonders for her rattled psyche—the kid was eager to explore the wonders of Big Pine and the vast lake that fronted it.

The plane settled to earth in a series of lazy spirals, and within a matter of minutes they were splashing along on its silver pontoons past an anchored buoy that read:

SLOW
NO
WAKE

A minute later, they came to rest against the Center's dock.

Two women stood on it. Both were waving at the approaching float plane.

"That's gotta be them," Jake shouted above the thunder of the engine. "That's our welcoming committee, Charly."

"Are those the two people you were talking about?" Charly shouted back.

"Must be them!" hollered Jake. After studying the fleet of canoes tied to the dock, he went on. "I'm going to be interviewing Dr. Cassidy for an hour or two, Charly. While I'm doing that, maybe I can arrange for you to go on a canoe ride. Sound like a plan?"

"Great idea, Dad!"

As soon as they stepped on the dock, the two women strode toward them, ready to shake hands.

"You must be Detective Becker," said Alix. She looked radiant in a lime green tank top and matching shorts. Without hesitating, she gazed deep into the man's warm, easygoing smile. She liked what she saw.

After a moment she turned. "And you must be Charly. Your dad mentioned on the phone that he'd be bringing you along. Aren't you the pretty one, though?"

She took the kid's hand and gave it a friendly squeeze. Then, speaking to everyone: "Let me introduce you to Dr. Rozzie Violette, the Director of Big Pine Research Center."

After Jake introduced the pilot, Captain Scott Brierly—who waved hello while lashing the seaplane to a post—the four new friends stood together at the center of the dock.

"Detective Becker," said Rozzie, who was looking quite adventurous in her khaki Australian bush hat, "I'm hoping that while you and Alix talk business, I can enjoy the privilege of taking Miss Charly for a ride in my antique canoe."

Jake lit up. "Rozzie, you must have been reading my mind. I was just telling Charly I'd try to get her a canoe ride."

Rozzie grinned. "Well, I *am* a psychic, you know?"

Jake looked at his daughter: "That okay with you, hon?"

"Sure is," piped Charly. "Dr. Violette, I want to see everything!"

Rozzie took her hand. "Great, we'll have some major fun, you better believe it. But from here on, you gotta call me Rozzie. Okay?"

"Sure thing, Rozzie!"

Then the woman in the funky hat turned to Jake.

"Don't worry, my canoe may be an antique—but the state law in Maine says you have to wear a life jacket on the water at all times."

Jake smiled again. "Thanks, Rozzie."

***

Rozzie hopped in as she pushed the canoe away from the dock, and Charly—now sitting in the prow—was amazed by the sky-blue expanse of water that stretched toward the distant horizon.

"Rozzie, look at the *size* of it! This is Moosehead Lake, right?"

"It sure is," said Rozzie, "all 118 square miles of it, honey. Did you know Moosehead is the biggest freshwater mountain lake east of the Mississippi?"

"Really?"

"Sure is. It's a whopper . . . nearly 250 feet deep in places. And if you look over to the west—see the big cliffs? Those things are 700 feet high. They've been a Maine landmark for hundreds of thousands of years."

Seated in the stern, Rozzie pointed toward the landmark with her paddle. "The history of Maine is quite interesting, and it's full of stories about those cliffs. They form what we call 'Mount Kineo' today, and they go way back to the last Ice Age more than 10,000 years ago."

Charly nodded. "Yeah, we learned about that in science class, Rozzie. Mountains of ice, two and three miles deep, and they pushed all the way down into what's now Kentucky and Tennessee."

Rozzie laughed out loud. "Things took a cold turn, that's for sure. But then it warmed up again—it always does, you know—and that's when the Native Americans started to arrive. The Red Paint People came first . . . a really mysterious group . . . and we know almost nothing about them. And then came the Penobscot and the Abenaki. They're still with us, you know?

"We've got an Abenaki village not ten miles from here. They were famous for making all these . . . all these religious pilgrimages up the sides of the cliffs. They'd go up there to pray and dance. The world they inhabited is fascinating to learn about."

Charly was twisting toward the stern to hear more. But a moment later, Rozzie's history lesson was cut short—by the loud roar of a motorcycle clattering along the dirt road that flanked the eastern edge of the lake.

"Speaking of the Abenaki," Roz shouted at her youthful charge in order to be heard over the sound of the Harley's engine, "there goes Melinda Birdsong, our famous Maine medicine woman!"

Amazed, Charly turned in the prow of the canoe to watch the big machine and its tiny pilot go thundering up the crest of a small hill . . . and then quickly disappear from sight. Charly could hardly contain her astonishment.

"That little lady on the motorcycle is an Indian *medicine* woman?" she shouted at her grinning companion.

"She sure is," Rozzie shouted back. "Didn't I tell you Big Pine was full of surprises? Melinda is not only a champion motorcyclist, she's also one of the most respected Indian psychics in America. Pretty cool, huh?"

Charly's eyes were shining with excitement. "Boy, I can't wait to meet her and start learning all about the world of the Abenaki!"

"You will, and soon, honey!"

Roz had begun to paddle again. "But that's enough anthropology for now. Tell me all about *you*. What grade are you in and what's your favorite subject?"

Charly grinned. She had turned again in the prow, so she could look back at Rozzie from time to time. "I'm in ninth grade at Boston Latin School," she told her new canoeing buddy.

"You know, it's on Avenue Louis Pasteur not far from the Harvard doctors' college.

"As for my favorite subject . . ." Now the youngster frowned thoughtfully. She was at the age when you take such questions very seriously. "I don't know, Rozzie. Actually, I . . . I like the arts a lot. Theater, literature, painting—that kind of stuff.

"My dad says I'm going to be the next Sarah Bernhardt. He says I'm always acting. Like, if I disagree with him about something . . . he's like: 'Stop with the acting, Charly. Who are you, the next Sarah Bernhardt?'

"I had to look in the encyclopedia to find out who she was . . . bet you didn't know she was Jewish!"

Rozzie was laughing out loud by now. "No, I didn't know that. It's not easy being a teenager, is it?"

"Nope."

"But you'll get through it, no sweat!"

"I hope so."

Rozzie had stopped paddling again. "So . . . I understand your dad is a police detective?"

"That's right. Homicide. He has a pretty tough job, I think."

The woman in the jaunty bush hat nodded thoughtfully. "I imagine he's pretty dedicated, huh?"

"He sure is, Rozzie. When he gets started on a case, you know, trying to solve a murder—he really throws himself into it. He doesn't eat much, and he barely even sleeps. And you can't really talk to him. His eyes get this faraway look. . . ."

Rozzie was looking carefully at her youthful companion. "Well, I'm sure he's a very determined policeman. But it's probably tough at times on you and your mom, huh?"

There was a long pause after this question. Surprised, Rozzie saw that Charly's face had changed. "Well, actually . . . my mom died, Rozzie."

The older woman's eyes widened. "She did? Oh, dear."

"Leukemia," said Charly. "I was only three, so I don't really remember much about her. Just her smile, a little. And I also have some pictures to look at. She was very beautiful."

Rozzie was biting her lower lip. "Oh, Charly . . . I'm sorry. So sorry!"

But Charly didn't seem particularly fazed by the disclosure. "That's okay, Rozzie. It doesn't bother me anymore, it really doesn't. Just once in a while . . . you know, my dad will get so busy. We have a wonderful nanny, Mrs. Whitney, she's very sweet, but. . . ."

Rozzie cleared her throat. "Well . . . that's good. That's very good. I'm glad Mrs. Whitney is a pal! And I'm sure you must have lots of other great friends, too?"

Charly smiled. "I do. I've got plenty of friends, Rozzie—and now I've also got you!"

The senior paddler produced a wide smile. "You sure do, honey, and we're gonna be great buddies. You wait and see!"

Charly nodded enthusiastically, and they cruised along in silence for a while.

Then, hoping to bring them back to the cheerful exuberance they'd felt at the start of their journey, Rozzie asked: "Charly, did you know you're sitting in a precious antique?"

"I am?"

"You sure are! This is an Old Town canoe we're paddling—and it was built more than 75 years ago."

Responding, Charly sent up a low whistle. It was one of her new skills as a budding teenager. "So, Rozzie, what you're telling me is . . . we're kind of, like, riding across Moosehead Lake in a little piece of history? Is that it?"

Rozzie was delighted. *What a bright child*, she told herself. For a moment, she felt a flicker of regret for the bright children she didn't have, and never would have. But the feeling passed quickly. Rozzie wasn't given to self-pity.

"Charly," she told her youthful charge as she powered the Old Town through a long U-turn and started back toward the distant dock, "Big Pine is famous for its canoes and its lake and its Native American tribes.

"But it's also famous for something else."

"What's that?"

Charly was grinning again.

"We make the best hot fudge sundaes in Maine!"

CHAPTER 30
A Meeting of the Minds

They were finally alone now, Jake and Alix, except for a brightly hued monarch butterfly which had decided to join them for a while.

They watched it flutter above their heads for at least half a minute, before it drifted off toward the stately pines.

"Want to stretch your legs?" asked Alix.

She was already moving down the sandy path that led away from the dock.

He kept stride. And kept smiling. He liked her breeze-blown red hair and her green eyes.

"Alix, you've really got a beautiful place up here."

He turned toward the azure surface of distant Moosehead Lake. "What a great spot for a research center. It's breathtaking."

She nodded. "Isn't it lovely? You should see the sky at night. We've got stars blazing all the way to the horizon—totally spectacular."

He grinned broadly . . . and was suddenly tempted to blurt: "Lovely, is it? Just like you!" He wouldn't give in to the temptation, of course.

He was here on official police business.

"I've got an idea," she said. "I'll show you around the Center, and we can talk while we walk. Whoops . . . pardon my rhyme!" She peered closely at him now. "How much time have you got?"

Jake sighed. "Only a couple of hours, unfortunately. I promised the Coast Guard Commander I'd have his plane back by five. He stuck his neck out for me and I can't disappoint him."

"You borrowed a Coast Guard plane to get up here?"

"I did."

She squinted at him through the bright summer sunlight.

"This thing you're working on must be pretty important."

"Trust me. It is."

***

They walked along silently for a minute or two. Then Alix brightened. "Jake . . . I meant to tell you back at the dock—your daughter is adorable. She looks just like you!"

Jake hesitated. "Well . . . thanks. But to be honest, I don't see the resemblance. To me, she's the spitting image of her mother."

"Then your wife must be very beautiful."

His expression didn't change. "*Was* beautiful. We lost her back in 1975."

Alix looked at him. "I'm sorry. I didn't mean to . . ."

Jake smiled. "Don't worry, Alix. I'm fine. It was a long time ago."

Nice going, knucklehead! Talk about sticking your foot in your mouth.

Alix felt like an idiot for a moment, but then she tried to ease up on herself—he *was* wearing a wedding band, wasn't he?

After all these years? He must have loved her very much.

She took a deep breath and did her best to change the subject. "Charly seems to have really enjoyed the plane ride, Jake."

He beamed. "She *loved* it, at least up until the moment when the pilot banked the plane for a 'National Geographic Photo Op' above Elephant Mountain. That's when she turned green and nearly lost her lunch.

"Fortunately, she managed to keep it together, or we'd have had a real mess on our hands!"

Alix laughed out loud. "The poor kid! But she seemed perfectly fine when she got off the plane."

"Yeah, she recovered pretty quickly, once she stopped with the picture-taking. She was having a ball with her new camera."

"You two seem close. That's very sweet."

"We are, and she is! I haven't had a free minute to spend with her lately, though, and that bothers me a lot. I invited her along today so we could spend some quality time together. Plus, I knew she'd really love the plane ride."

Alix liked what she was hearing. This guy was a terrific dad. And not bad looking either. He was certainly different from the men she'd hung out with in the past. Why couldn't she find herself a guy like Jake?

Suddenly, she found herself wondering: was *she* the problem, after all?

She began to study his features, looking for clues. "It must be very hard for you, raising a daughter by yourself, especially in your line of work."

"Nah . . . I love the kid madly. We do okay." Jake looked back at her. He was enjoying this. He liked her eyes. Liked her hair.

He'd never been big on redheads in the past . . . maybe he'd been missing something?

"Charly's really a cute name for a girl, Jake. It fits her perfectly."

"Well, her real name is Charlotte. She was named after my mother. Once we started calling her Charly, it just stuck—and she's been Charly ever since."

Alix nodded, then pointed. "Look, there she goes now, in the canoe."

They watched Rozzie paddling away in the stern of the Old Town for a few moments, and Jake threw his daughter a big wave. He grinned happily when she yelled back: "Hi there, Dad!"

They kept walking. Another monarch butterfly had arrived on the scene. Now he was spiraling through a series of loops near Jake's head. In the distance, a cavorting bluebird trilled his familiar theme.

"Okay, Jake," said Alix. She was all business now. "You came a long way to meet with me. How can I help you?"

He looked at her. "First of all, I want to thank you. I know you've got plenty to do, and I appreciate your time."

Is this guy always so polite? Alix was impressed.

"I called you right after I read the article about Big Pine in last week's *Globe* magazine. Fascinating stuff, I must say. I never even knew a place like this existed. It's all very interesting, but to be honest, I'm not much into this 'paranormal' stuff.

"I'm a cop, after all. You could say I'm old school."

She sent him a reassuring smile. "That's okay, Jake. You don't have to explain yourself. I didn't know about Big Pine, either—not until after I started my research, that is."

Frowning, he scratched his chin for a moment. "Alix, let me cut to the chase. We're hunting a serial murderer. The Police Commissioner is pushing us as hard as he can, and the Mayor's all over us to find this guy before he strikes again."

She reflected. "That sounds pretty intense. But I'm not sure how I can help."

He looked at her for a second. "Please try?"

"I'll do my best."

"Good. First, tell me about your theory of Som . . . som-balistic Telepathy. Heck, I'll never be able to pronounce that word!"

"Somnambulistic Telepathy." Alix smiled. Rozzie had enjoyed a good laugh while describing Jake's bungled pronunciation on the phone.

"Why don't you just call it ST?" she suggested.

Jake chuckled. "Good idea. ST, then. But tell me: do you really believe in that stuff? I mean, you gotta admit it's a pretty far-fetched concept. More like what you'd see on *The Twilight Zone*."

She reached out and took his wrist for a moment. "Jake, let me answer your question with a question of my own. And, yes, I *do* believe in the reality of ST. But here's my question: would you agree that Albert Einstein was one of the most brilliant scientists of the modern world?"

"Yes, sure. I'd agree with that. Who wouldn't?

"But what's Einstein got to do with ST?"

She sighed and shook her head. "I wish you'd been here for my lecture last week. I told them all about Oneirology. That's Greek for the study of dreaming."

He laughed. "Oh-na . . . what? You've sure got some heavy terminology going on up here, Alix." But then he smiled. "Jeez, I'm starting to sound like my partner. He's always telling me I talk like an encyclopedia!"

Alix smiled. "Well, it's simple enough: the word is pronounced oh-nye-ah-RAW-loh-gee." She blinked at him. "Don't worry, the name isn't important. The key point is that Einstein believed everything is interconnected, and usually in ways we can't fully understand. For example, electrons can affect other electrons, even when they're billions of miles apart in space.

"Einstein had a name for this weird aspect of reality— he called it *spooky action at a distance*. He was very interested in phenomena like ST. If you read his theories about spooky action, it becomes much easier to imagine that human beings might be capable of entering the dreams of other people—and perhaps even *participating* in them."

He gave her a long hard look. "Alix, I hardly know what to say. I can't go back to the Police Commissioner and the Mayor of Boston with Einstein's theory of spooky *gobbledygook*. I need something tangible. Help me out here, will you? They'll think I'm off my rocker if they find out I've come up here to consult with a. . . ."

"Crystal ball lady? Is that what you're thinking?"

"No, that's not what I meant." He thought for a moment and then grinned. "Well, maybe a little."

All at once they were both smiling broadly at each other. They were having a good time together. *He's got a sense of humor*, Alix told herself. *Good for him.*

"You know, my partner already thinks I'm totally nuts for wasting my time consulting with you."

Pretending to scold him, she furrowed her brow. "Jake, I'm surprised at you. I can tell you're a man with an open mind. Don't you enjoy being challenged by new *ideas*? You have to admit that strange things happen frequently . . . things that can't be accounted for with ordinary explanations."

He thought for a moment. "Okay, all this talk about 'spooky stuff' is fine, but I came here to ask for your help on a practical level. I'm working on a psychological profile for the type of person who'd commit these heinous crimes. I'm looking for any clues that can help me find this guy.

"He's planning to strike again, Alix. That much we do know. These guys don't stop killing until they're caught."

She sighed heavily. "Jake, I'm a sleep scientist. I'm not sure I'll be of much use."

"Give it a try, please? Maybe I could start by giving you some background. Maybe that would help you understand what we're up against."

"Okay. Fire away."

"All right, here's the latest. So far two women have been killed—and both of them were deathly afraid of being attacked in a nightmare, right before they died. The first victim called her girlfriend in the middle of the night in a total panic, fearing she was about to be assaulted in her sleep. The next day she was found murdered.

"The second victim kept a diary in which she'd written about her fear of being viciously attacked during a nightmare. She, too, was later found murdered."

Alix was gazing somberly at him now. "How sad."

"There's more. We've interviewed witnesses who saw each one of these women being harassed by a man who threatened them. According to those witnesses, the suspect told both victims: 'I'm coming after you tonight in your nightmares. You'll wish you were dead before I'm done with you.'"

Alix had stopped walking. Her grave face reflected her growing comprehension.

"So that's what we have to go on," said Jake. "In both killings, the suspect got himself thrown out of public establishments after threatening the two victims. They gave him the boot at a bar, and now he's suspected of later killing the young female bartender.

"And a cashier at a movie theater located near the Combat Zone—that's Boston's red-light district— refused his advances and then died horribly after he made several nightmare threats.

"In both cases, he was also ranting about a woman who had ruined him in the past. It looks like he thought both the bartender and the cashier resembled this woman, you know? He was delusional, if that's the right word.

"And there's more. At the movie theater, he claimed to be this Greek god Orpheus, who travels through the Underworld, the land of the dead. He told the movie cashier that *he* was Orpheus, while also threatening to invade her dreams as she slept. Do you see any psychological pattern here? Anything that might help us identify the killer?"

"I do," said Alix. "First of all, he sounds like a pretty intelligent guy, Jake. Ranting about dreams and Greek gods? Did you ever think he might be a teacher? Maybe even a classics professor of some sort?"

Jake was smiling.

"What's so funny?"

"That's *my* nickname—The Professor."

She stared at him. "Really? Why do they call you that?"

"The guys on—the other cops in Homicide—think I'm kind of brainy. They're easily fooled, believe me." He barked with sudden laughter, then grew serious again.

"But that isn't important. Let's get down to business. The clock is running, and I don't want to see any more women in Boston pay the price."

He gave her a searching glance. "What else can you tell me?"

She deliberated. "Okay, Jake . . . but first let me ask—why are you building a personality profile?"

"Well, it's a key step in catching the bad guy."

She stared. "Catching the *bad guy*? Is that standard police talk these days?"

She was teasing him now.

"Nope . . . it's just the way *I* talk. Actually, it's the reason I went into this line of work in the first place. To get the bad guys off the street before they can hurt people.

"You see, my baby sister . . ."

He suddenly fell silent.

Right in the middle of his sentence, Jake had stopped talking.

Perplexed, Alix looked curiously at him.

She waited.

Apparently, he had decided not to say more about the baby sister.

"So what's your professional opinion?" he asked. "How are we to understand such vicious, sadistic behavior?"

She thought for a few seconds. "Well, for starters, I'd say that men who commit these kinds of heinous crimes have one thing in common. They think they should have the power of life and death over other people. In their own eyes, they're like God. Many actually believe they've *become* God."

He was blinking slowly at her. "Keep going, please."

"Psychologically, the thrill-motivated killer tends to be a psychopath—someone with a disorder of character rather than a disorder of the mind. He lacks a conscience, feels no remorse, and cares only for his own pleasures. Above all, he wants to control the lives of others— usually by holding them in a grip of abject terror."

His face had lit up, and his eyes were shining. "This is good stuff, Alix."

"I'd also suggest that serial killers most often come from dysfunctional families. They experience what we call 'ulcerated relations' with their parents, most often with the father. They have strong feelings of resentment towards society—feelings triggered by their own failings. They endure a lot of sexual frustration, along with the pain of being socially ostracized.

"They don't think they're good enough to have real friends—or intimate relationships with the opposite sex."

He was looking intently at her. "Alix, how do you know all this stuff? I thought you said you were a sleep scientist."

Alix laughed. "What I didn't tell you was that I got my Ph.D. in psychology. So I do know a little bit about deviant behavior. And what I have to say next is not so good, I'm afraid. According to the data, once this kind of psychopath has tasted the sick gratification provided by a kill, he'll probably kill again."

Jake was glaring straight ahead. "That's what I was afraid of."

"One other aspect has often been noted in the literature," said Alix. "Most of these psychopathic killers want to relive the feeling of power they get by killing people. They want an instant replay on demand. So quite frequently, they'll take a trophy from the murder scene.

"You know, a piece of jewelry or underwear, something personal . . . a keepsake. Have you looked into that aspect yet?"

He shook his head. "Nope. We're not sure about that. It's still early in the investigation."

"Also . . . a serial killer will often follow the same method, carefully. For many of them, it's almost ritualistic. Have you found any patterns yet? Any similarities in behavior?"

But now Jake began to clam up. 'Yes . . . we *have* seen certain kinds of repetition . . . but I'm not at liberty to talk about them."

"I understand. No problem. But is he operating in a specific area or location? Does he return to the same area each time he strikes?"

"Well, yes. We only have two locations, remember— but they're fairly close. Sorry . . . I can't go there, either."

She was frowning hard now, doing her best to find a bottom line for him. "One thing I would say is that the serial killer literally chases his dream. He's got an inner fantasy going night and day, and he has to keep feeding it."

She held his gaze with her own.

"In my opinion, that's the key link between this kind of murder and ST. The killer seems to mistake his own inner dream life for outer reality—and in ways that normal people don't really understand."

Jake had stopped walking. "Alix, I can't thank you enough. This psychological briefing you've given me could prove to be very helpful down the line."

She sighed and frowned. "Well, I sure hope you find this guy before he kills again. And you know, Jake, you might also consider speaking with Rozzie. Don't forget, she's a gifted psychic. Maybe she could give you a different kind of perspective on your case. Why not?"

He offered her a bright smile, and his eyes were twinkling with mischief. "Oh, great. The Commissioner will love to hear that. As soon as I tell him, I can say goodbye to my career as a detective. *Sayonara*, Becker—you're *kaput*!"

But he was laughing, and she could tell he was intrigued.

"Seriously," he said. "It's my job to catch the bad guy with good old-fashioned police work, that's all."

He gave her a deep stare. "One thing you can be sure of, Alix."

"What's that?"

"We won't quit working until we put the cuffs on him and take him out of circulation."

***

"How was your canoe ride, sweetheart?" As usual, Jake greeted Charly with a monster hug. Rozzie was busy tying her antique canoe down at the other end of the dock.

"It was really fun, Dad! We found a baby loon sitting on its mother's back, and Rozzie said we were incredibly lucky to see that. The baby was really cute."

"Terrific, honey. But we gotta go now. Are you all set?"

As if answering his question, the seaplane's propeller screeched once and then began its usual whirling clatter.

Jake smiled as he turned to say goodbye to the Executive Director.

"Rozzie, thanks for entertaining Charly. It sounds like she had a great time."

"My pleasure," said Rozzie. "You've got a delightful little girl there, Jake. Smart, too. You should be very proud of her."

"I am, Rozzie, I am."

Jake gave his daughter an affectionate pat on the head.

Then Alix was shaking his hand. "It was very nice to meet you, Jake. I hope you catch the bad guy, and soon. Let me know if I can be of any more help."

Was she teasing him again? Hoping to find out, he gazed deep into her green eyes.

He found himself still hanging onto her hand. Had he forgotten to let go of it?

Right then Alix felt something flash through his gaze, something wordless but thrilling. A recognition? A connection? What?

She didn't understand what was happening. Not exactly. But she liked it. She liked it a whole lot.

As Jake stepped into the plane, he turned back to Rozzie.

"It's been a pleasure, Roz—many thanks!"

"No problem," she said. Then, laughing: "Hey, if you ever want any help with the *paranormal* aspects, I'm pretty well known in these parts."

He laughed cheerfully. "Thanks, Rozzie. If we decide to call in a psychic, I'll be sure to give you a yell!"

Then, at the very last moment, just as the plane door was about to close, Alix had a sudden thought. "Hey Jake," she shouted.

"Did you ever consider that your guy might be a *shrink*?"

CHAPTER 31
Breakfast, Interrupted

It was ten past seven in the morning, and the plate glass front window at Murray's Jewish Deli was already flooded with bright June sunshine.

Jake grabbed his friend's left shoulder and gave it a friendly squeeze.

"Murray, how you been doing?"

"Never been better," grinned the proud owner of one of Boston's most popular authentic Jewish delis. "Except for one thing maybe, which is not so hot."

"What's that?"

"I haven't seen *you* in here lately, Jake. Where the hell you been, anyway?"

The Professor shook his head. "Too much work, that's where. You know how it is, Murray. As usual, I've got a long day ahead of me . . . and I thought, what better way to start it off than with one of your famous cheese blintzes?"

The man in the apron laughed out loud. "Terrific! And I know what you mean about being swamped with work. That's the problem with America now. Everybody's too damn busy."

Murray laughed again, but beneath his flaring eyebrows, the deli proprietor's gaze had gone a bit somber, a bit fretful. "Still, you gotta eat, and you gotta eat *right*. Huh? I hope you haven't lost your taste for my food!"

"Not a chance, Murray. That will never happen, believe me."

The detective was looking toward the sandwich counter, where a middle-aged woman in a *Murray's Deli* apron was busy slicing up a stack of bagels. "When it comes to your food," he said, "I'm an addict for life. Only problem is, we've been up to our eyeballs in work the last few weeks, and I haven't been able to break away."

"So I hear, my friend, so I hear." Murray had fallen into line with his visitor by now; together they were filing past steaming ranks of brisket prepared for the lunchtime trade.

"Jake, I was just reading about those two murders. My God, how terrible for those poor girls! It was all over the front page."

Jake turned to stare at him.

"You read about the killings?"

"I sure did." Murray blinked slowly back. "The front of today's *Herald.* Don't tell me you haven't seen it yet? Hey, you're a big part of the story, Jake—I was impressed! There's a bunch of stuff in there about some maniac . . . probably a serial killer . . . and it said you've been consulting a psychic in Maine, trying to figure it all out."

Watching the detective's reaction, Murray's eyes widened with alarm. "Hey, did I say something wrong?"

The detective had stepped out of the sandwich line by now. "*I'm* in the story, up in *Maine*? What in the world? Murray, have you got a copy of the paper?"

Thoroughly puzzled, Murray peered at him. "Yeah, sure. It's back in the office. Come on, I'll show you."

Ten steps later, they were squeezing their way into a tiny office full of stacked coffee cups. The pages of the tabloid lay on a wide table, spread out between Murray's blue IBM electric typewriter and the ancient Friden EC-132 calculator he'd been using since the late 1970s. "There you go, Jake. Sit down, make yourself comfortable.

"I'll be out front. That cheese blintz is on *me*, whenever you're ready, my friend."

"Okay, thanks."

Jake was already sliding into the black-vinyl-covered chair that fronted the desk, even as he reached for the front page.

IS A SERIAL MURDERER LOOSE IN BOSTON?

Questions Arise as Cops Track "Surgeon-Like" Killer of 2 Women
By Mark Halliday

Special to the Herald—The recent killings of two Boston women, closely similar in many details, have raised questions about whether a serial murderer may be at large in an area stretching from the South End to the edge of the Combat Zone, a neighborhood of adult bookstores and X-rated strip clubs, according to police.

The two stabbing murders, which occurred in the small hours of June 9th and June 23rd, were reportedly marked by similarities that suggest a single perpetrator attacked both victims.

Those similarities also indicate that the murdered women were chosen at random by their assailant, before being stabbed to death, probably with a scalpel-like cutting device of the kind surgeons use, said police.

Describing the brutal slayings of a bartender who lived not far from the Combat Zone and a movie theater ticket-seller who also lived nearby, a highly reliable source inside the Boston Police Department Homicide Division said that "these two brutal crimes may very well be the work of a serial killer. I say that because both women were murdered in an identical manner, after being approached earlier by a stranger who had a large snake tattooed on the back of his right hand.

"There are just too many similarities," added the source, who asked not to be identified because he is not authorized to speak to the news media. He said his homicide team is now "working around the clock to find the killer."

The source also noted that the two murders involved some "spooky elements like you might expect to find in a horror movie." Those elements include eyewitness accounts suggesting that both women were harassed by a "ranting and raving" stranger who claimed to have paranormal abilities, the source said.

He added that the alleged assailant also claimed to be able to "travel through the underworld of the dead like the Greek God Orpheus" and to "invade the nightmares of other people while they were sleeping."

According to the source, the brutal stabbings were so vicious they left "a pond of blood" on the floor and "bloody smears" on nearby walls. The police investigation is continuing.

Stunned by what he'd just read, Jake was staring off into space now. Only one person in the Boston PD had ever described a "pond of blood" at the crime scene— and that person was Tony Rizzo.

"Goddamnit," Jake snapped at the sensational headlines of the tabloid, "I can't believe how *stupid* he is. Why not just make a public announcement warning the sonofabitch that we're on his trail?" Groaning and muttering, he swiveled his eyes down the wrinkled newspaper page . . . where he soon received another ugly shock.

The source went on to say that homicide investigators are so far "completely mystified" by the so-called paranormal aspects of the crime. "Right now, we're totally in the dark," he said. "This whole thing seems stranger every day . . . and it's already gotten so weird that the primary detective on the case—Jake Becker—has recently brought in a team of psychics to work on it.

"He was up in Central Maine just the other day, talking to some experts on nightmares and how to locate crime suspects using unorthodox paranormal techniques based on ESP. Right now, we're just hoping the killer doesn't strike again while we try to figure it all out.

"We don't want to create a sense of panic in Boston, but it's pretty clear the suspect will probably continue to kill until he's stopped. But stopping him is our job—and you can be damn sure we're going to get it done."

There was more, but Jake had seen enough.

After flinging the paper onto the desk, he stalked out of the office and back into the restaurant, where Murray was serving some other customers.

"Murray, I'm sorry but I have to get back to the station."

"What? You gotta take off? Hey, you haven't had your *breakfast* yet!" The deli mogul was staring at his customer as if he'd just stepped from a spaceship.

"I have to go," blurted Jake. "I'm sorry, but it's important. I'll be back to you as soon as I get a chance."

Murray reached out a hand, as if to stop him . . . but the detective was already hurrying toward the door.

***

He found Tony Rizzo hunched over a cup of early-morning coffee in the Homicide Department Conference Room.

He didn't apologize for interrupting his partner's first caffeine dose of the day.

"Tony, I just saw the story on the front of the *Herald*. Do you mind telling me what the hell's going on?"

Rizzo stared blankly at him.

"You leaked that stuff, didn't you?"

Rizzo didn't react at first. Then he set his cup down on the table. "I didn't 'leak' anything," he said. "I gave the info to that reporter straight up, but not for attribution."

"Mark Halliday?"

"That's right."

"A friend of yours?"

"I knew him in college. He's a good man."

"He's a goddamn *scribe*, Tony. We don't talk to scribes—especially about ongoing homicide investigations. You broke a cardinal rule."

Tony pushed his cup farther down the conference table. His bottom lip was sticking out.

"We've been spinning our wheels and getting nowhere," he told Jake after a bit. "I thought I'd throw a scare into our perp, that's all. Let him know the net is starting to close."

"Bullshit." Jake closed his eyes for a moment.

"What you actually did was compromise our investigation. You let him know what *we* know. That's bad police work. Plus it's just plain stupid."

Tony's face darkened. "I'd appreciate it if you keep those kinds of insults to yourself, Mr. Professor. Frankly, I'm getting tired of listening to your comments about my I.Q."

"In this case, the comment was warranted."

Jake was looking directly into Tony's eyes. His gaze didn't waver. "You didn't think, Tony. Leaking that stuff to the press was a terrible blunder."

"Really? I beg to differ, Mr. Professor." Tony's eyes were throwing sparks. "Lemme tell ya, when I was over in Narcotics—where I won half a dozen departmental citations for outstanding police work, I might add—we used the press all the time.

"A couple of times, in fact, we even planted false information in the *Herald* . . . and then busted some major drug suppliers in the middle of multi-million-dollar deals. Those were huge busts, and the dealers got caught because they were stupid enough to believe the disinformation we fed the newspaper."

But Jake was shaking his head. Angrily. "That kind of tactic might have worked in Narcotics—but this is Homicide. We do things differently over here. For starters, we don't try to manipulate the news media."

Tony scowled back at him. "No . . . instead, you spend an entire afternoon conferring with some lady-psychics up in Maine. But that approach doesn't seem to have been working too well for us either—or am I missing something?"

As if to underline his point, he reached for his coffee, lifted it to his mouth—and then made a loud slurping sound. "Deputy Stovall dropped by the office yesterday, in case you haven't heard," Tony continued. "He wanted to know where you were.

"When I told him about Big Pine, he started shaking his head. Then he asked me point blank: 'What the hell's he doing up there? How's he going to find a Boston serial killer up in the Maine woods?'

"I told him I didn't know." Tony slurped loudly again.

Jake took a step closer. "You don't know because you don't understand the background of this case."

Rizzo snorted. "Oh, yeah? Well, I do think I understand we're looking for a scumbag who gets his rocks off by cutting women—two women so far—and we ain't any closer to nailing the perp than we were when the first one got killed.

"I just figured it was time we scared the perp a little, that's all. So I called Halliday."

Jake's left eyelid twitched once . . . twice. *Easy*, he told himself. *Blowing your stack will only make things worse.* He took a deep breath. "Wrong move," he said at last. "You didn't scare him—you warned him, that's all. Your methods are just plain dumb, Tony."

Tony glared. "What methods are those, Jake?"

"Talking to the *Herald*, for one thing. Instead of tipping off the perp, you should have been focusing on the key elements that will take us to him. What you don't seem to understand is that we're looking for an extremely intelligent psychopath who's probably been trained in psychology. He may even be a shrink. If we're going to find him, we have to understand how he *thinks*.

"That's why I was up at Big Pine. The key to making this arrest will be knowing how the killer's mind works. That stuff you learned over in Narcotics—beating the information out of stooges who want to cop a plea and then using it to bust a supplier—won't work with this kind of suspect."

Tony's mouth had split open in an ugly grin. "Uh-huh. So . . . what you're telling me is, I gotta go study for a Ph.D. in psych at Harvard before I can take this motherfucker off the street?"

Jake sighed. "No. But you *do* have to open your mind up. You have to expand your understanding of how these psychopaths *think*. And that takes some knowledge.

"Even more important, it takes some imagination."

"Yeah, right." As if hoping to end the conversation, Tony reached for his coffee cup again. "I appreciate your advice, Jake, but I got my own idea about how we catch this guy, and fast."

"Which is?"

"I go round up a few of the drug snitches I used to work with on the street. I let 'em know what I'm looking for. Then I plant 'em against the nearest wall and I tell 'em if they don't help me find this asshole in two hours,

I'm going to use what I already got on them . . . which means ten years in stir, minimum.

"After they get done shitting themselves, they'll help me find the guy we want, and pronto."

Jake was already waving him away. "I'm not impressed, Tony. All that rough stuff you learned on the street—slapping your stooges around and making threats—isn't going to get the job done here. Why? Because a maniac like this guy is usually also pretty *smart*. You aren't going to find him sitting in a shithole rented room in the Zone, waiting for you to break his door down, no matter how many sick junkies you beat up en route.

"He's too intelligent to sit there passively, waiting for you and your goon squad to bust him—which is precisely why we need the psychological profile I've been putting together, with the help of that psych expert up at Big Pine."

Tony was still smirking. Still grinning sarcastically.

Unconvinced.

CHAPTER 32
Some Bad News for the Commissioner

Ten minutes later, the five men working on the Donovan and Mayhew killings (now minus Tony Rizzo, who'd just been pulled off the case) were sitting in the Conference Room, surrounded by styrofoam coffee cups and ashtrays that would soon be full of cigarette butts.

As usual, Jake started by conducting a thorough review of everything his team had learned so far about the perp.

The two remaining detectives on the team—along with two technicians from the second-floor lab—listened intently as Jake brought them up to speed.

"Our goal is real simple, gentlemen. We need to take this guy down and soon. To do that, we have to rely on solid, detailed, accurate police work. That goes without saying, of course. But in this kind of case, we also need to understand the importance of the *mind*.

"Nailing a serial killer isn't just about matching fingerprints and photographs and criminal records—and then breaking down somebody's door. Why? Because homicide frequently involves *ideas*—the kind of sick, warped ideas that can take over a perpetrator's life and turn him into a demented monster without a shred of conscience.

"If we're going to shut down the bad guy, we gotta understand how he thinks."

Jake gave the team a mild, inquiring gaze. "So let's ask ourselves: what's the sick idea that motivated the guy who killed Tracy Donovan and Elisa Mayhew?

"Let's ask ourselves," he continued. "What similarities did we find at the two crime scenes? Do those similarities tell us anything about the killer's sick idea?" He turned to the lab-tech supervisor, Bert Havrilak, sitting to his immediate left. "We found semen on both mirrors, right, Bert?"

"Correct," said Havrilak. He held up his black plastic notebook for a moment. "Same biochemical readout from both specimens."

Jake nodded. "Which tells us?"

"The same guy did both girls."

"Very good," said Jake. "But what *else* does it tell us, Bert? Does it suggest any *ideas*?"

Havrilak ran a hand along his close-cropped hair. "Well . . . we figure he must've jerked off in front of the mirrors. He was probably looking at himself as he did it. Watching himself, you know?"

Jake frowned. "Very good. Fine. So what does that suggest? Jerking off in front of a mirror, I mean."

Detective Steve Parks chimed in. "Okay, like . . . he wants to see himself as a big shot—a big powerful guy? Like, he's just finished . . . doing this chick, and he jerks himself off in the mirror? It's like, 'Hey, look at me—ain't I a great big deal?'"

Jake was smiling openly now. "Absolutely, Steve. You nailed it. And do you know what the psychologists call that kind of attitude? Huh? *Narcissism*. It's a psychological ailment. Do you know who Narcissus was, Steve?"

The younger cop shook his head.

"Narcissus was a Greek hunter, ancient Greece, who fell in love with himself. He used to stand around for hours at a time, staring at his own reflection in a pool of water."

Jake gave the team a long searching look. "His name is *also* interesting guys. It comes from the Greek word *narke*, which means 'sleep'—and also 'narcotic.' Fascinating, huh? And it's also interesting that Narcissus was eventually destroyed by an angry goddess named Nemesis—the goddess of Revenge. I hope we can be as effective as she was."

Detective Parks was nodding, but he looked puzzled.

"Okay, Jake, that's fine . . . but where does it take us?"

Jake held up one hand. "You'll see, Detective Parks. But let's back up a step and ask ourselves: what other similarities did we find while investigating these two killings?"

The other cops in the room were all scratching their heads and clearing their throats. Nobody spoke. They were wary of looking dumb in front of The Professor.

"Nightmares," said Jake. "The next similarity is *nightmares*. Now, what did Arthur Forbes tell us, right after the bartender at Mulligan's was killed?"

Detective Parks thought for a second. "He said this guy came into the bar on the day of the murder and told Tracy Donovan he was gonna attack her in her dreams. In her *nightmares*. That was how he put it."

Jake nodded cheerfully. "Correct! And what did we read in the second victim's diary?"

Parks didn't respond. But now Havrilak spoke up. "We worked all day on that diary," he told Jake, "and we took a careful look at every single sentence she wrote.

"Her last entry was full of stuff about nightmares, and about this asshole who'd been harassing her at the theater where she worked. Just like with that Forbes guy . . . this creep came into the Orpheum and threatened to attack her during a nightmare."

Once again, Havrilak was holding up his black plastic notebook. He scanned down the page with a finger.

"Get this: 'When I told him to buzz off, he started ranting about nightmares. Told me he'd sneak into *my* nightmares if I didn't do what he wanted!'"

The Conference Room had gone silent again. It stayed that way until Jake finally spoke.

"There's our *second* idea, gentlemen. Our perp seems to believe he has the power to invade other people's nightmares. Huh? He can move at will through your dreams, or so he believes. Now let me ask you all: was there a third similarity between the two killings?"

Jake paused for a moment, then answered the question himself. "The wounds," he said. "The wounds on both of the corpses." He turned toward the two lab guys. "Bert?"

"Yeah," said Bert. "A similarity, you bet. The two women had been cut with the same type of weapon. Fine-edged, you know. A super-sharp cutting surface. A surgical scalpel if you ask me."

Jake was smiling now. "Okay, there's idea number-three," he told them. "A surgical scalpel. Put them all together—all three ideas—and what do you come up with? What have you got? Maybe you've got a power-crazed narcissist who believes he can do the impossible by actually killing people in their dreams.

"You've got an educated guy who talks about Greek mythology. Remember, he tells victim number two all about Orpheus in the Underworld.

"Remember Tommy Ellington? Remember what he told us? This guy is intelligent. He's well-read. He understands psychology. He knows about dreams. And he's using . . . what, to kill his victims?"

Jake looked at them, one by one. "A surgical scalpel, that's what."

They were all staring back at him, waiting for the bottom line. But instead of offering them answers, Jake simply fed them more questions.

"Is he a psychologist, or maybe a counselor of some kind? Is he a psychology professor at one of the colleges or universities around Boston? And what about that scalpel? Is he a medical doctor, an M.D.? Is he a psychiatrist, a shrink who's also trained in surgery? Is he a twisted head-shrink artist who believes his own psychoanalytical bullshit?"

He paused and thought for a moment. Then: "You've all studied the composite drawing they did up in I.D. and Records, right? Based on the stuff we got from Forbes and Ellington and the guy who owns Mulligan's, we now have a drawing of him. And we're looking at what? A round-faced guy, mid-40's, kind of chubby, but also gone to seed. Really grubby, you know? He needs a shave, and he's got these big ugly bags under his eyes, like he's been living on the street for a while.

"Still, he's not that bad-looking. Underneath the wear and tear, he looks like a fairly friendly guy, pleasant enough features. Mild-mannered, at least until he pulls that scalpel out. He's thoughtful looking, not really a bruiser. He seems like the type who probably uses his mind, not his hands, to make a living.

"But is he also a psychopath? Is he a medical guy who got screwed up inside, maybe a medical guy who became obsessed with a sick idea, the same way Narcissus became obsessed with his own image?"

The other investigators looked at each other. They were frowning hard in their efforts to follow Jake's thread. Ideas! But before anybody could say a word, the telephone in the center of the conference table began to chirp.

"Hang on," said Jake. He grabbed it. "Becker here. What's up?"

"Hello, Detective Becker," said the voice on the other end.

"This is Marjorie Evans up in Commissioner Flaherty's office."

Jake didn't respond. He'd been expecting this telephone call, and now it had finally arrived.

"The Commissioner needs to see you, Detective Becker. In his private office.

"Right now."

***

Commissioner Flaherty was a beefy Irishman with snow white hair and the mottled complexion of a veteran cop with a passion for racehorses and Guinness Stout.

He did not seem happy to be greeting Jake.

"Sit down, Detective Becker."

"Yes, sir."

Jake sat.

The big man behind the cluttered desk had been a middle linebacker at Villanova, and the thick scar tissue along his nose told you he'd spent lots of time going up against pulling guards leading pitch-out sweeps.

"Can we go off the record, detective?"

"We can, sir."

"Good," said Flaherty. His hands were folded neatly on his desk. "So let me start it off by asking: why the fuck are the details of your murder investigation all over the front of Rupert Murdoch's shit rag this morning?"

Jake thought for a moment. "Well . . . we obviously sprang a leak."

The Commissioner barked with sudden laughter. "No shit? You sprang a *leak*? How long did it take you to figure *that* out, Sherlock?"

"Not long, sir."

"Who's the leaker and what are you going to do with him?"

"It's Tony Rizzo, sir. He's new in Homicide. A good cop, with ten years in Narcotics, but he's a cowboy who doesn't really understand what he's up against in Homicide.

"He made a bonehead move, thought he could scare the perp out of hiding by going public with some details from our investigation."

The Commissioner was scowling harder than a bulldog with a digestive ailment. "So what happens to him?"

"I think he needs to go back to Narcotics," said Jake. "He's a good cop, but unfortunately, the move to Homicide just didn't work out. I suspended him from our unit already per your approval."

"So be it," said Flaherty. "I'll have the deputy commissioner send the paperwork over right away." He gave The Professor another long brooding look. "That asshole's leak came at a bad time, Jake. Right before you walked in here, I took a call from the mayor. Needless to say, he's not happy."

"No?" said Jake. "I guess he wouldn't be."

"He told me what I already knew, Jake. The leaker's stupidity makes you and your guys look like a bunch of clowns. I'm sure those goddamn 'Staties' are laughing their heads off. Score one for the totally inept Massachusetts State Police. To say nothing of the totally inept Federal Bureau of Investigation.

"Do you have any idea how much those assholes enjoy it when we fuck up?"

Jake winced again. "Yes, sir. I do."

"So does the mayor. And to make matters even worse, he was pissed off even *before* the leak. Do you know why?"

"No, sir. I don't. Is it because the Red Sox are still in third place? I know he's a huge Bosox fan."

The Commissioner's red face turned even redder. "Don't fuck with me, Becker. The mayor is unhappy because we've had two young women brutally murdered recently, in circumstances that would suggest a single killer who didn't know either of his victims. Are you following my drift?"

"I am."

"Good. The perp cut them both to pieces," said Flaherty. "I'm told he slashed their arteries and they bled to death. Still with me?"

"I am."

"Good." The boss's hands were unfolded now, and the index finger on one of them was pointed directly at Jake's chest. "As up to date as you seem to be, detective, you probably also know that this is 1986 . . . and that we've got a citywide election coming up in a few months."

Jake nodded. "Yes, sir. I'm aware of that fact."

The Commissioner had begun rummaging in a drawer on the right side of his desk. "Goddamnit . . . where did she put those . . . oh, *here* we go."

He held up a short, stubby cigar. "Hav-a-Tampa," he told Jake. "I swear by them, especially in moments of stress. Want one?"

Jake shook his head. "No, sir. Thank you. I don't smoke."

There was a long pause while the Commissioner unwrapped the panatela and gripped its birchwood tip between his teeth. Then a match flared, momentarily bathing his features in a bluish light. "You're the point man on this investigation," he said thoughtfully, "and I was looking for you yesterday, so I rang your office."

He inhaled, then jetted a plume of gray smoke.

"They told me you were up in Maine, visiting some goddamn outer space think tank. Something like that."

Jake nodded. "Yes, sir. The Big Pine Research Center for the Study of the Paranormal."

The Commissioner's blue eyes widened noticeably. "The paranormal, was it?"

"Yes, sir."

The hulking former linebacker on the other side of the desk squinted through a cloud of cigar smoke. "I tried to call you up there but they said you couldn't be reached."

"Yes, sir. I was out of pocket for a bit, talking to a researcher."

The Commissioner thought about this reply. "Pardon my inquisitiveness, detective, but why the fuck were you up in Maine, doing the paranormal thing . . . when I've got two murdered women in Boston and the mayor riding my ass?"

Jake was nodding thoughtfully now. "Oh, that. Believe me, I can understand why you might . . . but the fact is, I'm working on a psychological profile of the killer. You see, we think he may be some kind of doctor, maybe a rogue psychiatrist who's obsessed with nightmares—"

But the rest of Jake's reply was cut off.

"Wait a minute, goddamnit," interrupted the Commissioner as he picked up the ringing telephone beside his huge right paw.

"Flaherty. Talk to me."

He sat immobile, listening, and his expression did not change. Smoke leaked ominously from the Hav-a-Tampa. Had it been packed with dynamite?

"Thank you," he finally said.

He hung up.

"We've got another one," he said.

Jake stared at him, wordless.

"A salesclerk at Filene's," said Commissioner Flaherty.

"They just found her slashed to death in a ritzy townhouse over on Beacon Hill."

CHAPTER 33
A Ton of Questions . . .
and Not a Single Answer

It was the same story all over again—but this time the details were even harder to fathom.

The victim, 25-year-old Tiffany Blake, had been cut to pieces the night before while visiting her cousin Amanda Hazlett in her posh three-story townhouse at 114 Mt. Vernon Street in the heart of exclusive Beacon Hill.

Somehow, the killer had been able to gain access to Tiffany's guest bedroom during the night.

Once again, no one on the premises had heard any sounds of struggle or screams of fear—even though the townhouse occupants had included four overnight guests sleeping in rooms near that of the victim.

Once again, the scene in the dead woman's bedroom was stark enough to make even a seasoned homicide detective like Jake pause and struggle for air.

This time, Jake didn't need Dr. Pino to point out the obvious—the gruesome fact that the victim had been slashed at least thirty times with a fine-edged weapon.

"This guy's MO is getting old," the medical examiner told Jake. "He cut her up like a damn watermelon. She must've bled out in a matter of minutes."

Jake didn't respond right away. He was examining the upscale bedroom, where the satin throw pillows and gauzy wall hangings were now defaced with reddish-brown smears of slowly congealing blood. Then he was circling the body spread-eagled on the floor and studying the tiny card that had been affixed to an adjoining doorway. It read: *Salle de Bain*.

"French for bathroom," said Jake.

He stepped inside and pulled the golden brass chain dangling from an antique lamp.

A minute passed, and then he walked back to rejoin the medical examiner.

"Dr. Pino, you should probably take a sample of the white cloudy substance on the bathroom mirror."

"Got it," said the man in the white coat.

"Same old same old," said Jake. "Am I right?"

"You probably are."

Jake thought for a minute. "How does a woman get slashed to death in a house full of guests, without anybody hearing a peep?"

"It's a puzzle, all right," said Dr. Pino. "So what next?"

Jake frowned. "Next I talk to the residents and their guests."

***

The Professor assembled everyone in the drawing room on the first floor.

They sat at a British eighteenth-century mahogany Hepplewhite dining table, where they were bathed in the soft glow from a leaded glass chandelier. The walls were painted in creamy pastels and adorned with bright swatches of lace, along with a couple of glittering brass sconces.

"I know this has been pretty tough on all of you, and especially you, Amanda," said Jake. "Can I just get you and your friends here to think back a little on what happened last night?"

"Okay," said Amanda. "I'll do my best, officer."

Amanda Hazlett was a tall thin woman whose brown eyes vibrated with shock and fear. "My cousin—Tiffany, I mean—got here about ten o'clock. She'd been working on a project. She builds these little dollhouses and stuff. She was really very good at it."

"All right," said Jake. He looked calm and relaxed, but the wheels were turning beneath. "Just take your time, Amanda, and try not to leave anything out."

"Yes, sir," said Amanda. Her mouth was trembling, and she kept fingering a pack of Marlboros on the mahogany table as if she wanted desperately to light up. "You know, we all played charades until probably two o'clock in the morning. We . . . we were drinking some wine—"

Amanda looked down toward the end of the table, where her husband Adam, a highly successful trader at First Boston, gave his salon-styled head a barely perceptible shake.

Jake read it in a flash: *Don't tell him about the pot, Mandy.*

"So we, you know, we drank the wine and played charades, and it got pretty noisy . . . lots of laughter . . . and we hardly noticed the time, until around two a.m. or so, give or take a few minutes.

"Well, all at once Tiffany said she was getting a headache" (here she looked at Adam and got another subtle head shake) . . . "you know, from the *wine*?

"So we told her, no problem, go on to bed, honey. We'll see you for brunch in the morning."

Amanda fell silent for a moment, and all six witnesses stared at the table. Amanda's lower lip had begun to tremble harder now; she looked as if she might lose it at any moment.

"Just take it slow and easy," said Jake. "Try to remember everything you can. You never know when the smallest detail might prove helpful."

"Okay, I'll do my best," said Amanda. But the trembling had only gotten worse. "Tiffany went up to bed, and that was the last we heard from her. Everything was peaceful, you know?"

She gave Detective Becker a panicky look and he wasn't surprised to see that her soft brown eyes were now glistening with tears.

"We played charades some more, maybe another forty-five minutes or so. Then the rest of us drifted off to bed. We never heard a sound after that. I remember noticing the mantel clock in our room. It pinged three times, right as I was falling asleep, so that had to be around 3 a.m.

"I slept pretty soundly, till almost nine, but I was still the first one up. I put the coffee on and started getting a bunch of stuff ready for the brunch. You know, the 'morning-after brunch' is a tradition around here."

The witnesses were all looking down at the table again. Amanda was wiping her eyes on a stiff brocaded napkin she'd found somewhere.

"Everybody was awake and up by ten or so, but . . . no Tiffany. So finally Adam said, 'You better call her.' I grabbed a cup of black coffee, with just some Sweet'N Low—I know the way she likes her coffee. . . ."

She paused and made a low sobbing sound, and they watched her gripping the edge of the table. Her knuckles were chalk white and her upper lip twitched and jumped.

"So I . . . I carried the coffee up to her room. I knocked a couple of times, no answer. Knocked again . . . still nothing. So I kind of . . . gently hollered, if you know what I mean? 'Tiffany, stand by, honey, I'm coming in!'

"Then I pushed the door open, real slow, you know, not wanting to be rude . . . and I found . . . I found . . . .

"Oh, my God!" Suddenly her shoulders were heaving and jerking and she was weeping fiercely: "Tiffany, Tiffany, how could this have happened? Who *did* this to you?"

Badly frightened, Amanda's husband was on his feet now and hurrying down the length of the table to stand behind her chair and slowly massage her shoulders.

"It's okay, baby. Just take your time. Just take it slow and easy, Mandy. It's going to be okay."

The table fell silent after that, except for the sound of Amanda's weeping. Jake was scribbling in a pocket notebook. He kept it up for more than a minute. When he looked around the table again, his face was calm and neutral.

"All right, Amanda, thank you. I know this isn't easy, believe me. But I need to ask: did anybody here notice anything at all after Tiffany went upstairs to sleep? I understand that you didn't hear anything coming out of Tiffany's room . . . but I'm wondering . . . did you *see* anything? Any signs of movement? Did you hear even the squeak of a door opening somewhere? Think hard, please. It's really important."

Another long silence at the table. Jake watched them shaking their heads and staring at the design of piled grapes and wheat shocks in the expensive carpet. Nobody said a word.

He gave it a good minute or so, then sighed heavily.

"All right," he said. From his front dress-shirt pocket he'd produced a small memo pad. "I'd like each one of you to write down your full names, addresses and phone numbers," he told them quietly. "I'm also going to give each of you my business card.

"It's really important, folks: if you do remember anything unusual from last night, any detail—no matter how small or insignificant it may seem to you—please call me right away. I'd also ask you not to leave the Greater Boston area until such time as the Police Department authorizes your travel."

No one moved. Ten seconds passed. Adam Hazlett's hand went up.

"Excuse me, detective, but Amanda and I were planning to visit her mother in New York this coming weekend."

Jake didn't hesitate. "I'm sorry," he said calmly, "but I'm going to have to ask you to postpone that visit for a while. Right now, we need all of you to stay in Boston and environs so we can reach you easily if we need to."

They were all nodding back at him now, white-faced and frightened. Jake didn't blame them for being afraid, either. How could Tiffany's killer have gained entry to her room?

How could he have slashed her again and again, without triggering a single cry of alarm from his hideously slaughtered victim?

Spooky, Jake told himself. Very spooky, indeed.

No wonder they're terrified.

CHAPTER 34
A Major Breakthrough in Chicago?

Saturday morning.

Seated before the teletype keyboard in the homicide communications complex, Detective Becker typed a request to NCIC.

TO: FBI National Crime Information Center
FROM: Jake Becker, Boston, Ma. ID #22-D61,
    Hom Div
SUBJECT: Info Request, Hom Div; MO Inquiry
REQUEST:

Boston PD Homicide investigating three recent murders involving fine blade cutting tool, probably scalpel. Suspect enters domiciles in early morning hours while victims sleep, but no signs of B&E. Method of entry is unclear in all three killings. Sending Boston PD composite drawing via closed-circuit video channel. No theft. Motive not yet determined. Victims appear to be carefully chosen and suspect reportedly (witnesses) visits them and warns them he will "attack them in their nightmares," then reappears and kills them within a day or two. One victim left diary saying alleged perp had a snake tattoo on one hand. Leaves "calling card" semen traces on mirrors at all three crime scenes.

Does NCIC have any matching MOs in National Files? Please advise,

J. Becker, Boston PD, Hom Div

Jake read the message over slowly and then hit the SEND button.

It was a long shot, but maybe something would turn up. The NCIC system had been operating for nearly two decades, after all; by now their files contained several million crime reports, fugitive descriptions and conviction/parole records.

Most of the stuff was computerized and teletype-networked to police departments all across the country.

It was worth a try.

Jake signed off . . . then rose slowly from his chair.

Time for another cup of coffee from the Jack in the Box fast food joint across the street? Right then, it was his only option, since the Police Department cafeteria was closed on weekends, and the coffee in the vending machines tasted like month-old crankcase oil.

For longtime coffee addicts like Becker, the Jack was the most convenient place to get a cup of coffee on weekends.

Let's go. He stopped by his cubicle for a moment to grab his raincoat—a line of thunderstorms seemed to have been camping out over the city for the past few hours—but just as he put his hand on the green London Fog, the phone rang.

"Hello. Becker."

"Jake?"

"Yes?"

"Lieutenant Vandergriff, over at CID."

"Yes, sir."

"I just talked to the Commissioner. Wanted to make sure we're all on the same page."

"Sure thing," said Jake.

"I'm sending through the paperwork on Tony Rizzo, who's been reassigned to Narcotics, effective immediately."

"Yes, sir. Got it. Thanks for keeping me in the loop."

"Sure thing. That's all, detective."

The line went dead.

Jake returned to his chair and sat motionless for a minute. Tony Rizzo would not be pleased, but he'd brought the reassignment on himself and there was nothing Becker could do about it. It was a damn shame, though, and now the hotheaded Rizzo would probably be his enemy for life.

Too bad, thought Jake. *He's not a bad guy . . . just too emotional and impulsive for his own good.* He watched the summer rain trickling down the one small window next to his cubicle. Suddenly the idea of coffee from Jack in the Box seemed pointless.

Sighing wearily, he reached for the folder that contained the composite drawing in HOM DIV/DONOVAN/MAYHEW/BLAKE.

***

Rozzie was scanning the front page of the weekly *Moosehead Antler*, and it didn't take her long to spot the story about the mega-rich developers from New York City who were scheming to build a $70 million hotel on 100 acres of prime lakefront property.

NYC Development Firm Planning to Build
Giant Hotel Complex on Moosehead Lake

"Goddamnit," Rozzie barked in her empty office, "Those bastards will *not* get away with this. It's time to put up the dukes!"

But then her thoughts were interrupted by the jangling of the office telephone. Would her aggravation never end? Sighing, she waited as always for the fifth ring and then grabbed it.

"Hello, Big Pine."

"Rozzie, it's me, Charly. I hope you don't mind me calling. I found your number on my dad's desk pad, and I didn't know who else to call."

Roz was pleased—and thoroughly startled—to hear her youthful voice. "Hi, Charly. What a nice surprise. What's happening, my friend?"

"Rozzie, I don't know what to do. I can't stop crying."

The Big Pine executive director fell back in her padded chair. In a flash, the Moosehead Lake development scheme was forgotten. "What is it, Charly? What's wrong, honey?"

"It's my boyfriend, Tanner. He broke up with me! And what's worse, he didn't even have the guts to tell me himself. I had to find out from Trisha. She told me she saw Tanner at the movies with this slut senior cheerleader. She said Tanner was kissing her and . . . and . . ."

Roz thought for a moment. How could she help? "Sweetheart, why don't you take a deep breath and try to relax? You're all wound up. Hey, everything's gonna be okay!"

"No, it's not, Rozzie." Charly emitted a loud sob.

"Everything's *not* going to be okay. I wish I was dead!"

Roz gripped the phone. "No, you don't, dear. You certainly don't. Look . . . can you tell me what happened? How long had you and Tanner been dating?"

"Since last Christmas. He's a junior, and I'm only a freshman . . . but he told me he loved me. Well, he lied! I guess he'd rather be with his little cheerleader."

"Have you spoken to Tanner about this? Have you told him how you feel?"

Charly sobbed again. "No! Of course not! What's there to talk about? He wouldn't have gone out with *her* if he still loved *me*."

Rozzie's attempt at therapy wasn't working—but she refused to give up. "Charly, trust me. You're disappointed now, but you'll get over it soon. Really, you just have to—"

"Boys are all pigs, Rozzie!" the kid cut her off. "I hate them all. I'm never going to let myself fall in love again for the rest of my life.

"I'll be a lesbian and I won't need boys ever!"

Rozzie groaned . . . but a moment later she thought she saw a way out. "You know what I think, Charly?"

"What?"

"I think Tanner did you a huge favor."

"Why? How?"

"Because it's a lot better to find out now that he's a jerk—rather than waste any more time on him. A leopard doesn't change its spots. Know what I mean?

"I'm sure you can do better than *that* idiot, Charly!"

There was a long silence while the kid weighed this advice. Then: "I'm sorry, but there's more, Rozzie. I've been having these terrible nightmares, too. I dreamed my dad fell off a roof or something like that. He just kept on falling . . . and he was screaming about some huge bug with lots of legs and a bleeding tattoo of a snake.

"It was so disgusting that when I woke up I almost threw up all over my bed. I'm worried something bad is going to happen to my dad. I can't lose him, Rozzie. He's all I have. What would I do if something bad happened to him?

"I don't think I'd be able to go on—not without my dad!"

Roz frowned. "Where's your father right now?"

"I don't *know* where he is. He's hardly ever home anymore. All he cares about is that stupid murder case. He doesn't even know about Tanner and me, because I never told him."

"Your father is trying desperately to find a murderer," Rozzie replied. "You do understand that, am I right?"

"Yeah, I guess so. But what about me? I need him, too."

"Of course you do, sweetie. And he loves you very much. Believe me, I could tell when you two were up here that he absolutely adores you."

Charly sent up an unhappy sigh on her end. "Yeah, okay . . . fine. But I never *see* him anymore—not since we got back from Big Pine. At breakfast all he does is give me a kiss on my head. Then he says, 'Love you,' and he's out the door.

"And he's never home at night to help me with my homework either. All Mrs. Whitney does is fold laundry and fill out her crossword puzzles. It's like she's not even *there* most of the time."

Rozzie pondered the situation. For the moment, she was at a loss.

But Charly was plunging ahead. "Mrs. Whitney told me she's worried about me, too. She says I'm not eating and I'm pale as a ghost. She told me I look awful.

"What am I going to do, Rozzie?"

The psychic nodded. "Charly, I've got a great suggestion. Why don't you talk to Alix? She's got a lot more experience at counseling people than I do. Besides, she's a *real* psychologist . . . and I'm just a fruitcake psychic. Hah-hah, just kidding! Anyway, I've got a feeling she could really help you right now.

"How about if I have her give you a call? Would that be all right?"

"If you say so, Rozzie."

A lengthy silence followed, during which Roz could almost read the kid's mind: *I sure wish I had a mom right now.*

***

Jake picked up. Listened for a moment. His eyes widened. The call was from the FBI in Chicago.

"Detective Becker? This is FBI Special Agent Fred Gustafson."

"Hello," said Jake. "What can I do for you, Agent Gustafson?"

"Well, it's more like, what can I do for *you*? I'm responding to your NCIC query of yesterday morning."

Jake's eyes were wide open by now.

"I'll be sending you a formal Teletype reply later in the day," said the FBI investigator, "but I wanted to put a voice behind it first. I figured it might be helpful to give you a personal heads-up on your three killings in Boston."

"Many thanks," said Jake. "What've you got?"

"Okay, for starters, we've got the killing of a well-known Chicago medical doctor, a famous surgeon. The murder took place in late May at his home in an affluent section of the city, Lincoln Park. Here's the possible connection to your three cases. First, the victim was stabbed to death with a fine-bladed cutting tool, probably a surgical scalpel, according to our lab guys. Also, he was killed in his own bedroom late at night—in a locked-up private dwelling with a state-of-the-art alarm system. No evidence of a break-in."

Jake was listening intently. "That scenario sounds very familiar," he told Special Agent Gustafson. "What else you got?"

"Plenty," said the special agent. "The crime scene was pretty grisly, with blood spattered on several walls. The Chicago PD took samples and asked for our help analyzing them. We did an initial biochemical assay, and we came up with an interesting finding.

"It seems that some of the blood on the walls wasn't the victim's, which means it almost certainly came from the killer."

Jake was sitting bolt upright in his chair. "Are you saying you think you might have some of the perp's blood?"

"That's right. We're certain the two samples we collected at the scene came from two different people, since they contained two different blood types. Right now, we don't know anything more than that. Unfortunately, we don't have the DNA analysis capability required for genetic fingerprinting, which could tell us much more about the killer's identity. That technology has only been available for about a year, mostly in England.

"It's a really powerful tool, but we have to send our blood samples over to a new biotech firm in London that does DNA analytics.

"Anyway, that's a much more complex operation. We sent them our blood work a couple of weeks ago, so we ought to be getting the results back soon. That should help us get a much more detailed look at the killer's identity."

"That's very good news," said Jake.

"Oh, and there's one more thing. Apparently, the perpetrator also left a drawing on a wall mirror in the victim's bedroom."

"Really?" Jake frowned. Squinted. He could almost sense what was coming next.

"Yup. It looks exactly like a snake," said Special Agent Gustafson. "Pretty weird, huh?

"A tiny snake drawn on the mirror—in the perpetrator's own blood. I made a special note on that, since you mentioned a guy with a snake tattoo on his hand in your report."

Jake nodded. He was thinking about Elisa Mayhew's diary.

"Thanks, Fred. That snake thing is very helpful. I think this might turn out to be our guy. What's the status of your investigation at this point?"

"Well, most of it's being run by the Chicago PD. One of their heavy hitters, a guy named Hank Jarreau, is in charge. He's the primary investigator on the case, and he's an experienced homicide cop. Jarreau is one of those hard-nosed Cajun guys. Grew up in a Louisiana bayou. Anyway, he's your man. I'll send you our formal update in a couple of hours."

"Sounds good, Fred." Jake meditated for a moment. "Say . . . I'm just thinking out loud here. If I can get to Chicago, have you got time to sit down with me?"

"Sure thing," said Gustafson. "Happy to help. I can probably get Detective Jarreau to join us as well. We're located in the Dirksen Courthouse Building on South

Dearborn—just take the Blue Line from O'Hare Airport and get off at the Jackson stop. We're at 200 Jackson. You can't miss it."

Jake was scribbling on a Post-It Note: *200 Jackson, Loop.*

"Sounds like a plan, Fred. I gotta talk to a couple of our people here, but I'll get back to you pronto to set up the time for a meeting. Okay by you?"

"You bet."

"Many thanks. Back to you ASAP."

Jake hung up. He sat motionless at his desk for a few moments, thinking about what he'd just learned.

Another locked crime scene, no B&E, and a scalpel-killer who attacks his victims while they sleep and then paints a snake on a mirror in his own blood. Once again . . . a narcissist acting out his inner torment while looking into a mirror?

All at once, his next move seemed clear.

This might be the break they needed to identify the killer.

Chicago, here I come.

***

Jake took the stairs two at a time, but when he pushed open the door marked HOM DIV HQ, he saw that his timing was bad.

Very bad.

The Commissioner was standing in the middle of the room, flanked by the Chief of Detectives and at least half a dozen members of the departmental brass. He was holding the usual smoldering Hav-a-Tampa cigar stub in his right hand, and the wooden mouthpiece had been gnawed down to a soggy mess.

"Good of you to join us, Detective Becker," said the Commissioner, "especially since you happen to be the subject of our present conversation."

He stuck the gnarled cigar end in his mouth, then pulled it out again.

"I just left the mayor's office. It was my third visit there this week, mind you.

"I'm sorry to report that he's not terribly impressed with your work."

Jake didn't reply at first. Then, choosing his words carefully: "We're doing everything we can, sir, and we're doing it as *quickly* as we can."

"Really?" The cigar was taking a terrible beating now, as the Commissioner ground away at it.

"Well, Jake, I'd like to *quote* the mayor at this point. May I do that?"

"Yes, sir."

"He just said to me, and this is an exact quote: 'Flaherty, we've got three women slaughtered in cold blood by a serial-killing maniac, and it looks to me like the guys on your homicide team are standing around with their thumbs up their asses—when they aren't busy leaking key details to the *Herald*, that is.'

"Quote, unquote."

Jake didn't say anything.

The Commissioner wasn't finished yet.

"Speaking of the *Herald*," he growled at his chief homicide detective, "it may interest you to know they received a letter this morning from a very unusual correspondent."

By now he was reaching into his suit coat pocket and retrieving a sheet of paper.

"It seems that the *Herald* has a new pen pal, Becker. They're planning to run his letter tomorrow. The lab techs are working on the original as we speak. I was going to hand deliver this copy to you right after our meeting . . . but now that you've arrived, I'll be happy to read you the contents myself."

"All right," said Jake. "Thank you."

"The letter is addressed to Mark Halliday, the *Herald* reporter who broke the story."

The Commissioner gave Jake a long baleful look, then opened the sheet of paper and read the handwritten letter slowly, carefully enunciating each word.

Halliday,

You tell your police snitch to pass the word—you can't stop me. I don't exist in your world. You get that? My only reason for being is to cause pain and death.

I'll continue to murder until my last breath.

The police think they're so smart. But they're just a bunch of dumb fools. They have no idea how powerful and destructive I've become. I am invincible! I will be known forever as the worst serial murderer in all of history. My victims will fill your morgues. I'll make Jack the Ripper look like a choir boy.

How, you ask? Simple. I have the power to travel through the Dream World and invade the nightmares of my victims. That's when I murder them. No one can escape. I live forever!

—The Surgeon

Jake reflected briefly. His brain was whirling—*I have the power to travel through the Dream World!*—and it was difficult to focus. He took a deep breath. Then: "Commissioner Flaherty, we just got what looks like it could be a break on the case. From Chicago."

"Really?" The cigar end glowed cherry red for a moment as the Commissioner took a deep drag.

"Same basic M.O., with only a couple of minor differences. Same kind of weapon, and he leaves a snake painted on a mirror—in human blood. I'd say there's a good chance this is the same guy who murdered the three women in Boston.

"Really?"

"Yes, sir.

"So what's next, Detective Becker?"

"I need to go to Chicago to talk with the FBI and the homicide detective who's running their investigation on the killing there. I think this could be the breakthrough we've been waiting for, sir."

The Commissioner nodded. Dragged on what was left of his cigar. "Okay, Becker, fine. Here, you better take my copy of the letter—your team will want to examine the contents in detail, I'm sure."

He handed the photocopy to the detective. "Before you leave, however, I've got one more question for you."

Jake nodded at him. "Fire away, sir."

"If you need to go to Chicago to get it done, why are you still standing in this room gabbing with us?"

"Yes, sir."

Jake turned.

Pushed his way back through the swinging double doors that led out of HOM DIV HQ.

Ten seconds later, he was hustling toward his office, where he made a quick call to Special Agent Gustafson and then another to United. The next plane to the Windy City was scheduled to leave Boston in three and a half hours.

Becker would be on it.

But not until after he called Charly and Mrs. Whitney, so he could make sure the kid would be okay during his absence.

CHAPTER 35
A Powwow at Big Pine

Alix and Rozzie were in the middle of a powwow in her office. It was ten minutes past four, only an hour after Charly's hysterical phone call to the BP Director.

"So . . . okay, I get it," said Alix. "The poor kid is miserable. She needs a mothering touch. What do you think I should do?"

Rozzie didn't miss a beat. "That's an easy one, Alix. Call Jake right now. Somebody needs to give him a whack on the head about Charly and that dumper-boyfriend of hers. Apparently, the dad is clueless."

Alix nodded. She liked the idea. But she also knew her request would require skilled diplomacy. "What should I say to him?"

"Once again, my dear, that's easy. Just tell him you wanted to find out how Charly's doing. Like . . . you heard from me that she was feeling down about her social life. That kind of thing. Look, it's pretty obvious . . . the poor guy's working day and night, trying to find that crazy killer. He's obsessed and I don't blame him.

"It's understandable that he'd be distracted, but that doesn't change the fact that Charly really needs him right now."

Alix concurred. "You bet she does. Remember being fourteen, Roz? Remember getting dumped?"

Rozzie moaned in assent. She thought for a few seconds. Then her eyes lit up. "Alix, listen. I've got a suggestion.

"Actually, it's *more* than just a suggestion. It's an official Rozzie Directive!"

"I'm ready." Alix had snapped to attention.

"You've been at Big Pine now for how long? Five weeks? Six weeks? Why don't you take a few days for yourself? Get away for a bit. Enjoy some soul time and recharge the batteries."

Alix was watching Roz closely. "Okay . . . not a bad idea. Continue, please."

Roz grinned slyly. "I checked the bus schedule right after I talked to Charly, and there's a Peter Pan running out of Bangor every day that will get you to Boston by late afternoon. I'll drive you over. Hey, I know how much you love riding in the Rozmobile!

"Seriously. You could help Jake on his case *and* spend some quality face time with Charly."

All at once, Alix's eyes were shining. "I like it, Roz. I like it a lot. But how do you suggest I go about setting it up?"

"Simple. Call Jake and tell him you were thinking about taking a trip to Boston. Tell him you want to get away from Big Pine for a few days and do some shopping."

Roz reflected for a bit and then frowned. "But please be careful. I promised Charly I wouldn't tell her father about the boyfriend horrors. And I can't break a promise to her—she's way too sweet for that! I hate to see her so sad . . . and she also seems terribly frightened about her dad in some strange way.

"When I talked to her, I got the feeling she was terrified about what might happen to her if she lost him. I wonder if maybe she's still struggling with her mom's early death, somewhere way down deep."

Alix sighed. "Poor kid. Losing her mother must've been tough." She thought for a while, then grinned at her pal. "Rozzie, I like your plan; it sounds like a winner."

"You bet it is, girl. And the best part is . . . it's also a wonderful opportunity for you to get closer to Jake. Do you see where I'm trying to go with this?"

"I do, my friend. And I thank you for it."

Rozzie's gung-ho smile blazed up again. "Don't forget, I have staggering powers as a psychic. And when it comes to Alix Cassidy, I can see into the future. I see you helping Jake to catch the bad guy and stop these terrible murders. I see you happy and content with him in the days ahead.

"I also see you growing spiritually and growing fast— even if there may be a bit of turmoil involved."

Rozzie reached over and patted her friend's hand.

"You're an old soul, Alix. You're here in this life to heal. That's what brought you to Big Pine, I'm sure of it. You think it was a coincidence? You've seen the other side, my dear. Not many people can say that. It's an amazing gift and I won't allow you to waste it."

For once, Alix was speechless, at least momentarily. But her eyes were now full of bright energy.

"I'll do it, Rozzie. I'll make the call." She gave her friend a searching look.

"You really think it's the right move, huh?"

"I do. As a matter of fact, I *know* it is. Now go ring that man ASAP!"

***

Fred Haskins was eyeballing the *Herald's* sports page when the call came in.

"Homicide, Detective Haskins."

"Thank you. I need to speak with Detective Jake Becker. Is he available?"

"Sorry, ma'am. You just missed him. Anything I can help you with?"

"Do you know how I can get in touch with him?"

"Not sure. He didn't tell me where he was going. I'm Detective Fred Haskins, his new partner."

"New partner?" Alix was confused. "Jake told me his partner was a Detective Rizzo."

"Ahhh . . . well, there's been an internal reorganization. Tony's been assigned elsewhere for the moment. But I'm filling in, no problem.

"Can I give Detective Becker a message from you?"

"Sure thing, Detective Haskins. Please tell him Dr. Alix Cassidy called from Maine."

There was a pause. . . .

"I see. Alix Cassidy. Pardon me, but you must be the psychic lady I heard about, working at that paranormal center up there?"

Alix chose not to answer this query.

"Please be sure to ask Detective Becker to call me. It's important. He probably has the number—but just in case he misplaced it, it's 207-555-2082."

***

On the fifth ring, Rozzie answered. "Big Pine."

"Rozzie, it's Jake Becker. I'm returning Alix's call. She said it was important. Is she there?"

"You're in luck, Detective Becker. She's sitting in my office at this very moment."

A second later, Jake heard her tell Alix, "It's Detective Becker. He wants to talk to you."

Then, with a sly wink (*you can do this!*), the BP director passed the phone to her friend.

"Hi there, Jake. How you doing?"

"Hello, Alix. It's good to talk with you again. As for your question . . . well, I've been better. Much better, in fact."

"Oh, dear. I'm sorry to hear that. More problems with the case?"

"I'll say. I'm sorry to report that we've had another one."

Alix took a sharp breath. "Another murder?"

"That's right. And it was brutal. A department store saleswoman. Same scenario. The killer accosts her during the day, threatens to show up in her dreams. Then she's found dead."

Alix was listening hard. "Oh, how dreadful. How absolutely awful."

She hesitated briefly. "Jake . . . I've been thinking a lot about you and your investigation. I've also been wondering how I might be able to help."

She breathed deeply and then took the plunge.

"As a matter of fact, I was just about to call you again—but you beat me to it!"

"Really?" said Jake. "You were going to call about our investigation?"

"Well . . . not exactly."

Alix closed her eyes, struggled for the right words. "You see, I talked to Rozzie. It seems she got a call from your daughter."

"She did? Charly called Rozzie?"

"That's right."

"But . . . why? I know they got on pretty well together, out on the lake. . . ."

Alix clenched her jaw. She wanted the next part to go right. "Ah . . . well, you know. Charly was kind of upset?

School stuff. Teen stuff, I guess. Anyway, she shared her feelings with Rozzie, and Rozzie sensed that she was feeling kind of blue. Kind of *down*, if you know what I mean?"

"Down?" said Jake. "Down about what? She hasn't said anything to me."

"No?" said Alix. "Well, that's understandable, I guess. I know you're totally caught up in your police investigation. It's not my business, of course—but Rozzie seems to think. . . ."

"Out with it, Alix. What's going on? Is Charly okay?"

"Oh . . . I'm sure she is. Really, I am. But school . . . you know, the social scene—she's kind of down about that stuff right now. She was sharing some pain, some anxiety with Roz. You know how maternal Roz can be. She's like a mother to half the staff up here at Big Pine."

"Uh-huh."

Alix pictured him alarmed and glaring on his end.

"Jake . . ." and she took another deep breath: "I . . . I have an idea I'd like to discuss. I don't want to intrude, you know that . . . but I thought, given the circumstances, and with your new murder having just occurred, and Charly's situation—"

She closed her eyes and then blurted it out in a wild rush. "I was figuring I might take a break for a few days and maybe come down to Boston? It's been more than 12 years since my last visit to the city. Well, to tell you the truth, I never *wanted* to come back. Not until now, that is.

"Anyway, I was thinking, if you approved . . . since you're so busy, maybe Charly and I could spend some time together? Maybe go shopping or catch a movie, something like that?"

Jake was silent for a few moments.

Alix held her breath.

How long was it since she'd last felt this much tension, this much suspense while talking to a man?

When Jake finally spoke again, he said, "Alix, I think that's a *great* idea!"

She let out a big sigh of relief. "You could help me with the case, for one thing," he went on, "and I need all the help I can get.

"But right now, I'm more concerned about Charly. What's her problem? Do you know? Can you help me at all?"

Alix tried. "Ah . . . well, Rozzie says it's just . . . you know, teen stuff."

He looked worried. "Boy stuff? *Sex* stuff?" he blared. "Is *that* part of it?"

Alix let out a slow breath. "Jake . . . I gotta take the Fifth! But really . . . Roz didn't sound too alarmed. I gather she thinks it's pretty normal. Just some adolescent turmoil erupting in Charly, know what I mean?"

"Okay, then," said Jake. But he didn't sound convinced, and she could tell he was grilling himself about whether or not he'd been paying enough attention to his daughter.

"Anyway, I do think you could help her," he added after a bit. "The kid does need some mothering, that's for sure. And I'd insist you stay at our place. We live in this great big old house . . . you'd have plenty of room and lots of privacy.

"When were you thinking of coming?"

She saw her opening and went for it. "Would tomorrow be too soon? There's a bus I can catch over in

Bangor, and Rozzie says she'll be glad to run me over there in her pickup.

"The schedule says I'd arrive in Boston's South Station around six p.m., if that works for you."

He laughed out loud. "Sure thing, Alix. I'd love to see you again—and I know Charly would, too. But there's a complication. I'm about to leave for Chicago tonight. We think we may have caught a big break in the case. So tomorrow's no good, but I expect to be back in Boston by Friday.

"How about I call you then to firm up our plans and make sure you can catch the bus on Saturday?"

Alix went for it. "That's even better, Jake. It will give me time to take care of some odds and ends up here at Big Pine. But are you sure Saturday afternoon around six will work for you?"

"You bet it will!" Suddenly, Jake felt much lighter, much quicker on his feet.

"I'll *make* it work, Alix.

"And I'll look forward to seeing you at the bus station on Saturday!"

CHAPTER 36
Some FBI Findings . . .
and a Hoodoo Drawing

He took the Blue Line train from O'Hare—a muscular, broad-shouldered man with a heavy black briefcase in his lap. It was full of laboratory findings and witness statements and diary entries and coroners' reports . . . all of which in one way or another focused on the word *murder*.

Jake Becker's bulging briefcase was a catalogue of violent death, which explained why he sat grim-faced and unsmiling as the elevated train clattered to a stop and the loudspeakers in the ceiling suddenly began to blare.

This is Jackson. Please watch your step as you leave the car. This is a Blue Line train to Forest Park. . . .

Outside the busy station, he discovered that it had begun to rain.

Jake was in the Windy City, all right. Amazed, he watched a sudden gale from Lake Michigan driving the deluge through the skyscraper canyons, then blasting it toward the narrow river that gave Chicago its name.

Half-running, his shoulders hunched against the storm, he crab-stepped along until at last he was standing in the great echoing lobby of the Dirksen Building with the water dripping from his raincoat.

He waved his badge at the security guard, stepped quickly past the electronic scanners, and was soon riding the elevator up to the Bureau's Chicago headquarters.

There a smiling receptionist kidded him for a moment. "Is it *that* wet out there?"

She hit a button on the console before her, and ten seconds later he was shaking hands with his FBI host.

"Detective Becker? Welcome to Chicago. I'm Fred Gustafson."

The special agent was a short heavyset man with a graying buzz cut and vivid blue eyes that bulged from their sockets, giving him the look of a startled frog at times. But his handshake was iron-hard, and his brisk, unsmiling demeanor made it clear that he was all business.

"How was your flight, Jake?"

The Boston cop laughed out loud. "No problems on the flight—but I'm glad our plane missed the monsoon I just walked through."

The G-Man was already leading the way down a narrow hall. "That's Chicago for you," he said, looking back over one shoulder. "But you get used to it after a while. Here we go, follow me."

Jake stepped into a small conference room, where a man with carrot-colored hair and a bone white fishhook-shaped scar riding his upper lip was seated at a long, polished table.

A veteran Chicago cop, he wore a standard-issue Glock in a leather holster under one shoulder. He stood up to greet them, and the steel hammer on the pistol winked once in the glare from the recessed lights in the ceiling.

"Jake, meet Hank Jarreau."

"Welcome to Chi-Town, Jake."

"Thanks, Hank. We really appreciate you and Fred giving us a hand on our cases in Boston."

The two men nodded back at him but didn't speak. The newcomers slid onto their padded chairs and Agent Gustafson reached for a pile of black plastic folders waiting at the center of the table. "Jake, I asked Hank to drop by because the Rogers killing is his baby," said Fred. "He read your NCIC request, and he was the one who alerted us to the MO similarities I told you about on the phone.

"Hank, why don't you fill Jake in on what you've got so far, and how it might relate to those serial killings in Boston?"

"Okay, will do," said Detective Jarreau. "One thing looks like *fuh shore*, the victim in Lincoln Park—Dr. Hoyt Rogers—he got hit with a sharp blade, probably a scalpel. Whatever, he bled to death quick. Huh?

"Deep slashes like that—you bleed out quick, *mouri*, know what I mean?"

"*Mouri*," said Special Agent Gustafson with a hint of a smile. "That's Louisiana Cajun for 'dead.' I think I mentioned that Detective Jarreau hails from The Big Easy and environs?"

Jarreau nodded his burly head and also smiled, but only for a moment. "The assailant jammed the damn thing between Dr. Rogers' ribs and never looked back."

He sighed heavily, as if saddened to be reporting such brutal details. "Then we get the lab report, and it says 'scalpel.' Huh? And we also find this little drawing of a snake painted on the mirror—painted in human blood.

"What gives? You mentioned semen on the mirrors in *your* cases in Boston—but we don't see any semen . . . all we find is this snake painted in blood. We're kinda puzzled . . . so we send a blood sample over to the

Bureau, and Agent Gustafson here gives us a hand with it.

"And what do the FBI lab guys find out right away?

"They find out that the blood from the snake drawing is *different* from the victim's blood. So it looks like we've got the killer's blood on the mirror, know what I mean?"

"We did the initial hemoanalysis ourselves," said Agent Gustafson, "but our lab tools are limited, and all we got was confirmation that the blood types were different. As I told you on the phone, we've sent the perp's blood sample off to London for a much more detailed DNA assay. This biotech stuff is brand-new in law enforcement, and London has the only forensics lab doing that kind of analysis right now. Their findings ought to help us learn more about the killer's identity."

Nodding, Jake scribbled a couple of words in his shirt-pocket notebook and then looked over at the FBI agent. "The use of the scalpel, that's one similarity to your Boston MOs," Gustafson went on, replying to the look. "Another is the locked room. No sign at all of any forcible entry. And get this: The Lincoln Park victim's housekeeper told us she was asleep in her room, two doors down the hall, and she never heard a peep during the killing.

"She'd been out of the house during the day—it was her day off—but she always returns to the mansion at night."

Jake was scribbling again. "That's not all," the agent continued. "She also told us there was a message left on the doctor's answering machine on the day that he died. Just a few words really, and the caller whispered them, so they were hard to hear.

"They were: 'I'll see you in your dreams, you asshole. Get ready to die.' We listened to the tape over and over again, as you might expect. The caller was probably male . . . but he had no really noticeable accent . . . and there was a whole lot of static along with the whispering, so we weren't really able to learn anything important about the caller."

Jake was looking back and forth between the two investigators. "It's hard to believe that call was simply a coincidence," he said. "Why? Because that's the exact same message our three victims got in Boston right before *they* died."

He turned back to Jarreau. "Did you interview any family members?"

"Yeah, *fuh shore* we did," said the Windy City detective. "The old man had two sons. One of 'em, Hoyt, Jr.—he's a big-shot lawyer right here in Chicago. A millionaire, heads up one of the major firms in the Loop. Huh? But he didn't tell us much. Said his father didn't have any enemies, as far as he knew.

"We also had him listen to the tape of the threatening phone call, but he drew a blank on that, too." Jarreau cracked his knuckles loudly—a nervous habit?

"Anyway, there's also a younger brother, a Michael Rogers. Hoyt says he's a psychiatrist in Providence, Rhode Island, but we haven't located him yet."

Jake scribbled, *Providence*, then thought for a minute. What was it Alix had said to him at Big Pine? *Did you ever consider that your guy might be a shrink?* Frowning, he scribbled again. Then: "Okay, thanks, Hank. So what do you make of the drawing in blood, anyway?"

Jarreau blinked slowly back at him. "It's a tiny snake, not much bigger than your thumb," he said after a bit. "Got these little red bands along the body, like a *hoodoo* thing, you know? Huh?"

Jake showed no expression.

Special Agent Gustafson was smiling broadly now.

"*Hoodoo*," he said. "That's a Cajun type of voodoo. Very spooky, right, Hank?"

The Chicago detective thought for a minute. He wasn't smiling.

"In some kinds of *hoodoo*, back in the bayous, you can draw a snake to make a curse. Huh?"

Jake was sitting up straight now. "A curse?" he said.

"Thas' right," said Detective Jarreau. "You draw the little snake, and in your mind, it's like, you know, you're painting it on your victim—the curse of the *Hoodoo*!"

Jake meditated for a few seconds. "Well, all I can say is—this damn case keeps getting stranger by the hour." He scribbled briefly and then sighed and closed his notebook.

"So where do we go from here?"

Special Agent Gustafson jumped in. "Lincoln Park," he said. "We're going to take a ride out to the mansion where the doctor was killed. Hoyt, Jr., has agreed to meet all three of us there at four o'clock sharp."

A moment later, they were all on their feet and headed for the door.

CHAPTER 37
A Showdown at the Mansion

With Special Agent Gustafson at the wheel, the unmarked Mercury Cougar zoomed north on Lake Shore Drive. At West Fullerton Parkway, they left Lake Michigan and swung past the green-leaved expanse of the Lincoln Park Zoo.

Detective Jarreau was talking about the White Sox—then mired in fourth place in the American League West—and their notorious lack of pitching.

"I was out at Comiskey on Saturday night," lamented the homicide cop, "and guess what? The Sox got hammered 13-2 by the Angels, huh?"

He made a low, moaning sound full of baseball despair. "*Fuh shore*, we ain't got shit for pitching. I mean, Bannister was bad enough. Huh? He gives up three in the first, two more in the second, then two in the third, and now we're down seven-zip. So they yank him and bring in Dave Schmidt.

"Did you know they're paying Bannister close to a million dollars a year—to do what? To pitch like shit?

"And guess what? Schmidt's first two hitters knock the ball into the lake. I kid you not. So now it's nine-zip, and we're still in the third inning. I mean, where the fuck is the pitching? Thank God they just fired Tony La Russa—maybe the new guy, Doug Rader, can help 'em build a decent pitching staff! Huh?"

Gustafson was barking with laughter.

"Sorry, Hank, but I got no sympathy for you. None whatsoever."

A National League fan, Gustafson turned to commiserate with Jake, who was sitting in the passenger seat. "I'm a Cubs guy, know what I mean? Which is . . . what? A recipe for total depression, that's what.

"Take my word for it, the Cubs aren't just bad. They're a national disaster. They're like the San Francisco Earthquake, or the Johnstown Flood, except they wear baseball uniforms. Really . . . they're so terrible, they're *historic*. They're so awful, I don't even go out to Wrigley anymore. Why bother? I just watch 'em on TV.

"I figure, shit, if I'm gonna be miserable all the goddamn time, why not be miserable sitting on my own living room sofa, where I can at least get an affordable beer whenever I want?"

Listening to the G-Man's tale of woe, Jake was laughing and nodding his head. "Hey, I feel your pain, Fred. But I don't have much pity for you and the Cubs, and do you know why? It's because I'm a Red Sox fan—which means I'm a victim of the worst curse in all of pro sports—the Curse of the Bambino!"

"Oh, yeah," boomed Hank, "I heard about that thing. A real nightmare, huh?"

"You *bet* it's a nightmare," said Jake. "The Red Sox have gone more than sixty-five years without winning a World Series—ever since they made the mistake of trading the immortal Babe Ruth to the Yankees back in 1920. The Bambino! Four times over that stretch, they made it to the Series, and four straight times they lost in seven games. You ask anybody in Boston and they'll tell you: The Red Sox were cursed forever the day they peddled the Bambino to the Yanks!"

Frowning thoughtfully by now, Gustafson was obviously impressed. "Jake, I gotta say, my heart goes out to you, pal. . . ."

But the special agent's next words were cut off by a loud blast of static from the police radio. *Six-niner, this is Control and Command. I've got a patch-in for you, six-niner. Long distance phoner, London, England. Over."*

Agent Gustafson gave the two of them a heads-up look: *London calling*?

He picked up the hand mike and flicked the plastic button on its side.

"This is six-niner, Gustafson. I read you, Command. What do you have again?"

Six-niner, I'm patching through a call from London. Go ahead, sir.

"Agent Gustafson?"

"You got him."

"Agent Gustafson, this is Alastair Bresnan at the Kingsford Lab in London. You remember, we spoke a few weeks ago, back when you first sent us those genetic samples on the Dr. Rogers murder?"

"Yeah, sure. How you doing?"

"Doing good, real good. But I thought I better call you right away. We went ahead and took a closer look at the protein assay on the perp's blood sample."

Gustafson nodded, then swung the wheel to the left. The Mercury lurched slightly as it turned onto Imperial Drive—the broad avenue where the murdered physician had lived.

"Okay, I really appreciate the heads-up, Alastair," the special agent said into his hand mike. "So what you got for us?"

The radio blared static again. When it subsided, they heard Bresnan say: "I think we maybe hit on something important here, Agent Gustafson. We asked the lab technicians to compare the DNA from the victim to the DNA from the perp.

"So they ran an x-ray crystallography scan on the bands . . . and now they're telling us the killer is a close family member. Maybe a brother or sister of the victim, or a parent, or maybe even a son or daughter."

There was a lengthy pause, during which Hank Jarreau and Jake Becker stared at each other. *Son or daughter?*

But then came more static . . . followed by a brief technical discussion about the crystallography findings.

After that Gustafson said goodbye and replaced the handset on its cradle.

"Hoyt Rogers, Junior," he said after a bit. Nobody else spoke. "Do we know much about this guy or what?"

Jarreau frowned. "He's probably clean, Fred. He's a prominent Chicago lawyer, moves in the highest political circles. He's got a rock-solid alibi, and he's been pestering us for weeks at Homicide, demanding we catch his father's killer."

"We don't see him as the perp. Huh?"

By now the Cougar was gliding to a stop at 470 Imperial Drive. Jake looked out the side window at the huge Victorian mansion with the sloping mansard roof and the sunlit gables.

"Okay, then," said Agent Gustafson. "Just so we know what we're going against."

He reached into his suit coat and patted the bulge under his right armpit. "That's probably his Lincoln Town Car in the driveway," he said.

"You might want to check your pieces, gents. Make sure you're good to go."

He looked carefully at the other two.

"Just in case we come up against something unexpected."

***

Wilma met them at the door. She stared at them.

"Hello," said Gustafson. "I'm Special Agent Fred Gustafson, FBI. I believe Mr. Rogers—Hoyt Rogers, Jr.—is expecting us?"

All three men were holding up their gold shields.

"Oh," she said. "Oh, absolutely."

Wilma was a heavyset woman with a wrinkled face and bloodshot eyes. The purple bags beneath them spoke volumes about the strain she'd been under in recent days. "Come in," she said. "I'll tell Mr. Rogers that you are here."

She led the way through a narrow vestibule framed by stained glass windows. Soon they were walking along a dim hallway flanked on either side by potted palms. Jake could hear opera music playing somewhere at the back of the mansion. An aria from *Rigoletto*?

Yes . . . hadn't that been Hoyt, Jr.'s alibi—he'd attended the opera that evening with friends, and had then spent the evening at home with his family in Evanston?

Soon they found themselves in the old man's elegant living room and staring curiously at a palatial fireplace, above which loomed the senior Dr. Rogers' solemn oil portrait. The assembled ranks of Chinese porcelains gleamed softly in the afternoon light filtering through a silk-curtained window. "Please sit down," cried Wilma.

She seemed distraught, almost on the edge of tears. But they quickly obeyed.

Hank and Jake dropped onto the two expensive ottomans, while Gustafson sank into a plush easy chair trimmed in glittering silver brocade.

Rigoletto suddenly ended.

The three of them watched the mahogany-arched doorway on the left side of the room, but no one appeared. Five minutes passed.

Jake looked at Hank. Then he looked at Fred. "He's a big deal in Chicago," said Agent Gustafson. "Hotshot lawyer. You know how they are. I think he likes to keep people waiting."

"Does he now?" said Jake.

"He keeps us waiting much longer," said Hank, "how about I go back there and hurry him up a little?"

But then they heard footsteps on the other side of the archway.

"Gentlemen, good day."

He was a slender dark-haired man with a few touches of silver at his elegantly groomed temples. His charcoal gray suit—Armani, of course, and well up in the three-grand neighborhood—had been tailored so perfectly it appeared to have been spray-painted onto his lean, athletic frame.

"Gentlemen," he said again. "I'm sorry to have kept you waiting. I was on the telephone to Riyadh."

"Please sit," said Hoyt, Jr. Jake watched him lower himself onto a narrow, straight-backed chair and cross his legs carefully.

The creases in his trousers were so sharp you could have cut a prime rib with them.

"Would you gentlemen like some coffee? Tea? Perhaps a glass of sherry?"

Gustafson waved the suggestion away. "Thank you, we're fine, Mr. Rogers. We appreciate you taking a few minutes to help us this afternoon."

"Glad to be of service." His voice was low, measured, without intonation.

"We just received some new information. We think it might have a bearing on your father's murder."

"New information?" said Hoyt, Jr. He gave the special agent a piercing look. "Nothing personal, Agent Gustafson, but I think it's about *time* you and your people came up with something new."

Gustafson didn't respond at first. His face remained expressionless. When he finally spoke, he sounded friendly, relaxed.

"There's new DNA evidence—from what we call 'genetic fingerprinting'—to suggest your father's killer was a close family member."

Hoyt, Jr., produced a ghastly smile. His upper lip wrinkled, then pulled back to reveal a row of evenly spaced, gleaming teeth. The teeth were large . . . too large, thought Jake, for the man's pinched little mouth. All at once Jake was remembering the Komodo dragon at Boston's Franklin Park Zoo—he'd taken Charly to see the monster-sized lizard only a few months before.

"A close family member?" echoed Hoyt, Jr. He was still smiling, but only with his mouth.

"Maybe a brother," Agent Gustafson cut him off smoothly. "Maybe a son, or a daughter. Somebody in the immediate family."

Gustafson gave the stylishly clad lawyer a searching look. "These DNA techniques are new, but they're also very powerful.

"We've been told by the lab folks that they're incredibly accurate, Mr. Rogers. Apparently, the statistical odds are quite high—millions to one, in fact— that your father was killed by someone in your immediate family."

The man on the straight-backed chair gazed at him for a few seconds, while his smile slowly went away. His features hardened, became metallic. The light dwindled in his eyes . . . for a few seconds, he looked like a glaring statue of himself.

"That sonofabitch," he said. His voice was pitched somewhere between a snarl and a growl. "That dirty bastard."

Agent Gustafson blinked at him.

"My younger brother," said Hoyt, Jr. "My brother Michael."

The upper lip shivered. The Komodo teeth reappeared. "I didn't want to suspect him at first . . . but now it's finally coming clear.

"It looks as if Michael killed my father, gentlemen— that dirty sonofabitch did it at last!"

Agent Gustafson didn't react. No expression. He looked like a veteran blackjack dealer in Vegas—flat-eyed, with nothing moving in his face.

"You think your younger brother killed your father?"

Hoyt, Jr., put both feet on the floor. "No question, now that you've got the DNA findings," he said with a sneer. "He's . . . he's the black sheep. A disgraced psychiatrist, a pathetic drunk. All his life . . . my father and I . . . my *late* father and I, we've been ashamed of him for years.

"But I never imagined he could be capable of murder."

His mouth twitched once, as if yanked to one side by an invisible force. Jake leaned forward on his sofa, watching the man intently. "He's a totally disreputable shrink, not a real doctor at all," said Hoyt, Jr. "He abused his patients, and he lied about that abuse. He stole patient information from a colleague's files.

"He drank like a fish! He's utterly disreputable, gentlemen.

"And he hated our father. *Hated* him. Had a nickname for him: The Prick."

After his outburst, the room fell silent.

A vacuum cleaner began to growl somewhere at the back of the house. "I called him right after . . . right after we lost Dad, and I'll get you that phone number before you leave. Well, he laughed at me. He actually mocked our father, even though he was dead!

"He showed no interest at all in attending the funeral. But of course, I wasn't surprised, not at all."

He frowned at the three detectives. "Where did you get the . . . the material you used for the DNA thing?"

Special Agent Gustafson gazed thoughtfully back at him. "Remember the snake that was painted on the mirror? In blood? We sent a sample to a specialized lab in England. It took a while, but we're told the results are indisputable."

Hoyt, Jr., nodded. "He must have been in Chicago on the night my father was killed." He paused for a moment, and then his eye opened wide.

"Oh, my God," he blurted. "That's it—the scalpel!"

The three lawmen looked at each other for a moment. Then Agent Gustafson spoke up. "Scalpel, Mr. Rogers?"

The lawyer was leaning forward in his chair now. His face had gone flushed.

"I just discovered it a few minutes ago, while I was looking over my father's possessions in preparation for our meeting. I hadn't noticed it before . . . but my father's plaque . . . a lifetime service award he got right before he retired? He kept that award in the Family Room, here on the ground floor. It's a polished mahogany plaque, and there had always been a scalpel, a top-of-the-line Ribbel, attached to the bottom of it.

"It was engraved with his initials, as I recall: 'HR.'

"But this morning, as I was looking the plaque over, I realized that the scalpel had been removed. It's missing."

A missing scalpel? Nobody spoke for a few moments. The three investigators were wide-eyed and sitting on the edge of their seats. They were watching the lawyer carefully.

Jake broke the silence. "We'll want to take that plaque with us," he said. "Fingerprints."

"Of course," said Hoyt, Jr. "Apparently, my brother stole the scalpel at some point during a visit. Then he somehow managed to get into my father's bedroom on the night of the murder. As you know, Wilma was sleeping a few doors down the hall. She didn't hear a thing. She slept right through it."

Detective Jarreau had one hand up. "We interviewed her at length, Mr. Rogers."

The attorney blinked at him. Rapidly. "Yes, yes, of course you did. Anyway, it's all coming clear now.

"Michael must have swiped the scalpel at some point, then used it to kill my father later."

"But you never heard anything about your brother visiting Dr. Rogers before the stabbing?" asked Jake.

Hoyt, Jr., stared back at him. "That's correct. It all makes sense now, because there was no theft, no burglary. . . .

"Look, detective . . . sorry, what was your name again?"

"Becker."

"Ah, yes. Jake Becker. Well, as I told Agent Gustafson and Detective Jarreau here . . . there was no burglary that night. Nothing in the house was disturbed.

"If you put that fact together with the stolen scalpel . . ."

Jake was sitting up straight now. His pulse had kicked up a notch.

"HR?" he said.

"Correct," said Hoyt, Jr. "Engraved on the handle. It was one of his proudest possessions."

Special Agent Gustafson had retrieved a small spiral-bound notebook from his suit coat. "So you think your brother stole this . . . this 'HR scalpel' from the plaque?"

"I do."

"Better go get it," said Detective Jarreau, "so we can look at it ourselves and maybe check it out for fingerprints."

"No problem," said Hoyt, Jr. He was already on his feet . . . and it took him less than a minute to retrieve the damaged plaque and hand it to the Chicago investigator.

"Ask yourselves," he pressed on, while the burly detective examined the piece of evidence in minute detail, "why would a stranger have wanted that scalpel? Can't you see how the pieces fit together? My brother was a disgraced doctor and a violent alcoholic. He hated our father's legendary role as a supremely accomplished surgeon.

"What better way for him to gain revenge than by stealing Dad's honorary engraved scalpel and then using it to kill him? You're welcome to take the plaque with you for fingerprinting, if you wish—but I don't see any point, really . . . since everybody in our family and lots of our friends have handled it frequently over the years."

The three cops thought for a minute, then nodded agreement.

Hoyt, Jr., was scowling at them by now.

Jake watched his upper lip pull back, again revealing the too-large teeth. "Quite frankly, gentlemen, you seem a bit slow on the uptake here. I've been waiting nearly a month for you to nail my father's killer . . . but all I ever hear is: 'We're working on it.'

"No offense . . . but is that the best the FBI and the Chicago PD can do—'We're working on it?'"

Once again, however, Agent Gustafson declined to respond. He was writing something in the spiral-bound notebook. After a bit, Jake said quietly: "Do you know where your brother might be right now, Mr. Rogers?"

Hoyt, Jr., closed his eyes for a moment. "The last I heard he was living in Providence. He'd rented a room . . . had been teaching at a local community college. He had a telephone for a while, but then it was shut off for nonpayment. I'll get you the number before you leave, if you want to check the phone company's call records.

"Anyway, he lost *that* job, too, a few months ago, and he was pretty much just drinking all day long. For all I know, he could've moved back to Boston, where he'd lived for fifteen years or so before Providence. Or maybe he went on to New York or Hartford. Who knows?"

"Where'd he live in Boston, do you remember?" Jake was also scribbling busily now.

"Downtown mostly. As I recall, his last Boston address was a rundown apartment building on Kneeland Street. I can get you the actual address if you want."

Jake scribbled again: *Kneeland—Combat Zone?*

They sat motionless for a few more seconds. Then Hoyt, Jr., clapped his hands and rose to his feet. He glared . . . then pointed a long finger at Special Agent Gustafson. "I've decided that I'm going to Boston in the morning myself, gentlemen. I figure that's Michael's most likely move at this point. I'm determined to find him, and I intend to bring along a skilled private detective—a man I've worked with before on several difficult cases.

"I can assure you that we will locate my brother, regardless of how long it takes."

But now Detective Jarreau stepped in. The homicide investigator had risen slowly from the ottoman.

His great bulk quickly dwarfed the little man in the perfectly pressed suit.

"Mr. Rogers," he said. "I need to make a point."

Hoyt, Jr., shot him an angry look. "A point about what?"

"About your last comment," said Detective Jarreau. "*Fuh shore*, you got a right to go to Boston, just like anybody else. But if it was me, I'd want to save my ticket money."

Hoyt, Jr., didn't budge. "What are you getting at, detective?"

Jarreau grinned. "What am I getting at? Well, for starters . . . as soon as we leave your fancy little living room here, we'll be on the horn to the Providence and

Boston Police Departments. We'll be working twenty-four seven to find out where your brother is hiding. I'm sure Detective Becker here will help us with that."

He sent the miffed attorney a slow, lazy smile. "*Got it?*"

Hoyt, Jr.'s face was a mask of outrage.

"And there's one more little thing."

"What?" snapped the man in the Armani.

Detective Jarreau produced his sweet Southern smile again. "It's *fuh shore* that you can fly to Boston tomorrow if you want. That's entirely your affair.

"But the first time you interfere with this murder investigation, I'll put the fucking cuffs on you myself."

Now he leaned toward the angry man in the $500 Italian shoes.

"Are we clear on that, Mr. Rogers?"

***

Back in the unmarked Mercury and headed toward Lake Shore Drive, the three homicide investigators quickly reached an important decision.

"I don't like this guy," rumbled Detective Jarreau. "I haven't liked him from the beginning, know what I mean?"

"I do know," said Jake. "I'm not crazy about him myself."

"He's got a silver spoon up his hiney," said Jarreau. "Huh? He's one of them guys thinks his farts are fragrances by Dior."

"You got that right," said Special Agent Gustafson. "But I don't think he's the perp."

"Why not, Fred?" Slumped against the backseat of the car, Jarreau had gone into angry bulldog mode.

"He doesn't have the stomach for it," said Gustafson. "He's a silk-stocking lawyer who loves to go to the opera. Murder takes *cajones* the size of Texas grapefruit, and he doesn't own 'em."

Gustafson turned to look at the other two for a moment. "Plus, he's got an ironclad alibi.

"Ten people talked to him at the opera on the night the doctor was killed . . . and his wife swears he spent the rest of the evening with her in their bedroom."

Jarreau was glaring. "Yeah, you're probably right. But I don't trust the sonofabitch. He's slippery, you know?"

Jake laughed. "True enough. But you have to remember. He's a lawyer."

Jarreau snickered. "Okay, so he didn't do it. But I think he knows more about who did than he's letting on. Why's he so hot to go to Boston? What's the real deal between him and his brother? Have they hated each other from day one? Somehow, it don't add up."

Agent Gustafson was piloting the big Cougar onto Lake Shore by now. He thought for a minute. Then: "So what you want to do, Hank?"

The big Cajun didn't mince his words. "I say we put a tail on him right now. Watch him until he gets on the plane." He gave Jake a look.

"How about if I keep you in the loop, Jake? Then your guys can pick him up as soon as he lands in Boston?"

Jake nodded. "Sounds like a good move, Hank. Let's do it."

Gustafson was already reaching for the hand mike and passing it on to his colleague in the backseat.

CHAPTER 38
Welcome to Boston!

Saturday morning, eight o'clock.

Having raced home from Chicago and grabbed a few hours of badly needed sleep, Jake Becker was now neck-deep in the manhunt for the vicious psychiatrist, Michael Rogers, M.D.

While more than a score of detectives and rapidly recruited patrol officers banged on doors and interviewed the locals all across the Combat Zone and its contiguous neighborhoods, Jake's in-house team was working virtually nonstop to build the enormous file of homicide-related information that would eventually nail down the location of the killer.

Like the flashing ganglia in a gigantic brain, Jake's command post was moment by moment upgrading and expanding an ever-increasing amount of data related to the four murders. Assisted by a rank of endlessly flickering computers and a platoon of trained clerks searching through reams of archived biographical data and thousands of arrest records, Jake's bloodhounds were focusing most of their efforts on two long rows of corkboards that ran the length of the Homicide Division Squad Bay.

The boards were covered with scrawled notes, crime scene photos, composite sketches of the alleged killer, biographies of the murder victims, statements from witnesses and descriptions of physical evidence such as Elisa Mayhew's leather-bound diary . . . along with a continuously updated psychological and behavioral profile based on Jake's discussions with Dr. Alix Cassidy and several forensic psychologists in the Boston area.

Taken together, the information on the boards formed an enormous catalogue that would allow the investigators to pinpoint potential locations for their chief suspect with growing clarity and precision.

As the long day wore on, Jake & Co. felt certain that the noose was closing on their prey.

Already a team of police investigators in Providence had discovered a key fact: Dr. Michael Rogers had been fired from his teaching job at a local community college three months earlier, after being charged with "inappropriate behavior with a female student" and also with "stealing funds from a student club he advised."

He'd also exited his modest apartment in a working-class section of the city . . . and had then departed Providence for Boston, according to two of his former colleagues at the school. Apparently, the bad guy had decided to return to the Hub, which meant he was probably living once again in the city that had been his home for the previous twenty years.

They were making progress, no question about it. But it was *slow* progress, and the pressure on Jake's homicide team was growing by the hour.

Each time the Commissioner rang him, the message was the same. Work harder, work faster, no excuses, get it *done*—or we'll find somebody who can.

By now the tension was taking its toll on Jake's crew of weary gumshoes. On two separate occasions, angry arguments over the interpretation of evidence and differing theories about what it meant had exploded into shouting matches and waving fists.

Detective Haskins, normally a calm and thoughtful investigator, had completely lost his cool at one point and had flung his half-full cup of coffee against the nearest wall, while roaring at his startled colleagues: "We're standing around with our dicks in the air, and that asshole is about to strike again. Can't somebody here give us something *new*, for Chrissake?"

It was ugly, and Jake knew it would soon get uglier. Because of Rizzo's foolish leak to Mark Halliday, the city was swamped under a tide of relentless media coverage of the murders, with grisly "serial killer" stories and photos dominating the front page each day.

By now even the staid and traditionally reserved *Boston Globe* had joined the feeding frenzy and was publishing one breathless story after the next about "screaming and helpless women bleeding to death after being slashed wide open."

Indeed, the entire city of Boston seemed caught up in a terrifying nightmare, with panicked women telling TV and print reporters they were afraid to leave the house at night and were checking and rechecking their locked doors every hour on the hour.

It was brutal, and it was utterly grueling.

But Becker kept on working.

There was no alternative and no time for rest.

Then, somewhere around five o'clock, as he sat at one of the coffee-cup-and-ashtray-littered conference tables that dominated the squad room, Becker checked his watch and jerked upright in his chair.

Alix Cassidy was due at South Station in less than 60 minutes.

Fine with me! Jake was looking forward to seeing her again. He needed a couple of hours to recharge his batteries, anyway. But first he'd swing by the house and pick up Charly, after which the two of them could zip across town to meet the Peter Pan bus that would be bringing the Big Pine sleep scientist to the Hub.

Hurrying through the underground garage that flanked the Boston PD, Jake smiled cheerfully.

Okay, Dr. Cassidy, you better be ready.

Here I come!

***

Six hours before Jake headed off to pick up Charly, Alix had settled happily into her seat aboard the Peter Pan bus. Her spirits were high and her green eyes were shining—especially after she realized that the empty adjoining seat would probably *remain* empty, since the bus doors had been closed and the driver was already nursing the accelerator.

Yes, they were now underway. Moving quickly, she lifted the arm rest . . . and discovered that she now had plenty of extra room in which to stretch her legs.

Bon voyage, Alix Cassidy!

But then she got an unpleasant surprise, as a tall man's long shadow fell across the empty space beside her.

"Excuse me, *Madame*. Is this seat taken?"

Gunther Sverdlow.

Her heart sank like a heavy stone in deep water.

"Oh, hello, Alix. What a nice surprise!"

She sent him a blank stare. *You knew damn right well I was on this bus . . . so why are you playing dumb?*

She would do her best to remain civil, however.

"Hello, Gunther. What are you doing here?"

He produced one of his reptilian smiles. "I was invited to Boston to meet with the Swiss Ambassador. I believe your Secretary of State, Mr. George P. Shultz, will be in attendance. The Ambassador is hosting a state dinner this evening at the Swiss Consulate, and he felt that my presence would be helpful."

His features coiled into another lizard-like grin. "And where are *you* off to?"

"*Swiss Consulate, whoopee-do!*" Alix told herself. But to him she said: "I've got some shopping to do, that's all." She had zero interest in the man at this point. Why couldn't the fool see that?

"Is this seat spoken for?" he purred and then pointed at the empty chair beside her.

"Gunther . . ." *Think fast, Alix!*

"I'd really prefer it if you sat somewhere else. It's going to be a long ride, and my legs tend to throb—*like your penis!*—after a bit. No hard feelings, but I really do need to stretch out and elevate my legs."

She took a quick glance around the half-empty bus. "Actually, it looks like there are plenty of other empty seats if you don't mind."

Good for you, Alix. You found a way to keep the shithead at a safe distance!

The somber scientist frowned, but soon recovered.

"Of course, of course. Whatever pleases the *Madame*! But if you should find yourself in need of some stimulating conversation during the ride, just let me know."

Please kill me now, she wailed inwardly. Then: "All right, I'll keep that in mind, Gunther."

But I wouldn't hold my breath if I were you.

***

Sitting in Jake's unmarked police cruiser outside Boston's South Station, Jake and Charly were eagerly awaiting Alix's arrival.

"There's the bus, Dad—I see it coming!"

Charly was pointing off to the right, where the Peter Pan logo gleamed through the cloudy overcast. Together they watched the exhaust pipe belch a cloud of black smoke as the bus pulled into Bay 42.

Jake took a glance at his watch. "Looks like she's right on time, honey."

Alix was the fifth passenger off. Before she'd taken five steps, dad and daughter were at her side. As they approached, Jake took a long, hard look at her face . . . and for a moment he was struck by the way she seemed to resemble all three of the Boston women who'd been murdered.

Same fiery red hair, same vivid green eyes.

Déjà vu?

But then he blinked, and the uneasy moment passed. An instant later he was taking her hand.

"Welcome to Boston, Alix." Jake gave her an affectionate hug.

"Me, too!" Charly chimed in and then lit up as Alix bent to deliver a friendly cheek kiss.

"Thanks for picking me up, guys."

While they were waiting for the bus driver to open the luggage compartment, a gentleman named Sverdlow sauntered into view.

"Hello, Alix."

"Oh, hello, Gunther. Let me introduce you to Boston Police Detective Jake Becker." *That should get his attention.* "And this is his daughter, Charly."

Turning to Jake, she added, "Gunther is also spending the summer up at Big Pine."

"Nice to meet you, Gunther."

Jake reached out to shake his hand. The detective's greeting was friendly enough, but his instincts told him that Alix didn't like this guy one bit.

A moment later, he treated Gunther to one of his patented "gorilla handshakes." The Swiss researcher didn't much care for it, either; he grimaced in pain as the bones in his right hand were powerfully compressed.

All of which was just fine with Alix. After pointing out her suitcase to Jake, she said, "See you around, Gunther."

Then she, Jake and Charly headed toward Jake's car. *Goodbye, Dr. S., and good riddance!*

"How was the bus ride?" Charly asked.

"It was heaven," laughed Alix. "I had a whole row to myself, so I could really stretch out. That made a huge difference."

Jake was watching her carefully. "Who *was* that guy, Alix? He had an attitude, I could tell."

Alix nodded. "He's one of the hotshot lecturers at the conference," she said.

"Like you?" asked Jake. With a smile he popped the trunk and placed her suitcase on top of what appeared to be a rifle case.

Alix stared at it for a second and then switched her gaze to Jake's right shoulder, where the strap that held his 9mm Smith & Wesson was plainly visible. Catching her glance, he quickly buttoned his sport coat to hide the weapon.

"You must be famished," he told Alix.

She grinned. "I'm so hungry I could eat a house! But I'm more worried about you. I know you just got back from Chicago late last night. Aren't you exhausted?"

He smiled at her. "No way, Alix.

"As soon as I saw you step off that bus, all my fatigue vanished."

She smiled back at him and then patted his shoulder. "I'm flattered, Jake . . . but I suspect the real story here is that you're simply the Superman of the Boston Police Department!"

Charly sent up a boisterous laugh. "Alix, you're funny!"

All at once, Jake was feeling better. It was the first laughter he'd heard from his daughter in several days.

"You *talk* funny, too," Charly added.

Alix pretended to be astonished. "What . . . because I don't have a Boston accent or *pahk* my *cah* in *Hah-vahd yahd*?"

Jake chuckled. "Charly, stop being rude to our guest. Be nice."

"It's okay, Jake," said Alix. "I think both of *you* talk funny. You oughta hear yourselves. *Fah* out, *Chah*-lee . . . jump in the *cah*!"

Now all three were laughing, and Jake looked happier than a New England clam enjoying a mud bath.

"Where are we going for dinner, Dad?"

"I knew you'd get around to that subject in a hurry," said Jake. "And I have a great idea. Let's head over to Murray's. You're in for a treat, Alix. Okay with you, Charly?"

"You bet. I love the food there."

"Ever eaten in an authentic Jewish delicatessen, Alix?"

"Nope, can't say that I have."

"This is your lucky day," said Jake.

***

"Well, well. Look what the wind just blew in. If it isn't Detective Jake Becker and his adorable daughter!"

"Hi, Uncle Murray," sang Charly, who'd been calling the deli owner "uncle" ever since she was a toddler.

"And who might *this* charming lady be?" Murray gave Jake a sly wink.

"Murray, let me introduce you to Alix Cassidy from Atlanta. She's going to be visiting us for a few days."

"Nice to meet you, Alix. Hey, you made a very good choice when you decided to spend some time with Jake. He's a real gentleman. One of the nicest, in my humble opinion."

Poker-faced, Alix nodded.

"How much did you pay Murray to say that to me, Jake?"

Charly howled. She was enjoying the Murray-inspired banter as always. But now the deli impresario was shaking a long finger at the detective. He scowled and pretended to be outraged. "Jake, the last two times you've run out of here like you had red ants in your pants without even touching my food.

"I've still got two of your Reuben sandwiches waiting for you in my freezer, and I'm not letting you outta here until they've been eaten, old buddy."

He cut loose with his booming, trademark laugh and then turned to Jake's daughter.

"Hey, Charly, you wanna hear a good joke?"

"Sure."

"Okay," said Murray, who had long regarded himself as the second coming of Jackie Mason. "Why do so many Jews go to India?"

"I give up, Uncle Murray."

"Because they got a *New Delhi* there!"

His round shoulders jiggled with merriment. Then he roared and waggled his handlebar mustache at Charly, who gave him a quick round of applause, followed by the ultimate accolade: "Totally cool!"

Murray smiled at his appreciative audience and then said, "Let me get you some *noshes* while you decide on your dinner."

He returned to their table loaded down with a basket of bagel chips, a bowl of zesty chive dip and a dish full of Kosher dill pickles. He plunked the goodies in front of them and piped, "Okay, gang, what'll it be?"

Without delay, Charly made her move. "Can I have the open brisket sandwich with garlic mashed potatoes and a black cherry soda?"

"Same for me," said Jake, "but also with a cup of coffee, please. Your turn, Alix."

She looked at them for a second. Then she leaped. "Okay," she said. "I'm in your hands, folks, so I'll take my chances. Make mine the same."

"You're very brave, Alix," said Jake. "Trust me—your taste buds are going to thank you for that decision."

He turned back to the deli mogul. "Murray, you can start us off with some matzah ball soup."

***

Five minutes later, when Murray spotted Jake coming out of the men's room, he hustled over and grabbed the detective's arm. "She's beautiful, Jake. Is it serious?"

Jake opened his mouth to reply, but Murray couldn't wait. "You know, it's about time you found yourself a good woman."

The homicide cop stiffened slightly. "Whoa . . . not too fast, Murray. We just met, you know? And this is business . . . she's here to help me with the murder investigation. She's a lecturer at this paranormal institute up in Maine, just for the summer."

Jake paused. His features softened. "But you're right about her looks. She *is* beautiful, isn't she?"

"She sure is, Jake. And while we're on the subject, how's that investigation of yours going, anyway?"

Jake frowned. "Too slowly as far I'm concerned. But we're making progress, Murray. Keep your fingers crossed, will you?"

Back at the table, Jake started to talk about the case, but Charly quickly cut him off.

"No shop talk, Dad. You promised."

He grinned. "You're absolutely right, Charly. Case closed."

Then he turned toward their visitor, who asked, "What are your plans for tomorrow, Jake? I was hoping Charly could keep me company. We could do some shopping, maybe go to a movie?"

"Terrific idea. You two could *schmy* around together."

"*Schmy?* I never heard that word before."

Charly was laughing again. "It means to goof around, just have some fun."

Alix gave her a wink. "Okay then, I'd love to *schmy* around with you tomorrow."

"You okay with that, honey?"

"Sure, Dad. Can we go to Faneuil Hall?"

He nodded. "As long as you promise to bring home some chocolate chip cookies."

"My dad's favorite place on earth is the Boston Chipyard," Charly told Alix. "They make the best chocolate chip cookies anywhere."

"Wonderful. I love chocolate chip cookies, too," Alix exclaimed. "They're my absolute favorite treat."

Charly produced a ringing laugh. "There you go talking funny again, Alix!"

All at once, Jake realized he was feeling terrific.

"Okay then, it's settled. That works out perfectly for me, too. I have to meet with the Commissioner in the morning, and I'll be tied up until midafternoon.

"So why don't we plan on meeting up later in the day? Maybe go out for an early dinner? How's that sound?"

***

After enjoying Murray's hospitality to the max, they headed back to Jake's place.

The unmarked car pulled up to a stoplight and he turned to look at his visitor. "You must be pretty bushed after that long bus ride."

Alix laughed. "You got that right, Jake. But it's nothing a good night's sleep won't fix."

"Don't worry, you're going to have your own bedroom, and nobody will bother you!" Charly blurted from the backseat.

There was an awkward pause after that . . . which Jake quickly covered. "Charly, thanks for managing our guest's accommodations so efficiently."

"You'll even have your own portable TV set!"

Alix smiled and looked back at her youthful friend. "Thank you, honey. Sounds like I couldn't have done any better at the Park Plaza!"

"I hope you'll stay a long time," said Charly.

Now the two grownups were laughing hard. "Come on, let her breathe, Charly!"

Ten minutes later, they were standing in the living room, which featured a leather-covered sofa, two black glass coffee tables and a large walnut-stained desk covered with Charly's science project on "Protecting the World's Endangered Species."

"Home sweet home," said Jake. "I'm sure Charly will ask you to help her with her science project. She's been working on that thing for a solid month."

Alix nodded and smiled. "You can count on it, Charly. The first rule of science is that we always help each other."

"See there, Dad?" Charly laughed out loud, "I told you she'd want to help me, didn't I?"

Jake nodded. "Okay, but you two should also take plenty of time for fun.

"Alix, I'll show you the Family Room in a minute. That's where Charly watches all her favorite sitcoms. She's a huge *Cheers* fan!"

Alix lit up. "*Cheers*? Hey, I'm a big fan myself. Great show. I love that Woody Boyd!"

Charly was thrilled. "Me, too—he's the coolest bartender ever!"

Alix smiled. "Charly, I already feel like I'm right at home."

"Are you ready to examine your quarters, Alix?"

When she nodded, Jake led her down a long hallway floored with shining squares of terrazzo tile. The walls were decorated with family photos and several of Charly's drawings and watercolors. A few more steps and he turned into the spare bedroom, which contained an antique rocking chair and a queen-sized bed covered with a lavender-hued spread. The promised portable TV set gleamed from one corner.

"Your home away from home," said Jake.

"It's very nice," said Alix. "I really like the way you've decorated the room, Jake."

"Charly deserves most of the credit," he replied. "She picked out that rocking chair herself, over at Jordan Marsh."

Alix nodded. "What a great kid."

"Couldn't agree more," Jake smiled. "Listen, I've got a few things to take care of. Why don't you just settle down and relax for a while, catch your breath for a bit, and I'll wait for you out on the porch?"

"Sounds good to me, Jake."

"Would you like some coffee or tea? Maybe a cold beer or a glass of wine?"

She looked at him for a moment. "Maybe later?"

"Fair enough, then."

But now Charly had arrived to join them in the spare bedroom. She carried a big stuffed animal with pale gray fur and blue button eyes. It was Eeyore the Donkey—the famous "Woe is me" character from Winnie the Pooh.

Carefully and lovingly, Charly perched the droopy-eared doll on their guest's pillow. "Alix, I'm going to loan you my best buddy for tonight, but you have to bring him back tomorrow.

Alix smiled. Her eyes were shining.

"I'm honored, honey. I truly am. I'll be sure to bring him back to you first thing in the morning."

Charly leaned back on her heels and cut loose with the donkey's trademark bellow: "*EEE*-yore! *EEE*-yore!"

Not missing a beat, Alix bellowed right back at her: "*EEE*-yore!"

They both laughed . . . but then Charly grew more serious.

The teenager was looking deep into her new friend's eyes now, and her lips were trembling slightly. "Alix, I should tell you . . . Eeyore is very, very important to me. See, he used to belong to Dad's younger sister, my Aunt Rachel. She died when she was only six years old. This doll was her favorite toy from what Dad told me.

"Dad gave Eeyore to me when I was just a kid, in memory of Aunt Rachel. I've treasured him ever since!"

"Oh, Charly," said Alix, "I'm so terribly sorry to hear about your Aunt Rachel. How awful for your poor father."

But the child didn't seem to be listening now. Her face had changed. She seemed a bit frightened . . . a bit confused . . . maybe even on the edge of blurting out something that troubled her? Was the kid about to burst into tears?

Alix looked over at Jake for guidance, but his suddenly dark face was closed to her. It was a blank.

"I'll tell you about it later," he said quietly, and then fell silent.

When Charly finally did speak again, her voice was soft and muted, almost a whisper.

"Eeyore will make sure you're *safe*, Alix."

Alix nodded and smiled.

But her mind had begun to race.

Eeyore will keep me safe? she asked herself, as the smiling father and daughter quickly departed the guest room.

Safe from what?

CHAPTER 39
Alix Looks . . . and Then Leaps!

He poured her a glass of sparkling zinfandel, then one for himself.

It was almost nine o'clock now, with the crickets chirping away in the backyard hedge. A thin slice of moon gleamed bright as silver in the midsummer sky. Neither of them spoke for a while . . . until at last Alix sighed with contentment and broke the silence.

"What's that marvelous fragrance I'm smelling, Jake? Do you know what it is?"

He smiled. "I suspect those are Mrs. Whitney's azaleas. She's got a green thumb, no question about it."

"Your housekeeper is also your gardener?"

"Well, not officially. She grows her roses and azaleas and violets on the side. She loves it and she's quite good at it apparently." He leaned toward her.

He was grinning a little now and obviously enjoying himself. "Are you a gardener, Alix?"

She shook her head and then took a sip of wine. "Not really. But it does sound like a lot of fun. It must be quite rewarding to grow a prizewinning yellow rose. On the other hand, scientific research is pretty demanding. I run from morning to night, and no matter how hard I work, I never seem to catch up."

"I understand," he responded. "I think homicide is the same way. Once you get pulled into a case, you can forget about the rest of your life."

He paused for a moment to stare into his wine glass. "I have to be careful to give Charly all the attention she deserves, and I do.

"She's the only person I ever seem to have time for. Ever since I lost Ruth to Hodgkin's . . . you know . . . Charly was only three years old then and. . . ."

He trailed off.

She was gazing intently at him. "I was very sorry to hear about your wife and your sister, Jake. What happened to Rachel?"

Jake paused, and his face darkened noticeably.

"Unfortunately, she was kidnapped and murdered by a criminal psychopath."

"Oh my God, Jake. That's awful. How terrible that must have been for you."

Jake didn't speak for a while.

Alix was watching him carefully and saw how his eyes burned with remembered pain.

"It was tough," he said quietly. "All those years, each time I visited Rachel's grave, I'd also spend some time visiting Ruth, who's buried in the same plot. Those trips to the cemetery got to be pretty difficult."

Then he shook his head and fought his way back into the present moment. "Well, the important thing is that I got over it somehow. And I guess I . . . I guess that experience was a big part of why I became a cop, you know?"

She nodded. "I understand, Jake. I'm amazed that you were able to go on without falling apart. That says a great deal about your inner strength!"

Jake smiled back at her. His expression had softened. "It's okay now, Alix. All of that took place a long time ago. And Charly and I have done fine. We get along great. But I do miss Ruth now and then. After she died, I guess I kind of lost interest in everything but work.

"I turned into a workaholic cop, and that's pretty much what I've been ever since."

Alix didn't speak for a few moments. The crickets were singing even louder now, and they could hear a lonesome dog barking somewhere in the distance.

"I think you're very brave, Jake. And Charly obviously loves you very much. You've been a good father to her, and that's all that matters."

Jake smiled again. "Have I? I hope so. Thank you for saying so. Most of the time, I feel like I'm just putting one foot in front of the next. Doing my best and hoping it's good enough."

"I'm sure it's not easy," Alix hurried on, "when you lose the person who forms the very center of your world."

She looked up at him from her glass. "I lost someone, too, although he didn't die."

He frowned at her. "You lost a husband?"

She sighed again, more heavily this time. "No, I've never been married. But I did lose the man I loved most in the world. For a while there, I thought I'd probably spend the rest of my life with him.

"But it ended badly, very badly."

"I'm sorry."

She sent him a wan smile. "He didn't die tragically like your wife, but for me he might as well have."

Jake looked into Alix's green eyes. "Life can be pretty tough at times," he said. "And this is one of those times for me. I've got a maniac running loose out there on the streets, a real psychopath, and so far we haven't been able to even slow him down, let alone catch him.

"As soon as you and Charly hit the sack, in fact, I've gotta run back down to the station and see how my team is doing."

She thought for a few seconds. "Any idea at all what's motivating the guy?"

Jake set his glass down on the porch railing. "Well, as I told you up at Big Pine, he's obsessed with nightmares. He told all three of his victims that he planned to visit them in their dreams. You know, somnam . . . somnam . . . what's that scientific term again?"

"Somnambulistic Telepathy."

"Right. Well, the really strange part of this whole thing is that all three women who died left behind reports that they'd actually dreamed about him right before their deaths—and both were terrified that he actually *could* invade their sleep."

Alix didn't speak for a while.

The crickets kept up their love songs.

Then she said, "That's just plain amazing, if you ask me. Listen, Jake . . . I've got an idea. Starting tomorrow, why don't I give you a custom-tailored course in sleep science and ST? It couldn't hurt, right?

"At the very least, knowing more about this stuff could help you understand the killer's obsession better, don't you think?"

Jake nodded eagerly back at her. "That's a terrific idea. Let's do it!"

Alix reached over and patted his hand. "I think you'll find the science involved isn't really all that complicated."

Somehow they'd both risen to their feet by now. "I know you're pooped, Alix," said Jake. "It's already coming up on ten p.m. Let me walk you back to your room, and we can say good night.

"Tomorrow, let's jump on these serial killings with both feet, whaddya say?"

But saying goodnight wasn't quite as easy as that.

They stood in the doorway to her room for a few moments, reluctant to part . . . until all at once Alix leaned into him and kissed his cheek. For a few moments his arms were around her, holding her close. Their lips nearly met . . . but he managed to pull away at the last second.

"Good night, Alix. Thanks for coming to Boston."

She smiled at him, her eyes full of light. "There's no place else I'd rather be, Jake. I hope you know that."

"I feel the same way, Alix."

They were looking into each other's eyes now.

What they didn't see was Charly's door twenty feet down the hallway . . . as it slowly inched open.

Nor did they see the delighted smile on Charly's face, as she watched the visiting sleep scientist from Big Pine lean forward to plant a kiss on her father's cheek.

The cheerful daughter and the smiling houseguest went to bed after that, and the house fell silent . . . but not for long.

Soon Jake was jumping back into the unmarked cruiser for the quick ride back downtown.

Duty called. He knew he had a thousand things to catch up on after stepping away from the investigation for the past few hours. Taking care of them was a lot more important than sleep.

***

When he returned, it was almost dawn. He poured himself the usual glass of cold milk, then padded silently through the dark house toward his own room. It took him only a few seconds to shed his clothing and slip into the warm, welcoming comfort of the king-sized bed.

He was dozing—nearly sound asleep—when something touched his arm. He flinched visibly . . . then peered through the dim light of early dawn at the woman who now stood beside his bed.

She was smiling calmly at him, and her eyes were bright with a single teasing question.

He nodded.

Already naked, she slid in beside him. They embraced.

The first birds of the bright new day were already beginning to chirp outside their window.

CHAPTER 40
Out of the Past . . . a Monster

After working on her science project for an hour, Charly had kissed them both goodnight and gone to bed.

Jake and Alix were alone.

They sat at the big dining room table, relaxing over tall glasses of iced tea. The stereo played a Barbra Streisand classic from 1981, a slow-paced duet with Barry Gibb of the Bee Gees, *What Kind of Fool*?

> *There was a time when we were down and out,*
> *There was a place when we were starting over.*
> *We let the bough break,*
> *We let the heartache in.*
> *Who's sorry now?*

Jake looked at her again and again. He couldn't stop smiling. "Alix, Alix," he said. "I'm so pleased you've come to Boston."

"Thank you, Jake. I am, too."

"Chicago wasn't much fun," he continued. "It's kind of strange, but lately I've been noticing . . . *no* place is much fun if you aren't there."

"I feel the same way about you," she said.

Alix took a sip of tea. "So tell me . . . where are you? With the investigation, I mean?"

Jake thought for a moment. "I think we broke some new ground out there. We paid a visit to the murder victim's oldest son."

"We?"

"I went there with an FBI agent and a Chicago homicide detective. This famous doctor had been killed in his mansion four or five weeks ago. So we went out there and met with the son."

She nodded. He drank some tea. He was silent for a while, thinking.

What kind of fool
Tears it apart,
Leaving me pain and sorrow?

"The thing is," said Jake, "the FBI had just gotten some results from this high-tech lab test. Genetic fingerprinting. Ever heard of it?"

She frowned. "I don't think so."

"These days, it's amazing what they can do. At the crime scene, they'd found some blood on a mirror, and they looked at the DNA. It didn't match the victim's blood, so it had to be from the killer. Anyway, they put it through a centrifuge, and they pulled out some DNA.

"After running some additional tests, they were able to tell that the old man had actually been killed by someone in his immediate family."

He paused again. He was looking at her curiously. "Alix . . . is something the matter? You okay?"

Her eyes had gone strange. Fearful.

"A . . . a well-known surgeon in Chicago, you say? Killed by somebody in his immediate family?"

Jake nodded. "Yeah, that's it. It was a brutal killing, too. The poor guy had been cut to pieces by a scalpel. According to the medical examiner, he'd been slashed in the ribcage and bled to death. So we talked to the older son. For a while, we were wondering if *he* might be the killer . . . but he seems to have an airtight alibi. Plus, he's a hotshot lawyer out there, a really heavy hitter. From what we've been told, he's got some powerful political connections. All things considered, he's just not a likely candidate for cold-blooded murder.

"Anyway, we sat down with him. Right away, he starts telling us that the killer has to be his younger brother, this whacked-out psychiatrist, Dr. Michael Rogers . . . who's probably living right here in Boston."

Alix's right hand shot up to cover her mouth. She looked dazed. Stricken.

"Oh my God, Jake!"

He stared at her. "What? Hey, are you okay?"

Amazed, he watched her lurch sideways, arms flailing . . . watched her struggle to get to her feet . . . watched the glass of iced tea go flying. An instant later, the contents splattered against the fruit bowl in the middle of the table.

She was on her feet. Her face was contorted with pain and her mouth was a slash of anger.

"Goddamn him!" she shouted at the dumbfounded man on the other side of the table. "Goddamn that dirty sonofabitch. I know him. I know him, Jake.

"That filthy scumbag. I *know* him!"

By now Jake was also standing up. Stunned, he was reaching across the table, trying to put a calming hand on her shoulder. But she would have none of it. Enraged, she slapped the hand away.

"Alix," he said. "What in the world is the—"

"That vile sewer rat!" she roared, and he couldn't believe what he was hearing. "That lying piece of shit!" Then she began to run. She took three steps and slammed head-on into Charly's science project.

She went down hard, but then bounded to her feet and ran toward the front door.

He hurried after her, as dumbfounded as he'd ever been in his life. "Alix, what is it? What is it? Will you please slow down? Can we talk about it?"

They had reached the front porch. Alix paced back and forth, hugging herself frantically. "I'm cold," she told him. "I'm freezing! That sneaky bastard . . .

"I'm cold, Jake. I'm so cold."

Once again he reached for her, and once again she slapped his hand away. Her mouth was jumping and her eyes were wild, wild.

"That dishonest shithead . . . he lied to me. He *raped* me if you want the truth. Oh, he didn't use violence to rape me. He did it with *lies*.

"Filthy lies, and then *more* lies!"

Jake was hanging onto the porch railing now. "You mean . . . you're saying . . . are you saying you had a *relationship* with this guy?"

"I am. I did. He's a vicious psychopath, Jake. He exploited his patients and got one of them killed. The poor kid was a disturbed Vietnam veteran with PTSD. It happened twelve years ago. Rogers was working as a shrink at the VA Hospital in Boston, and he wound up with the vet as a patient. He manipulated him, lied to him.

"Then he discovered the kid had this power, this amazing power."

She glared fiercely at Jake.

"Somnambulistic Telepathy," she snapped. "That's how all of this started. The vet had been hideously injured in Vietnam, both physically and mentally. He'd witnessed rape and torture. He had killed people, and he believed he'd been cursed for the things he'd done.

"He believed he was the victim of a deadly curse!"

Now she whirled and glared again. A light had just flashed on in the house next door.

Jake blinked at her. "The neighbors," he said.

"Alix, we gotta go back inside."

But she was frozen to the spot. "I had a patient," she growled. "In Atlanta. I'd just gone to work at the SDC. This young woman came to me suffering with terrible nightmares. She had been the vet's fiancée, at least for a while, before she decided that she couldn't marry him— a man whose face had been burned halfway off."

By now Jake had managed to take one of her hands in his own. "Alix," he said softly. "Alix! Listen to me."

She tried to pull her hand away.

"*Listen* to me," said Jake. "Whatever this is . . . whatever happened, it's over now. It's done. It doesn't matter.

"It's over, do you *hear* me?"

Alix's eyes were still wild. "The dirty bastard—he's back, Jake! He's back . . . and now he's killing people. He must have snapped completely. He must have gone insane."

"Listen to me," said Jake. "We'll work together. We'll help each other."

He was leading her back into the house now. "Whatever happened back then, it's over and done. Over and done! It wasn't your fault, Alix. You didn't know what you were dealing with.

"How could it possibly be your fault?"

Together they staggered over to the sofa and fell onto the cushions. She was breathing raggedly now, and her voice had gone hoarse from weeping. "It was a terrible time for me, Jake. Terrible. I was so lonely, so miserable. I'd been through this awful relationship . . . and I was full of self-loathing. And he took advantage of that.

"The brilliant Dr. Michael Rogers. He sweet-talked me along. He told me I was beautiful and smart and charming and fun to be with. . . ."

She sent up a low moan of anguish, then looked at him. "Goddamn, I *hate* that prick. I'm glad I turned him in. I vowed I wasn't going to be destroyed by his manipulative lies! It took courage . . . but I reported him to the medical authorities, and in the end, *he* was the one who got destroyed!"

Jake was massaging her shoulders, trying to ease the terrible stiffness in her muscles. "Look, we'll find a way to deal with it," he said. "We'll work the case together. The Boston PD is already closing in on him, Alix. We think he may have moved back here from Providence, back into his old neighborhood . . . which is why we're pounding on every door in and around the Boston Combat Zone.

"We've already gotten a few hits from witnesses who claim to have seen him in Boston, and it's probably only a matter of days—maybe even hours—before we'll have the sonofabitch in lockdown.

"We'll work on it together, do you hear me?"

He was staring into her face now, searching her features for a sign of hope.

But all at once her eyes went huge again.

"Oh my God," she said.

"What?" said Jake.

"Nightmares," said Alix. "Somnambulistic Telepathy."

She shuddered, and her green eyes burned with sudden horror.

"He knows how to hurt us," she said.

Jake felt a wave of dread ripple through his gut.

"He can hurt us, Jake. Hurt us bad. All of us. Me, you . . . even poor Charly. He can attack us in our nightmares anytime he wants.

"He has the power to kill us—just like he killed those innocent young girls!"

Jake had opened his mouth to reply, but he was interrupted.

A shadow had fallen across the carpet—the shadow of a young girl in a nightgown decorated with tiny pink roses.

Her face was a mask of pure terror.

"Charly!" Jake shouted. He had risen to his feet without knowing it. "How long have you been listening to us?"

Charly sent up a wailing cry of fear. A helpless sob.

"I heard everything, Daddy. We're in danger, aren't we? Is he going to kill us?"

***

It took them nearly an hour to comfort the child and put her to bed.

Thirty minutes after she'd finally drifted into broken sleep, Alix staggered off to Jake's bedroom. He paced the living room carpet for a few minutes, then picked up the wall phone in the kitchen and dialed PD Dispatch.

It took the on-duty sergeant less than ten seconds to punch the call through to Fred Haskins's unmarked.

"Haskins here. Talk to me."

"Fred? Jake. What's the latest?"

Jake's new partner sighed unhappily. "We're doing all we can, but we don't have anything solid yet. We've knocked on every door in the Zone, and nobody's seen the perp."

"Where are you right now?"

"I'm parked out front of Tootsie's. We just interviewed everybody in the joint. We struck out. So now it's on to the next club."

Jake deliberated. "You've been showing his picture around?"

"Sure have. We did get a few hits earlier tonight. A couple of bartenders and a dancer remembered seeing him four or five nights ago. They even remembered the snake tattoo. But nobody we've talked to has seen him during the last few days."

Jake had begun to pace the length of the telephone cord, three steps each way. "So what's next?"

"Next is we're going to drop by some of the illegal after-hours clubs. They'll probably panic when they see us coming."

"Okay," said Jake. He grunted in frustration, then tightened his grip on the phone. "You find anything, you call me pronto."

"Will do."

"And get some sleep."

"Maybe."

"Eight a.m. sharp," said Jake. "I want the entire team in the Conference Room."

"Roger that."

Jake hung up slowly, frowning, then began to rub his eyes. After a while, he reached into the refrigerator and poured himself a glass of cold milk. Then he closed the refrigerator door and started for the bedroom.

He eased in next to Alix and spent the next minute listening to the soft patter of rain on the glass. He could tell from her breathing that she wasn't asleep, but there wasn't anything more to be said. So he just rested one hand lightly on her shoulder.

The two of them lay there, not moving. Not sleeping. Rain fell against the window.

***

An hour before dawn broke, the first *Herald* delivery trucks began dropping their bundles at newspaper boxes scattered all across the Boston metro area. The front pages carried a screaming headline.

2nd Letter Ridicules Police Investigation
'NIGHTMARE SERIAL KILLER' THREATENS TO KILL BOSTON DETECTIVE & FAMILY NEXT

The letter from Dr. Mike to the paper was printed directly beneath the headline. Once again, the sneering message had been sent directly to the *Herald* reporter who'd broken the original story. After a brief intro, the letter ran as follows.

To Mark Halliday

> *It's been amusing to watch the feeble attempts by the police to catch me. Why can't they get it through their brain-dead heads that I can't be stopped? And I will obliterate anyone who dares to try!*
>
> *Never before has there been a monster with such evil power.*

You tell Detective Becker that his ass is cooked. Royally! Doesn't he have a 14-year-old daughter? And what about his new squeeze, Alix Cassidy, who stole my life? Who stole my dreams of fame and fortune? She's toast, Halliday!

As for that pretty little girl of his . . . the one they call "Charly"? She's going to pay, too. Tell Becker she's next on my hit list.

Make no mistake, Halliday.

I'm going to take my time killing all of them— and I'll enjoy it!

—The Surgeon

CHAPTER 41
Alix's Haunting Nightmare

Alix woke up slowly, inch by uneasy inch. Something wasn't . . . right.

Something had glimmered nearby. Something pink. *What*?

She took in a sharp breath, almost a gasp. Was she looking at a pink jewel of some kind? Was she seeing a bright charm plucked from a vivid pink bracelet?

No . . .

It was a tiny eye.

My God . . . she was staring into the face of a pink-eyed rat!

She watched his mouth fall open, heard him squeak—

As he crawled slowly up her thigh!

Yeeeeekk!

Had Alix screamed?

Or was it the rat?

"What the hell?"

This time there was no doubt. It was Alix who had just screamed, even as she whiplashed her legs back and forth in a desperate effort to dislodge the slimy rodent before he could reach the soft flesh between her thighs.

She had cried out, all right—but somehow she knew her terrified shriek wouldn't be heard.

Where am I . . . and how did I ever get here?

No answer.

But she *needed* an answer . . . before the pink-eyed rat made his move!

She looked wildly around the room. There was just enough light filtering through a torn curtain to let her make out her surroundings. A cement floor. A rusted pipe hanging from the ceiling. And cold. Bone-chilling cold.

Oh my God, she told herself, *I'm naked. That's why I'm so cold!*

It was true. Her arms were covered with prickly goosebumps, her lips purple with gathering frost. Somehow, she must hide her nakedness! Now she was scrabbling across the cement—exposed, exposed. Pursued by her new pink-eyed friend!

She could feel the rough cement tearing at her flesh and leaving droplets of blood everywhere.

She could also see how his tongue was lapping them up . . . a diseased tongue covered with sores that leaked pale green pus.

Yes, his pink eyes were *controlling* her.

Try as she might, she couldn't free her tortured gaze from his. Now she was crawling onto a mattress—a lumpy, foul-smelling mattress coated with urine and feces.

She tried to vomit but produced nothing more than heaving air.

While the starved rat licked his hungry chops.

"Get away from me!" Had she screamed those words, or only thought them?

Paralyzed.

Utterly helpless. Her limbs were frozen inside an enormous iceberg.

Then she spotted them: the faded bloodstains on the far wall. Pale brown, pale lavender in places: Whose? *Whose*? And why did this basement room look so familiar? What was it about this dismal scene that she recognized, however dimly?

Oh my God . . . was this the *place*? Was this the room where poor David Collier had blown his brains out?

No. *No.* That nightmare had ended twelve years before. That tragedy was *over*, goddamnit! Never again would she have to visit that foul basement, the scene of the greatest tragedy she'd ever witnessed.

"Hello, Alix," said the pink-eyed rat.

She took in a huge breath and forced the words from her voice box.

"Rats can't talk!"

There was a chuckling sound. A trickle of dark laughter.

"This one can."

Had she been drugged? Had she snapped and been dragged into the locked ward at the state mental hospital? "Who are you?" she raged.

"You coward—come out of the shadows so I can see you."

Again, a chuckling sound. "Just look into my eyes, honey. Look into my eyes and you'll *see* who I am."

Alix had no choice. She was desperate now, and she had to obey. She looked. She gagged.

"No . . . it can't be you!"

"You've aged well, Alix. I forgot how beautiful you are," said the pink-eyed rat.

She flared instantly. "Well, I can't say the same for you, Michael. You look like the same piece of shit I once knew. What's it like to live the life of a pink-eyed rat?"

"You're about to find out, my dear. I've waited twelve long years for this moment, and I plan to make it last until you beg me to end your agony. How could you ever forget the special time we shared together right here in this room?

The rat sat up on its haunches and rubbed its forelegs together.

"You ruined me, Alix. I was utterly disgraced and humiliated because of what you did to me. Well, guess what? It's payback time. You're going to suffer, dear heart, and there's absolutely nothing you can do to stop me. Nothing!"

Despite her peril, Alix felt a flash of anger. "Don't get all high and mighty with me, Michael. You broke my heart. You betrayed me *and* your profession. You violated your oath—*do no harm*—and you're responsible for that poor boy's suicide. You deserved everything you got. As a matter of fact, if it had been up to me, I'd have had your balls cut off and served to you on a silver platter.

"You're nothing but a repulsive pink-eyed rat."

A pause, while the diatribe sank in. Followed by more laughter. "Still got that old spunk, eh, Alix? I always liked that quality in you. But it won't help you now. Not with what I've got planned.

"Here, take this."

Two scorching bitch slaps, one to each cheek, quickly brought her back to reality.

She bristled. "How dare you hit me? Who do you think you are?"

"Why, I'm just a pink-eyed rat waiting to devour your flesh, bite by delectable bite. I'm going to eat you alive, Alix. Isn't that what pink-eyed rats do?"

She stiffened again. "You can go straight to hell, Michael. You'll fit in perfectly with your new rat friends. This is just a nightmare. As soon as I wake up it will all be over—and you'll be back in the sewer where you belong.''

The rat snickered. "You think it's going to be that easy, Alix? Do you believe for one second I'm going to let you get away? If so, you're totally delusional. You are *mine*, cunt. Do you hear me? I own you."

The rat held up a soiled, battered doll.

"Do you recognize this, Alix?"

"How'd you get that? Give it back. It doesn't belong to you. It's Charly's."

Oh my God. That's what she meant: it will keep you safe!

"What have you done, you bastard?"

The rat sneered. "You'll find out in due time, my little peach. You're going to be seeing a lot of me, Alix. I'm going to haunt you, night after night, until I've had my fill. Then I'm going to lead you to the edge of a mountain cliff and shove you straight into oblivion."

"You tell me now how you got Charly's doll!"

"Why, I simply took it. Just like I'm going to take your life and turn it into a living hell. For twelve years all I could think of was how to get back at you for what you did to me. And then, just like that, you suddenly appeared—as Becker's new fuck buddy. What are the odds of that happening?

"Becker's a fool, Alix, if he believes he can stop me. And to think that before you fucked me over, you and I had the Nobel Prize within our grasp. It was *my* discovery, not yours. You stole it from me, bitch. And now I'm going to destroy you . . . along with Becker and his little donkey-doll daughter.

"Before long you'll all be with my father in his hell hole."

"You're insane, Michael. Don't do this. I'm begging you."

She watched him shake with sudden laughter. "You like my new stage name? I do. My dead prick father must be glowing with pride. Maybe he's even bragging to his new hell mates about his infamous son, *The Surgeon*. He always wanted me to follow in his footsteps.

"Well, guess what? Now I have!"

He held up his beloved surgical weapon, so that she could examine it carefully. The scalpel was engraved with the initials "HR," and he gave her a few seconds in which to study it. Then he placed the cold metal against the nipple of her right breast.

She shuddered . . . but her thoughts were elsewhere. They were focused on a more frightening threat. Still shuddering, she opened her mouth wide. "No . . . please, don't hurt Charly. She's just an innocent child!"

Those were her final words to the rat, however.

A moment later, she felt herself being shaken, roughly shaken by someone else's hands.

A man's hands.

"Alix, wake up. Wake up. You were having a nightmare. It's over. You're with me, Alix. You're safe!"

As her eyes regained focus, she cried out, "No, it's *not* going to be okay, Jake. This is terrible.

"I've just seen the devil . . . and his name is *Michael Rogers*."

***

Ten a.m. Saturday.

Six men sat in Conference Room B: Detective Sergeant Jake Becker and the five other investigators in his squad. All six were waiting for a very important Boston Police Department procedure to begin.

The procedure was known as "getting your ass reamed."

It began promptly at ten o'clock, when the door to the conference room swung open and a chunky red-faced man named Sam was suddenly confronting the men at the table.

"Good morning," snapped Sam Vandergriff, the CID Lieutenant of Detectives.

It was easy to read the anger in his eyes. "I'm glad to see everybody's here, and I'll get straight to the point.

"What the fuck is *wrong* with all of you people?"

They stared back at him, expressionless. No one spoke. The red-faced man walked to the head of the table, where a chair had been reserved for him. He didn't take it. He just stood beside it with his shoulders hunched way up.

He looked like a starved pit bull about three seconds after he learns that dinner has been canceled.

"Detective Becker, do you want to try and answer my question?"

Jake thought for four or five seconds.

"You want to know what's wrong with my squad? Is that the question?"

"Correct. You've got it, Becker. Congratulations. And may I tell you *why* I've asked you that particular question?"

"Please do."

"It's because we've got a serial killer terrorizing the City of Boston, detective. Okay? We know who the asshole is. We know what he looks like. We know his MO—the way he threatens these women and then shows up and attacks them late at night. We know about the scalpel he uses and the weird shit he leaves behind on mirrors. Okay?

"Hell, we even know, within a few blocks, where the jerk-off probably *lives*. And we've also got several recent photos of him from his brother in Chicago. Think about it. Think about it hard. We've got all that . . . and yet we can't bring him down.

"Instead of taking him in, we've been standing around with our *schlongs* hanging out, while the good citizens of Boston tremble with fear."

POW! The red-faced man's large right fist crashed into the worn surface of the conference table. "I want to know what you and your people have been doing for the last twenty-four hours, Becker. I need something to tell the Deputy Commissioner. I need something solid for him, you understand? See, for the last several days, he's been ringing my little telephone upstairs, oh, every fifteen or twenty minutes. Every time I pick up, he asks me the same question. Do I want to go back to directing traffic? Do I? Huh? Huh?

"Do I want to spend my shifts making out traffic reports and detailing fender benders? And the answer is no, I do *not* want to do that, Becker! I want to continue in my current role as the hard-charging Lieutenant of Detectives. Know what I mean?

"So give me something, detective. Give me something I can tell the Deputy."

There was a long silence, before Jake finally said, "We're all over the Zone, Lieutenant. We're covering it like the dew covers Dixie."

Jake turned and glanced down the table. "Detective Haskins, why don't you fill the Shift Commander in on the details?"

Haskins nodded. He didn't look happy, but you could tell he would do his best.

"Okay," he said slowly, frowning a little. "The entire squad worked 'til three this morning, along with three detectives we borrowed from Sergeant Schmidt's squad and eight uniforms. We hit all the bars, all the strip joints, all the flops.

"We put the squeeze on thirty or forty of our top snitches. We worked our best leads, showed our photos up and down the street."

Haskins stared glumly at the man standing stiffly beside the empty chair. "We talked to a couple hookers who said they'd seen the perp drinking at The Climax. And a bartender thinks he served him at the Club Galaxy four or five nights ago. But that's the last time anybody remembers eyeballing him."

The lieutenant nodded, then reached into his shirt pocket. He removed a pack of Tareytons. He shook one from the pack and took his time lighting it. "So where are we, Detective Haskins? You think he's gone underground? Think he's hiding in a cellar somewhere in the Zone, and we just haven't found it yet?"

"Could be," said Haskins. "Or maybe he ran. He's got to know we're onto him. I mean, his older brother in Chicago . . . we've got enough I.D. from the brother to take him down the minute he shows up on our radar.

"So maybe he ran. If he did, he could be anywhere."

"No shit?" said Vandergriff. He was gritting his teeth. "Anywhere? Now *there's* a clever deduction."

Now his broad face grew even redder. "I assume you've covered the bus stations. Amtrak? Logan? You've got photos of him posted at all the major transportation centers around Boston? You been talking to the airlines? I mean, you've done all of the basics, right?"

Haskins sighed. "Yup. All of it. But nobody's made him yet. We've been running him wire to wire, 24/7, for a solid week. We just haven't hit pay dirt."

The lieutenant took an angry drag on the Tareyton. Gray smoke jetted from his nostrils. "Okay . . . Detective Becker? I need you to give me the lowdown on this. Okay? The straight skinny. No fiddle-fucking around. What's your plan, detective?"

Jake looked at him. "My plan?"

"How are you going to find this shithead and take him down?"

Jake pondered the question briefly. "Well," he said. "For one thing, we've been doing some background work. The perp used to be a psychiatrist at the VA Hospital in Jamaica Plain. Spent more than ten years there apparently. We're talking to his former colleagues. According to what we're hearing, he had some pretty strange ideas about psychiatry. We're trying to understand how his mind worked."

Vandergriff glared. "What? You're talking to his *colleagues*? Pardon me, but I don't get that. How the fuck will that help you make the collar, Becker? Don't we know enough about him already?"

Jake started to answer—"Well, the guy had a long history of abusing—", but then he was interrupted. The conference room door had just swung open again. It was

Flaherty this time . . . and he looked even more pissed off than the lieutenant.

"Well now, what've we got here?" growled the Commissioner. "Is this the Ladies' Sewing Circle or what?"

Nobody answered him.

"Sam, what's the latest?"

The lieutenant stopped chewing on the end of his Tareyton. He looked like the firing squad was about to attach the blindfold.

"Sir, the latest is, we don't have dog shit."

The Commissioner blinked several times, and then his features sagged. "Why am I not surprised to hear that, lieutenant?" He turned to face the six men at the table.

"Maybe it's because the Boston PD has been standing around like a platoon of fucking wooden Indians for more than a week now. Is *that* why I'm not surprised?"

The room remained silent.

"Becker," said The Commissioner, "I came down here to give you a message. It's straight from Chief Rooney, who's spent the past four days going nose-to-nose with the mayor."

Now he took a step toward the conference table. He was scowling and sneering, and somehow doing both at the same time.

He looked like a bleeding club fighter who's just gone ten grueling rounds and lost on a split decision.

"You're the point man, Becker, and the shit stops rolling when it reaches your desk. You're the Squad Supervisor on those three ten-sevens, am I correct?"

"Yes, sir," said Jake.

The Commissioner produced an especially ugly smile.

"You've got forty-eight hours, pal.

"Nail that insane asshole—or we'll find ourselves a detective who can get it *done*."

CHAPTER 42
"Cut the Tail off the Donkey!"

"All aboard," shouts the bus driver.

"This Peter Pan bus is heading nonstop to the Dream World. We'll be leaving in exactly five minutes!"

Charly clambers aboard. She's thrilled and excited. *Oh, what a great ride this will be. What fun I'm going to have in the Dream World!*

The bedside clock reads 3:24 a.m.

Charly has just entered what will be the final REM stage of some very troubled sleep.

Now she scoots into the first seat on the left, right behind the driver. She settles back to enjoy the ride.

But then, out of nowhere, comes a menacing voice.

"Is *this* what you've been looking for, sweetheart?"

All at once the driver has turned toward her. He's holding up a familiar-looking doll.

By its tail. As if responding to the sudden attention, the floppy-eared doll suddenly belts out a familiar line: "Thanks for noticin' me!"

Charly feels a jolt of fear. "Why, it's *you*, Eeyore! I've been looking everywhere for you! Where have you been?"

"He's been with *me*, that's where. And I intend to keep him. He's mine forever!"

Amazed, Charly stares at the stocky, blue-eyed man in the plastic-billed Peter Pan cap. "Who . . . who are you?"

"Oh, that's an easy one. I'm Dr. Mike."

The driver grins back at her. An ugly grin. "I'm the person who's going to destroy your life, my little friend."

Charly feels a flash of anger. "You give Eeyore back! He's mine. You had no right to take him!"

The Peter Pan driver is quite impressed. This little girl is full of piss and vinegar. Just like dear old Alix. How wonderful!

He gives Charly a cold blank stare. "I'm going to say this one time and one time only. Do you understand?"

When she doesn't respond, he shouts at her. "I can't hear you!"

Now she's intimidated. "Yes . . . yes, *sir*."

"That's much better. Now you will shut your trap and do exactly as I say. Got it? Or I'll cut Eeyore into donkey filets."

Charly gasps. "Please don't do that! Please!"

"You tell your dumb-ass donkey father he can't stop me. Did you get that? You tell him I'm going to destroy you all."

She gapes at him. She's terrified . . . but she's also brave. She's going to stand up to him. "Stop talking about my father that way! My father is the best policeman in the whole world—and he won't quit until he catches you and puts you in jail where you belong."

The driver grins like an evil toad. "Yeah, right. Fat chance. He'll never catch me and you know it."

He sends her a long slow wink. "You know, it's really too bad the way that nasty boyfriend of yours dumped you.

"It's just very sad . . . the fact that he likes that *other* girl a whole lot more than he ever liked you."

She doesn't reply at first. Suddenly her eyes are full of tears. But Dr. Mike doesn't have any sympathy for her. Instead of comforting her, he grabs Eeyore by his blue-furred neck and squeezes tight.

In a flash, Charly starts coughing and choking. She feels like she'll explode if she doesn't get some air! Only when the man in the Peter Pan cap loosens his grip on Eeyore's throat is she able to regain her breath.

He's glaring now. He's enraged. He's holding up something made of metal . . . something that shines and glitters.

"Do you know what this is?"

She shakes her head.

"It's a scalpel," he growls. "It's very useful, my little friend. A doctor can use it in the hospital to make people feel better."

He chuckles. He winks. "Or you can use it to cut off a donkey's tail—like *this*!"

He lifts the blade, threatening the doll. She shrieks, "No, please don't hurt Eeyore! He didn't do anything to you. He's just a poor old donkey."

"Really?" He laughs softly, happily. "I hope you don't mind . . . but I'm going to carve your little donkey friend into bite-sized pieces. Is that okay with you, Miss Charly?"

She's sobbing uncontrollably.

"I think I'll start with his tail. Good idea?" Dr. Mike is toying with her now, swinging Eeyore back and forth, back and forth, like a hypnotist putting a subject under. Terrified, she catches a glimpse of something tattooed on the back of his hand—a deadly-looking snake!

All the while, the hapless doll keeps moaning out his familiar donkey sounds: "EEE-yore! EEE-yore! It's . . . ohhh-kayyy!"

"Please don't hurt him, mister!"

Dr. Mike sighs. "Don't you want to have some fun, Charly? How about if we play a little game? You, me and Eeyore? It's called 'Cut the tail *off* the donkey'—and I'll go first!"

With a sudden flick of his wrist, Dr. Mike slashes the doll.

All Charly can hear are the desperate grunts of her sad-eyed and now tailless donkey.

"Daddy!" she howls. The tears are running down her face.

"Daddy, please help us!"

Jake, asleep in the next room, opens one eye. He hears the second "Daddy!" He leaps to his feet.

A moment later, he's running down the hall.

"Daddy . . . this man . . . this man tried to cut . . . this man tried to cut Eeyore!"

He stares at her, thunderstruck.

"What man, honey? What man did that?"

She sobs. She gasps. "The man . . . the man with the snake tattoo on his hand!"

Jake stares at her. "A snake tattoo, Charly?"

"Yes!" She's sobbing and sobbing . . . and then looking at her bed, looking at the floor.

"Daddy—he's gone! Eeyore was sleeping right here beside me—and now he's gone!"

Oh my God, thinks Jake. *This can't be happening.*

But it *is* happening. They spend the next 20 minutes searching high and low for the little doll. They tear the bed apart, examine every inch of the sheets and blankets and pillowcase, looking for the donkey with the pink bow on his tail.

Full of dread, they comb the rest of the room . . . and find nothing.

Wide-eyed, Charly stares at her father. "That man in the dream—he took Eeyore, didn't he, Daddy?"

Jake has no answer for her. He has no answer for himself. He holds her in his arms while she weeps and trembles.

This cannot be happening to us, he tells himself. But he knows he's wrong.

How long will it be before Dr. Mike visits Charly's nightmares again?

How long before he decides to start using his scalpel on Jake's beloved child?

***

Halliday, this is my third letter to you and The Herald. *Today I want to ask you a riddle. Okay by you? Here it is: What do a saw, a hammer, some nails and some plywood have in common?*

Ask Detective Jake Becker! If he's as smart as they say, he'll quickly figure it out.

Make no mistake: I'm going to destroy Becker's life and all he lives for. I know all. I will watch. I will wait. And it won't be long now. His life may be almost over, but his agony will never cease.

First donkey-daughter, then you, Becker—and finally, my sweet Alix!

Build Jake, build. Hurry, but have no hope. Bang, Jake, bang—hammer the final nails into the coffins that will imprison your loved ones for all eternity.

Hey, Jake—you ever heard that funny old riddle?

Q. What'd one casket say to the other in the cemetery?

A. Is that you, Coughin'?

Hah-hah! Whee! Why not laugh? It's too late for tears, Jake. It's all over.

—The Surgeon

The first task for Dr. Mike after exiting the Greyhound bus terminal in Baltimore was to find a bathroom.

It had been five days since his last dump, and his stomach ached horribly. He knew he could wait no longer—or he'd wind up crapping in his pants.

Indeed, it had nearly happened several times already on the long ride from Boston. During that endless sojourn, the nightmare stalker had entertained himself more than once by watching the shocked faces and listening to the angry mutterings of the other passengers as he let go a series of ass-rattling stink bomb farts.

Yeah! At one point, just for the sheer *fun* of it, he'd even risen from his seat and wandered happily about while distributing his scent. At times during the long ride, the entire bus had smelled like a three-day unflushed toilet.

It was a fitting metaphor for the monster he'd become.

But at least he'd had the sense to get the hell out of Boston! After his letters to Mark Halliday and the sensational coverage of "The Surgeon" in the *Herald*, the cops were undoubtedly closing in on him.

Remembering the stark front page headlines he'd been triggering of late, Dr. Mike could only smile with satisfaction.

IS JACK BACK?
Is Boston's Vicious "Surgeon" Killer
A Reincarnation of London's Ripper?

Yes, things were working out very well. And the best part of all was the knowledge that his secret power was "portable." Ever since the night when he'd murdered his hated father—then asleep in Chicago—by sneaking into his dreams (even though Dr. Mike was during those same moments dozing and dreaming on the plane ride home to Boston), The Surgeon had been reveling in his ability to kill whenever—and wherever—he wished.

Because he operated entirely in the Dreamtime, it didn't matter where his body was located in space. No way! Thanks to his toll-free expressway into the world of other people's nightmares, he could torture and kill his victims *anywhere*. So why not hang out in Baltimore? After spending all of 1970 there as a Visiting Fellow in the Johns Hopkins Addictive Substances Clinic, he knew Crabtown inside out.

They'd never find him here. Never!

Bring it on, he told himself as the exhaust-belching Greyhound rumbled into the city's rundown Transportation Center on O'Donnell Street.

Dr. Mike is ready to kick some ass!

His first order of business—right after the huge shit he'd take in the nearest men's room—would be to drink himself into a stupor.

He knew the perfect place for that: the locally infamous Cat's Eye Pub on Thames Street in Fells Point.

Fells Point was a seedy, rundown section of Baltimore frequented by half-loaded yuppies and drifting sailors in search of hookers and cheap drinks. Dr.

Mike remembered the neighborhood quite well from his fellowship year, and for good reason: he'd spent more than a few nights at the "Eye," boozing and whoring.

Now it would be his home away from home.

He was on a roll, and he knew it. Fells Point would fit him like a glove. In this shabby world of endless red brick row houses and cobblestoned streets intersected by trash-littered alleys, he'd never be noticed. This was a world full of wailing tugboat whistles and yellow streetlights burning dimly in the fog that hovered endlessly above the murky water.

Home sweet home for Dr. Mike!

Hurrying along the Thames Street corridor that flanked the Inner Harbor, en route to the Cat's Eye, he soon had the good fortune to stumble upon a good old-fashioned bitch fight.

Two strung-out and disgustingly ugly hookers were battling it out over a prime stretch of real estate on the corner of Thames and Nugent Streets.

He watched the two of them go at it. "You get the fuck off my corner, you motherfucker," shouted Bitch No. 1, "or I'll carve you out a brand-new asshole. Do you hear me?" Enraged, she was pounding Bitch No. 2 with her fists. No way was she going to surrender her spot.

If she didn't deliver the bread tonight, her pimp would beat her senseless, or maybe worse.

He watched them and smiled. Yes, this was exactly how he'd handle Alix! Carve her out a new asshole!

He laughed out loud, and the alpha hooker didn't like it one bit.

"What *you* looking at, ass breath?"

"I wouldn't fuck you if you were the last piece of ass on this planet," Dr. Mike yelled back at her and then moved on. Onward! He huffed along, desperate for a drink, until at last he reached the corner of Thames and South Broadway.

There he instantly recognized the vivid neon sign hanging above the battered door. The closer he got, the clearer the image became.

Suddenly he was looking into a freakish eye with a slit-like golden-yellow pupil that stared angrily back at him.

It was the eye of a king, a regal black panther—the baddest bad ass in the entire feline kingdom! But this bad-ass owned only one eye; the other socket was hollow. Spooky! Had the dark orb been taken out by some rock-throwing drunken sailor?

Grinning fiendishly, Dr. Mike stared long and hard at the dead socket . . . and then an amusing thought crept into his mind. *Bad-ass cats despise pink-eyed rats!* And wasn't *he* a pink-eyed rat? What could be more perfect?

Face it: he'd been drawn to Fells Point by a karmic force, a force he didn't understand—but a force that could not be denied. He was *meant* to be here.

But the hour was growing late. *Snap out of it*, he commanded himself. *After you've found a place to hide, the time for real nastiness will arrive.*

Ready to rock, he took a deep breath and pushed on the door.

The joint was packed wall to wall . . . but it didn't take more than a few seconds for Dr. Mike to spot what he wanted. To reach the jam-packed bar, he'd have to maneuver his way through the crowd of rowdy happy hour suburban yuppies and local construction workers enjoying a cold one after work. Okay . . . why not have some fun along the way? Why not pinch a few asses en route to the bar? Did he really give a shit if they called him a lech?

It was *true*, wasn't it? Right then, he knew the soft feel of a girl's ass would drive his blood to where he needed it the most: below his belt.

The first two coeds didn't bat an ass cheek as he groped them. As a matter of fact, they actually seemed to like it. But bitch number three was onto him and was soon yelling "Asshole!" to his face.

Well, she'd be calling him much worse before he was finished with her! Yes, he'd certainly come to the right place.

But hang on, he needed to slow down. Before he got too drunk, he should ask the bartender for some practical advice.

"Any idea where a guy can get a room around here?"

The bartender had heard that piercing scream, "Asshole!"—and he gave the disheveled derelict in front of him a sharp glance.

"What was that all about?"

"No big deal," snapped Dr. Mike. "Just another nasty broad with a nasty mouth. She didn't like it when I pinched her butt, that's all.

"Say, can you help me find a place to crash tonight?"

The bartender sized him up quickly. This guy wasn't looking for a room at The Ritz.

"Down the street," he growled, while his hands darted among the beer glasses. "Follow the Inner Harbor down to 24 Broadway Avenue, right where Thames and Broadway intersect. You'll spot a joint called 'Mama's Place.' You can't miss it.

"She'll have a room. Always does, provided you got the bread to pay her a week in advance. She rents by the hour, too, if that's what you're interested in."

For the first time in many a moon, Dr. Mike decided to be polite. "Thanks *mucho*, my good man."

He smiled at the bartender for a moment, but his cheerful grin soon vanished.

Face it, he had some unfinished business to take care of—and there would be nothing friendly in the way he managed it.

Yeah.

Dr. Mike was about to *call* on a few folks.

Too bad for them.

One by one, he ticked off the names on his mental list.

Charly.

Jake.

Alix.

CHAPTER 43
A Plea for Help

Later that night, after Jake and Charly had fallen asleep, Alix lay there wide awake.

Her mind raced with troublesome memories and sudden flashbacks during which she'd be sitting in a psych class at Wellesley, or walking across campus, or writing a paper on Freud at one of the long oak tables in the library. A few moments later, she'd be watching her mother at the stove, watching her shake green onions into a pan as she whipped up a delectable Sunday morning omelet.

Unable to drift off, Alix twisted and turned. *Nearly three a.m.* Struggling to find a cool spot on the mattress, she listened to Jake's deep, regular breathing for a while.

Somewhere near dawn, she found herself standing above a patient in the SDC Atlanta sleep lab, with the EKG tracing dancing on the screen and the brainwave monitors beeping softly in the background.

Wait a minute—what's that? That shadow in the window?

For a moment, she thought she'd seen a tall figure leaning against the glass, his dark baseball cap slanted low on his forehead, so that she couldn't make out his eyes. . . .

Now she looked down at the patient on the table. Something wasn't right. She *felt* it, and she asked herself: *What's wrong with this picture, Alix?*

The patient's eyelids fluttered and twitched, a sure sign that REM sleep—the world of the Dreamtime—had begun. Alix watched her eyelids flicker, then jump. Gradually she became aware of a background sound, music from somewhere, a golden oldie playing softly, way back in the deep recesses of her struggling mind:

Out of the mist your voice is calling . . .
It's twilight time.

Alix took in a sharp breath. That music out of the past, that popular song by The Platters—*Twilight Time*—how had that long-ago music crept into the mists that drifted through Alix's wandering brain?

Each day I pray for evening,
Just to be with you.
Together, at last, at twilight time!

She looked down at the patient on the lab table.
Then she saw them.
Lines of bright red blood trickling from both of her sleep subject's eyes!
Oh my God, no! Leaning in closer, Alix watched vivid drops of blood creep along her subject's cheek.
Was this real? Was it happening? *She's hemorrhaging. . . her brain must be bleeding out through her eyes—I have to wake her up!*
She reached out with a trembling hand, intent on grasping the patient's shoulder. But before she could make contact, she heard a low ripple of male laughter begin on the other side of the lab.
Her eyes went there . . . and then to the large silvered mirror that hung above a second table.
That mirror had been positioned so that observers could watch a sleep subject's breathing and facial movements from a safe distance, without fear of waking the sleeper.

What? In the mirror! *What?*

There was something moving in the glass. She stood stock-still above her sleeping subject, watching . . . a gleam of light. A flash of soft greenish light, and then . . .

A hat!

And beneath it, *his* face—the same face she'd feared and despised and dreaded for so many years.

"Hello, sweetheart. I'm back."

She didn't speak. How could she speak? Her mouth was a clot of horror, as if it had been packed with some warm, gooey paste. And her arms were heavy, so heavy she couldn't lift them. She could barely breathe, she felt so heavy, so terribly heavy and unable to move.

With a brutal shock, she realized that *she* was now stretched out flat on *her* back.

She was the sleep subject now. The sleep subject who lay helpless on the bed. . . .

It was *Alix!*

And there he was, looming directly above her, smiling sweetly and holding the long glittering blade gently in his right hand.

"Hi, honeybell! So nice to be with you again. May I show you my little plaything?"

She opened her mouth to respond—but produced nothing more than a little air, a faint hissing.

Now he held the gleaming surgical tool directly above her eyes.

"Can I tell you a story about my plaything, Alix? Can I tell you a little tale . . . a tale full of sound and fury, signifying nothing?"

Wild-eyed, she stared up at him. "Wha . . . what? A story?"

"A tale told by an idiot," he crooned at her. "The story of a young man who grew up all alone. A very lonely young man . . . a man whose father did not *appreciate* him.

"My story, Alix. *My* story!"

Paralyzed, lying helpless on the table, she waited to hear the story.

"See this?" he was asking her now, with the scalpel looming right in front of her eyes.

"See this crafty little device, my sweet? This is a surgical scalpel." And he waved it slowly back and forth through her terrified gaze.

"It's a real beauty, of that you can be sure—and it was one of The Prick's proudest possessions. If you look closely, you'll see his initials embossed right there on the steel: HR.

"Can you see them, Alix?"

She didn't answer. Somewhere deep in her mind, in the farthest reaches of her crawling mind, she was calling out: "Jake . . . *help* me, Jake!"

"It was very sad what happened between my father and me," said Dr. Mike. He sighed deeply, heavily. "It nearly killed me to see the disdain he felt for me moving through his sadistic eyes. I struggled and I suffered . . . all those years . . . and then *we* met. You and me, Alix.

"We found each other in the darkest hours of the storm. We were going to build a wonderful new life together. You and me, Alix—you and me!"

She shuddered on the table. *Jake, please . . . Jake!*

He was moving the blade along her thighs now. Whisper-soft, the polished steel caressed her thighs. "His proudest possession—and I took it from him. I made it mine, Alix; I made it mine!

"Do you see the greatness of what I did? Do you see the *triumph* of it?"

On the word *triumph*—he flicked his wrist and she felt the sting of the razor-sharp blade cutting into her flesh.

Then all at once her world was shaking, shaking, crashing through space and tumbling back to earth.

"Alix! Alix! Wake up—it's okay, honey. It's just a nightmare. It's okay!"

Jake was holding her in his arms, rocking her slowly back and forth, soothing her with whispered words of love.

She clung to him . . . hung on his strong arms . . . struggled to believe that the nightmare had really ended, that it was over at last.

Then she felt it.

The wet. Down there between her legs, in her most private place. *The wet*!

Frantic, she pulled her nightgown up.

In the pale dawn light of the bedroom, she saw the blood.

"Oh my God, Jake!"

"What? What, honey?" He stared at her as if she'd just arrived from outer space.

"He cut me!" she cried out to him. Her voice was jagged with new terror.

"He cut me in the nightmare . . . and now there's blood on my legs!"

She turned to him then. Clung to him. "Do you understand, Jake? Don't you get it? He cut me in a nightmare, and now there's blood on my legs.

"*My* blood!"

***

Desperate times called for desperate measures. And this was certainly a desperate time. Why? Simple. Alix knew that without Rozzie and Dr. Jacobson by her side, she, Jake and little Charly might all die at the hands of Michael Rogers.

But Roz and Stan could help her fight back!

Gripping the telephone so tightly her knuckles blanched, Alix dialed Big Pine.

Please, Rozzie, be there. Please. I need you!

The phone in the director's office rang once, twice, three, four times—and on the fifth ring Rozzie answered.

"Hello, Rozzie here."

"Rozzie," she shouted, "it's me, Alix!"

"Oh, good! How the hell are you, honey?"

"I'm in terrible trouble. That's how I am."

Rozzie took a sharp breath. "What? Why? What's happened?"

"Rozzie, David Collier is still on the scene somehow. He left something behind."

"What? I thought you said you saw him kill himself."

"I did. And that's something I'll never forget. But there's more to the story than that . . . even though I don't understand it. Something uncanny happened right before he died. Do you remember how I told you I saw a strange energy jump from Collier to Rogers right at the end? A spooky energy?"

"Of course I do. You said you saw something pass between them."

"That's right. Now I know what it was."

"What?"

"Don't you see? Rogers is now carrying the dark energy Collier passed on to him right at the end of his life. That energy has given Rogers the ability to use

Somnambulistic Telepathy. And now he's attacking me with it. He wants revenge."

Roz was silent for a moment. Alix could hear the wheels turning.

"You did what you had to do, Alix. The sonofabitch got everything he deserved."

But her friend wasn't listening. "Oh my God," said Alix. "Rogers is 'The Surgeon'!"

Roz was struggling. "How could that be?"

Alix's eyes were huge, and the words came rushing out. "Okay. This is what happened. Jake just got back from Chicago, where he found out that the Boston serial killer also murdered his own father back in Illinois. When he told me that, I became hysterical."

"What are you saying, Alix?"

"The killer is Michael Rogers. The same shrink who fucked me over twelve years ago. He's the Surgeon! And somehow he knows we're on to him. I've had horrifying nightmares ever since I learned he was a killer. Rogers is threatening to cut me to pieces, the same way he murdered those innocent women."

She gasped then, and Rozzie heard her fighting for self-control. "Jake and Charly are the best things ever to happen to me, Roz! I can't let them be hurt because of what I did. How could I ever fall in love with a man as evil as this?

"What's wrong with me?"

Rozzie made a sputtering sound. "Nothing is wrong with you, honey. You've got your head screwed on as tight as anybody I know."

"Would you come to Boston, Roz? I need you here with me. Now."

Roz was fighting mad. "You bet I will. Wait until you see me in action, sweetheart. We'll nail his ass to the wall, or my name isn't Rozzie Violette!"

"I was hoping you'd say that."

Rozzie smiled, but then frowned. Her friend was in terrible danger, and she wanted desperately to help.

"Wait a minute—I just got an idea," said Roz.

"What?"

"Melinda Birdsong. I'm going to bring her with me— if I can talk her into it, that is."

Alix took a huge breath. "You're kidding. Melinda *Birdsong*? The Abenaki medicine woman? How in the world will *she* be able to help?"

Rozzie was quick to reply. "Think, Alix. Melinda is a gifted psychic, a really heavy hitter . . . and she's also meaner than a hungry snapping turtle. She doesn't take the slightest shit from anybody. If there's anyone on the planet who will know how to move through the Dreamtime—and how to deal with a shithead psychopath like Michael Rogers—it's Melinda."

Alix remained silent for a few seconds. "Damn," she finally breathed, "you might be right, Rozzie. Melinda certainly knows her stuff . . . and she's utterly fearless. I realized that the first time I saw her climb aboard that screaming Harley of hers."

Rozzie nodded. "It's perfect, Alix—I'll call her right away. Meanwhile, have you considered the idea of asking Dr. Jacobson what he thinks of all this crazy stuff?"

Alix was nodding on her end of the line. Grimly.

"He's my next call, Roz."

***

"Stan, it's me, Alix."

"Hello, Alix. How are things going up in Maine?"

The words came rushing out. "I'm in trouble, Stan. My life and the lives of two of my best friends are in terrible danger.

"ST is back!"

Dr. Jacobson listened intently, while she wept and begged for his help. It didn't take him long to respond. "Okay, I'm on it. I'm already moving toward you, Alix.

"I'll help you every way I can."

"Oh, thank you. Thank you, Stan! I'll give you more of the details once you get here. Listen, you're going to have to help me enter the Dreamtime. Literally, I mean. *Physically!*

"It's the only way we'll be able to stop him."

Dr. Jacobson hesitated. He knew better than to ask too many questions.

"Hang on, Alix. Just do your best to stay calm. I'll get there as fast as I can."

"Thank God," said Alix. She hung up. She cried for a moment longer, but then took a deep breath and set her jaw.

Her life-and-death struggle with ST was about to begin.

CHAPTER 44
Enter Private Detective Boohar

They were in the middle of studying the lab's DNA-assay—a 47-page report crammed with high-tech gobbledygook—when the telephone rang in Fred Haskins's cubicle.

"Haskins here."

He listened for a minute, frowning, then cupped the mouthpiece with one hand.

"It's the Duty Sergeant out on the front desk. The tail got it right, Jake. Their first stop after Logan Airport was the Boston PD. He followed them right to our front door. Hoyt Rogers and that private detective he hired just walked into the lobby a minute ago."

Jake nodded. "Okay, no problem. You say he's got the private detective with him?"

"That's correct," said Haskins. "A guy named Boohar."

Jake stared at him. "You're making this up."

"I'm not," said Haskins. "Alan Boohar. What should I tell them?"

Jake thought for a moment. "Well . . . I guess we gotta talk to 'em for a minute. Courtesy, you know?"

"No problem."

"The thing is, we're probably going to need Rogers' help at some point. He's sitting on a ton of info about his younger brother."

Jake sighed with aggravation.

"Tell the Duty Sergeant we're coming up front to greet our visitors."

"Will do," said Haskins.

***

Hoyt Rogers, Jr., wore a pinstriped gray suit and a sleek gold bow tie woven from Hong Kong silk. He was also carrying a neatly rolled up umbrella, although it was a cloudless day in Boston.

After shaking hands with the two detectives, he pointed the umbrella at Jake.

"Detective Becker," he said, "it seems obvious that your team needs some professional help."

"Does it?" said Jake.

"Roger that," said Hoyt, Jr. "Nothing personal, Becker."

He pronounced it as BECK-ah.

"Your people here in Boston are clearly in over their heads."

Jake and Fred looked at each other.

"I want to introduce Mr. Alan Boohar," said Hoyt, Jr. He pointed the umbrella at the fat man in the narrow-brimmed hat who flanked him on the left.

"Mr. Boohar is a private investigator, and he's got impressive credentials."

"Hello, Mr. Boohar," said Fred.

"Pleased to meet you," said Jake.

"I've asked Detective Boohar to join me in the search for my brother," said Hoyt, Jr. "Believe me, he's damn good at what he does."

"I'm sure he is," said Fred. "And I also like his hat. Mr. Boohar, is that what they call a 'bebop' hat?"

The gumshoe didn't seem pleased by the compliment. "No," he said bluntly. "It's not a bebop. Not at all.

"It's actually just a slimmed-down fedora."

"Okay," said Fred. "A slimmed-down fedora. Now I understand."

Jake gave Fred a warning look.

Knock it off.

"Why don't we go back to the squad room," he told their two visitors, "and I'll bring you both up to speed on our investigation."

***

Jake took them through it, step by step, for more than twenty minutes. Hoyt, Jr., listened intently, with his rolled-up umbrella propped on his knee.

"Okay, so what's the problem?" he asked when Jake had finished.

"The problem?" said Jake. "It's pretty simple really. We've looked high and low, night and day, but we haven't been able to find your brother, Mr. Rogers. At least not yet.

"We've got a nationwide APB out on him, but no luck so far."

Hoyt, Jr., stared at him for a few seconds. "I understand all that, Detective Becker. What I *don't* understand is why your people can't get the damn job done. We think Michael may be living in a rented room somewhere around the Combat Zone. That's the area where he lived a couple of years ago, before he went down to Providence to teach at that community college.

"Detective Boohar here has managed to locate two of his previous addresses. They're right on the edge of the Zone.

"Have you and your men checked out that area of the city?"

Haskins glanced at a poker-faced Jake. "We sure have," he said after a bit. "And we're continuing to look for him, there and elsewhere in Boston."

Hoyt, Jr., nodded impatiently. "Well, he couldn't have gone too far. My brother was down and out, gentlemen. Totally broke. His drinking was out of control. He probably moved into yet another rented room after he returned from Providence. I mean, think it *through*. Have you searched that area carefully? Did you put plenty of officers on it?"

"Oh, we did, we did," said Jake. "But nothing has turned up yet, Mr. Rogers. However, we do want you to understand that we're giving it our best effort here in the Homicide Division of the Boston Police Department."

Hoyt, Jr., produced a sour smile. "Well, I hope so," he muttered at them, "especially given the fact that three young women have been brutally murdered so far."

Fred Haskins's lips were tightly compressed. "Mr. Rogers, I can assure you that we know how many young women have been murdered so far. It's uppermost in our minds right now."

Hoyt, Jr., didn't seem impressed by this statement. "That's fine," he said. "But we need to ratchet up the pursuit, if you will."

"Ratchet it on up?" said Haskins. "Is that your thought?"

"Exactly," said Hoyt, Jr. "That's why I've engaged Detective Boohar here. He has some very good ideas of his own."

He turned to the gloomy-looking private eye, whose slimmed-down fedora now rested securely in his lap. "Go ahead, fill them in, Alan."

Boohar blinked rapidly at the two cops. "First off," he said, "I'm gonna walk the streets in and around the Combat Zone with several photos of this Michael Rogers. I'm gonna be asking folks if they've seen him of late."

He gave them a look of fierce determination. "I can tell you this much: I won't stop until I hit pay dirt."

Both policemen nodded in agreement. "That makes good sense," said Jake. "But of course, we've already asked most of the 'folks' around the Zone that same question and we came up empty. No pay dirt at all."

Detective Boohar sent Jake a thin, cold smile. "No offense," he said, "but I'm really wondering if your people have been assiduous enough in their pursuit of this felon."

"Assiduous?" said Haskins. "I don't think I know that one, Mr. Boohar."

"*Determined*," snapped the private eye. "I'm not down on the police, understand. But in my experience, most of them do tend to go home at five o'clock, the moment their shifts have ended.

"Nothing personal, Detective Haskins . . . but I like to believe that I work at a higher level of determination."

Jake and Fred sat motionless for a few seconds, thinking. Then Jake said, "Mr. Boohar, we can't stop you and Mr. Rogers from talking to the 'folks.' But I do need to warn you that if you do that, you'll be in danger of interfering with a police investigation."

Hoyt, Jr., made a snorting sound. "Wait a minute," he said. "I'd ask you to remember that I'm an experienced attorney, Detective Becker. I'm well aware of my rights as a citizen."

Jake didn't flinch. "Here's the bottom line, Mr. Rogers. If you're out there questioning the 'folks' and you wind up alerting the suspect and triggering his flight, you'll be subject to immediate arrest. And if you *do* run across anything that's relevant to our ongoing investigation, you'll have to report it to me and Detective Haskins immediately."

He looked both newcomers in the eye. "If you hold back the smallest detail, you could be locked up for obstruction of justice—and under Massachusetts law, you could find yourself waiting for days to get a bail hearing."

Hoyt, Jr., was standing up by now. He was also pointing the umbrella again. "Are you threatening me, detective?"

"No, sir," said Jake. "I'm advising you, that's all."

The angry lawyer produced another snorting sound.

Then he turned to his glowering sidekick. "Let's go, Alan. It's obvious that the Boston Police Department isn't terribly interested in catching this killer."

But Fred Haskins was holding up one hand. "My card," he said. "If you two come across anything of note—anything at all—I will need to hear from you. Are we clear on that?"

Hoyt, Jr., delivered another sour smile. "Sure thing," he said. "You bet we are." He sent the detective his icy stare. "And that cuts both ways, gentlemen.

"As soon as you locate my younger brother—or rather, *if* you locate him—I expect you to notify me immediately."

Jake nodded and smiled. But he was watching their arrogant visitor intently. All at once, he was remembering a detail from Alix's most recent nightmare. At the time, the detail hadn't seemed terribly important. But now it had triggered a thought in Jake's racing mind.

"Before you leave, Mr. Rogers, may I ask you a quick question?"

The hawk-eyed attorney leaned toward him. "Of course. That's why I'm *here*, detective. Fire away."

Jake nodded. "Well, as I'm sure you know . . . we've been searching through thousands of different personal documents and phone records and the like, searching for any information that might give us a clue as to your brother's whereabouts."

The lawyer was glaring at him, poker-faced.

"I understand, Detective Becker. So what is your question?"

Jake spoke without hesitating. "Does the name Fells Point mean anything at all to you?"

The lawyer's eyes widened slightly at the sound of the name . . . but he gave no other sign that he recognized it at all.

"Fells Point, did you say?"

"That's it," said Jake. "No big deal . . . we happened to run across that name in a document search the other day. We found the name on a postcard your brother had sent to a colleague—another VA psychiatrist—a few years ago, and he wrote on the card that he'd had 'a great time in Fells Point over the weekend.'

"We were wondering if that name might mean anything to you."

Hoyt, Jr., paused for a second, then blurted in a rush: "No, I can't say the name has any special meaning for me. Nothing at all. I'm sorry."

He turned to look at the private eye. "Are you all set to go, Alan?"

"Yes, sir, I'm ready to roll."

A moment later, he and the trailing Boohar were exiting the police station and hurrying back toward their waiting cab. As soon as they jumped in, Rogers was in the driver's face.

"Logan Airport," snapped the impatient attorney, "and if you want a good tip, you won't waste any time getting there."

"Got it," barked the cabbie, as his foot hit the gas pedal.

Boohar gave the lawyer a quizzical glance. "The *airport*, Mr. Rogers? Wait a minute—I thought we were going on to the hotel."

"Not any more we're not," growled the frowning lawyer. "That asshole Becker just tipped his hand."

Boohar was so flummoxed he didn't speak.

"Fells Point is a rundown neighborhood in Baltimore," said Hoyt. "It's on the waterfront—a seedy area full of battered taverns and sailors looking to get laid. I'll bet you a thousand bucks my brother's hiding out there."

Boohar's mouth was hanging open. "But . . . but how can you be so sure?"

Attorney Rogers growled impatiently. "Because, number one, he's probably not in Boston, or he'd have been found by now. His picture's plastered all over town, don't forget. Number two, my brother lived for a while in Fells Point when he was training at Johns Hopkins some years back. He hung out in a couple of bars there whenever he wasn't working or studying.

"He even took me there a couple of times, and then proceeded to get drunk and act like a complete horse's ass.

"Anyway, he loved Fells Point. And he was also terribly proud of his fellowship at mighty Johns Hopkins. He never stopped bragging about it, or reminding my father that he was working at 'one of the great healing institutions of the modern world.'

"It all fits perfectly, Alan. Becker found those two words on a postcard . . . but apparently, he doesn't know they refer to a rundown neighborhood in Baltimore where my brother loved to hang out. It's the perfect hiding place for a drunken loser like Michael Rogers— and my gut tells me he's living in a flophouse in Fells Point as we speak!"

Now he whirled around to bellow at the cabbie: "Come on, pal, step on it—we've gotta catch a flight!"

Boohar was struggling to take it all in. "Okay, I get it. But why don't you start by contacting the Baltimore police? Isn't that the logical next step?"

The lawyer sneered while waving the suggestion away. "Because *I* want to be the one to find my brother, and not the cops. Why? Because the police will shoot first and ask questions later. And if that happens, I'll never get a chance to tell that dirty bastard how much I despise him for killing our father.

"Now stop with the questions and just do what you're told."

Boohar obeyed, but his downturned mouth showed how he felt about it. Until now, the Chicago gumshoe thought he'd seen everything. But he hadn't seen Hoyt Rogers, Jr., yet, had he?

Face it: the hotshot lawyer was an out-of-control dickhead. Why the hell hadn't Boohar turned down this job?

Well, it was too late now.

***

The cab screeched along the city streets toward the highway tunnel that would take them toward the airport.

But neither of them happened to notice the unmarked gray 1983 Chevy Camaro that trailed them at a steady distance of about 50 yards.

Nor did they spot the Camaro's driver, Sergeant Ralph Hannigan of the Undercover Unit, who'd been assigned to tail Hoyt Rogers, Jr., and his private gumshoe the moment they landed in Boston.

***

"Before you hit the tunnel, pull over at a pay phone!" roared the brutally impatient Hoyt Rogers, as they sped through the city. Now he was waving a fifty-dollar bill.

"Do you see this, cabbie? Get me to a phone and it's yours, my friend."

Locked on the waving bill, the Yellow Cab driver's right eye had nearly fallen out. Now he was alternately gunning the engine and hitting the brakes again and again, as he searched desperately for a phone booth along the city sidewalks.

"Come on, come on," Hoyt, Jr., fumed at the befuddled man behind the wheel. "Do you want this dough or not?"

The cab lurched drunkenly along, with the tires squealing and the engine howling . . . but in the end it was the lawyer and not the driver who finally spotted the pay phone in front of a Mobil station on the opposite side of a downtown street. The driver blinked helplessly at first . . . but then quickly redeemed himself by ignoring the NO U-TURN sign and instead making an outrageously illegal U-ie.

And so what if the slick maneuver cut off a trash truck and forced two passenger cars to swerve out of his path to avoid a collision? All three of the pissed drivers were now pounding their horns in disgust.

Hoyt, Jr., loved the move by the Mario Andretti wannabe. "Good work, pal! Tell 'em all to kiss your ass!"

Then he turned to Boohar. "I need some change—I never bother to carry any."

"Okay, lemme take a look." Boohar was now digging through his pockets . . . and coming up with a pile of nickels, dimes and quarters.

Hoyt jumped from the car, then ran to the booth and inserted the coins. Next he dialed his private number.

"Attorney Rogers' Office."

Hoyt was relieved when the call was answered by his executive assistant Helen Crossman. She had a tendency to leave early on days when he was out of town, and he'd rebuked her for it more than once.

"Helen, it's me. I need your help."

"Of course, Mr. Rogers. What is it?"

"I need you to call the firm's travel agent and get me on the next available flight to Baltimore. As soon as you find seats, put me in first class and Boohar in coach. Got it?"

"Excuse me, sir. Who is Boohar?"

"Alan Boohar, the private investigator I hired to help find my brother. And while you're at it, have them make hotel reservations for us at the Baltimore Four Seasons on Oriole Drive. Make sure my room is on the Concierge Floor.

"Oh . . . and you better make the reservations for a week just in case."

"I'll do it right away, sir."

"Do it yesterday, you hear me? I'll call you from the airport within thirty minutes, so you can give me the flight information. If you strike out on the commercial flights, tell them to charter me a private plane.

"It's imperative that I get to Baltimore tonight—and I don't give a damn what it costs!"

***

The race was on. After zooming through the Callahan Tunnel and then onto the airport highway, the taxi and its two frantic passengers skidded to a stop outside Terminal A at Logan. Moving as fast as he could, Rogers paid the cab fare and tossed the promised fifty-dollar bill onto the front seat, a disdainful move that forced the driver to scramble for it.

A moment later, he was leading the charge through the terminal and sprinting toward the nearest line of pay phones. Within half a minute, he had Helen back on the horn.

"Mr. Rogers, as you requested, we've booked two seats for you and Mr. Boohar on United Airlines flight number 6802 due to leave Logan at 8:35 p.m. and arrive in Baltimore at 10:20. I'm sorry, sir, but First Class was completely sold out so I booked you in coach. I hope that's okay."

"Fine. It'll have to do. What about the hotel reservations?"

"All set. Two rooms at the Four Seasons. As you requested, sir, your room is on the Concierge Floor."

"Okay. Now what's on my schedule this week? I'll have to cancel all my appointments."

"Let's take a look. Well . . . for starters, you've got a lunch date with Bill Wrigley at the Harvard Club on Wednesday."

"Shit, I've been trying to get him out to lunch for months. See if he's available the following week, will you? What else?"

"You've got a tee time Thursday afternoon with Mayor Washington. The newspapers say he's been very ill recently, so he probably won't be all that disappointed if you cancel on him."

"All right, do it. And tell him I hope he's feeling better. I need his influence greasing the wheels on that Michigan Avenue condo project we're doing with the Pritzkers."

"Will do. Oh, and there's one more appointment. You've got a 10 a.m. on Friday with a grad student from Kellogg who's looking for venture capital to start a high-tech computer company. Something to do with miniature computers you can carry around with you."

"What? Miniature computers? And you carry them *around*? How about cars that fly? Does he want to pitch that idea, too?"

The super-smart lawyer hooted with derisive laughter.

"Get real, Helen. Cancel the idiot. Why should I waste my valuable time on that kind of far-out bullshit?"

CHAPTER 45
A Severed Head

Charly had gone to bed an hour ago.

Now she stood at the bottom of a rumbling escalator. Her heart was pounding, and her brain was racing along at a hundred miles an hour.

Where am I? How did I get here? And how am I supposed to climb that thing . . . with the stairs running against me?

To make matters even worse, there were no railings!

The noise was deafening. The chains, the gears and the motors were clashing. The tortured metal screamed so loud it made her head ache. Chaos! Was she dreaming?

Yes . . . this had to be a nightmare.

With a groan of horror, she realized the worst.

He was here! The one who'd tried to hurt her before. The one who'd attacked Eeyore.

He was back . . . and she knew he would try to hurt her again.

As if confirming her worst fears, the mellow voice floated above the clattering steps of the down escalator.

"Hello, Charly. How nice to see you again. Do you remember me?"

She clamped her jaw shut. She wouldn't answer!

He gave her his evil grin. "Say hello to your tailless donkey friend, Charly."

In a flash, her determination to remain silent evaporated.

"Give him back," she demanded. "He's mine!"

He only chuckled. He was enjoying this. She watched helplessly while he tightened his grip on the poor animal's neck. Anguished, she listened to the desperate donkey's hopeless pleas for mercy: "EEE . . . yore! EEE . . . yore!"

He grinned again.

"You didn't do what I told you to do, Charly. You disobeyed me."

His grip tightened. Charly wanted to scream. *I'll suffocate if he doesn't stop!*

How could she rescue her friend? Only one way. Somehow, she would have to climb the escalator, climb against the descending steps and take him back. But how? It was impossible.

Okay, you gotta do it, she told herself, and with a sudden burst of energy she leapt onto the tumbling metal stairs and began to fight against the gravity that ruled them. One step, two steps . . . somehow, she was gaining ground. Maybe she could make it.

Hang on.

Her legs flailed and thrashed against the air.

Hang on . . . you can do this!

But her adversary was only toying with her. As soon he spotted the desperate progress she was making, his foot went to the control pedal. The escalator responded with a vicious growl and began to speed up, tossing her head over heels, all the way back to the bottom.

Her knees were raw now and her hands were cut and bleeding. And no wonder: the stairs on an escalator are outfitted with shark teeth!

Charly howled as they slashed her . . . and then howled again when they ripped into her defenseless toes.

A giant gash on her forehead dripped bright red blood into her mouth. She was choking on it. But she had to keep fighting.

Up she went—weeping and clawing and battling the metal stairs—and then down she went, bleeding and wailing and begging for it to stop. But it didn't stop. It would *never* stop. Again and again she fought the vicious machine . . . and all the while, *he* stood at the top, looming far above her, chortling and squeezing the donkey's neck tighter and tighter and tighter. . . .

Soon he was shouting. "No more cut the tail off the donkey bullshit, Charly. Let's have some real fun, whaddya say?"

Now she was staring at his glittering scalpel.

"No, please don't!"

With one quick slash, the deed was done.

"NO!"

Eeyore's severed head hit the floor with a thud, then rolled onto the top step of the escalator.

Charly was paralyzed. Helpless. Unable to breathe. Stricken dumb, she watched the donkey's head come bouncing down the steps, bouncing along on a collision course with her own head. The escalator was moving faster and faster now. Eeyore's head was bounding from step to step, getting closer and closer, while his haunted and frantically bulging eyes stared into nothingness.

And then—

Just before impact—

Charly was horrified to see that it *wasn't* Eeyore's head . . .

But the head of her father!

"Daddy, Daddy!" she screamed.

Instantly, Jake and Alix were untangling themselves from each other and bolting from their bed.

In five seconds, they were at her side.

"Charly, Charly, wake up. You're having a nightmare."

Her eyes shot open. "Daddy," she cried out. "Daddy, you're safe. You didn't die on that escalator, after all!

"Please don't leave me ever again!"

Jake held her close. "I'm not going anywhere, sweetheart. You had a terrible nightmare. That's all it was, honey. A terrible nightmare."

But Jake knew better.

He knew what was coming next.

How long would it be . . . before it was *his* turn to climb the *down* escalator?

Chapter 46
A Visit to South Station

He awoke to the sound of Alix breathing peacefully beside him.

The bedroom clock told him it was nearly four a.m. He braced one elbow against the mattress and then rested his head against his palm, so that he could look down on this woman he loved. Her eyes were closed. Her red hair lay in silky tendrils against the pillow.

Alix, he told himself with a smile, watching her breathe, *my sweet, sweet Alix*.

But then there was a slight tapping sound at the window, as if a restless knuckle had begun to worry the glass.

He looked over . . . squinted . . . and looked more closely.

A stick-like shadow, but soft-edged and limber, was inching along the panes.

What the . . .

It couldn't be.

Impossible.

As his eyes slowly adjusted to the predawn darkness of the bedroom, he caught his breath.

There was a snake crawling on the window.

His heart froze. A snake? Yes. It was moving slowly along the glass . . . and leaving behind an oozy scarlet secretion.

Blood?

Holy shit, Jake told himself. Moving quickly, he slipped away from the sleeping Alix and rolled to his feet. He felt the cool floorboards meet his toes. Then he glided soundlessly toward the window on the other side of the bedroom.

Soon he got another shock.

The closet door had begun to move. Amazed, he watched it creak slowly open, as if it were being pushed gently from within. What the hell was going on? His head felt strange . . . had his exhausted brain been packed with soggy cotton?

It came to him: *I'm dreaming. I must still be lying on the bed.*

He blinked and groaned . . . and then the realization hit him with the force of an electric shock: this was a nightmare. And he couldn't wake up. He couldn't escape.

Stricken and feeling utterly paralyzed, he watched the closet door swing slowly open . . . until he was looking squarely into a wide, grinning face.

Into a mouth twisted by a vicious sneer.

"Hello, Professor. It's good to meet you at last."

The words hung on the air like sparks of fire, then winked out one by one.

Jake opened his mouth to reply, but found no words.

The presence on the other side of the room sent up a slow, guttural laugh.

"You know what I hate most about you, Jake?"

Jake struggled. His tongue was a dead wooden clapper trapped inside a broken mouth.

"I hate the way you refuse to *believe* in me," chuckled Dr. Mike. "You're such a bright guy, such a gifted detective. So brilliant! And yet you refuse to admit that I can *do* this."

Dr. Mike sighed unhappily. "Despite all the evidence, you refuse to acknowledge that I have this power over you—over you and your lovely Alix and your sweetly irrepressible daughter, our little girl Charly."

There was a long silence, while the helpless homicide detective writhed on the bed.

You sonofabitch . . . I'll kill you dead!

Dr. Mike sighed. "How can I convince you that I'm real, Detective Becker?" The presence on the other side of the room chuckled again; he was enjoying himself fully.

"Oh . . . wait . . . I have a terrific idea!

"What if you were to run a little errand for me, Professor? Huh? Do you want to run a little errand for Dr. Mike? Don't worry, it's an easy assignment. All you gotta do is visit the Greyhound terminal in Boston.

"It's right there at South Station, remember? Atlantic Avenue? I'm sure your police duties have taken you there on occasion."

Jake was struggling to understand. *The Greyhound terminal? South Station? Why?*

The presence emitted another creepy laugh. "Well, now. I guess I should explain. I understand that little Charly is quite heartsick these days, Jake. Am I right? Seems she lost her little donkey doll, eh?

"Seems like somebody cut his fucking head off. Am I also correct on *that* fact?"

Jake was gritting his teeth. Would his heart explode?

"Locker Number Twenty-Four," said the presence in the closet. "If you want Charly to see Eeyore smile again, you'll have to take a look inside Locker Number

Twenty-Four. Just take a look in that locker, Jake . . . and I'm sure you'll wind up a-*head* of the game, if you follow my drift. Hah–hah!"

The door was already beginning to close.

Jake shuddered . . . crushed his teeth together . . . jerked awake.

That was Dr. Michael Rogers, he told himself. That was the killer. But it can't be real—it was only a nightmare!

He lay motionless in the dark, blinking slowly and listening to the pounding of his own racing heart.

While Dr. Mike's final words replayed themselves.

Again and again . . .

Locker Number Twenty-Four.

***

They sat together in the breakfast nook and sipped from steaming cups of English tea, while Jake told Alix about the astonishing nightmare.

"The strangest part was how *real* it seemed," said the puzzled homicide detective, after describing the vivid 4 a.m. assault by the sniggering Dr. Mike. "I know it was only a dream . . . but I could have sworn that Rogers was right there in the room."

Alix was watching him carefully. "Jake, you aren't going to like this—but you need to understand: Rogers *was* in the room."

The detective's eyes widened with surprise. "Come on, Alix. Are you really trying to tell me . . . ?"

"Yes, I am. I've been waiting for you to wake up, Jake. I know it sounds insane . . . but ST is real, and so is Dr. Mike. He's got the power now. Don't ask me how, but he's got it.

"He's a fucking serial killer. Don't you get it? If we're going to have any hope of stopping him, we have to start by accepting the obvious: Michael Rogers is able to slip in and out of other people's nightmares, and he's able to kill them while they sleep."

Jake shook his head. "I'm sorry, but you're asking me to believe in something that can't be real. ST defies logic, Alix. It also violates science."

She was glaring at him. Angry. "Tell that to those poor young women—the three women in Boston who were brutally killed while they slept."

Jake scowled. "You don't know how they were killed, and neither do I."

But Alix had heard enough. She set her cup of tea back down on the table. "Look, I know I can't convince you about the reality of ST, because I know you won't listen, and I know you won't keep an open mind.

"But can I at least ask you to do me a personal favor?"

He blinked at her. "A favor?"

"That's right. For me? Just a simple favor for *me*?"

He was smiling in spite of himself. "Okay, but I think I know what you're going to ask me to do, and I don't like it."

She'd taken his right hand, and now she held onto it. "Just go to the bus station like he suggested. Open the damn locker, Jake. If there's nothing to ST—if Mike Rogers is simply a figment of our imagination—then the locker will be empty and you'll have proved your point.

"What can you lose?"

Jake sent up a bitter laugh. "Alix, if I go to the Boston Greyhound Station in order to look for a doll's head in a locker . . . I'll feel like an idiot!"

She was still holding his hand.

"Will you do it, Jake? Please?

"Will you do it for my sake?"

***

The Greyhound manager quickly agreed.

"Okay, no problem," he told the homicide detective, after inspecting his gold shield and the search warrant from the Boston District Court. "Don't worry. I got a master key that opens all the lockers at once—from the back."

The two of them hurried along the upper level of the massive Boston South Station transportation complex. The rotunda was jammed with passengers making their way into the city for another day of work.

In the distance, they could hear the roar of bus engines and the loud hissing of pneumatic brakes.

"You working on a big case or what?" asked the Greyhound factotum as they passed an Au Bon Pain bakery and then a jam-packed McDonald's at the north end of the concourse.

Jake smiled. "As far as I'm concerned, they're all big, Mr. Rafferty."

The manager nodded. "Can't go into details, huh? I get it."

Jake looked at him calmly. "Let's just say somebody's life is at stake. We may be able to learn something very helpful by examining the contents of that locker."

Mr. Rafferty nodded. "Okay, then, here we go." They had reached the big metal rack of numbered lockers.

Moving swiftly, the little man in the gray uniform slid his key into the master lock at the back of the device.

Then he leaned to one side and began pawing around in Number 24.

Jake waited.

"Okay. Just one item in here, detective. Looks like . . . hey, what the hell is *this*?"

He was holding up what appeared to be the severed head of a floppy-eared doll.

Jake gazed uncomprehendingly at his guide. He'd stopped breathing. "Can I take a look at that, please?"

"Sure thing."

A moment later, the stunned detective was staring into the black button eyes of a donkey doll's amputated head.

He felt a wave of dizziness sweep over him, followed by a wave of icy dread.

It couldn't be.

But it was.

He was now holding the mutilated head of his daughter's missing doll, Eeyore.

Mr. Rafferty peered at him. "You okay, Detective Becker?"

Jake shook his head. Struggled to clear it.

"Yeah, I'm fine. No problem. Just a little surprised, that's all."

The Greyhound rep had begun to close up the lockers again.

"No offense, detective, but you seem a little bit spooked."

"I do?"

"Yessir. You look like you just saw a damn ghost!"

CHAPTER 47
Preparing for Battle—on the "Dreamscape"

Dr. Jacobson arrived first, in a bright blue Ford Fiesta he'd rented at Logan Airport.

As soon as he walked through the front door of Jake's place, a weeping Alix Cassidy toppled into his arms.

"Oh my God, we're so glad you're here!" She couldn't stop hugging her close friend and longtime mentor.

"Hey, no problem, no problem at all," said the rumpled sleep lab director in his soothing "Don't worry, I'm in charge now" tone of voice.

After returning Alix's frantic hugs and shaking hands with Jake, he stepped back and examined his deputy.

"Alix, no offense intended, but you look terrible. What in the world have you been doing up here?" He was squinting at her now, searching for further signs of mental stress. "Didn't I warn you to take it easy at that . . . that Big Pine conference of yours? Didn't I tell you to make sure you kept your cool?"

Alix was nodding . . . nodding and wiping away the tears. "You were right, Stan. I don't know how it happened exactly, but I've gotten into a . . . a life-threatening situation. This is the worst thing I could have imagined. It's all so complicated, so incredibly complicated that I hardly know how to begin telling you about it."

He groaned and shook his head. But a moment later the big man in the pale blue windbreaker was taking a deep breath and smiling at her and doing his best to calm her down.

Thank God he's here!

Jacobson reached across the space between them and took her hand. Still smiling, he held it gently in his own big right paw.

Then he led her over to Jake's leather sofa where they both sat down.

"So, Alix. What was it you were saying just now? Something about a death threat?"

She nodded. "That's right. Okay, I better just get right down to it, Stan. As I told you on the phone, ST has resurfaced."

Stan stared at her, expressionless. "Really? Somnambulistic Telepathy is *back*? Are you sure?"

"I am. There's been another episode."

She was biting her lower lip. Her tears had begun to glisten again.

Stan waited.

"The blunt fact is that I've been experiencing some very strange nightmares—some terrifying dreams in which a man you may remember is chasing me with a scalpel, and he's absolutely determined to kill me with it. And there's no way I can escape.

"He's a serial murderer, and he's already killed four people—three innocent young women and his own father."

Dr. Jacobson was no longer smiling.

"Let me get this straight, please. You've been dreaming of 'a man I may remember'? Who might *that* be? Sorry, but I don't get it."

Alix's hands began to shake again. "Dr. Michael Rogers," she said quietly.

The two of them looked at each other. "Do you remember Dr. Michael Rogers?"

Dr. Jacobson didn't answer for a few seconds. "Are you talking about that disgraced psychiatrist you turned in, back in the mid-seventies? *That* guy is back in your life?"

She closed her eyes as she struggled to hang onto her composure. "Not in my *life*," she said. "In my *nightmares*. He's invaded my dreams. He cut me in a nightmare, and when I woke up, I was actually bleeding from the cut.

"Real *blood*."

She leaned back on the sofa and took a deep breath.

The words came tumbling out as she told him the entire story from beginning to end.

***

Just as Alix was finishing her dreadful tale, the front door banged open.

Within seconds, Alix was bear-hugging the Big Pine Executive Director and once again blinking back tears.

"Rozzie, I can't tell you how glad I am to see you!"

Alix turned to the glowering white-haired woman beside her. "Melinda, welcome! Thank you so much for agreeing to help us."

The Abenaki medicine woman produced a small tight smile.

Alix took a breath. She was shaking a little, and they could all see how she was struggling for self-composure. "Roz, having you and Melinda here is a lifesaver for me. I feel better already."

Rozzie lit up. "Hey, we're just glad you're okay, honey."

But Alix had already turned toward the sleep expert. "This is Dr. Stanley Jacobson, my boss at the sleep lab in Atlanta. Rozzie, I've told you all about him. You have no idea how relieved I am that he was willing to drop what he was doing and rush here to help us."

A moment later, Roz was lunging toward the scientist from Atlanta.

"Good to meet you, Stan. Alix tells me you're wearing the pants when it comes to understanding the dynamics of sleep and dreams."

Owl-like, Dr. Jacobson peered at her. "The pants?"

Rozzie chuckled. "Figure of speech! According to Alix, you wrote the book on brain activity during REM sleep."

Alix was shaking her head. "Geez, Rozzie, go easy on him, will ya? The poor guy just got here!"

"I'm fine," said Stan.

But then he rubbed his hands together, and they could tell he was ready to get down to work. "Melinda, let me join the others in welcoming you. As you know, I'm a sleep scientist. The place where I'm most comfortable is inside a laboratory."

He frowned then, and they could tell he was choosing his words carefully. "My field is science, but Alix has told me about your important work—and I want you to know that I greatly respect the world of the paranormal and your own expertise as a Native-American healer."

Once again, the medicine woman delivered her calm, deliberate smile. Then she muttered something that sounded like "kag-ah-nah!" . . . which he assumed meant "thank you" in Abenaki. Nodding, he shook her hand vigorously. "This is an extremely difficult and complicated situation," he said thoughtfully. "Whether we're talking about sleep science or the paranormal dynamics that may be involved in dreaming, one fact seems pretty clear.

"We're going to need all the help we can get!"

***

Alix was the first one to mention the struggle that lay ahead. "I'm sure we all understand that we've got some difficult days in front of us," she said. "So I thought I'd start by explaining why it's so helpful to have Dr. Jacobson on the team."

She looked around the table and saw four faces at full attention.

"As most of you know by now, Stan is a renowned authority on the dynamics of sleep and dreaming."

Dr. Jacobson quickly began waving one hand at her, as if trying to brush her words away. "I *used* to be an expert maybe," he told them, "but that was a long time ago. For the last ten years or so, I've spent most of my time as an administrator.

"Running a big research lab is a full-time job, believe me."

Alix nodded. "Your modesty is much appreciated, Stan, but the truth is you've *forgotten* more about the mechanics of sleep than most sleep researchers know." She gave him a sharp glance. "And that's great—because we're going to need every bit of your knowledge and expertise in the days ahead."

Stan still looked a bit uncomfortable, but at least he was smiling now. "I'll do my best to help, Alix. You know that."

"I sure do," said Alix, "and I'm very grateful. Make no mistake: the challenge we face is quite dangerous. As a matter of fact, it's unlike anything I've ever heard about as a sleep researcher."

Jake was clenching his jaw by now. "Stan, I need to be sure that Alix won't be facing any needless risk in this situation. Huh? As you now know, she's been having these dreadful nightmares that somehow appear to involve a serial killer. I'm not prepared to accept the possibility that her life could be threatened if things should get out of hand.

"In my opinion as a homicide detective, she's facing a great deal of danger and—"

But then Melinda suddenly cut in.

"What Alix must face is . . . *curse!*"

The table fell silent. No one moved. At least ten seconds passed before Alix said, "Can you tell us a little more about that, Melinda?"

The medicine woman had tilted her head back slightly. Eyes half-closed, she appeared to be gazing at the ceiling. "In the world we do not see," she said in her low, singsong voice, "there are many unknown forces. There are powers that must be respected."

She lowered her eyes and looked at each member of the team in turn. "Sometimes, once in a very great while, these forces will fall out of balance. The powers will become . . . *antagonistic.*

"If there is a breach in the space-time during that period, a dark energy can be released into the realm of those who walk the earth."

The others looked at each other. *Those who walk the earth? The human race?*

"When the break takes place," Melinda continued, "the earth-walkers experience it as a curse. They face a dark energy that will harm them again and again, until the balance is restored among the powers and the curse is released."

She held up both hands and closed her eyes.

"This is what happened in Vietnam. Mekong Delta . . . murder, terrible murder. And then once again into the world—once again into the world comes the curse! And now it lives inside the cutting doctor.

"It lives now in the doctor with the knife: *The Surgeon's Curse!*"

This time the silence in the room lasted even longer . . . until Jake finally broke it with a heavy sigh. "Melinda . . . go easy, will you?

"We knew we were confronting a serial killer, but you make him sound like *Frankenstein.*"

Melinda sent him a calm, level gaze. She didn't speak, because she didn't have to. Her expression said it all.

You're right, Jake. We are dealing with a Frankenstein: this is the real thing.

Alix was the first to recover her wits. "Melinda, thank you so much for joining us. You have no idea how much we need you now."

Melinda nodded slightly.

Frowning, Alix was doing her best to measure her words carefully. "Okay, let's go back to Michael Rogers for a minute. On the level of human psychology, the bottom line here is pretty simple. You don't have to be an expert on the paranormal in order to grasp it.

"To put it bluntly: we're going to have to figure out how to enter a serial killer's nightmares . . . and then neutralize him somehow."

She was staring fixedly at Stan now. "I've already explained the whole thing to Dr. Jacobson. He understands that Somnambulistic Telepathy—ST—is real, and that our serial killer is committing his hideous crimes while he dreams.

"We don't understand the mechanism involved, but whether these crimes are being caused by abnormal psychology or by a curse—or maybe even by *both*—there's no longer any doubt that Dr. Michael Rogers has learned how to kill people by invading their nightmares."

There was a long, uneasy silence at the table . . . until Rozzie suddenly lifted one hand. "Just one thought from the peanut gallery over here, gang. I can't hope to keep up with Melinda, that's for sure . . . but I do have nearly thirty years of experience as a psychic, and I can tell you all one thing right now.

"Whatever this 'force'—this 'energy'—might be, it knows we're onto it.

"During the last couple of weeks, I've been picking up vibes all over the place. Just the other morning, I was watching one of our cute little mourning doves hunt for seeds down near those big oak trees at the edge of the lake. All at once, I spotted a dark shadow.

"That shadow went streaking across the grass. A few seconds later, *ka-pow*! A red-tailed hawk dropped out of the sky like an F-4 Phantom Jet and took that poor little dove's head off!"

She paused, then visibly shivered. "I watched that happen, and right away I got a flash. I told myself, something's coming, Rozzie. Something's coming your way . . . and it's not going to be a pretty sight!"

Jake was shaking his head again. "Guys, I gotta be honest. All of this sounds pretty weird, pretty off the wall to me. And also pretty dangerous.

"I want to make absolutely sure that nobody gets hurt here—and especially you, Alix."

Dr. Jacobson was nodding, but he was also showing signs of impatience. "Okay, Jake, I hear you, and thanks for the input. I'm not sure what Rozzie's hawk incident means—but I learned a long time ago that keeping an open mind is absolutely essential in science. I also need to remind everybody that we've got some very specific tactical problems to solve, whether they involve a 'curse' or not."

"He's right," said Alix. "What we haven't figured out yet is how the person who infiltrates the killer's nightmares—that's going to be me, of course—will be able to protect herself from real injury and real death, if and when he attacks in the Dreamtime."

She paused.

As if on cue, Dr. Jacobson suddenly was talking in a low, urgent voice.

"We're on terra incognita here, for sure," he said. "But there *is* one strategy that just might work."

They waited.

"Hypnosis," said Dr. Jacobson. "Hypnotic suggestion."

They stared at him.

"I can tell you that there's been a great deal of recent research to show that people can be programmed through hypnotic suggestion to wake themselves up from a nightmare on command."

They blinked slowly back at him, while doing their best to take it all in.

"We'll have to think long and hard about this," the expert said slowly. "But it may be possible to hypnotize Alix and give her a hypnotic suggestion—what we call a 'hypnagogic code word.'"

Jake was the first to respond. "Okay, fine," he said. "But what kind of code word would it be, Stan? How would it work and what would it *do*?"

Stan deliberated briefly. His eyes swept around the table. "The concept is simple," he said. "When the killer attacks Alix in the Dreamtime, she says the word to herself, and the hypnagogic code *wakes her up*.

"If she can escape a nightmare whenever she needs to—simply on her own command—the killer's power over her will be broken."

He looked around the table again, and now his jaw was set. "Once Alix has the protection of the code word going for her, she may be able to find a way to bring this maniac down."

Maybe. And maybe not. Now they were all looking at Melinda Birdsong. Did the Indian medicine woman believe Dr. Jacobson's strategy would actually work?

But they might as well have been gazing at the Egyptian Sphinx.

Calm and serene, her eyes appeared to be focused on some distant landscape.

And her enigmatic expression told them nothing at all.

Chapter 48
The "Nightmare Team"
Goes into Action

It was time to begin the journey into Alix Cassidy's horrifying nightmares.

But it wouldn't be easy. Or safe.

One mistake, and the Nightmare Team knew they could lose her forever.

Dr. Jacobson explained the risks to them during their first rehearsal, which took place on Sunday evening in Jake's crowded living room.

"Okay," said the sleep expert, looking rumpled as always. "Before I outline the specifics on what we'll be doing, let me give you the good news."

Jake nodded at him.

"Stan, I'm glad to hear there *is* some good news."

"You bet," said Stan. "Here it is. We are a *go* at the Brigham and Women's Hospital starting tonight at 11 o'clock sharp. Fortunately, the director of their sleep lab is a longtime colleague of mine. We've attended a lot of research conferences together over the years, and when he heard about the perilous situation we're in, he agreed to let us use the sleep lab right away, even on a Sunday night.

"We'll have two skilled techs, one of whom is a polysomnography specialist, to help us manage Alix's sleep session."

Rozzie looked quizzically at him. "Hang on, doc. Poly . . . what? I'm an expert on ESP maybe, but I haven't spent a whole hell of a lot of time in sleep labs."

"Not me, either!" blurted Melinda Birdsong. "This is not my world—but I will do my best to help."

"Okay, thanks, Melinda. And I'll do *my* best to be clear." Stan was smiling a little. "Here's the drill, folks. We're going to be using the latest equipment in a polysomnographic or 'sleep physiology monitoring' study of Alix's brainwaves while she's asleep in the Brigham lab. That facility simply duplicates an ordinary bedroom, by the way.

"The bottom line here is that we'll be observing the electrical activity in her brain with an electroencephalograph, or EEG."

Jake was frowning now. Hard.

"The EEG is essentially a glorified voltmeter," said the sleep expert. "Jake, how much do you two know about the physiology of sleep?"

The professor didn't hesitate. "Only what I've learned from Alix."

"All right, I'll try to keep it simple then. The human brain runs on chemical processes which generate tiny bursts of electrical energy along the neurons, or brain cells. All right? And when I say tiny, I do mean tiny. We measure that electrical output in millionths of a volt."

He paused for a moment to let his description sink in.

"But with the EEG, believe it or not, we can track these mini-voltages quite accurately. And that's crucial—because they'll help us identify the different stages of Alix's sleep. But the EEG isn't entirely accurate, and it doesn't give us a complete picture of brain activity during sleep.

"Most nightmares occur during the stage of sleep known as 'Rapid Eye Movement,' or REM." Stan took a long look at his Atlanta assistant before continuing. "If we can tell exactly when Alix enters REM sleep, we'll be ready when this . . . this maniac visits her in a nightmare. To accomplish that, we'll place electrodes on her chin to measure muscle activity—often a sign of intense dreaming during REM sleep . . . along with electrodes at the left and right outer *canthus*, which is a corner of the eyelid that contains a nerve complex."

He thought for a moment. "I'm not going to get into the technical stuff. All you need to know is that we feed all the data into a Grass machine, which quickly analyzes it and then identifies the subject's stage of sleep. Of course, we also get help with that from an electromyograph, or EMG, which monitors the sleeper's overall muscle tension."

Here Rozzie let out a burst of nervous laughter. "Say, that's a lot of *electro* stuff, doc. How does the machine pick up the vibes Alix will be putting out as she wanders through Dreamland?"

"Simple," said Dr. Jacobson. "We also attach special sensors to her scalp and to her legs. They record everything that's happening in both her brain cells and her muscles, and they quickly pass it on to the Grass analyzer. Some of the data will be interpreted by a small onboard computer.

"This is brand-new technology, of course, but the results so far have been quite accurate."

Roz nodded. "Okay, got it. But what's the bottom line?"

Dr. Jacobson looked calmly at them. "It isn't very complicated," he said after a bit. "With the help of the sleep technicians and the technology, we'll know exactly when Alix goes into REM sleep. At the same time, the EMG will be measuring her state of muscular agitation.

"When this Rogers monster comes after her in a nightmare, we'll know it instantly. We'll be standing by and ready."

He looked at Alix. "Your job will be to get all the information out of him that you can. Find out where he lives, what he does each day—when he's awake, I mean. If you bring us the right information, we may be able to use it to track him down in the daytime world. Then Jake and his team can lock him up while we look for a way to neutralize his ST."

Stan leaned toward Alix. He searched her face intently. "But remember, Alix, if Rogers goes after you with the scalpel, his attack will be physically *real*. If he cuts you, you will bleed. And if he cuts you badly enough . . ." but he didn't finish the sentence.

"Anyway, the moment you see him beginning to make a move, you must instantly wake yourself up with the code word I will give you via hypnotic suggestion."

But now Melinda chimed in. Her eyes were burning with intensity. "Remember, too—when he comes after you, we will all hear the voice of the curse. You will hear it and so will we!"

They stared at her.

"The voice of the curse?" Jake finally asked. "This curse thing . . . it can speak?"

Melinda bent her small frame toward Jake. "It is not human, this voice. It will come through the air like the voice of a hawk as he dives for the kill. You will hear it, Alix . . . when this monster comes for you, you will hear the voice of the curse.

"And we will hear the echo, right in the lab. There will be an echo—the voice of the curse!"

The room fell silent. A question hung in the air. No one seemed to want to ask it.

Then Jake finally spoke up.

"Stan, all of this sounds very scientific, very plausible. But Alix's life will be at stake here. What if she *can't* repeat the code word for some reason?

"What happens if she can't find a way to wake herself from the nightmare?"

Stan looked around the room. He didn't seem to like the question much. "If she gets stuck in the nightmare and our instruments tell us she's undergoing maximum stress—which means she'll be experiencing maximum terror—then we'll do our best to intervene."

Jake's mouth fell open. "Your *best*? Wait a minute.

"Are you saying you might not be able to bring her back in time?"

The sleep expert released a deep sigh.

"Jake . . . I'm not going to kid you. I don't know if we'll be able to wake her up. Okay? You have to remember, this is the very first time—the first time *I'm* aware of, anyway—in which a scientist will be conducting a sleep study from *inside* a nightmare."

He thought for a second. "And this won't be just *any* nightmare, remember—because everything that happens to Alix while she's under will also be taking place in the *real* world."

Jake reacted quickly. "Goddamnit, Stan, there are too many risks here. I'm sorry, but this stuff is way too dangerous! If that maniac goes after her with his scalpel and we can't intervene . . ."

Jake stopped right there. No need to say more.

His words hung on the air of the living room, vibrating ominously, until Alix finally spoke.

"We don't have a choice, Jake. You know it and I know it. That monster is going to kill again, and probably sooner than later.

"It's the only way. I have to go in. I'm the only one who can stop this psychopath from killing more women. I don't see any other options, do you? Trust me: I've *got* to do this."

She met Jake's eyes for a moment. He saw the fear, the outrage burning there.

Then Melinda spoke again. "Do not fear so much. You will hear the voice, Alix. You will know what to do. It will come from within—you will feel it within—and you will know what to do. Not so much fear, please?

"You will be protected by the code, and you will know what to do!"

Jake was shaking his head. "Okay, Melinda, I guess I gotta take your word for it." He sighed and turned to Dr. Jacobson.

"What time are we due at the lab?"

"Eleven p.m.," said the scientist. "Two hours and twenty minutes from now."

Alix turned to Stan. "Okay," she said. "When do you plan to hypnotize me and give me the code word?"

Dr. Jacobson took a deep breath. "I'm ready when you are, Alix."

***

The Brigham and Women's Sleep Disorders Service was located at the Faulkner Hospital in the Jamaica Plain section of southwest Boston, and the Nightmare Team arrived there promptly at 11.

Silent and frowning, they walked together up the winding sidewalk that led to the glass-walled lobby of the Faulkner—the bright and spacious building which housed the half-dozen labs and consultation rooms of New England's best-known sleep study and neurological research complex.

At the front desk, a weary-looking staffer greeted them. She had been waiting for their arrival.

"Welcome to the Faulkner Sleep Lab," she told the nervous-looking fivesome. Then, after a quick round of introductions: "Dr. Jacobson, I'll page Dr. DeWitt now. I've been told that he and his staff are ready to assist you."

Five minutes later, they were shaking hands with Dr. Boyce DeWitt, one of Boston's leading sleep experts.

"Stan," he intoned as he led them along a labyrinth of offices and then pushed through a pair of swinging metal doors, "before you get started and I leave you with our two outstanding sleep techs—Derek Haas and Mitzi Hamilton—I want to tell you how much I admire the work you've been doing in Atlanta."

He paused for a moment, then reached to the wall and threw a switch. The indirect lighting panels flickered once and then came alive.

All at once they were standing in a huge laboratory full of high-tech instruments. "I thought your study of REM sleep epilepsy broke some important new ground, Stan."

"Many thanks, Boyce." Dr. Jacobson was doing his best to smile . . . but handling compliments had never been his strong suit. Now they were walking along beneath a large wall-mounted placard: QUIET—SLEEP STUDY IN PROGRESS.

Another few steps and they'd entered a private room containing a bed and a gleaming lab table outfitted with two electronic monitors. An adjoining bathroom would give Alix the privacy required for changing her clothes and attending to her personal needs during the hours ahead.

Soon they were all assembled in the control room, which overlooked the laboratory-bedroom and featured several silently blinking monitors and computerized instrument panels.

They stood there for a few seconds, squinting in the overhead light and trying to take it all in. Then a side-door swung open and they found themselves shaking hands with the two techs, Mitzi and Derek, who'd be monitoring the EEG and EMG input throughout Alix's approaching journey into the Dreamtime.

All eight of them huddled briefly around the softly flashing command console, while Dr. DeWitt rattled off a few preliminaries.

"Under the Brigham Sleep Disorders Service Protocols," he read from a clipboard, "I'm required to note for the record that the medical supervision of this sleep study involving Dr. Alix Cassidy will be provided by my good friend, Dr. Stanley Jacobson of the Sleep Disorder Center of Atlanta, Georgia."

He looked up from the paperwork for a moment—just long enough to give Alix a bright, supportive smile. Then his eyes went back to the clipboard in his hands.

"Tonight's study will be conducted entirely within the precincts of the Brigham and Women's Faulkner Center Sleep Laboratory. During this study, all of Brigham's legally mandated strictures regarding medical procedure and patient privacy will be carefully observed."

A moment later he was smiling broadly and shaking hands all around.

"No worries," he told them. "Believe me, you're in capable hands with Derek and Mitzi—there's nobody any better at monitoring sleep physiology than these two!"

He riffled through his paperwork one last time, took a final look around the now-humming laboratory . . . and then headed back toward the swinging metal doors.

They were on their own now.

Alix's nightmare confrontation with Dr. Mike was about to begin.

CHAPTER 49
The Hawk and the Surgeon

Twenty minutes later, the last of the electrodes had been fitted to Alix's scalp and eyelids. From this point forward, every millivolt generated by her brain stem—the command center for most sleep and eye movement functions—would be counted and studied by the computer-driven machines that stood ranked like chattering robots around her bedside and in the control room.

"How you doing, Alix?" Having taken up his position behind the control room microphone, Dr. Jacobson was already examining the dials on the Grass machine. Flickering erratically from time to time, that high-tech monitoring device would soon be analyzing the flow of sensor data in real time. "You okay?"

"I'm ready to go, Stan," said Alix. The others nodded in agreement.

"All systems go!" barked Rozzie, doing her best to lighten the dark sense of foreboding that hung over the lab. "Alix, don't forget to say hello to Dr. Mike for me—with a swift kick in the ass!"

Nobody laughed. "Alix," said Dr. Jacobson, "I want to remind you of one thing. If you do get into a confrontation with . . . with our adversary, you'll need to remember that whatever happens in your nightmare will also be happening in the world of reality."

Alix nodded calmly, but her taut face betrayed her fear. With Dr. Jacobson's approval, Jake had slipped quietly from the control room into her temporary sleeping quarters. Now he reached across the bed to take her hand. Dr. Jacobson didn't protest.

"If he makes any sudden move toward you," the scientist continued from his perch in the control room, "any move at all, you must immediately repeat the hypnagogic code word I implanted in your subconscious."

Alix nodded calmly, but beads of perspiration gleamed along her forehead.

"You are *not* to wait and see what develops," added Dr. Jacobson. "Do you understand, Alix? If he moves in your direction at all, you must go *instantly* to the code word. Which is, please?"

"Collier," she replied. "I ought to know it by now, Stan. You made me repeat it at least six thousand times."

Dr. Jacobson didn't smile. "One more thing," he said. "Just for the record, I need to point out that if the monitors start telling us you're in trouble, we will try and intervene. If the EEG and EMG reading rates start climbing toward max out, we'll do our best to wake you up.

"I'm not sure we'll be *able* to, of course. To my knowledge, this kind of situation has never occurred before. But I promise you we will do our very best."

"I know you will, Stan."

She nodded, but barely. Jake saw how the skin around her mouth had gone bone white.

"Good luck, Alix."

She nodded . . . and then got a surprise. Melinda Birdsong's arm was around her shoulders and pulling her close.

"Alix," said the Abenaki healer in a low, urgent voice, "please remember, help will come from within. When you hear the cry of the hawk, which will be the voice of the curse, do not fear. Help will come from within, and soon."

Alix nodded. "Thank you, Melinda."

Alix managed a brave smile. Her eyes went out to each member of the team.

They stayed longest on Jake.

She took a deep breath. Her gaze steadied as she mouthed the three words, "I love you."

Then she said, "Let's do this."

***

The Brigham Sleep Lab fell silent then, except for the gentle hum of the instruments. After a quick thumbs-up to the two technicians, Dr. Jacobson reached out to the Command Panel and pushed the illumination switch.

The recessed lights above began to fade. Half a minute later, the entire laboratory bedroom settled into twilight mode.

Alix's eyelashes fluttered once or twice, then settled. Her eyes had closed. The technicians watched the muscles around her mouth twitch erratically for a few seconds and then sink toward rest.

Alix felt silly at first. In spite of the emergency they faced, and in spite of the personal danger she was about to confront, trying to sleep while half a dozen people monitored your every breath was just plain . . . ludicrous. For a moment she found herself wondering what her *own* sleep subjects must have thought each time they were put to bed during the dozen years she'd spent as a researcher in Dr. Jacobson's lab.

But it was also true that she hadn't slept for 36 hours and was utterly exhausted.

Within fifteen minutes, they saw her right calf jump once, before twitching briefly and then relaxing.

The EMG responded instantly with a soft pinging sound, almost musical.

Mitzi leaned in for a closer look at her dials.

Alix was half-asleep now. . . .

> *Alix is trying to picture the seashore. Myrtle Beach . . . Sea Island. How she'd loved those childhood rambles along the snow-white sand, and the breeze rippling the whitecaps at the surf line!*

(Her eyeballs twitch. Her leg jumps again. The EEG screen lights up with pale blue numbers from the canthus sensors: VX-17/2X19V/Synchron22KZ.)

> *The lighthouse! Her favorite fantasy . . . her favorite escape. The candy-striped lighthouse at Cape Hatteras, and she's sitting in the Captain's Chair. She's sweeping the horizon with her eyes. She's enjoying the electric blue Atlantic, and the gulls hovering, screeching just outside the lighthouse window, so close she can almost reach out and touch—*
>
> *What?*
>
> *Touch WHAT?*
>
> *Her . . . hand! She looks down: what's that . . . that THING in her hand? Is it a scorpion?*
>
> *You're kidding, right?*
>
> *Its tail flickering . . . and the drop of poison hanging from its flickering tail.*

(Her eyeballs twitch and twitch again. The EEG screen and the eyelid sensors light up in pale blue numbers: VX-17/2X24V/Synchron33KZ.)

A scorpion? But how? Where? She wants to shake it free, fling it out of her hand . . . but before she can move, before she can even think . . .

She hears. . . .

On the winding metal stairway of the lighthouse:

First the cry of a great bird, a predatory bird: ki-ki-ki-ki-ki . . . and the bird's savage cry rising like an approaching siren, rising and rising until it ends in a hawklike scream of attack: ki-ki-KEEEEEEE!

Then, echoing through the sudden silence: footsteps.

Oh my God.

She knows who it is. She has always known. Instantly and forever, she knows who it is.

It's him again.

***

3:19 a.m.

The Nightmare Team went on full alert, and for good reason.

Both the EEG and the EMG needles had swung deep into the Red Zone.

Watching the gauges leap and then drift, Dr. Jacobson seemed to be growing more alarmed with each passing minute.

The two Brigham sleep specialists didn't look happy, either.

"Dr. Jacobson, we're getting some pretty intense REM activity," said Mitzi Hamilton, who was perched above her computer screen like a mother hen watching an unsteady chick. "We're coming up on the maximum readout, sir."

Dr. Jacobson grimaced. He didn't need the data to understand the obvious. One look at Alix Cassidy's rapidly twitching eyelids and her tightly bunched calf muscles, visible at the edge of her flung-back nightgown, sufficed to show the sleep guru that a blaster nightmare was fully underway.

When Alix's right leg shot out and kicked the air several times, even the normally placid Dr. Jacobson looked fearful. "She's going through a major neuronal discharge," he told the grim-faced team, "and it's probably going to get a lot worse before it gets any better."

Jake didn't take this pronouncement well. His body language said it all. He looked like a pumped-up middleweight just before the opening bell. "How's she holding up, doc?" he glared at the unhappy-looking scientist.

When Dr. Jacobson didn't reply immediately, he repeated the question in a loud, commanding voice: "I asked you how she's holding *up*."

Dr. Jacobson looked at him. "Hard to say," he murmured after a bit.

"We're on the edge of the unknown here, Jake. You know that."

Nobody moved. Nobody spoke.

Then Melinda Birdsong rose from her chair. Her broad face had darkened. Her eyes were closed. Amazed, the others watched her rock back and forth on the balls of her feet.

She was hugging herself and rocking steadily, and then in a high-pitched, wailing voice she uttered a cry that did not seem human: *ki-ki-ki-ki-ki*!

Rozzie was also on her feet by now. "My God," she said. "The hawk!"

Her eyes were flashing; they were darting wildly around the sleep lab.

"That's the raptor," she told them in a rush. "It's the cry of the hawk. That's what I heard at Big Pine, right before that poor mourning dove was killed!"

For a few seconds, they all stared at each other, paralyzed. The two lab techs looked like they were in shock. Then Jake finally broke the spell.

"Rozzie . . . what the hell *is* this? What's going *on* here, do you know?"

Rozzie blinked back at him. "I think Dr. Mike has arrived, Jake. I think he just entered Alix's nightmare."

Jake didn't respond at first. Then he whirled to face Dr. Jacobson.

"Stan, what do you think? Is that sonofabitch coming after her or what?"

The scientist winced as if he'd been struck. "Jake, I can't answer that. All I can tell you is what the data's telling me—she's going through some very deeply turbulent REM sleep right now. Usually, that kind of turbulence means a nightmare has begun, or maybe a series of nightmares.

"As for their subjective *content*, we really have no idea."

Jake thought about it for a few seconds. His face had grown somber now and his eyes were cold.

"I don't want her taking any unnecessary risks," he said in a voice tinged with anger.

"Same here," said the lead researcher.

"So is it time to pull her out? Wake her up? Hell, for all we know, he could be attacking her right *now*."

Dr. Jacobson was studying the data points, as they flashed across the bar graphs orchestrated by the Grass machine.

"A little longer," he said. "Let's let her run with it a little longer."

Jake looked at Rozzie for a moment: *Whaddya think, Roz?*

Her eyes shot her answer back at him: *Stan's the man, Jake. Let's run with it a while longer.*

Melinda Birdsong had fallen silent. Her eyes were still closed.

"Okay," growled Jake. "But let's stay alert. I know it's late and we're all tired—but let's stay on our P's and Q's, huh? Everybody okay with that?

"First sign of any real trouble, let's pull her out of there!"

Dr. Jacobson nodded. "That's the plan, Jake. We'll give it ten more minutes and then see where we are, okay?"

Jake nodded.

The lab was quiet now, except for an occasional electronic beep from the Grass machine.

***

He stood facing away from her, looking out a porthole window toward the distant Atlantic. He would not let her see his eyes.

"Hello again, Alix."

She opened her mouth to reply, but produced only a rush of empty air.

Had her vocal cords been paralyzed?

"Don't you want to say hello to me? It's been such a long time, Alix."

She struggled. She fought. But she could manage only a single word. It was more like a strangled cry: "Michael!"

He turned slowly toward her, and she saw how vile, how corrupted his face had become.

His distorted features sagged and bulged, as if he were wearing a rotting death mask. And his once-lively eyes had gone dull, listless. When he finally spoke, it was the sound of a tomb opening. It was the sound a warped door makes as it groans against its hinges in a dungeon.

"Alix . . . do you remember that day we spent together in Harvard Square? The day we bought ice cream cones and laughed? The day you called me your 'Woolly Bear'?"

She nodded. "Yes, I remember."

He chuckled and winked. "Ah, the joys of taking a stroll down Memory Lane! Why, I'm feeling so damn nostalgic, I could almost cry!"

A half-smile crossed his face.

"Tell me, Alix—do you remember the first time I fucked you?"

She didn't reply. Her face was cold and stern. She wasn't looking at him.

"No? You don't recall our first fuck? Well . . . how about the first time I stuck my finger up that tight little ass of yours? Remember how much you loved it?

"Why . . . you squealed like a pig in heat, you hot little bitch, you!"

She closed her eyes for an instant, while the pain of the memory went slashing through her.

Then: "You betrayed me, Michael. You betrayed yourself, and you betrayed me. You lied and you abused the trust of your patients.

"I'm sorry, but I have no respect for you. As a matter of fact, I despise you."

She turned to look at him. "The truth is that you aren't just a scientific fraud.

"You're also a murderer.

"You're an insane psychopath."

He didn't respond at first. The sun went behind a cloud . . . and it was very strange the way the lighthouse suddenly began to go dark.

She was standing in a pool of freezing shadow now. He loomed just outside it.

She saw something glittering in his hand.

He laughed ominously. "Well, the betrayal cut both ways, honeybell."

He gave her an icy sneer. His lips were twisted with disdain. "You turned me in to the medical authorities, darling, and as a result my life was destroyed. All because of you! I lost my license to practice medicine. Then you stole my discovery—Somnambulistic Telepathy—and made it your own.

"You took everything I had, you deceitful bitch."

He stepped toward her pool of shadow. "In the end," he said softly, almost tenderly, "you turned out to be just another cunt . . . just another lying, sneaking cunt."

Like a bolt of killing electricity, the word *cunt* went through her.

It took her strength. It left her utterly weak and nerveless, so that she toppled backwards onto the great wooden wheel that turned the searchlight.

She lay spread out on the wheel now—she was helpless and powerless, without a molecule of remaining strength.

"I've waited a long time for this," said Dr. Mike. "I've waited twelve years for this single moment, Alix. Do you know what I'm going to do to you?"

She could only stare at him, wide-eyed and paralyzed.

"I'm going to do some *chest surgery* on you, bitch!"

He lunged. She saw the blade flash. Saw it zoom toward the flesh between her ribs.

At the very last moment, just as the metal began to bite into the skin below her heart, she managed to scream the single word that might save her.

"COLLIER!"

***

Jake spotted it first. He grabbed Dr. Jacobson's shoulder.

"Blood!" he shouted. "She's bleeding, Stan. Fuck . . . she's bleeding on the sheets.

"*Do* something. Hurry!"

A moment later, the entire team had rushed from the control room to Alix's bedside. Bending over her, Dr. Jacobson raised one hand. He was about to try and shake her back to consciousness . . . but before that hand could reach its target, Alix's eyes shot open.

"Oh, my God," she shrieked at the stunned Nightmare Team. "He cut me. He wanted to . . . he nearly . . . he cut me . . . he wanted to . . ."

Then Jake took her in his arms and held her and wiped away the trickle of blood that seeped from her ribcage.

"It's all right, Alix. You're safe. It's okay, honey."

He looked around the room wildly, glared at the rest of them, then back at her. His stern face blazed with anger.

"You're safe now, Alix—you're safe with *me*!"

Chapter 50
The Surgeon Makes His Move

Their plane was half an hour late, but at last Hoyt, Jr., and Boohar arrived in Baltimore.

They hailed the first cab they spotted.

"Run us down to the Cat's Eye in Fells Point. And I'll need you to wait there for us." Without a moment's hesitation, Rogers had just waved goodbye to another fifty.

"Why the Cat's Eye?" Boohar asked.

"It was my brother's favorite hangout. I'm hoping that he still boozes there. Maybe we can find somebody who knows how to find him."

The cab barreled north from the airport on I-95, then swung east on Pratt Street toward the city's recently opened National Aquarium and Harborplace shopping mecca.

At Calvert Street, they ran into a traffic backup caused by two motorists in a fender bender. They were standing beside their mangled cars and screaming at each other.

"Come on, come on," snapped Hoyt, Jr., who seemed close to having a stroke. "Can't you get *around* these assholes?"

The cabbie started to reply, but Boohar cut him off. "Hoyt . . . don't look now, but we've picked up a shadow."

The elegantly clad lawyer glared back at him.

"A shadow? What the hell are you talking about?"

"We're being tailed," said Boohar.

Hoyt glared even harder. "You're kidding me."

"Nope." Boohar was shaking his head. "Two cars back—see that black Chevy Impala? He picked us up on the airport access road. He's been with us ever since." Now the detective turned to confront the high-powered lawyer.

"Trust me, Hoyt. I've been in this business a long time. We've got a tail, and he's a cop."

"But how?" spluttered Hoyt, Jr. "How, Alan? Nobody knows we're in Baltimore."

"It's that goddamn Becker," said Boohar. "He must've put a tail on us back in Boston. They saw us get on the plane at Logan . . . then they tipped off the cops here in Baltimore."

Boohar thought for a moment. His eyes lit up. "Shit, for all we know, he's had them bird-dogging us ever since Chicago. Anyway, the Baltimore PD now has us on their radar. We gotta *do* something, sir."

The lawyer snarled angrily, then turned to the frightened-looking cabbie.

"You heard him. We've got a tail. Ditch him!"

The cabbie's eyes widened. "Ditch him? How? We're backed up in traffic, man."

"I don't care how you do it," snarled Hoyt. "Just *do* it, goddamnit!"

The cabbie looked around desperately for a few seconds . . . then brightened.

"Okay, see that side street off to the left? That's Water Street. It's partially blocked off, lots of construction. But if you know what you're doing, you can sneak between the pylons and hook a left onto the Jones Falls Expressway."

Hoyt rolled his eyes.

"Don't talk about it, buster—*do* it!"

441

The cabbie nodded and his foot went to the accelerator. The tires screeched as he yanked the wheel to the left, and the cab rocked through a perpendicular turn.

Hoyt watched the black Impala pull out of line to follow them. Seconds later, when the cab again slewed through a vicious left turn and shot onto a nearby freeway ramp, the Baltimore undercover cop at the wheel of the Impala missed his cue and flew past the turnoff.

They were roaring north on the Jones Falls now, alone and tailless.

"Good work," said Hoyt. "Now find an exit as fast as you can and get us down to Fells Point." The lawyer's mouth made a thin, angry line.

"As soon as the tail reports that he's lost us, the Baltimore cops will start knocking on doors throughout the neighborhood."

Furious, he scowled at Boohar.

"Becker's not stupid, Alan. He must've seen how I reacted when he asked me about Fells Point. So I'm sure everybody in the Boston Police Department now understands why we hightailed it to Baltimore.

"We gotta find my brother before the goddamn cops do!"

***

Soon they were zipping south on Broadway and then left onto Thames.

At the crowded pub, the private detective pulled out an old photo of Michael Rogers and showed it to the bartender.

"Have you seen this man before?"

The bartender focused for a second. "Nah, never seen the guy."

But with twenty years of practicing law behind him, Hoyt could sniff a lie in a heartbeat. "Come on, pal. Give it to me straight. Maybe this will help your memory a little?"

The ante this time was a $100 bill. Hoyt wasn't fucking around.

It worked.

"Now that you mention it, I *do* remember seeing a guy like that come in here the other night. But hey, he was a mess, okay? Wrinkled clothes, greasy hair, lots of dirt under his nails. He caused a ruckus, too. Some woman got real pissed at him. She was beating him over the head with her pocketbook and swearing at him like a raped ape.

"She kept screaming, 'You asshole! How dare you touch me, you piece of shit?'

"The deal was, he'd squeezed her ass. So right away I warned him, 'Pal, if you ever do that again, I'll go upside your head with this here Oriole bat I keep under the bar!'"

Hoping to demonstrate, the bartender was reaching for his weapon—but Hoyt waved the gesture away. "Let's cut to the chase, huh? Did the guy say where he was staying?"

"Nope. He must've been new in town . . . 'cause he asked me if I knew where he could find a cheap room."

"Oh, yeah? What'd you say?"

"I told him there was a boarding house a couple blocks up Thames Street, Mama's Place, where he could rent a room by the day—or by the hour, if that's what he was looking for.

"I don't know if he went there or not, but it might be a good place to start looking."

"Thanks, buster. You can keep the change."

The bartender stared at him. "What change? You didn't order nothing."

"Keep it anyway."

***

A summer night.

The full moon hangs like a glowing lantern above the sand dunes. She's sitting in the beach house kitchen, petting the cat.

A fluffy-haired, emerald-eyed Maine Coon cat with a licorice-drop nose. Her beloved *Puddy*.

The ocean breeze ripples against the screen door of the kitchen, and she's full of joy, full of happiness. How wonderful that *Puddy* has returned to her!

Now she looks down. The cat's mouth has fallen open. His porcelain-like teeth, his gleaming white teeth . . . like two rows of polished fishhooks winking and gleaming in the overhead light.

The portable radio, the little Zenith plays softly at her elbow, a mellow golden oldie from way back in 1958.

It's the Danleers, doing their classic doo-wop hit, *One Summer Night*:

> *One summer night, we fell*
> *In love;*
> *One summer night,*
> *I held you tight.*
> *You and I, under the moon*
> *Of love . . .*

She looks down . . . and the fishhooks wink in the unsteady light. Then a soft, low-pitched voice says, "Nice to see you again, Alix."

She freezes on her chair. Has the cat somehow spoken? Has *Puddy* found a human voice? Or is she dreaming this? Is this another nightmare?

A sudden feline shriek of pain . . . as her cuddly pet rises in front of her stunned gaze—rises and rises until he's hanging upside down, writhing and whining in agony and hanging by his tail!

Then the shadow appears. The shadow simply materializes out of thin air. It's the shade of a husky middle-aged man in a baseball cap, and the cap is pulled way down low over his eyes. Her heart races as she sees what the shadow is holding in his right hand, even as she hears once again the dreaded syllables uttered by the dreaded voice.

"So nice to see you again, Alix. And look who I've brought with me for a little visit!"

The shadow lifts his right hand slightly—the hand with the tail in it—and Puddy shrieks in agonizing pain.

He's only a shadow, she tells herself, *and a shadow isn't real. A shadow cannot hurt you. Puddy isn't really here. You're only dreaming this. This is only a nightmare, Alix. He cannot hurt Puddy. That will not happen tonight.*

But now he's chuckling again, and he's letting the cat swing a little. He's singing to her, crooning the next lines from that long-ago love song by the Danleers:

> *You kissed me, oh, so tenderly*
> *And I knew this was love*
> *And as I held you, oh, so close,*
> *I knew no one could ever take your place.*

He chuckles again. "Don't you get it, Alix? Why are you so slow? Don't you understand the Sea of Dreams?"

She struggles . . . she wants to leap up . . . wants to race across the kitchen, fly through the screen door to safety—but she knows she can't desert *Puddy*. How can she leave Puddy behind?

It's too late now, anyway—it's too late to run . . . because when she looks down to see why her legs aren't working, she discovers that she's bound by thick ropes to her chair.

"Look into the cat's eye, Alix," says the shadow of Michael Rogers.

She does. She doesn't want to . . . but she can't help herself. All at once, she's gazing into the green eyes of the terrified feline. She's staring into a pair of pain-blinded eyes, eyes hypnotized with sheer horror. And something's moving there. Something's growing there. An image . . . in the wet black pupil of the cat's eye . . . a *face*.

A face that's full of rage, full of unspeakable anger.

It's the face of an old man . . . a glaring old man whose open mouth is running with scarlet blood.

"Do you remember the man I told you about, the man I knew as *The Prick*? That's his face, right there in the eye of the cat!"

A wave of dread rolls over Alix, a cold black dread so intense that she nearly vomits. Where has she heard that nickname before? What were the circumstances? How has his face suddenly appeared in the terrified eye of the cat?

Now the shadow looms above her, the shadow with the cat twisting and groaning beside it. He chuckles softly, softly.

"Alix . . . why are you such a slow learner?"

All at once she's watching a glittering shaft of metal as it presses against the soft warm flesh at the base of Puddy's throat. *The Surgeon's scalpel!*

"The Sea of Dreams," he tells her softly. "Do you understand now how I can travel there, Alix?"

He chuckles.

"The Sea of Dreams . . . what is it if not the great ocean of the collective human unconscious?

"Don't you get it, Alix? Don't you understand that *the dreams of all of us are but a single eternal dream we all share*?"

The blade presses closer. Her stuttering brain races to grasp the stunning realization: he's going to cut Puddy's head off!

He's laughing again, with the scalpel sunk deep in the cat's fur.

"I killed The Prick, Alix. It's true! After all those years of humiliation, all those years of sadistic torment, I found a way to steal his beloved scalpel! I took his most precious keepsake, the shining symbol of his greatness. Then I snuck into his nightmares and jammed this blade into the space between his ribs and slashed him to death!

"So how was I able to accomplish that glorious task? That final triumphant victory? I did it through the power of the CURSE, Alix.

"Do you hear me? It was the CURSE that gave me the strength to bring down The Prick! Because the CURSE is alien, Alix. It is *ALIEN and it is eating our dreams.*

"It is the CURSE that devours our dreams, and the CURSE is the ALIEN—"

Flash of the scalpel—

Puddy is about to die. Somehow she must save him!

With the very last of her failing strength, Alix bellows into the face of the grinning shadow.

"COLLIER!"

She instantly snaps awake.

***

She came howling up out of the freezing darkness, and even as she awoke, she was raging at them.

"He's being controlled by a *monster*, do you hear me? Something alien has him in its grip. That's why he does what he does without caring. It's why he has no remorse.

"The monster is not human. It comes from another *place*."

"My God," said Jake. "What are we doing here, Stan? Talk to me, goddamnit! What are we *doing* here?"

Dr. Jacobson's face was ashen. He stood there thunderstruck.

Then, with his voice shaking: "I can't answer that, Jake. Who could? We're in over our heads now. We've entered another realm entirely. We're dealing with the totally unknown here."

But now they all looked up. The door of the control room had just slammed open.

It was Mitzi Hamilton, looking frightened.

"Dr. Jacobson," she said in a rush, "I think you should know we just lost the input from the eyelid sensors, and the EEG has started behaving erratically. Apparently, there was a huge burst of electrical energy during that last nightmare. . . ."

They waited for more, but it was Alix who spoke next. "The REM explosion. That was it. Do you remember, Stan . . . that research I started doing a few years ago? I told them about it during my first lecture up at Big

Pine—the biochemical cascade and then the surge of brain energy. That's what just happened. I just went through it. The REM explosion is real, Stan.

"It must be the trigger that allows ST to take over a sleeper's brain."

Openmouthed, they stared at her. But a moment later, before anyone could respond, Rozzie was muttering at them. With her eyes narrowed to slits, she was moaning and growling like some ancient Priestess of the Night.

"There will be a light," she groaned again and again. "On the far shore, there will be a guiding light. Melinda, you sang of it on the day that Alix first arrived at Big Pine. I heard you sing it in the tongue of the Abenaki.

"You told me about it in a dream that I've dreamed again and again, ever since the day Alix first came to us.

"On the far shore, Melinda, you said there will be a light and that it will see Alix home—but only after she has looked into the eye of the CURSE!"

Jake was glaring at her now, half-crazed with fear. Then, turning back to face Dr. Jacobson: "What the hell *is* this, Stan? What is it, and how do we *stop* it?"

Alix had begun to shudder. Her eyes were rolling in her head. "I have to go back in," she bellowed at them. "I have to go back in and confront it . . . now!"

Desperate, Jake yanked on the scientist's arm.

"Stan! What gives? Help us. Stop her. *Do* something, or by God, I will!"

"I have to go back in," cried Alix. She was already sliding back down onto the bed. She was already fading out of their world again.

They watched her eyelids fluttering, fluttering.

"I have to confront it, Jake."

As if agreeing with her, Melinda was rocking back and forth again. Once again, she uttered her unearthly cry: "ki-ki-ki-ki-ki-KEEEE!"

Alix shuddered. She made a roaring sound, the sound of a creature tortured beyond all endurance.

A moment later, she was back asleep again.

***

She stood in front of the antique mirror, checking her lipstick.

But . . .

The top half of the mirror had begun to bulge weirdly. Then a huge bubble suddenly formed in the glass. She looked closer . . . and she saw it.

A green-eyed cat was trapped inside the bubble.

A deep male voice began to echo inside her head. "Welcome to The Prick's Playhouse, honeybell!"

Horrified, she felt a wave of bitter vomit flash into her mouth, then slowly subside.

"What?" she wailed in her terror. "What do you want, Michael?"

"Why . . . it's perfectly obvious, isn't it? I want you to *look into the mirror, Alix*—The Prick's Playhouse Mirror!"

She was powerless to refuse.

Her eyes found her beloved pet in the bubble, found the trickle of blood that leaked from his injured mouth. Then with a *cracking* sound the glass bubble burst open . . . and she heard Puddy wailing in anguish and frightened within an inch of his life.

She opened her mouth to scream . . . only to discover that something was crawling into it. She tried to scream, but instead she coughed violently . . . and then spat a tangle of pale yellow slugs onto the jagged shards of the broken mirror.

They were crawling on the glass now, the greasy slugs, crawling and bleeding and being cut to pieces.

Hi, Alix. I'm back. So nice to be with you again! Would you like to join me on a quick tour through The Prick's Playhouse?

He reached for the scalpel.

"Sit down, Alix. You've been on your feet all day long, dear."

She opened her mouth, ready to tell him: "Go fuck yourself!"

But her tongue had frozen . . . it wouldn't move.

She looked around—and slowly discovered that she *was* sitting down. How had he gotten her onto this hard, straight-backed chair?

She remembered.

This was a nightmare.

He controlled it.

He could do whatever he wanted with her, *whenever* he wanted.

He could tie her up. . . .

Look! Her shoulders were bound so tightly to the chair that they'd gone white. They were completely drained of blood.

"Honeybell," he said now, "ain't we got fun?"

She tried once again to howl at him: "Fuck you!"

But her mouth had stopped working. With a stab of horror, she asked herself: *Will I be able to utter the code word when I need to?*

"Alix," he crooned now, enjoying himself fully, "I want to give you a brief lecture on the Art of Surgery. Okay by you?"

She stared blankly at him, uncomprehending.

"Let's start with the basic tool, the scalpel itself," he said brightly.

He was holding the "HR" blade at eye level, as if reading the inscription on its side. "As you can see, this is a Number Eleven Ribbel, long regarded as one of the finest cutting tools in the entire world."

She was watching the blue-steel edge of the Ribbel, hypnotized.

As if by magic, her bonds had been released. She was suddenly on her feet.

"Bend over, bitch!" Dr. Mike commanded.

"Please," said Alix. "You don't have to do this. Please."

But her willpower had deserted her. He was controlling her nightmare and he knew it. Now her wrists had been expertly tied. Now she was bending over a lab table, with her white ass totally exposed. There was no way she would be able to free herself.

He laughed quite joyfully.

"You're fucked, honeybell. You never should have stolen my discovery. You ruined me, Alix. Why did you do that?"

She felt an overpowering urge to fight him now. "Fuck you, Michael. You can go straight to Hell."

"And you can shut up. Watch how easy it is!" Suddenly he was covering her mouth with duct tape. "Look at that beautiful ass of yours, honey bucket. You know, you always did have a gorgeous bottom. Pearly-white! And the way you *squirmed*, the way that pearly-white ass of yours just squirmed and squirmed. . .

"You loved it, you little bitch! You were so hot, I thought you'd burn a hole in the bed." He laughed happily. So happy! "But now we're going to enjoy a different kind of adventure, you and me. We're going to put on a demonstration of chest surgery with the help of the world's finest cutting tool, the mighty Ribbel."

Remembering something, he roared with laughter. Then she heard him boast.

"My father was a magician with the Ribbel, honeybell. He played it the way Heifetz played the violin. To this day at the American College of Cardiology, they'll tell you that Hoyt Rogers, Sr., was the greatest heart surgeon in the history of open-heart valve repair."

His words stopped.

The table disappeared.

Now she was back in the chair, bound hand and foot with tight hemp ropes digging into her skin.

Rogers leaned in, grinning and gasping, his face aflame with hatred. "But they're wrong, my sweet. They're wrong. Because the greatest is his son! Yes, me . . . Michael Rogers, the most accomplished cardiac surgeon of our era—little Mikey Rogers, who's ready to show you what he can do!"

She tried to scream through the duct tape. But it was hopeless. With a jolt of pure horror, she realized: *I won't be able to say the escape word.*

He was taking his time, enjoying the moment and giggling like a naughty schoolboy. "Wait until you feel the bite of the Ribbel in your chest. Now *that* is what I call pain, my honeybell!"

He waved the blade for a moment, then leaned in closer. "I know you're going to enjoy it, and I surely don't want to miss the moment when you start screaming in pain!"

He reached out with one hand and tore the duct tape from her mouth—and in that one flashing moment she heard a voice screaming from another dimension, from another realm entirely: k*i-ki-ki-ki-ki-KEEEE!*

In that same shuddering instant, she seized her chance.

"COLLIER!"

***

This time she didn't even return to the Nightmare Team in the laboratory.

Perched on the edge of sleep, she took a single gasping breath and dove back down into the Dreamtime.

He was waiting for her, of course—with the scalpel poised and ready to strike.

In the sleep lab, meanwhile, Melinda Birdsong was once again rocking herself back and forth. With her dark eyes clamped shut, her stern face might have been a tribal mask. Was she now lost in a dream herself?

Numb with shock, the team in the sleep lab watched the Abenaki medicine woman rock like a metronome, while uttering the hawk cry and shaking like a wind-whipped leaf.

A moment later she threw her head back and sent up her unforgettable chant.

> *Naaaaaii-eeeeeeh-wah!*
> *Naaaaaii-eeeeeeh-wah!*

Then there was a single blinding flash of light, during which Rozzie screamed three words she would never forget.

"Curse of *Morpheus!*"

In that same blazing instant, Dr. Mike raised the scalpel, about to lash out.

But this time, instead of uttering the escape word, Alix Cassidy looked him in the eye and said in a low, flat voice what she had finally come to understand.

"Your power is broken, Michael."

His head jerked back, and he looked at Alix in scornful disbelief.

"What? Huh? Broken? What do you mean, *broken?*" He looked deep into her eyes, then gave her a puzzled, searching frown.

"Ah . . . have you forgotten that you're trapped in The Prick's Playhouse, dear heart?" His voice was so low-pitched that she could barely make out his words.

"You're lost in another nightmare, and I'm holding the Equalizer. You're fucked, honey bunny. In this world, I run the show. Got it?

"At The Prick's Playhouse, Alix Cassidy is totally fucked and she's about to die!"

She smiled.

In this moment of terror—this supremely terrifying moment with everything at stake—Alix Cassidy calmly smiled at Dr. Mike.

"I've beaten you, Michael."

"Beaten me? Ha!" His blue eyes were enormous. He was breathing raggedly now, breathing as if underwater and fighting for air. "You're trapped in the Playhouse, and I'm holding a razor-sharp scalpel three inches from your eyes.

"I am The Surgeon, bitch—*I am The Surgeon!*"

"No," she said. "You're beaten. That's what you are. Beaten. Your power is broken, and you are defeated. Do you want me to demonstrate?"

But instead of answering, he lunged.

She shouted: "COLLIER!"

A light winked above the chair—a flash of green lightning—and she was instantly gone.

Dr. Mike blinked frantically at the space where she'd once sat bound to the chair.

"What is this?" he asked himself over the sound of the rain on the window. "What the fuck is *this*?"

And then . . . just like that—a blink!—she was back in front of him, peering deep into his eyes and smiling all over again. "Do you see what's happening, Michael? Do you see that I can move in and out of any nightmare, just like you? Do you see that I have the power, too?

"You're beaten, Michael. It's over."

He lunged.

"COLLIER!"

And the space before him was empty again.

He staggered forward, waving at the transparent air. The entire room had tilted strangely; it seemed to be revolving in slow circles, with him standing dazed and confused at the center . . . until his growing rage finally climbed into his mouth and he screamed so hard the window rattled and shook.

"Come back here, you dirty bitch—I HAVEN'T FINISHED WITH YOU!"

But she was gone for good. She had escaped . . . and with growing horror he saw that she would *always* be able to escape his power—by uttering the one single word he hated most to hear: *Collier*.

***

Stunned and disoriented, Dr. Mike opened his eyes wide. What the fuck was going on? Why was he awake? Never before had he been awakened while torturing one of his victims in a nightmare. . . .

And what was that pounding noise . . . the hammering sound that seemed to be shaking the entire room? Amazed, he looked wildly around the shithole. That pounding . . .

The door!

Somebody was beating on the door with his fists. And he was shouting. Shouting things that all at once made Dr. Mike's blood run cold.

"Michael? This is Hoyt! Are you in there? Open up, goddamnit! I said this is *Hoyt!*"

His brother Hoyt? No. It couldn't be. How had that dickhead traced him to Baltimore? What could he possibly want? Grunting with the effort, Dr. Mike dragged himself from the filthy mattress and staggered toward the door.

His hand shook as he yanked at the rusted chain.

The door swung open and he blinked wildly in the sudden surge of light from an open hallway window. Two men stood in the doorway. Both were glaring at him.

"My God," said Michael Rogers. "It's you. How . . . how the fuck did you find me?"

"That doesn't matter now," snapped Hoyt.

Without hesitating, he pushed past his disheveled brother and strode into the center of the rented room.

Boohar followed, with his intent eyes swiveling from the rumpled mattress to the maniac standing beside it.

"All that matters now is that I'm here," growled Hoyt.

"But . . . but *why?*"

"It's simple. I'm going to put you where you belong, asshole."

Dr. Mike stared at him. "Really? And where is that?"

"In the Illinois State Prison, on Death Row."

A slow smile spread across Dr. Mike's face. Then he emitted a slow, guttural laugh. "Oh, I see. *Now* I get it! Mr. Bigshot Lawyer, Mr. Hoyt Rogers, Jr., the famous attorney—you're gonna lock me up."

He tilted his shaggy head far back and laughed again.

"Do you mind telling me what I did wrong in order to deserve such a drastic punishment?"

His brother didn't answer the question. He left it to the detective.

"You're under arrest for the murder of your father," said Detective Boohar. "I'm a licensed private investigator, and I'm authorized to put the cuffs on you."

Hoyt nodded. His mouth was a jagged line of hatred. "You're coming downtown with us, you fucking scumbag."

Dr. Mike smiled again. "Am I, Hoyt? And where will we be headed, my dear brother?"

Hoyt gazed at him for a moment. His face was cold, empty. "We're going down to the headquarters of the Baltimore Police Department."

Dr. Mike's eyes widened a little, but he was still smiling.

"I don't think so, you fucking little twerp."

The two brothers were glaring openly at each other now.

"Hoyt, have I ever told you," drawled Little Mikey, "exactly what I think of you?"

The Surgeon's face was changing now; all at once he looked twenty years younger. He looked like a kid again . . . a naïve and confused little kid . . . except that his eyes were vibrating with a lifetime of bottled-up rage and hatred.

"You're a sawed-off little pissant in a thousand-dollar suit, Hoyt. You're an ass-licking suck-up who spent his entire childhood sniveling back at the brutal tyrant who was our dear father."

Hoyt's face had gone bone white. "Really, Michael? Tell me, please: why don't I recognize the man you're describing? Is it perhaps because I'm a millionaire partner in one of Chicago's most successful law firms?"

"Is it because I'm now the president of the Illinois Bar Association—and probably the next governor of Illinois?"

But Dr. Mike wasn't listening now. Slowly, unobtrusively, one hand had snaked out to the battered kitchen drawer on his left. Now that hand was moving, feeling for something –

Then it was holding The Surgeon's scalpel high in the air.

"Recognize this, Hoyt?"

The two other men had stiffened. Boohar's left hand went to the bulge that protruded from under his right shoulder.

"This was our late father's most beloved trophy," said Dr. Mike. "Do you remember how he always kept it inside that glass case on the wall in the family room?"

But the lawyer didn't answer. Instead he looked over at Boohar, who was now pointing his Smith & Wesson at the center of Dr. Mike's heaving chest.

"Drop it," said the private eye.

Dr. Mike thought for a moment, then laughed. His eyes were shining now; he actually seemed to be enjoying himself.

"I have no *intention* of dropping it," he said. Then: "Look at me, Hoyt."

The lawyer glared back.

Nobody moved. Hoyt was staring directly into his brother's eyes. Dr. Mike was smiling gleefully. In spite of the tension, he seemed to be enjoying himself.

"You have ten seconds before Boohar pulls the trigger," said Hoyt. "And while you're counting, I'll just say goodbye by repeating the one word I've always used when talking about you with our father:

"*Loser!*"

The word flashed between them—even as the look of burning hatred raced between their eyes—and in the same instant, Dr. Mike whipped the glittering scalpel through the air and slashed his own throat from ear to ear.

A bright red wave of blood shot across the space between them and drenched the front of the lawyer's expensive suit.

For a moment, Dr. Mike just stood there, tottering on his feet and still smiling. Then they heard him hiss with the last of his breath:

"This isn't over for you, Hoyt—it's only *beginning!*"
He fell . . . and just as his body hit the filthy linoleum tiles, the door exploded open and four armed men in bulletproof vests came bursting into the room.

"Nobody moves," shouted the first man through the door, who was brandishing a Sig Sauer automatic. "Hands in the air!

"Baltimore Police—drop that gun and get your fucking hands in the *air!*"

They all stood there for a few more seconds . . . until it was obvious that the dead man wouldn't be moving anymore, and that the two living men posed no further threat.

Then the police began looking around the room.

Startled, the lead cop spotted something on the floor.

He looked closer . . . and then bent down to retrieve the mutilated child's toy that lay there.

Torn and ragged, it was a blue-furred doll of some kind—a headless and tailless donkey covered with dust.

THE END

EPILOGUE

Three weeks later, during a jam-packed award ceremony on the fifth floor of the Boston Police Department, Detective Jake Becker was presented with the Homicide Division's Highest Citation of Merit for "directing the team of investigators who successfully apprehended one of the most dangerous serial killers in the history of Massachusetts."

While the TV news cameras ground away and the print reporters scribbled in their notebooks, Commissioner Ryan Flaherty sang the praises of the man who was now being described everywhere as "the hero of the manhunt for The Surgeon."

Intent on getting all of the PR mileage he could out of this moment, Flaherty didn't hold back.

"This award goes to Detective Becker for his great skill in using all the traditional methods of police work in stopping The Surgeon," said the beaming commissioner. "Along with a team of incredibly dedicated investigators, he employed the tools of standard police investigation—everything from state-of-the-art fingerprinting techniques to highly effective interviewing of witnesses to insightful psychological profiles and composite drawings. He used them with consummate skill to prevent a maniac from further terrorizing our city.

"What Detective Becker and his team accomplished in a very short time was nothing less than remarkable. Not only did they manage to locate the serial killer only a few moments after his suicide—with the outstanding help of the Baltimore Police Department—but they were also able to identify a silver heart-shaped locket he'd taken from one of his victims, which showed beyond a reasonable doubt that their suspect was indeed 'The Surgeon.'

"I should also point out," added the upbeat commissioner, "that Detective Becker and his team were able to use some recently developed tools in forensic biochemistry—tools that allowed them to bring state-of-the-art, gene-based identification techniques to bear on this case.

"In the days ahead, these same genetic breakthroughs are going to change forensic science from top to bottom . . . and the Boston PD is proud to be on the cutting edge of this key technology."

Now a wave of excited applause rolled across the crowded auditorium as a dozen flashbulbs went off. Sitting at Jake's side, Alix Cassidy reached over and squeezed his hand. Then she whispered jokingly in his ear, "I sure hope he mentions all the brilliant work you did in the Dreamtime, Jake!"

The detective grinned happily back at her . . . even as Charly squeezed his other hand and told him, "I'm so proud of you, Dad! I can't wait to tell all the kids at school—you're the real deal, for sure!"

Then, after giving the recently repaired and freshly groomed Eeyore a mighty hug, she cut loose with a triumphant: "It's ohhh-*kayyy*!"

Sitting in the second row, newly close friends Rozzie Violette and Stan Jacobson applauded and smiled warmly at each other.

Then Murray Fisher leaned in close and burbled in his friend's ear.

"Jake, you're gonna be the most famous guy who eats lunch every day at my deli!" Murray shook with laughter and then added, "Tell you what. Soon as I get back to work, I'm gonna put up a sign announcing a major change in my sandwich lineup at the deli. You remember my *Mishegoss*, right? Yiddish for 'craziness'? Corned beef, chopped liver, pastrami, Russian dressing and cole slaw on rye?

"Hey, lemme tell ya, we're talking about Boston's most famous deli sandwich, okay?

"Well, from now on, it's gonna be known everywhere as the Becker Boomer!"

Six years later.

The hugely successful Chicago lawyer paused in front of the mirror in his lavishly appointed downtown office.

Smiling contentedly, he began to adjust his silk bow tie.

But just as he tugged at the knot . . . something moved in the glass.

A ripple . . . a flicker of something scaly . . . something that undulated for only an instant across his startled field of vision.

He leaned in for a closer look.

But the snake-like image was gone.

All he saw was his own supremely self-centered face—the face of a man accustomed to winning every battle in which he chose to fight.

It was nothing, he told himself, as he turned away and headed off to work on his next $400-an-hour legal case.

Nothing at all.

ABOUT THE AUTHOR

Douglas Volk is a veteran corporate executive who also writes dark thrillers that are "hard to put down" (*Maine Sunday Telegram*). The author of *The Morpheus Conspiracy, The Surgeon's Curse,* and *Destiny Returns* (coming December 2019), he also served as CEO of the Volk Packaging Corporation.

One of the most interesting things about Volk's approach to novel writing is the way he uses the tools of business to build his thrillers from the ground up. After assembling a team of specialists with firsthand knowledge of sleep science, crime scene forensics, psychiatry and law enforcement homicide investigation techniques, he taps into the team's expertise throughout the writing and editing process in each of his books.

Thanks to this "team approach," his paranormal crime thrillers have often been praised for their credibility and convincingly realistic detail.

Volk's novels also frequently include another of his major concerns: the painful and deeply disturbing impact of the "betrayal" of U.S. soldiers who fought in Vietnam by their own government. As a U.S. Army veteran himself, he's passionately committed to telling stories about that tragic betrayal whenever he can.

Douglas Volk lives in Maine with his wife of more than 45 years. They have two adult children and five grandchildren.

Coming December 2019: *DESTINY RETURNS*
This time the paranormal Curse of Morpheus has overtaken a millionaire lawyer in Chicago—a ruthless criminal who knows how "bad dreams" can kill!

PROLOGUE: *March 2001*

It was a presentation that Charlotte "Charly" Becker and her proud father—retired homicide detective Jake "The Professor" Becker—would remember for the rest of their lives.

The unforgettable moment began when a burly, broad-shouldered man named Eddie Janovik pinned a gleaming blue ribbon and a gold medal to the front of Charly's Chicago Police Department uniform jacket.

"Patrolman Becker," said the unsmiling and stern-faced Janovik—aka the "Chicago PD Superintendent"—"it's my proud duty to present you with the 2000 Harrison Award for Outstanding Bravery in the Line of Service as a Chicago police officer. Your act of courage in disarming an assailant who threatened the life of your partner with a lethal weapon was only the latest act of valor in a long and honorable tradition of heroic service by the officers of the Chicago Police Department.

"Being a police officer is one of the hardest jobs in the world, and it often requires the kind of heroism you displayed during that incident last year."

A few seconds later, the Superintendent was carefully affixing the golden disk with the familiar Latin motto (*Fortitudo et honoris*) to the blue serge fabric of Charly's jacket.

Seated in the first row of the PD Central Auditorium, the retired homicide detective was blinking back tears . . . and then lifting his right hand to his forehead in a loving salute to his daughter.

Watching him, Charly smiled back.

At that moment, she was remembering a rainy summer afternoon—about eight months earlier—when she and her partner crept into position beside the door that led into No. 801 at the Pleasant View Housing Complex in South Chicago. . . .

***

Showdown.

Patrolman Becker—a 28-year-old Chicago PD rookie street cop—placed the palm of her left hand beneath the butt of her Smith & Wesson 9mm semiautomatic.

Stone-faced with total concentration, Charly was "steadying the muzzle"—just as she'd been taught a few months earlier at the Police Academy.

On the other side of 801, an intoxicated male adult suspect was at that moment screaming with rage: "Get the fuck outta my face before I kill you, bitch!"

Listening hard, Charly took a deep breath, while her calm and cool partner sent her a nod of confidence-building approval. "You looking good, Charly," said veteran Patrolman Reggie Carter, who'd been "working the street" for the past 11 years and had survived dozens of these "domestic dispute" police calls. "You ready to go?"

"All set," said Charly.

"Fine and dandy," said Patrolman Carter. He was whispering now. "We're gonna be fine and dandy. Just follow my lead, got it?"

"Roger that," said Charly. She was doing her best to sound calm and unemotional, but the two words wobbled a bit as she spoke them. Her hands shook a little, too, as they did their best to steady the S&W.

This was Charly's fourth day on the job at the Chicago PD.

The two of them were crouching at both sides of the door now, with their weapons trained and the safeties off. The trouble with these domestic disputes was their unpredictability; one false move and an unlucky cop could end up taking an ambulance ride—or maybe even a ride to the morgue on downtown Jackson Street.

But there was no turning back now.

It was a humid, drizzly afternoon on 78th Street, deep in the violence-torn South Side of Chicago. Patrolman Becker and Patrolman Carter had taken this call ten minutes before, while eating bean burritos with guacamole dip at a Taco Bell located eight blocks to the east.

Six-niner, this is Dispatch—got a DD at 78th and Causeway, Pleasant View Apartment complex. . . 911 caller in 801 says her boyfriend is armed and threatening her with a gun.

They'd left their bean burritos on the table.

Now Patrolman Carter was holding his right hand in the air.

"On my mark," he whispered.

"Gotcha," whispered Charly.

With that, the older patrolman used the knuckles on his left hand to rap against the door. Then they waited.

They could hear Fleetwood Mac singing in somebody else's apartment, about four doors down the hallway. It was one of their classics, an oldie called "Dreams," from way back in 1977.

> *Thunder only happens when it's raining*
> *Players only love you when they're playing. . . .*

Reggie Carter rapped his knuckles again. He also said in a loud voice: "Chicago PD, open up."

Nothing. Just the radio going down the hall.

> *Now here I go again, I see the crystal visions;*
> *I keep my visions to myself. . . .*

Charly was holding her breath.

Then two things happened close together.

First, she heard a scream of tires racing down 78th Street eight stories below—probably some stupid hot-rodder showing off.

Second, right after the squealing tires, the battered apartment door swung open.

Behind it, like a scowling jack-in-the-box still quivering at the top of his spring, loomed a huge man with a gun.

For a moment, the three of them stared at each other. Then the gunman shouted something—Charly thought she heard: "I don't talk to no *poh*-leece!"

His pistol was up and cocked. It was also pointed directly at Charly's partner. Behind him, a weeping woman was kneeling on the floor and holding two terrified children in her arms.

They were frozen in place. If they'd been a marble sculpture, it would have been named: *Terror*.

The gunman's finger was on the trigger. It was trembling. And the muzzle was pointed directly at

Charly's partner's chest. But nothing happened for a while . . . as the distant radio played on and on.

It's only me who wants to wrap around your dreams,
And have you any dreams you'd like to sell?

Charly took the leap.

She dove forward. Like a middle linebacker exploding into a ball carrier's ribcage, she went head-on into the gunman's midsection. He flew backwards and his pistol flashed. The round went sizzling away into the sound of Fleetwood Mac. Another moment passed—or was it a year?—and then the suspect was flat on his back and Patrolman Carter had the S&W against his skull.

"Another move, you dead," said Carter.

The suspect didn't move. Within a few seconds, Reggie Carter had turned him over and was kneeling on his back while he applied the handcuffs. Soon there was a loud clicking sound which told them the assailant had been restrained. But Charly was still sitting on the floor.

She was staring at her left leg, four inches above the knee, where the blood was now pumping from her femoral artery. Her eyes were wide with fear. Shuddering with the effort, she crawled up to a kneeling position. She was still studying the left pants leg of her blue uniform, watching it turn redder with each beat of her heart.

"Fuck!" screamed Patrolman Carter. "Aw, fuck! Charly?" He was also staring at the reddening pants leg. It was arterial bleeding, and he'd seen it before; if it kept up, he knew she'd bleed out within a few minutes.